THE STRICKLANDS

THE
STRICKLANDS

By EDWIN LANHAM

Introduction by
LAWRENCE R. RODGERS

UNIVERSITY OF OKLAHOMA PRESS
Norman

Library of Congress Cataloging-in-Publication Data

Lanham, Edwin, 1904–1979
    The Stricklands : a novel / by Edwin Lanham ;
introduction by Lawrence R. Rodgers.
     p. cm.
    ISBN 0-8061-3419-4 (alk. paper)
     1. Labor unions—Organizing—Fiction.
2. Depressions—Fiction. 3. Oklahoma—Fiction.
4. Brothers—Fiction. 5. Outlaws—Fiction. I. Title.

PS3523.A612 S77 2002
813'.54—dc21

                           2002066843

The paper in this book meets the guidelines for permanence
and durability of the Committee on Production Guidelines
for Book Longevity of the Council on Library Resources, Inc.

1   2   3   4   5   6   7   8   9   10

*No living people or actual events
form the basis of this book.*

Introduction

Lawrence R. Rodgers

WHEN *The Stricklands* appeared in March of 1939, its publisher, Little Brown, was confident it had a bestseller on its hands. Lanham had already written four well-regarded novels, and his fifth was poised to be his breakout book. Early reviewers acclaimed his latest work, calling it Lanham's "finest novel to date and one of the surest on the contemporary American scene."[1] Set in the lean Depression years, it tells the story of two brothers, one a farmer's union organizer and the other an oil-field worker turned outlaw, facing environmental hardships readers would have found as topical as the evening newspaper. A decade earlier, Edna Ferber had proven Oklahoma to be reliable literary terrain when *Cimarron* finished 1930 as the nation's number-one bestseller (and supplied the story for the 1931 movie of the same title that won the Academy Award for best picture). Ferber's tale, which included a larger-than-life account of the famous 1889 land run, was set in the rowdy days surrounding statehood. Nonetheless, despite a thirteen-day state tour to research her subject, *Cimarron* was, to her surprise, criticized for its less-than-accurate recreation of the region's history by pioneers who had lived through it. Ferber produced a novel that state historian Angie Debo would dismiss as "rooted in nowhere."[2]

In contrast, *The Stricklands* is steeped in authentic regional detail. As a period piece, it not only recreates, with map-like clarity, the feel of the landscape in Oklahoma's hardscrabble Cookson Hills region but also captures the undertones of despair felt by the era's least prosperous classes. Immersed in a national farm emergency, as well as labor and race tensions, Lanham's Oklahoma is a land in crisis. The story is, in the largest sense, a familiar Depression tale. It dramatizes what happens when the institutions that individuals once believed in have failed them. Hardworking folk have lost faith in the ability of banks, the press, law enforcement, and local and national government to improve their lives. What remains is a contested territory of social negotiations and pressures among competing groups of poor and rich whites, African Americans, and Cherokee, Creek, and Choctaw Indians, who together reflect the rich range of Oklahoma's distinctive cultural mix. While, as one character says, "The red man and the black man both got a grudge against the white man" (25), they all share a grudge against the rich man.

The attention that Lanham gives to examining the relationships among these groups is almost unprecedented in American fiction. A tangled web of vested interests complicates all their interactions. A WPA dam-building project that will put five hundred unemployed laborers to work will also flood out the Stricklands' and others' homesteads in order to create a recreation area for the wealthy. Despite having the strongest legal claim on the area, the Indians of the Five Civilized Tribes remain the region's "forgotten men" (13). The same white workers who elicit our sympathies in their daily class struggles are also racist and refuse to join the Southern Tenant Farmers' Union because it admits blacks. As such tensions suggest, Lanham's racial landscape extends well beyond a simplified account of black/white division. Indeed, the author's three-dimensional view of race is one of the novel's most compelling features. Writing in *The Saturday Review of Literature*, Oliver LaFarge celebrated *The Stricklands* as "built out of the very soil of the Oklahoma hills. Hillbillies, share-croppers, Indians, Negroes, politicians, all the strange new melange that makes Oklahoma the strangest and most interesting of states, are genetically part of the story." Sensing a literary sensation in the making, he pronounced it "a good bet for the Pulitzer Prize."[3]

And, indeed, Oklahoma would become the staging ground for the novel of the year. But in an almost tragic instance of ill timing, that novel would not be *The Stricklands*. Within days of its publication, John Steinbeck's *The Grapes of Wrath* was released, and as quickly as Steinbeck's already bright critical star continued to ascend, *The Stricklands* receded from view. A fine novel was eclipsed by a national sensation. The two share some conspicuous similarities. They both commence in the identical eastern pocket of the state. They express comparable radical political sympathies for displaced tenant farmers and come to the same familiar conclusions about the farming crisis, collectively rooting its causes in drought, poor crop management, low commodity prices, and, especially, nefarious corporate and banking farm practices. Echoing a Joad-like tenuousness, a character in *The Stricklands* observes: "There's only seven inches of soil between us and starvation." Most notably, Steinbeck and Lanham share a thematic interest in dignifying the daily struggles of the man and woman furthest down. Such mutual sympathies are best embodied in the outlaw mystique accorded to Tom Joad and Pat Strickland. Both become multiple murderers, yet their crimes reflect less the acts of wrongdoers than those of men with laudable intentions driven to extremes by the pressures of their respective worlds. Sharing a similar faith in a morality borne of individual conscience, both authors thus draw a firm opposition between justice proper and the law.

The Grapes of Wrath and *The Stricklands* are, nonetheless, hardly the same novel. Where Steinbeck realizes the epic, even biblical, dimensions of a poor family journeying to California, Lanham devotes himself to the farm population who stayed behind. In this way, *The Stricklands* offers a useful corrective to Steinbeck's mythically powerful but historically problematic account of Depression-era Oklahoma. Unlike the Texas-born Lanham, Steinbeck's milieu was California, not the Southwest. Where Lanham had spent time in his setting and knew it like a local, Steinbeck had journeyed once along Route 66 and talked to some Oklahoma migrants. When Steinbeck famously turned the tree-covered Ozark hills in Sequoyah County into the Dust Bowl and the state into an arid wasteland radiating outward from a single highway, he created enough regional furor to lead Representative Lyle Boren to denounce *The Grapes of Wrath* on the U.S. House floor as a "dirty, lying, filthy manuscript."[4] By contrast, Lanham's setting is convincingly etched amid "crusty limbs of blackjack oaks" (3), the "slow malignant waters of the Canadian" (185), a Cherokee stomp dance, and hills filled with men who are "mean because they don't git enough to eat" (92). If Boren's real frustration was Steinbeck's failure to represent Oklahoma in its best light, *The Stricklands* offers no soothing corrective. However, if as the son of a tenant farmer Boren's indignation arose from seeing an entire state population encapsulated into a single derogatory "Okie" label, he would recognize in *The Stricklands* an essential appreciation on Lanham's part for creating a heterogeneous mix of characters that are convincing products of the Oklahoma soil.

As the criticism that greeted Steinbeck and Ferber suggested, Lanham's ability to condense the essence of Oklahoma into a novel was no small feat. The challenge owes in part to the fact that the state's most characteristic feature seems to be its inability to be characterized. Historically, by telescoping the several-century process of eviction, occupation, and ownership occurring all across the West into the span of a few decades, Oklahoma "deviated more from the general pattern of state evolution" than any other state.[5] As the terminus of the "Trail of Tears" and the site of some two dozen all-black towns, it has also represented a unique crossroads of diversity, the only location in the country at the beginning of the twentieth century "where the three 'founding' cultures of American society coexisted in significant numbers."[6] The state's irregular circumstances permeate its identity to the extent that the most comprehensive written history is ordered around the idea of Oklahoma's "anomalies."[7] Is Oklahoma the southern part of the North, the northern edge of the South, Southwestern, Midwestern, Western? A part of the farm belt, the middle border, the prairie, the Ozarks, or the Great Plains? Mountainous? Hilly or flat? The answer is yes. It is a state that, in encompassing so many labels, seems, finally, to be aptly defined by none. Two native historians labeled it "an obscure southern Middle Western state."[8] The U.S. Census Bureau has, since 1910, grouped it with Arkansas, Louisiana and Texas in the less than clarifying category "West South Central."[9]

A full appreciation of Lanham's impressive command of his setting relies on comprehending a crucial division in Oklahoma geography. Drawing a line on a state map from the upper right corner in the northeast to the bottom left in the southwest (thereby creating two triangles with the panhandle attached on the west) sets out a rough estimation of two altogether different cultural and geographic regions. The western and more northern part is plains country, defined, like other western states, by sparse vegetation, aridity, distance, and rugged frontier values. Phrased more lyrically, this part of Oklahoma is a place "where habits learned in humid areas are bound to fail."[10] In contrast, the southeast section, through which the action of *The Stricklands* moves, retains the title "Little Dixie" by virtue of natural features and Confederate sympathies. The area's topography is heavily forested, hilly, irregular, and prone to erosion. It is generally unpromising agricultural land. As Lanham worked on his novel, this region had the highest tenancy rate in the country, nearly 70 percent in the Depression. (The pattern of tenancy had been established while the area was under Indian rule and allowed no white ownership.) Three quarters of its farms were under one hundred acres. Per capita income hovered around two hundred dollars per year (a little more than half the national average). Subsistence tenant farmers like Jay Strickland were the norm. By such measures, it was a suitable setting for one of the novel's major strands, Jay's fight to create the Southern Tenant Farmers' Union.[11]

The difficulties that Jay faces in trying to organize the union mirror the near collapse of political radicalism in Oklahoma by the Depression. During the intense partisan bickering that preceded the application for statehood, the territory's farmers' union, by cooperating with organized labor, was able to exert significant influence at the constitutional convention. During early statehood, the Oklahoma Socialist party had the largest membership in the country relative to its population, peaking at 11,000 in 1914.[12] Its primary constituents were tenant farmers who saw in the party an organized means of combating landlords and creditors. What the small landholders sought was, in effect, identical to that which Jay Strickland calls for in a speech to attract new members: he wants to organize "to better conditions, to git long-time land tenure and in the end to git every tenant a piece of land of his own" (62). The utopian idealism underlying Jay's demands was no less in evidence in the real world of Oklahoma politics. But a mix of naiveté and systematic suppression by opponents and an unpopular anti-war platform by the socialists effectively ended the party's state reign by the late teens. While not countering this historical

reality directly, Lanham's willingness to leave open the possi-
bility that better things await the Jay Stricklands of the world
suggests his powerful belief in the capacity of individual sacrifice and toil to rectify the world's inequalities.

Jay seeks advancement through organized, communal, and
racially equitable means. He represents, in this sense, a progressive, modern approach to combating the ills of poverty—
thereby symbolizing the best hope of the future for Oklahoma's
exploited classes. As a bank robber, his brother Pat represents
a contrasting, if more dramatic approach. The details surrounding Pat's flight from justice, his escape from jail, and a
series of events too significant to give away in an introduction
may lack the social relevance underpinning Jay's labor fight,
but Pat's story is not without its own symbolic weight. Repre-
senting a rapidly fading set of values out of the old West, he is
a lone individual driven by good motives who through a com-
bination of violence and will battles a system that seeks to con-
tain him. He is thus a reminder of the untamed earlier days of
Oklahoma and Indian Territory. His fate, compared to that of
his brother, tells us much about the region's transition from a
bandit-filled territory at the edge of civilization into a modern
state with a full claim to cultural citizenship. His trajectory is
noticeably akin to that of real-life outlaw and fellow eastern
Oklahoma son of a bootlegger, Charles Arthur Floyd. Dubbed
"Pretty Boy" by the press, Floyd became a folk hero for robbing the same country banks that were foreclosing on farmers.
Made the subject of a song by Woody Guthrie and eulogized in
The Grapes of Wrath, he emblematized an exhilarating if short-
lived triumph of the have-nots over the haves. After Floyd was
shot by FBI field agents in October 1934, as many as forty
thousand people converged on a cemetery near Sallisaw to
attend the largest funeral in Oklahoma history. In modeling
Pat on Floyd, Lanham not only smartly tapped into the insa-
tiable public thirst for tales, fictional and otherwise, of the era's
most notoriously misunderstood badman, he also created one

of the few radical novels that can claim to be a page-turner.[13]

As a farm novel, *The Stricklands* was unusual in its radical sentiment. However, in *The Stricklands'* celebration of the essential dignity of people of the soil and the general appeal of farm life, it joined a surprisingly large array of other novels that focused on farming. One study has identified over 140 such novels set in the Midwest that were written between 1890 and 1962.[14] The most familiar among these include Willa Cather's *My Ántonia* (1918) and Ole Rölvaag's *Giants of the Earth* (1927). Other Oklahoma farm novels appearing alongside *The Stricklands* include John Milton Oskison's *Black Jack Davy* (1926) and *Brothers Three* (1935), Nola Henderson's *This Much Is Mine* (1934), Dora Aydelotte's *Long Furrows* (1935), William Cunningham's *Green Corn Rebellion* (1935), and Alice Lent Covert's *Return to Dust* (1939) and *Months of Rain* (1941). Set in and among the institutions that surround farm life—rural churches, schools, Sunday picnics, small-town main streets— these novels cluster around similar themes reflecting the capriciousness of the environment and the virtue of labor. Their central characters are often pioneers and immigrants who look to farming as a means of assimilation. Celebrating soil as the soul of identity, they glorify the essential virtue of rural settings. Conventional plots and flat characterization limit all but the best of these novels. Set alongside them, *The Stricklands* represents a striking contrast in literary achievement. Not until Rilla Askew published *The Mercy Seat* in 1997 would Lanham's Oklahoma setting host a story as complex in its rendering of the interconnected effects of race, class, and setting on character.

Lanham's early biography is hardly one that presaged either the subtle craftsmanship that characterizes all of his fiction or the sheer abundance of his published work.[15] Born in Weatherford, Texas, he came from genteel Confederate stock. His grandfather, Samuel Willis Tucker, was a Texas governor, and other relatives included congressmen and a prominent judge. After his father died when he was four, Lanham was shuttled between Texas and the East, where he attended prep school in Maryland and New York. While still a teenager, he took work on a freighter and traveled around the world. Returning after eight months, he lived in New Hampshire briefly before entering Williams College, but dropped out in his junior year. His writing career began after he gravitated to Paris and became a fringe member of the expatriate crowd radiating around Robert McAlmon's Contact Publishing house. Contact, a press equally praised and condemned for its racy, experimental work, included in its stable of writers Ernest Hemingway, William Carlos Williams, and Gertrude Stein. At McAlmon's urging, Lanham joined this elite group when he drew on his sea experiences for his first novel, *Sailors Don't Care*, which Contact issued in 1929. While working on the novel, he met and married Joan Boyle, a fashion designer and sister of the radical writer Kay Boyle. He followed with two semi-autobiographical novels. The first, *Wind Blew West* (1935), which set out themes he would develop further in *The Stricklands*, focuses on the multigenerational dynamics of a Texas family farm. A sequel, *Banner at Daybreak* (1937), is a postwar-generation story of living abroad and then returning to Texas. By the time he published *Another Ophelia* (1938), *The Stricklands*, and *Thunder of the Earth* (1941), which won a Texas Institute of Letters Award, he was not only churning out fiction at a remarkable rate, he had also come to be known as a fine wordsmith with a talent for adept storytelling. Whether focusing on sea life, Paris, New England, New York, the frontier Southwest, or depression Oklahoma, he displayed a gift for rooting out the essence of the regions about which he wrote.

Nonetheless, like so many American writers, his abundant talent could not always pay the bills. Divorced and remarried by the 1940s, he supplemented his novel writing with work as a journalist. His writing took a fresh turn after the mid-forties as he began contributing large numbers of short stories to both popular magazines like *Saturday Evening Post* and to mystery journals. He followed with a number of well-received murder mysteries, which made him a favorite of the pulp fiction crowd. When Lanham died in 1979 at the age of seventy-four, his contemporary reputation hinged almost entirely on his stature as a mystery writer.

Reprinting *The Stricklands* thus not only offers the opportunity to revive a less familiar period of Lanham's career, it also makes available one of the most powerful regional novels of its day. Such a claim, however, both points to its merit while also limiting its scope. Despite Flannery O'Connor's contention that "the best American fiction has always been regional," in American literary quarters, identifying a work as "regional" has tended to confer on it substandard stature, whereby a label like "local color" suggests a fascination with quaint, out-of-the-way settings apart from a real world somewhere else (a farm, for example, versus the city). By such measures, despite whatever a Hawthorne, Twain, or Faulkner may reveal about the essential spirits of their respective regions, their novels are more celebrated for articulating universal values than for bringing local cultures to life. Finally, a similar claim can be made for *The Stricklands*, even as it merits notice for its regional authenticity. It takes on universally relevant themes about the means by which individuals seek to overcome their powerlessness.

Notes

1. Stanley Young, "Edwin Lanham's Vigorous Western Saga," *New York Times*, 5 March 1939, 7.

2. Angie Debo, "Realizing Oklahoma's Literary Potential," *Oklahoma Libraries*, 16 July 1966, 72.

3. Oliver LaFarge, "Men Alone and Men Together," *Saturday Review of Literature*, 4 March 1939, 19.

4. Quoted in Warren French, *A Companion to* The Grapes of Wrath (New York: Viking, 1963), 125.

5. Arrell Morgan Gibson, *Oklahoma: A History of Five Centuries* (Norman: University of Oklahoma Press, 1981), 3.

6. Murray R. Wickett, *Contested Territory: Whites, Native Americans, and African Americans in Oklahoma, 1865–1907* (Baton Rouge: Louisiana State University Press, 2000), xi.

7. Gibson, *Oklahoma*, 3.

8. Alice Marriott and Carol K. Rachlin, *Oklahoma: The Forty-Sixth Star* (Garden City NY: Doubleday, 1973), 16.

9. Merrill Jenson, ed., *Regionalism in America* (Madison: University of Wisconsin Press, 1951), 101. The best overview of Oklahoma's environmental diversity is Gary L. Thompson's "Green on Red: Oklahoma Landscapes," in *The Culture of Oklahoma*, ed. Howard F. Stein and Robert F. Hill (Norman: University of Oklahoma Press, 1993), 3–28.

10. Peter Wild, ed., *The Desert Reader* (Salt Lake City: University of Utah Press, 1991), 2.

11. Information on farm statistics and state labor history has been culled from sources that include: Robert Lee Maril, *Waltzing with the Ghost of Tom Joad: Poverty, Myth, and Low-Wage Labor in Oklahoma* (Norman: University of Oklahoma Press, 2000); Jim Bissett, *Agrarian Socialism in America: Marx, Jefferson, and Jesus in the Oklahoma Countryside, 1904–1920* (Norman: University of Oklahoma Press, 1999); Sheila Manes, "Pioneers and Survivors: Oklahoma's Landless Farmers," in *Oklahoma: New Views of the Forty-Sixth State*, ed. H. Wayne Morgan and Anne Hodges Morgan (Norman: University of Oklahoma Press, 1982), 93–132; James R. Scales and Danney Goble, *Oklahoma Politics: A History* (Norman: University of Oklahoma Press, 1982); and Kenny L. Brown, "Progressivism in Oklahoma Politics, 1900–13: A Reinterpretation," in *"An Oklahoma I Had Never Seen Before": Alternative Views of Oklahoma History*, ed. Davis D. Joyce (Norman: University of Oklahoma Press, 1994), 27–61.

12. Manes, "Pioneers and Survivors," 113.

13. Information on Floyd can by found in Michael Wallis's *Pretty Boy: The Life and Times of Charles Arthur Floyd* (New York: St. Martin's, 1992); and "When Outlaw Died, Outpouring of Respect Overwhelmed Town," *Kansas City Star*, 30 October 1998, 30.

14. Roy W. Meyer, *The Middle Western Farm Novel in the Twentieth Century* (Lincoln: University of Nebraska Press, 1965).

15. My biographical information was drawn from three main sources: David Sours, "Edwin Lanham," in *American Writers in Paris, 1920–1939*, ed. Karen Lane Rood, vol. 4 of *Dictionary of Literary Biography* (Detroit: Gale Research, 1980), 244–46; Robert McAlmon, *Being Geniuses Together, 1920–30* (New York: Doubleday, 1968); and "Lanham, Edwin Moultrie, Jr." in *The Handbook of Texas Online*, <http://www.tsha.utexas.edu/handbook/online/articles/view/LL/fla58.html>

THE STRICKLANDS

✤ *Jay* ✤

YOU can see the trees dead from last year's drought all through the close green woods of the hills. You can see the crusty limbs of blackjack oaks lifted up like arms in prayer above them dark green leaves. Them trees are dead and will rot to the roots and blow over in the first big wind but all around them new life is growing and the spring is turning into summer and the moss is on the limestone rocks on the hillsides like fur on a squirrel. It's fresh and green again and the drought is a year away and nature forgets, I reckon, like men and women forget. If there was only some way to make men remember the world would be a better place to live in. But they forget and nature forgets and each year they hope fer something better and they try to live on hope. It's deep-rooted in them like it is in nature and like a seedling all they want is a drop of water fer themselves and a ray of sunlight.

Jay Strickland drove along a narrow road in the shallow valley. It was still moist from recent rainfall and the loam was a dark red, following like a stream the contour of the countryside, winding among boulders and tree stumps into the wild silent heart of the hill district. Partly hidden from the road by a field of green corn was a farmhouse, a three-roomed building with weathered clapboard walls and a stone chimney, with roof shingles silvery as moonlight. Behind the house slabs of limestone were spaced like steps down a lumpy hillside to the cornfield, where there was a low fence of smooth gray-and-green stones. The fence encircled the field and ran close beside the road, and Jay's eyes turned to it.

I always git that feeling of peace and remembering when I see that old fence. Some of them mossy stones I wedged in place with my own hands and you could tell my age by some of them, the little ones that was the biggest I could carry then and I couldn't even lift 'em to the top of the fence, and then the hefty ones I was so proud of when I toted 'em down from the hill. Many's the time I shot fox-squirrels off that fence with my twenty-two and year after year I hoed suckers out of that cornfield. This is home, all right. This is the land I was born on and born to and it's a fine feeling each time I come back to it.

Jay turned his five-year-old car into a lane leading to the farmhouse. He sounded the horn, and when he entered an open space before the house he saw his father sitting in the smooth hollow worn in the topmost stone of the steps. Jay waved his hand and got out of the car.

"Jay, is that you?"

"Sure enough, Dad. . . . Say, you're lookin' fine."

"Come up to the house, boy, come up to the house. I'm glad to see you." Crosby Strickland wore a faded hunting-cap and his face was thin and brown beneath it. His nose was long and high-bridged, and his cheeks were sagging and leathery, with deep hollows.

Dad is gitting old, all right, or he wouldn't have to put a hand on the porch pillar to pull himself up. It's good to grip his hand again and see them gray eyes of his, but his fingers is stiff as pieces of wood and his hand on my shoulder is a dead weight.

"You don't come out as often as you ought to, Jay."

"I'm kept pretty busy, Dad."

"I know you are. But it seems I only see you when we got trouble, Jay. . . . But you're a help to us then, and Christ knows there's plenty trouble now."

Jay nodded, and looked with a frown at the hard red ground beside the greenish stone steps.

"Set down, Jay, anyhow. How would you like a swaller of corn?"

Jay looked up into the branches of the post-oak tree beside the house and grinned. "I sure would, Dad."

"Set down, son, while I fetch the jug."

I wonder did Dad make that keg fast yonder in the top of the tree or did Belle do it. He always did swear that whisky aged better in a keg swaying in a tree-top than any other way and God knows he's right because everybody says that old Crosby Strickland makes the best corn whisky in the valley, the best in Oklahoma, maybe. Many's the time I've hoisted a keg up yonder and tied it in a crotch.

Crosby Strickland brought an earthenware jug out on the porch and sat down beside Jay on the stone step. Jay crooked his thumb through the handle of the jug and let its weight lie along his forearm as he drank some of the whisky.

"It's a good batch, ain't it?" Crosby said with an anxious lift in his voice.

"It's as smooth as ever, Dad. The best there is."

"Belle gives me a hand with it, Jay, now that you and Pat are gone." There was a moment of silence and the two men looked at each other.

We're both thinking the same but he don't want to start talking about it yet. I hate to see the old man feel so bad and I wish to Christ Pat had used better sense.

"The thing I don't like, Jay, is that these hills are gittin' busy as a main drag. They got this here plan to dam up the valley to make a lake and the talk is they want to buy up all the land in the valley."

"I know about that lake, Dad. It will give work to about five hunderd men."

"I don't want to have to leave this farm, boy. But the trouble is with all them Gov'ment men in and out somebody's liable to stumble onto the still."

"I wouldn't worry about that, Dad. Nobody gives a damn these days."

"No, but it's aggravatin'. Anyhow, nowadays people can drive over to Arkansas and buy their whisky legal. I don't sell corn like we used to, Jay, back in the old days when I had you and I had Pat, too, and I don't git nothin' fer it." He took a tobacco can from his hip pocket and as he shook tobacco into the crusty bowl of his corncob pipe his hand trembled.

"I wish both you boys had stayed here in the hills," the old man said slowly, staring at the cornfield. He took off the hunting-cap, and his long gray hair fell across his forehead, where the skin was blue-white and drawn tight over his skull.

Jay cleared his throat. "Dad, have you heard from Pat?"

"Belle went out to look fer him this morning, Jay." Crosby struck a match to light his pipe, taking his time, sucking the flame down into the bowl. "She thinks she knows where he's at."

"She would if anybody would. I reckon Pat will head back this way, all right."

"Sure he will. There's no better place to hide out than these here hills. Once he gits off into the blackjack they can hunt from now to doomsday and never find him."

"Has Belle got any notion where to look?"

"Well, they was always going off into the hills together, to places they knowed about, and maybe there was a sort of agreement. Belle was positive certain she would find him."

"Pat will have to leave this part of the country," Jay said. "He can't hide in them hills fer the rest of his life. Damn it, I wish he'd listened to me."

"He's a reckless boy, a foolhardy one. That devil was always in him, even when he was a boy. You helped to keep it down, Jay, because Pat admires you and he always tried to be like you. If you'd of stayed home you might of stopped him. You're steady, Jay, and I don't quarrel none with your idears, but you'd be better off here and I wish to Christ you'd never left."

"I don't know," Jay said. "I doubt if I could of done anything with Pat. It was bound to happen, the way things was. There ain't no work fer Pat and he felt he had to git his hands on some money. I reckon he done it fer Belle and Billy as much as anything."

"I reckon he did."

"There just ain't no chance fer people like us, Dad, that's the whole thing. Poor people don't never have a chance, not from the day they're born, unless they stick together fer their own good. But Pat always wanted to act by himself."

"I'm not saying you're wrong," Crosby said in a slow, careful voice. "I know things have been bad fer us and I can see why you couldn't stand fer it, neither of you. It made you want to go out and fight to make things better and it made Pat want to go out and kick the world in the pants. I wish to Christ I could of stopped him."

"It was bound to happen, Dad."

"I reckon so, but Pat ain't really bad, Jay."

"Of course he ain't."

Crosby gave his head a shake and looked at Jay strangely down his long nose, with a tense, nearsighted expression. "You can see the difference in your faces, Jay. You both got that thin mouth, but yours is stiff and Pat's has got that droop at the corner, that damn-you look. You put that together with his red hair and that hellion laugh and you got Pat."

"If it wasn't fer that red hair of Pat's he might of got away," Jay said. "It was his red hair they recognized. I guess there ain't a doubt it was Pat done it."

"Oh, sure, he done it." Crosby sighed and picked up the jug.

"If they catch him it's ninety-nine years in the Pen, Dad. That's the penalty fer armed robbery down in Texas."

"Ninety-nine years," Crosby said slowly, putting down the jug. He had not taken a drink.

"We've got to git Pat out of this part of the country, all right," Jay said. "Sure enough we do."

"Belle rode off early this morning and she ain't come back. Maybe she found Pat." Crosby shook his head and spat tobacco juice that clung like a brown spider to a stalk of broomweed beside the porch. "The whole state is on the watch fer him. There was a couple of Laws passed through here asking questions, and that Lamar Baker was out this way and he asked about Pat, too, but friendly."

"I don't know how friendly," Jay said. "Because Lamar Baker come right out of the valley here don't mean he's our friend. He's always lookin' fer his chance and I wouldn't put nothin' past him."

"Him and Pat always been friends, Jay."

"Maybe so. But let me tell you something, Dad. Lamar is runnin' fer county attorney, and it ain't but three weeks to primary day. He went to a union member over by Boggs and he give him twenty dollars to deliver that Boggs ballot box on primary day. I seen Lamar and I told him that was where he made one big mistake and it would sure as hell defeat him fer county attorney. I told him we was organized over to Boggs and we made up our minds in a body and our votes wasn't fer sale and when that box is opened on primary day there won't be no union votes fer him. I told him he was goin' down Salt Crick and he was pretty sore."

Crosby smiled and nodded. "Anyhow, he asked me a lot of questions, it seemed like, but I didn't tell him nothing."

Jay put one hand on his father's shoulder. "Pat is sure lucky to have you and Belle to come back to, Dad. You've been a good father to both of us." Jay's fingers tightened on the thin muscle and bone of Crosby's shoulder. "Don't you try to put any of the blame fer Pat on yourself, Dad. We both of us know you're a grand old man."

"I'm glad you said that, son. I done my best, Christ knows." Crosby turned his face to Jay, his eyes squinted. "I'm an old man now. I'm about played out, Jay, and you're a comfort to me. You make up fer Pat, and I don't mean to say I ain't proud of Pat. He's a fine boy and I'm proud of his spirit even if it took him on the road he took. By Jesus, I like a man with fight in him, and you and Pat both got plenty of that, but by Jesus Christ, I ought to be able to do something fer the boy now he's in trouble. That's what a father's fer."

Crosby bent his head, and Jay was silent, waiting for his father to look up. When he did he turned his face to Jay and his lips drew back in a smile, showing his spaced yellow teeth. He said slowly, "What the hell, Jay, let's down some of that corn."

"Here's the jug, Dad."

The old man took the jug in both hands, and the crooked smile still turned up the corners of his lips. "Why, Christ," he said, "that one little corn patch yonder has made enough good whisky to fill a lake in this here valley." He laughed and lifted up the jug.

He's himself again, old hard-bit Crosby Strickland. He's a fine old man and I'm proud to have him fer my father and it's mean to see the way things are and to know how he feels about it. He thinks he missed being the kind of a father he ought to been and God knows he done his best to discipline Pat. But he never could be real strict with him or with me, even when he knowed he'd ought to, and he used to call on me fer advice even when I was just a shaver. And every time Pat got into a mess it give him a laugh because it was only bad boy trouble then. I remember he'd say *Why, the little pip-squeak got away with it* whenever he caught Pat up to something, like when he found him with that can of tobacco he stole from the store, caught him rolling his first cigarette. *God damn it, Jay, what are we going to do with him?* he used to say, and he'd like to die laughing. And there was the time at the barn dance when we was up in the hayloft with them other kids and Pat had his underlip stuck out and he was feeling his red hair and he wanted to go home and he'd be damned if he'd stay. They was dancing to "Old Dan Tucker" and when the music stopped the men stepped outside where the jugs was and when they come back the fiddler cussed and stomped his boot-heels on the floor and the whole party had to turn out to look fer the fiddle. But they couldn't never find it and it busted up the party and we was halfway home when it come to Dad what had happened. I remember he slapped his leg so hard that his horse jumped half out of its skin and the old mare us two was riding double on shied into the ditch. *Damn you, Pat*, the old man yelled, *what did you do with that fiddle?* And Pat yelled back *I chucked it down the well* and he dug his heels in the old mare's fat sides. I remember Dad was roaring and yelling like a locomotive at a crossing while we galloped on down the road, but he didn't try to overtake us. And when he come up to the house Pat had already took off into the woods with a blanket. All Dad said the next morning was *You're a spiteful little bastard, Pat. Someday you'll git your rear end in a sling.* . . . And that's just what has happened, but I guess Dad still thinks of Pat the same way, only a kid, restless and reckless, and even now, after he robbed a bank, he thinks the same. But still you can see the sadness in his face and I guess he feels he's to blame. The smile wrinkles he used to have at the corners of his eyes are crow's feet now, and his skin is like horsehide and sags from his chin. He's an old man and he's lonely and just because he tries not to catch my eye it's plainer to see that he ain't happy in his mind. I hate to go off and leave him but I got to do it.

Jay got to his feet, and Crosby raised his eyes anxiously. "You ain't leavin', Jay?"

"I've got to, Dad. There's an Indian down the road I want to see."

"Who's that?"

"He calls himself Joseph Paul. You know him."

"Sure, I know that Creek. I got a walnut stick he carved fer me. Bought it fer two bits." Crosby stood up beside Jay. "What do you want of him, Jay, more of this union business?"

"That's right."

"You won't git no Indians in the union."

"If I don't it won't be fer want of trying."

"Them fullbloods will stick together among theirselves, but they won't sign up with no tenant farmers' union, Jay. They stay to theirselves."

"Maybe so."

"I know that. I know them Indians, Jay. So long as one of 'em has got a stalk of corn it belongs to the whole caboodle. You got to admire that part of it."

It ain't no use to talk that over with him and it ain't never no use to argue with Dad.

"As soon as Belle comes home, Dad, I want you to let me know," Jay said. "Send Belle into town in the truck to fetch me."

"All right, Jay."

"And if she finds him, Dad, we got to git hold of some money somehow. We got to git Pat safe out of this part of the country."

"Don't I know that, Jay!"

Crosby followed Jay to the car, standing by while Jay started the engine, saying: "It was fine to see you again, son. Don't make it so long between visits."

"I'll git out again as soon as I can, and the minute you hear from Pat you let me know," Jay said. As he drove away he glanced at the mirror above the windshield and saw his father reflected small and stiff.

I want to git away fast and put trees between me and the house like I could leave behind me the sadness there and not have it follow me along the road. But that I couldn't never do. I sure do hope Belle finds Pat and when she does and I see him I'm going to talk to that boy and I'm going to tell him fer Dad's sake and fer Belle and Billy he's got to behave. He's in deep now, just too damned deep.

Jay drove very fast the two miles along the valley road to Joseph Paul's house, a one-roomed shack on the slope of a hill beside a rocky field that the Indian had left off farming in disgust several seasons ago. Jay stopped his car at the side of the road and started up the hill.

Yonder's that fullblood setting in the shade whittling on a walnut stick. He's got that white pith helmet he always wears setting back on his head and his brown forehead is wet with sweat you can see rolling down the creases of his fat face. It's funny how a man as poor as him can be so fat. You can see it in rolls on that hairless chest with his shirt open like it is.

"Hello, Joseph Paul," Jay said.

"Long time no see you, Jay." The fat Indian got to his feet and held out his hand. His face was solemn; the clasp of his fingers was strong. Jay sat down on a sun-bleached chopping log with hardly any bark left on the smooth hardwood.

"Make plenty stick, two-t'ree chair," Joseph Paul said with a spread of his hand toward the walnut whittlings. "Sell him in town."

"Dad said you made him a walking stick."

"Ay-uh." The Indian deposited himself with care on a rickety wild-cherry chair with a plaited hickory bark seat. He sat quite still with his palms on his knees, looking at Jay.

"Doing any work these days, Joseph Paul?" Jay asked.

"Make stick and chair. Work damn plenty."

"Sure." Jay smiled and watched the Indian take off his pith helmet and fan his face.

I remember Joseph Paul a little fellow with big black eyes

and his hair cut in bangs and then a thin young farmer and now a fat Indian setting in the shade. He never puts out nothing but still that's Indian.

"There's been a lot of rain," Jay said. "Crops ought to be pretty fair this year."

Joseph Paul shrugged his shoulders and looked at the rocks and weeds of his field with a certain placid eloquence.

That look of his tells a lot. It tells how the fullbloods wanted to hold their lands in common and how the white man broke them down and how when the land was finally allotted they got the rockiest and the wildest hillside land where they couldn't grow a stalk of corn. And it tells me how to go about it.

"You don't farm fer nobody else, do you?" Jay asked.

Joseph Paul shook his head.

"I wondered if you did. Lots of Indians do."

"Some do, Jay."

Jay lit a cigarette and heard the Indian saying: "See Lamar Baker two day ago."

Jay took the cigarette out of his mouth with a slow deliberate motion and blew smoke against the end of it to scatter the ashes.

"Him ask about Pat," Joseph Paul said. "Pretty busy fella, Lamar. Him talk damn plenty. Him want Indian vote."

"What did you tell him?"

"Don't know not'ing. Don't say not'ing."

"That's just as well," Jay said. "I guess you know they claim Pat robbed a bank down in Texas and maybe Lamar wants to find him and git the credit. I don't know. He's running fer office. Maybe he wants to know because he's a friend of Pat's. I wouldn't know which it was."

The Indian's faint smile showed broken yellow teeth. The lobes of his ears joined his brown cheeks in a point toward his square jaw and when he smiled his ears moved. His black eyes looked steadily at Jay.

"Joseph Paul, I guess you know I'm working fer the Southern Tenant Farmers' Union?" The Indian nodded and Jay watched his face as he talked. "I'm starting a drive now. Fer one thing I want to git the spinach workers organized solid before the next crop is made. We ain't going to have people cutting spinach in the fields fer four cents a basket no more, Joseph. We'll strike the whole industry if we have to and we'll git ten, twelve and maybe fifteen cents." Jay waited for the Indian's nod and kept watching his face. "Joseph, I've got to have your help."

You can't never tell what he's thinking. You can only speak your piece and wait fer his answer. But he listens to me.

"We need the Indians in the union and the Indians need the union, Joseph. Some of you Creeks pick spinach and a few farm tenant land. Our program in the end is to git land of their own fer all them people. It's time the farmers here in Oklahoma had a square deal, and I don't need to tell you, Joseph, that the Indians never had a square deal. You Civilized Tribes Indians are the forgotten men in this part of the country. You was drove away from your homes in the old South by soldiers with guns who hunted you out of the hills like animals and put you in chains like animals. You was marched into the wilderness, into the swamps, and you died like flies coming to the Indian Territory, to the land they promised you fer as long as the grass grows and the water flows. But they didn't keep that promise very long. You fullbloods wanted to hold your lands in common because the wise men of your tribes knowed that if it was allotted individually the white man would beat you out of it. But it was allotted and look what you got — rocky upland farms that will hardly grow a stalk of corn. Like that field of yours yonder, Joseph Paul."

"My pappy follow Chito Harjo," Joseph Paul said.

"Who's that?"

"Chito Harjo — Crazy Snake. Him Creek chief and him say fer Indian keep land all toget'er, all one, all fer tribe, and white man attack Indians in camp fer powwow. Crazy Snake catched, put in chains. Hair cut off. Him die."

"I know about Crazy Snake," Jay said. "He knowed what he was talking about. He knowed that allotment was just a way to cheat the Indian and we know now that he was right. Your father had a hunderd and sixty acres of land allotted to him, didn't he, Joseph?"

The Indian nodded, and spread his hands.

"And you got forty acres left," Jay said. "You maybe wouldn't have that, if it wasn't your homestead and is tax exempt and can't be mortgaged. The other hunderd and twenty acres

was took away from you years ago and Crazy Snake knowed
that would happen. He knowed the fullblood would be fair
game fer cheating and exploitation. And now to make a living
most of you got to farm another man's land and plow his fields
and harvest his crops and you're no better off than slaves, no
better off than the slaves your tribe used to own in the old
South. Did you ever stop and think of that? I tell you, Joseph
Paul, the Indians can't go on retreating. There's no place to re-
treat to. You've got to turn around and make a fight and you've
got to do it together and you've got to do it with other people in
the same fix. What you-all need is organization, our organization. You can help us and we can help you." Jay paused, then
lowered his voice. "You go around a lot, Joseph. You see plenty
of Indians of all tribes and you could help us out. How about
it? Will you do it? Will you join up?"

"Sure," Joseph Paul said, and Jay grinned and took out his
handkerchief to wipe his face.

"Pretty good speech," the Indian said, with a faint smile. "But
no call to make it, Jay. Sure me help."

"I thought you would, Joseph," Jay said. "I hoped you would.
Now this is what you can do. You can sound out the Indians
you know and git those who think our way to talk to their
friends. We want to git the idea moving, we want to start them
talking union, and then we'll follow it up. This is my plan, and
I'd like to know what you think about it." Jay stopped to light
another cigarette, watching the Indian through the smoke. "I
thought we'd have a stomp-dance off in the hills some place, a
stomp-dance and barbecue, and we'll git as many Indians together as we can, and you'll talk to them and maybe I'll make a
speech. What do you think?"

Joseph Paul took a pipe from the forepocket of his overalls.
The bowl was a .50 caliber cartridge shell, soldered to a metal
stem. He shook a small amount of tobacco into it from a sack
and tamped it with his little finger. He lit the tobacco and took a
quick, delicate puff, then turned to Jay with a placid, Oriental
look. He said quietly: "Indian like stomp-dance."

"Spread the idea around some," Jay said. "How about a Saturday night, a couple of weeks from now?"

"Big stomp-dance come pretty soon. Soon as moon big Indian have stomp-dance over by Boggs. Plenty eats. Dance all night. You go t'ere, Jay?"

"That's Cherokee, ain't it?"

"Cherokee. All day big powwow, Jay, play Indian ball. See plenty Indian t'ere."

"Yes, I reckon it's worth a try, Joseph, but them Indians are lined up in politics. I don't believe we'll git no place. The point is I want to start things moving quick as I can. I've got a drive under way among the nigros and there'll be a barbecue over to Tanzey on Saturday. Why don't you come over?"

"Maybe so."

"There'll be plenty of roast pig. Bring along a few friends, Joseph, the ones who are interested."

"Okay."

"Our slogan is land fer the landless," Jay said. "Some day we aim to abolish farm tenancy altogether, and right away we're putting in co-operative stores where a man can git his money's worth. And fer them that has land we're going to help put through Farm Security loans that will give you five years' tax exemption and forty years to pay off. And if we can keep a progressive government in this country we'll have them debts wrote off the books. And listen here, Joseph Paul, the Tenant Farmers' Union is the Indian's friend and we want every Indian in the district to bring his grievances to us and we'll take 'em up and we'll git action on 'em. You can depend on that. We're all together in this. We've all got to work together, Indians, nigros and whites. That's what we've got to make people see, Joseph. We've got to break down prejudice and work together and everybody's got to help."

He don't put out much but you can depend on this Indian. He shakes your hand the way a man ought to do it.

"I've got to head back to town now, and I'll see you Saturday at Tanzey," Jay said. "Right?"

Their hands still were clasped and Jay stood looking at the bleak wall of the house and the strip of gunny sack nailed across a broken windowpane. "If you hear anything about Pat, Joseph Paul — if you do, let me know."

"Sure do, Jay."

Jay went down the hill to his car, and before he got in he

turned and waved to the Indian, who was standing at the head of the path. Joseph Paul moved the white sunhelmet in a slow arc, and Jay got in the car. He turned it around and drove back out of the valley, following a road that ran along the northern ridge, dense with second-growth yellow pine and blackjack oak. Among the trees it was impossible to tell the contour of the valley; and even from the wild ridge top trees almost screened all vision.

I hate to think of the valley filled with water, of water covering up them trees where I've hunted squirrels and treed coons all my life. I know them woods like some people know a city's streets. The Government's done some fine work and I reckon this here lake will help the country, but I don't like to see that valley dammed up. Everybody's got their heads full of soil erosion and resettlement and God knows it's got to come, but the way they go about it shows it's the people with money they think of first and the farmers and the workers last. They build a dam in the valley first of all to make a lake where people can go swimming and enjoy themselves, people from town and not the farmers living here now. And they'll have lodges around the lake and guys from Mehuskah will bring their blonde women out here fer the week end. It will be just a God-damned whorehouse on the side of the lake, and the farmers will be moved off somewhere else to farms maybe a little better. But still, the Government will build 'em new houses and give 'em bottom land on easy-purchase terms. They'll be better off. Some good will come of it, all right, and it's progress and they'll reclaim some eroded land with the irrigation, but it will be a grab bag fer the Mehuskah politicians and fer people like Lamar Baker. He's already got his finger in it and I reckon he'll git plenty. He knows how to do it and that's all he's after, grabbing money and gitting ahead, grabbing somebody else's money and gitting ahead of somebody else. You'd never think he come out of the valley, and God knows he don't never come back to it except to canvass votes or hunt possums.

The road climbed higher on the slope of the ridge, and down below Jay saw the site where the dam would be built. There was a clear view of it from a clearing at a fork in the road where stood a schoolhouse of ocher native stone, known as the Sour

Tom School. One fork of the road led down below to a covered bridge across a creek; the other turned southwest toward Aldine. Jay stopped the car at the side of the road by the schoolhouse.

I ought to drive on about my business, but there's something about that little woman . . . I just want to stop and talk to her fer a minute, and by God I'm goin' to do it. I got plenty of time.

Jay got out of the car and walked across the bare clearing to the schoolhouse. The door was open and he looked in.

Hot damn, with that sun on her hair, with that white soft skin, with that laughing look about her, and she's teaching in an Indian school. If I could just be sure about her. If I could know what she really thinks and what she's after, and she must be after something. That's the hitch, she's after something and what it is I ain't got.

She had not seen Jay and she had not seen his shadow on the pine floor. Fifteen little Indians sat at their desks watching a white rabbit in a cage of chicken-wire at the end of the schoolroom. The small brown faces and round dark eyes all were turned toward the rabbit and it was absolutely silent in the room, with not a furtive whisper, not even the movement of a hand. On the blackboard was written:

This is a rabbit.
He has pink eyes.
He has long ears.
He can sit up.
His name is . . . .

She looked up and saw Jay and her smile was sudden and warm and there came with it a faint flush that brightened her face and made her blue eyes sparkle. Her eyes were a light clear blue, intense in contrast to her black eyebrows and hair.

"Jay, hello!" She got up from her desk and came toward him.

"I was just passing by," Jay said. "How are you, Leona?"

She called to a small brown girl: "Emma Paul, you take the crayons out of the top drawer of my desk, and Martin Goback, you give everyone a sheet of paper. You may all make a drawing now." She smiled again at Jay. "Let's go out by the well where it's shady, Jay. I want to talk to you."

She always says that: *I want to talk to you.* It sounds like it means something but it's her way and I guess she says it to everybody just like that. But she talks mostly about herself and it's plain I don't interest her much, not in the way she does me.

"At least they like to draw pictures," Leona said. "That's one thing I've found out. But they work so tight and small and I can't make them draw free and splashy the way they ought to."

"You still having trouble with them kids?"

"Plenty of it. Jay, I can't even get them to name the rabbit. They just won't respond. I'm teaching them exactly the way they told me to in the demonstration school, but it doesn't do any good. Listen, I bought that rabbit myself, and I built the cage for it, and they like to watch it, but they won't talk about it. They won't even give it a name. Did you see what was written on the blackboard?"

"Sure."

"That's the way we teach, the activity method. You know, make them participate. Before, I had a little horny frog and I wrote on the blackboard: *This is a toad; he has horns; he breathes through his skin; he does not make warts.* You see, we try to stop all those superstitions, like if you step on a toad it will rain and all that. But these fullblood children just won't help me out. I suppose I'll have to name the rabbit myself. How do you like Hoppy?"

"Hoppy?"

"For a name."

"Oh, sure." They were leaning against the stone wall of the well and Jay watched the light and shade on her face, the blue-black sheen of her hair.

"If you just ask them a question it scares them near to death. They hang their heads and look around at the other kids and they answer in soft little voices that slip out of their mouths like lizards scuttling from under a rock. I'm about ready to give up. I've been teaching school for three years, Jay, and that was all right, but I wish I hadn't transferred to the Indian schools this spring. The pay is better, but heavens!"

"Indians ain't the same as white kids," Jay said.

"You don't need to tell me that. I simply can't make them come to life."

No matter what she says she can make it sound like it's just fer me, even when she's talking about herself. Most little women are like that but this here little woman stands on her own two feet like most of 'em don't.

"Anyhow, Jay, tomorrow is the last day of school."

"Is that right?" Jay said. "What do you aim to do this summer, Leona?"

"I don't know. Go home to Tulsa, I suppose. I'd like to take a trip to Colorado where it's cool."

Her sort of woman would have too many wants. I couldn't give her what she's after and I'm a fool to go panting after her like a hound dog. She wouldn't be a wife fer a man in my line. She'll have to have a feller who's a success in the world and makes plenty and can send her to Colorado Springs fer the summer. But she's got something. She thinks about herself and them big blue eyes of hers take everything in and she's got that look like she could tame a cage-full of panthers. I guess any woman with looks like hers is too damned sure of herself and knows she can git whatever she's after. . . .

"I wish I wasn't making such a botch of this school, but I can't make those kids act human." She smiled at Jay. "I don't think I'm the schoolteacher type, do you, Jay?"

"You sure ain't," Jay said. "But give them time, Leona. After a while they'll open up. I know Indians. What you'd ought to do is keep two or three of 'em together after school and let 'em play with that rabbit, not just sit and talk about it. And you let 'em draw, if that's what they like. Those kids don't have nothing. They don't have colored sticks and white paper at home. You just let 'em make plenty of pictures and you'll git along with them."

"I want to understand them, Jay. I want to know more about the Indians, about how they live and what their homes are like. I ask them questions, but I can't get them to tell me anything."

"Indian homes ain't much," Jay said. "They got nothing. Just a shack and a cook-stove."

"They have their folkways and customs and that's what I want to study. I'd like to be kind of an expert on Indians."

She ain't interested in whether the Indians are starving to death. She wouldn't open her eyes to that and she ain't concerned with their troubles. I guess she feels the same way about white people. She don't know what exploitation and suffering is and she don't care. She's like the rest of 'em in this part of the country, when they want to explain away conditions like that they say: It's poor white trash and if you gave 'em anything better they wouldn't know what to do with it. They been saying that in the South since the Civil War and they salve their conscience that way and I reckon she thinks the same. It's a waste of my time and I know it.

"Jay, did you ever go to a stomp-dance?"

"A stomp-dance? Yes, why?"

"Well, I'd sure like to see one. Lamar Baker told me that there's a big one off in the hills pretty soon and that white people can go to it."

"How come you know Lamar Baker?"

"I met him over in Tulsa a couple of years ago when he was stumping for the Governor, and one day a week or two ago he passed by here and stopped for a drink of water."

"Is that so?"

"He was real surprised to find me here, and he stopped in to see me once or twice in Aldine."

"I just about grew up with Lamar," Jay said. "I've knowed him a long time."

"That's what he said. Jay, I want to go to that stomp-dance. Will you take me?"

"I wish I could, Leona."

"Well, can't you?"

"I'll be too busy."

"You shouldn't let yourself be so busy all the time. You're working too hard. And, Jay, you're never going to get anything out of it."

"I ain't lookin' fer anything."

"I mean you'll never get ahead that way. Jay, I wish you'd be practical about it."

Jay shrugged his shoulders.

"You're a trial, Jay, you sure are. Listen, I've got to go back to my class. Those little fullbloods may be on the warpath in there."

They started back to the schoolhouse, and at the corner of the building she stopped and put one hand on his arm.

"Oh, Jay."

"Yes?"

"I'm sorry about your brother."

It only just come into her head. All this time she's been thinking of herself and it just come into her head. I'm a God-damned fool to waste my time.

"I reckon Pat's safe in Mexico by now, Leona."

"Do you think so?"

"He's had time to make Mexico, all right. I ain't worried about Pat."

"That's good. I'm glad to know he's all right, Jay."

They walked on to the door and she took his hand. Inside the schoolhouse a little girl giggled.

"Good-by, Jay. Come back soon."

"I sure will, Leona."

Jay walked back to his car. He drove away on the road to Aldine, increasing his speed as the road improved.

Just the warm feel of her hand can make me forget all I was thinkin' and I'm a fool all right. But I guess maybe she likes me a little. Her face is always bright and smiling and she holds onto my hand that way. I guess she would learn. She's from Tulsa. She's a big-town girl. She never had to find out how hard it is fer some people to live and if she did maybe she would think different. I ought to take her with me someday up in the hills and let her see fer herself. That's what I'll do. I'll let her see kids with gunny sacks to sleep on. I'll let her see four people sleeping in one room, half of them on the floor, with nothing to eat but cornbread and molasses and sometimes a chunk of salt pork and cream gravy. That ought to make her see things different and that ought to make her see that I got to go on in the work I'm doing.

It was three miles to Aldine, and fifteen miles beyond it to Mehuskah. On the upland, where the rain water dried more quickly, the narrow road was slick with dust and the oak trees along it, the sassafras trees and the trumpet vines, were powdered with dust already blown loose and dry. At each end of the road

that ran through Aldine and formed its principal street was a
signpost: ALDINE, POP. 380. On the outskirts of the town the
houses stood under shade trees beside cornfields and truck gardens, but on the main street there were no trees. On either side
the town presented a blank brick face and there was only a cluster of people at the corner by the domino parlor. One of the two
hotels, the cotton gin, and the grist mill had been boarded up
for years and the machinery was rusty and silent. Jay drove
quickly over the rough street, and again was in a residential section on the road to Mehuskah.

That's where she lives, that white boarding-house set back
under them elm trees. It's a lonesome place, I reckon, fer a gal
like her. I remember when it was a city to me, when I was a kid
and we used to come here to the store in a wagon. In them days
we called it Aldine City. I'd never seen so many people together
all at once as there was of a Saturday then, crowded four deep
along the boardwalk and in and out of the drugstore and the
hotel and the general store with the horse collars on the wall and
the flypaper and the ax-handles and the hoes and rakes and the
clean store-clothes that smelled so new. I remember that first
time I was scared to git out of the wagon. Maw was alive then
and she stayed in the wagon with me, setting there in her poke
bonnet looking straight ahead of her because she didn't want to
git out on the boardwalk in her bare feet, even if she had come
there special to buy herself a pair of shoes. The man had to bring
'em to her out of the store and she tried 'em on in the wagon. It
was a long ways to town and back then by wagon and team, but
now we got this black-top road all the way from Aldine to
Mehuskah, and Mehuskah is the big town and they call Aldine
a "ghost town" with its trade gone to the city and the railroad.
It sure ain't Aldine City no more and it's like to fall to pieces
now and I remember when the hotel was crowded and I used to
go out to the gin and watch the compress work. I guess when I
was a kid if I'd of seen a place the size of Mehuskah I'd of turned
tail and run. Who'd of thought then of a place with paved streets
and an eight-story building and thirty-three thousand people
in it, by the Chamber of Commerce figures, anyhow?

Jay had to drive along the main business street of Mehuskah
to reach his three-roomed frame house near the M. K. & T. rail-

road tracks. He drove across the railroad crossing and turned left off the paved street with a bump. He had to steer a careful course among the deep and dust-filled holes in the road. Here, beside the tracks, were two rows of weather-white houses, in front of which in the afternoon sunlight women and children sat in chairs in the tiny yards, or on the balustrades of sagging piazzas. In one yard there was a bed with springs hanging to the bare ground and a shabby patchwork quilt spread over it. Three small boys sat solemnly on the quilt and watched Jay drive by. Jay's house was the last in the row and the yard in front of it was larger. Just beyond a picket fence there was a two-acre cornfield and for the house and field Jay paid twelve dollars a month rent. Because of the rains his corn stood tall and green with silky tassels swinging and he was sure to make a crop. The shabby house, the color of a sweaty dun horse, stood beside the cornfield like a farmhouse, except that it did not have the settled, much-used appearance of a farmhouse. There were no washtubs hanging on the wall, no intimate and revealing indications of the poverty of daily life. Somehow it could be told that the door of this house was never locked; the building had the emptiness, the lack of interest or personality, of a deserted house. Only the partly drawn shades in the windows indicated that it was lived in.

Jay opened the door and stopped with his hand on the knob when he saw a battered straw suitcase in a corner. The handle of it was patched with baling wire and the straw was broken through in several places and streaked with grease and dust.

"Hello," Jay said. He went into the living room, a bare dusty room with a calendar the only ornament on the faded wall, with a table and two chairs and a curved-back sofa that was solidly propped on a block sawed from a two-by-four plank. Sitting on the sofa was a thin Negro. He got to his feet and grinned at Jay.

"Is you Jay Strickland?"

"I don't believe I know you," Jay said, and his thin lips drew tightly together. When he was suspicious his eyes narrowed into lines that paralleled his high cheekbones and he looked as brown and unbending as an Indian.

The Negro was still smiling. "I thumbed my way down from Memphis, on th' road. Sid Bowlder sent me this way."

"Oh, sure," Jay said.

"He told me y'all needed somebody to help out down heah."

"That's right, we do. Set down." Jay dropped into a rocking chair and threw his left leg over the arm.

The Negro sank back on the sofa. "My name is Rock Island Jones. I been workin' fo' Sid around Memphis, but befo' I share-cropped down in Arkansas. I'm an Arkansawyer."

Jay took out a tobacco sack and rolled a cigarette. He tossed the sack across to the Negro and took a match from a small china shoe on the table.

"What did you say your name was?"

"Jones — Rock Island Jones. They calls me Rocky."

"Rock Island after the railroad?"

"Yeah, my pappy wo'ked on th' Rock Island."

"I can sure use you, Rocky," Jay said. "Glad you could come down. How is Sid?"

"He doin' fine."

"Uh-huh," Jay said. "You can start in right off if you want to. Saturday evenin' there's a barbecue over to Tanzey, about fifteen miles south." He looked hard at the intent, intelligent face of the Negro. "We got lots of work to do, Rocky. We got to organize them farm workers and fix it so they can earn a living like human beings instead of animals." He paused and shook his head slightly, frowning. "It ain't been easy through here. We got that same old trouble, the whites and the blacks. The idea has got around that the Tenant Farmers' Union is a nigro union and a lot of white men have stayed out of it. A lot of men who want to belong have stayed out because of that."

"You can't have no Jim Crow unions," Rocky said.

"I didn't say Jim Crow."

"You knows what I mean."

"I mean we don't aim to have no Jim Crow union. We got that trouble, though, and that's one thing we got to beat."

"They done told me it was kind of slow down heah," the Negro said. "You'd ought to git the union organized strong befo' it's too much talk of Jim Crow."

"Of course we ought," Jay said impatiently. "But look here, we won't have no terror like there was over to Arkansas. We got to go slow here, but still we ain't going to lay off organizing the nigros because the white farmer has got his eyebrows up.

We got to go ahead with that work, just like I'm going ahead now to git the Indians in line. I reckon it will be a sight easier to organize Indians and nigros together than it will white men and nigros. The red man and the black man both got a grudge against the white man."

Rock Island Jones nodded, and Jay turned his head and blew on his cigarette, scattering the ashes.

"We never had no rank-and-file movement here in the state of Oklahoma before," Jay said. "This state has been controlled by political forces since the Civil War and it's different from the old South. It's different from Arkansas. We ain't got so many sharecroppers here. It's renters mostly, and urban workers who go out to cut spinach and pick cotton in the season. We can't git a hold on them people unless we educate 'em to it, and that takes time. We can't start a rank-and-file movement overnight. We got to go slow. It's too easy to put the fear of God into 'em if we run into any trouble, and we don't want to go out and organize no topheavy union without no leadership. We got to build that leadership, too, and the time will come when we got all them hunderd and sixty-five thousand tenants and sharecroppers in this state organized solid. But we got to go slow at first. We got to git the organization rooted."

"Up Memphis way they thinkin' it ought to go faster," the Negro said.

"You'll see fer yourself how we're goin'," Jay said. "Already we got a good membership in the eastern part of the state. We're doing things, Rocky, and you'll see. Now over at Tanzey Saturday something ought to come off. It's a good barbecue and we'll have a crowd and we'll need some good speaking. I'm going to make a talk and I guess I can count on you."

"You sure kin."

Jay smoked his cigarette in silence. The sun had sunk from sight behind the ridge west of town and in the warmer light the harsh outlines of the frame houses and the Katy freight-shed farther along the tracks were softened and the grimy paint appeared more pure in color.

"I got to find me a place to sleep," the Negro said.

Jay took the cigarette out of his mouth. "You can bunk here. I got a folding cot, an old army cot, but it's comfortable."

"That will do jus' fine."

The sun is sinking into them long green waves of trees in the hills and I wonder if somewhere out yonder in the blackjack Belle has found Pat.

Rocky stood up and went for his suitcase. Looking at him, Jay said: "I've got some overalls I can let you have."

Rocky glanced down at his tight-fitting suit.

"You're a farmer now," Jay said.

"Man, I was raised with a hoe." The Negro grinned. "I was choppin' cotton when I was so-high. My first suit of clo'es was a flour sack. Yes, sir."

Jay got up and went into the next room to take down the cot. He stood a moment by the window looking at the glowing western sky. The stub of the cigarette drooped from the corner of his lips and smoke from it rose to his squinted eyes. He stood looking off toward the hills.

If Pat is anywhere out yonder in the blackjack it's damn sure that Belle will find him. . . .

ℬelle

❧   ❧

A SLOW, twisting smudge of smoke rose from the burned-out fire, white against the dark green trees and then a thin blue against the colors of the sunset sky. Belle Strickland sat with her back against a cedar tree watching the twist of smoke spread and break into butterflies of motion against the orange sky. It was very quiet in the gully, and airless, and her forehead was wet with perspiration. The fire was near enough for her to feel its heat on her face, but the smoke that the smoldering greenwood gave off kept the mosquitoes away.

It's hard to set here and wait and wait and not know whether he's coming or whether he means to come or whether he's safe. If he does come he'll look fer me here and all I can do is set and wait. . . .

Belle wore overalls and a blue cotton shirt with sleeves rolled high on her round solid arms, which were scarred with insect bites. Her large-boned, handsome body was sprawled carelessly on the ground at the base of the tree, in complete repose, but her eyebrows were drawn together in a constant frown that wrinkled her pale and lightly freckled forehead. She had taken off her man's felt hat, into which was thrust an eagle feather Joseph Paul's wife had given her, and her blonde hair fell in an un-combed mass to her shoulders. She lay looking steadily at the western sky.

Pretty soon now it will be twilight and then night, but the moon is coming on to full and there'll be light. Maybe he'll come by night. It was eleven o'clock when I got here and that makes seven hours I been waiting and all that time I ain't touched the jug. I ain't been near the cleft of that cedar tree except that once when I moved the jug into the shade. All day long and all alone and I ain't touched it and I ain't going to touch it until Pat gits here. And he's got to come. Where else would he go to but here? He always said we'd meet in Cedar Gully and he's got to come. He'll find me here waiting and he'll find the jug full up and he'll say honey, Belle, sweet honey, darling, I knowed you'd be here waiting fer me and if you wasn't I'd of blowed my brains out. . . . Pat, you got to come. Pat, you got to be here. Pat. . . .

Belle suddenly rose to her feet and started toward the tree where the jug was. She was startled by the sudden clear sound of a horse snorting, and spun around. But it was her own sorrel saddle-horse, hobbled and cropping grass on a gentle slope that led to the sheer bank of the gully. Her saddle was slung astraddle a fallen tree, with the skillet still tied to the pommel, the cooking supplies still packed in the saddlebags.

I *will* have one drink, just one, and then I'll unpack the things and fix myself some supper. Tomorrow Pat will show up and maybe tonight. I know he'll be here but I can't go on just waiting unless I take a drink.

She lifted the jug from the cleft where it was securely wedged and twisted the cork out. She crooked her thumb through the handle, threw back her head and raised the jug to her mouth. Her blonde hair fell down her back, shining in the sunset. The corn whisky was warm, but even so it was smooth, and she took a long burning drink, then lowered the jug and gasped a moment for air, blowing out her breath.

"You aim to save me a swaller, I hope?"

Belle whirled around, her mouth open, her blue eyes wide

and anxious, and the first thing she saw was Pat's hair redder than the sunset.

"My God, Pat!"

"Hello, Belle."

I can only stand and look at him and my heart thumps so and my knees are weak and he got here after all and I knowed he'd come. I knowed that nothing could keep him away but he only just stands there looking at me with that sweet curving smile of his lips and his hair so red and rumpled on his head.

"I might have dropped the jug, Pat!" Belle laughed. "It would of served you right. I wish I'd dropped it." Her voice was caressing. "Where did you spring from?"

We just stand here looking and it's been three months now since I seen him. His face is thinner and he looks tired but he's still got that smile of his. . . .

"I been watching you fer a long time, Belle. I couldn't make out whether it was you, not until I seen that sorrel horse. I thought you was some Indian down here."

"Did you ever see an Indian with cornsilk hair?"

"I seen that eagle feather in your hat."

"Oh."

"Well?" Pat said.

Belle smiled at him.

"Don't I git a kiss?" Pat did not take his eyes from her face.

"I thought it was the jug you was anxious fer."

"I hope you left me anyhow a swaller, that's all."

"It's the first I took of it, Pat."

"I bet."

"Look and see fer yourself."

Pat leaned his rifle against the cedar tree. He straightened with his chest thrust out and his teeth shining in the amber light of dusk. He went a step toward her and took the jug from her hands, then his arms went on around her and he hugged her close to him. "Little Belle. Hot damn! It's good to see you."

She turned up her face and he kissed her hard. His hand ran through her rumpled blonde hair, his palm caressing it. They breathed each other's breath, their faces pressed together.

"I was scared you wouldn't be here, Belle."

"Gee, I was scared you wasn't coming."

"I had to walk through the blackjack. It took me a long time."

They held each other tightly and Belle stood with her head thrown back, her eyes closed. Pat bent to kiss her with his head on one side like a puppy picking up a toy.

"Pat, what a beard you got!"

"Two days of it. You better bring me a razor."

"Pat!"

"Yeah."

"Don't you drop that jug!"

"The jug's okay."

"The cork ain't in it." She turned away, and Pat raised the jug; some of the corn whisky had spilled on his hand. Belle bent over and licked his fingers, laughing. He pushed her away and lifted the jug to his mouth. He took a deep drink. "Oh, God bless Dad. Oh, that's good. How is he, Belle?"

"He's fine."

"And how's Jay?"

"All right, Pat. Working hard. Look here, it'll soon come dark. Pat, when did you eat last?"

"Not all day, Belle."

"Oh, my poor dumpling. Oh, Pat, I'll shake something up quick as I can. I'll fry some eggs, Pat, and I brought some bacon and coffee."

"I wonder," Pat said. "How about that fire?"

My Lord, I'd clean forgot that they're after him and he robbed a bank and run away and they recognized him and the Laws are looking fer him. He has to hide himself away and be careful and never know when they're after him and when they'll come down on him with guns and I guess they'd shoot him first and talk afterwards. We're just about at the end of everything and what is there to do? But I oughtn't to let him know I feel that way and I oughtn't to let him think about it. We've got to be happy together just fer now, anyhow just fer now. . . .

"I think it's safe, Pat."

"I guess so. Nobody lives near Cedar Gully. Hell, it's all right. I'll git some firewood, Belle." Pat kicked his way into the bushes, and Belle began to unpack the saddlebags.

"Hey, Belle, what's this? What's this in the pot?"

"It's fer tomorrow, Pat. I shot a couple of fox-squirrels and I put 'em there to soak."

"Squirrel stew!" Pat said. "Belle, nobody can make a squirrel stew like you can."

"There's a patch of hickory trees down the gully a piece, Pat, and I knowed I'd catch me some squirrels yonder. I brung along the twenty-two just fer that."

"Through the eye each time, I bet," Pat said fondly. He looked at her as she knelt in the twilight by the fallen log, her hair pale against the cherry darkness of the saddle leather.

"Say, Belle, guess what I brung fer Billy — How is Billy?"

"He's fine, Pat. He sure does miss his Dad."

"I want to see that boy. Belle, guess what I brung him — a little gun and you pull the trigger and it makes a flash like a real pistol going off. It's got a little battery in it."

Belle glanced at him over her shoulder. "Pat, I don't know I like that fer Billy. I don't want him playing with guns, even toy ones."

"Oh now, say," Pat said. "I want him to be as good a shot as his Maw and Dad."

Belle sighed. "Pat, how about that firewood?"

"Okay, I'll git it — But, Belle, you take a look at that little gun. It sure will tickle Billy."

He walked farther along the gully, kicking in the grass, and when he returned with his arms full of wood Belle had built up the fire and her face glowed in the warm light. He piled the wood to one side and sat down. He stretched out his legs, sighing.

"I'm about done in, Belle. I ditched my car fifteen miles yonder, other side of the blackjack, and I rode shanks' mare the rest of the way."

Belle sat cross-legged beside the fire putting strips of bacon into the frying pan. He watched her movements and his eyes lingered on the strong sure sweep of her arms, the exciting lift of her breasts as she leaned forward to hold the skillet over the flame. Pat sprawled out on the grass and reached for the jug. He pushed himself back to a sitting position and leaned against the tree. The bacon had begun to snap and hiss like snakes in the frying pan. Belle turned it with a forked stick of greenwood. In the firelight her face was placid and the shadows along her cheekbones were shadings of tenderness and content. She began to take the bacon out of the skillet and spread it to drip on a nest of green leaves.

The last time I cooked fer Pat was before he went away, before he went down to the oil fields. I knowed then he oughtn't to go and I tried to tell him so but he wouldn't listen. I wonder if he had in his mind then what he was going to do, or I wonder if he went away just to work in the oil fields like he said. It wasn't fifty feet from here that we built our fire and it was pretty chilly and we had a couple of blankets and I thought then he'd be gone maybe a month and he'd git tired of working and come home to me again. All he wanted was a little cash money and I thought that when he'd saved a few dollars he'd come home again and I never thought he'd come home like this, with the Laws after him. I guess I'd clean forgot about that car he stole in Mehuskah and the time he done in prison, and I never thought he'd take and rob a bank.

"Pat, it was you done it, wasn't it?"

"Done what?"

"Down in Texas."

"Oh, sure." Pat laughed. "It was easy, Belle, and it was funny, too. It was a laugh. There was four of us and we had us two cars. I was riding with Clyde Winter and we parked on the main drag, right opposite the bank. We set there and waited, and way out on the other side of town them other two pulled a stick-up of a filling station and then they high-tailed it out of town. We was settin' in front of the bank and as soon as we heard them sirens we walked inside. The Laws was out after them other two and all we had to do was to walk into that bank and pull our guns and take the jack and then we had plenty of time to git away. We walked out slow, like we'd just been in to change a bill, and we got into the car and drove away and that was all there was to it."

Belle sat back on her heels, watching him, and he saw the intent, anxious expression of her eyes.

"What's the matter?"

"I was just wishing you didn't have that red hair, Pat." She broke six eggs one by one into the frying pan. "Pat, what happened to the other fellow?"

"You mean Clyde?"

"The one with you."

"That's Clyde Winter. They got him, Belle. . . . He was to go West with them other two and we broke up and they was in the car the filling station job was done in and they caught 'em. It was after we all met down near the Red and split up the jack and them others was on their way to Colorado and they caught 'em up around Amarillo. It was in the papers."

"I didn't see it."

"It was in the *Dallas News*. But they don't know they was in that bank job."

"I wish you hadn't done it, Pat."

"All I got was six hunderd bucks when we split it up." Pat spat into the fire. "Only six hunderd bucks! There was just twenty-four hunderd cash in that little tin-can bank." He reached in his pocket and took out a wad of bills. "Here, gal, buy yourself something pretty, something blue to go with them eyes."

Belle looked at the money in his hand. Her eyes blinked rapidly and he saw the glistening highlight of the fire on her cheeks.

"Belle, what's the matter?"

"It's shameful to think you got to spend your life hiding out, Pat. I wish you hadn't done it."

"Oh, it ain't as bad as all that. This will blow over, Belle. Look here, I'll drift out West and git located and later on you can come out and meet me."

"And rob a bank out yonder, Pat?"

"Now, honey, don't be like that."

"Well, what would you do, Pat?"

"Honey, don't read me no lectures. You sound like Jay."

"I wish you'd listened to Jay." She looked at him, her face intent in the firelight. "Gee, Pat, we could be happy as two squirrels in a hollow tree if we just had the chance. If we just only had the chance. If you could just keep out of trouble long enough."

"And what?" Pat said. "And starve to death?"

"We could always git along."

"Belle, I ain't going to see you in pick-up clothes and living on salt pork and dried peas in the hard years. Belle, you'd ought to be dressed in silk every day, silk from the skin out and patent-leather shoes. Some day we're going to have us a pretty house, maybe one of them stucco bungalows, in some big town, maybe out West somewheres. Out West where they never heard of Pat Strickland."

"Such things don't come easy, Pat."

"I'll make 'em come easy. You watch and see, honey."

"Pat, here's your supper. The coffee ain't quite ready, but here's your bacon and eggs." She squatted on her heels by the fire, watching him eat. "Hon, there's going to be work in the valley this year."

"Work?" Pat said with his mouth full. "What work?"

"They aim to build a dam and all that and there'll be work fer five hunderd men."

"Yeah?" Pat grinned at her. "Maybe we can grab off that payroll some day."

"There you go." Belle sighed.

"I'm hot, Belle. I couldn't git me a job working anyhow, anywhere. You know that."

"Yes, I know. I was just thinking anyhow now there *is* work."

"Relief work, I bet."

"W.P.A., Pat."

"Yeah, relief work. . . . Take a look at that coffee, gal."

She took the coffeepot off the fire. "Give it a minute to settle."

"Put some of them eggshells in it."

"I did already."

"Listen to me telling you how to cook!" Pat laughed.

"I've just been thinking," Belle said. "Pat, what *are* you going to do?"

"Oklahoma is too hot fer me," Pat said, "and Texas is poison. It's plain I got to head out West, Belle, and I been thinking some about Mexico. We could hole up down there fer a couple of years, you and me. But still and all, there's California. What I'd ought to do is drift out yonder way and git located and then I'll take and send fer you and Billy. How would you like that?"

"Wherever you are I want to be, Pat. But why don't I go West when you go?"

"I don't know. Maybe so. Why not? But I only got six hunderd bucks."

"That would keep us until you found work out yonder."

"Yeah, maybe."

Belle went over and sat beside him, her back against the tree.

"Pat, I'm going to talk to Jay."

"How is old Jay?"

"He ain't been out to see us in a long time now. He works so hard."

"I admire Jay," Pat said. "I sure do." He swallowed some of the coffee. "You ain't talked to him since this last happened?"

"No."

"I'd like to see old Jay."

"I'm going to git him out here, Pat."

"I'd sure like to talk to him."

"Pat, Jay will know what to do. He'll help us all he can."

"Sure he will." Pat grinned. "What a team we would of made, me and Jay, the two of us. But he always had them serious ideas in his head. You got to admire him fer it, but I wish he was more free and easy like us. He's wasting his time with that union of his. He'll never git nowhere at that work he's doing. But he's okay. He's an okay son of a bitch — just so long as he don't read me no lectures."

"Still and all, I wish you'd listened to him."

"Well, I didn't. Pass me that jug, honey."

She gave him the jug and he took a deep drink. Then he put his arm around her. She leaned against him, her head on his shoulder. Looking at the dying fire, she said softly: "I wish you hadn't listened to them men, honey."

"What men? Say, what are you talking about?"

"Them men you robbed the bank with. I wish they hadn't put you up to it."

"Nobody put me up to nothing, Belle." His fingers tightened on her arm.

He was always ready fer anything. He never could take a dare and of course they put him up to it. Left alone Pat wouldn't have gone bad and he ain't bad now, not really. He's just a boy like he used to be, like he was when we was married, like I hope he always will be. He ain't the kind fer the Laws to be after. He ain't bad and he knows it, too.

"That's your trouble, Pat. You was always so wild and reckless. If anybody puts you up to anything you've got to go him one better. Now ain't that so?"

"We had to have some money, Belle, and I just had to rob that bank."

"It made me feel awful bad," Belle said. "We thought you had a good job in the oil fields and everything."

"That job petered out."

"We thought you had that job, anyhow, until one day there it was in the paper. It sure did make me feel bad."

"What did they say in the paper, Belle?"

"I still got the clipping. I kept it fer you. But you couldn't see to read it in this light."

"Let's have a look at it."

Belle took a man's wallet from the pocket of her overalls and opened it. She unfolded a newspaper clipping. Pat struck a match and read by its light:

Jackville, June 23: The Public State Bank was held up and robbed today by two men a few minutes after two other bandits, apparently belonging to the same band, had stuck up a filling station on the west side of town. Several thousand dollars was taken.

The robbery occurred one minute before closing time. The desperadoes shut the doors of the bank and rifled the vault in a leisurely fashion. They tied the officers of the bank and one depositor who was present with copper wire and escaped without attracting attention. It was an hour before S. W. Roberts, the cashier, wriggled free of his bonds and gave the alarm. If the robbery had taken place ten minutes earlier the men could have taken the $10,000 payroll of the McNaughton Company.

The match burned Pat's fingers and he dropped it into the grass.

"Now God damn, Belle, there was ten grand that got away from us."

He struck another match and she saw his intent face in its light.

One of the bandits has been positively identified as Pat Strickland, an oil-field worker with a police record. His red hair made him readily recognizable.

The match went out and Pat leaned back against the tree.

"Pat," Belle said.

"Yes."

"What if they catch you?"

"They won't never catch me, honey."

"But if they do, Pat, what would happen?"

"Don't you worry about that."

"I mean what could they put you in jail fer?"

"Oh, that," Pat said. "Ninety-nine years."

All his life in jail. If it happens life ain't worth living. I couldn't go on all my days without him. I'd kill myself. I'd have to do it. I couldn't go on without Pat. . . .

"That's the rap fer armed robbery in Texas, Belle. Ninety-nine years. But they ain't never going to catch me."

"Let's don't talk about it, Pat," Belle said. "Pat, if you don't quit hugging that jug I'm going to git me a divorce so you can marry it."

"I'm sorry, honey. You thirsty?"

"Sure I am."

His teeth flashed in the firelight as he watched her drink from the jug, three full swallows. She lowered the jug, breathed deeply several times, and drank again. Pat whistled softly.

"Still and all I ain't even up with you," Belle said. "Pat, look over yonder by the saddle and you'll find a couple of blankets."

"You go easy on that jug while I'm gone." He walked over to the saddle and unstrapped the blankets from the saddle-skirt. He spread them both on the ground, one on top of the other, and they lay down together.

"Honey, I'm back home again," Pat said. "This is like the old days back again. I sure have missed you."

"Have you, Pat?" Her head was snuggled into the curve of his arm. "Some nights I wake up aching and crying fer you."

And that's a fact and it's mean when you can't sleep and you

got to git up and walk up and down on the porch in your bare
feet with old Crosby snoring inside and you look up at the stars
and the moon and everything is so damned awful. It's bad to be
alone and a woman ought to have her man with her all the time.
He ought to be there for her to care for and think about and
worry about and love the loneliness away.

Pat's arm was tight around her and he slid his hand under the
cotton shirt. His palm was warm on her skin.

"Pat?"

"Yes."

"What about them other women?"

"What women are you talking about?"

"Well, you been gone a long time."

Pat chuckled. "You're the only woman I ever had eyes fer,
Belle."

"Don't try to tell me that. I know you better, Pat."

"That's the truth. I don't like them big-mouth Texas women."

"You just didn't run across one that caught your eye, I guess.
Ain't that it?"

"My eye is already caught. My eyes are so full of you I can't
look where I'm going."

"Some men think a woman will believe any kind of a lie they
tell 'em."

But I know it's true and I know Pat is mine like he says and
whatever happened he's mine and whatever happens anyhow
tonight we're here together and after now I don't want to
think. . . .

Crickets were humming in the tall grass and fireflies drifted
like falling stars into the gully. Off in the distance there was the
cry of a screech owl. The sound was lonely and there was an
aching silence after it. Belle turned and crushed her face against
Pat's chest, her hands clutching his arms.

I oughtn't to cry. I don't want to cry. Tonight we ought to be
happy and gay and I tried to be but I been waiting all day and
worrying and afraid he wouldn't come and he did come with his
red hair and that tired look around his eyes and that strain and
worry in his face and it hurts me deep down. What chance have
we got fer anything now the way things is? What chance have
we got fer anything after tonight?

Pat bent his head to her ear and whispered: "Honey, now please don't cry. What's the matter?"

"Everything is so low-down." She raised her face, wet and glistening in the firelight. "Pat, darling, just you kiss me."

Pat leaned against the tree. His eyes were squinted in the early morning sunlight and he looked steadily across at the opposite side of the gully. The slanting sunrays shivered in the gleaming dew of a patch of clover.

"I ought to ride home pretty soon," Belle said.

Pat kept looking straight in front of him. The bank of the gully was sheer red clay and on the slope at the base of it there was tall grass and clover.

"Pat, what are you staring at?"

"You know what, Belle?" He looked up at her. "There's a bee-tree down yonder and it ain't too far. I been watching bees and they come off that clover and make a straight line down yonder into the gully. How would you like some wild honey?"

He's only just a boy and it's good he can find something like that to think about. It's good he can set and think of wild honey instead of all them Laws out after him. He's only just a boy.

"How about it, Belle? Do you want some wild honey?"

"Sure I do."

"You can take it home to Dad. Come on, let's find us that bee-tree."

The way he lopes off ahead of me he's like a hound dog after a coon but it makes him happy and I'm glad he can find an interest. He's only just a boy.

"Belle, bring along that hatchet."

"All right, honey."

A man has always got to think of something else. He can't just set and be content. His head is like a little boy's pocket full of everything, with fish-hooks and a jackknife and marbles and a piece of rock candy and a couple of screws and a tenpenny nail and a live green turtle and Pat's head is just like that. Now he's out after a bee-tree like it was the only thing in the world he had on his mind, like he was out here in Cedar Gully just to git some wild honey and then we'd go on home again just like everyday people and we'd eat the honey with flapjacks in the morning and then he'd go out and chop suckers out of the corn and come home at noontime tired and wash his face and hands in the pan on the porch and eat hearty and go back to the field and tramp home at sundown and after supper we'd set on the porch and watch the moon come up and listen to the hoot-owls and the mocking birds and I'd sing him songs and we'd be so happy just the two of us without no worries and without the woods full of Laws looking fer him. . . .

"Belle, come on down here. Belle, I found it!"

"I'm coming, Pat."

"And bring that hatchet."

"I got the hatchet."

Pretty soon I got to go home and leave him here alone and I got to make sure nobody sees me and back-trails me to Cedar Gully and I got to git hold of Jay and bring him out here and the three of us will set down like we used to and talk and whatever Jay says to do I know will be right. Jay is so straight in his head and when he says something he says it because he's thought about it and there's no other thing fer him to say. He'll know just what to do, if there's anything to do, if there's anything at all to do except wait and worry and know that some day they'll catch up with Pat and if they don't he'll go out and he'll rob another bank and some day he'll be caught. I guess Jay's right that there ain't no chance fer people like us the way things is and there ain't no chance fer Pat. . . .

"Here's your bee-tree, Belle."

Pat stood with his hands on his hips looking at a dead hollow tree. There was an opening at the base of the hollow and another farther up, just above Pat's head.

"I bet it's chock-full of honey, Belle," Pat said. "We got to build us a fire."

Anything that can bring that smile back on his face makes me glad. That tired look is gone today and his face don't look so thin. He worries me so but all he's thinking of now is a bee-tree and I'm glad a little thing like that can make him forget but I can't forget or stop thinking that any time any minute yonder in the trees there'll be men with guns, some of them Laws with ten-gallon hats and black shirts and pants and short black boots and with big cartridge belts of red-brown leather hanging low on their sides. All them hard-faced men looking fer Pat and he's just a boy, just a redheaded boy looking fer some wild honey fer his wife and Dad.

"Belle, help me gather up some wood."

"Sure I will, honey."

Pat was kneeling by the tree, building a fire at the lower opening of the hollow. Belle went into the bushes in search of wood and when she came back with her arms full the fire was burning.

"Pat, what do you want with a fire?"

"Ain't you ever smoked out a bee-tree?"

"No, I ain't never."

"You don't find 'em often around here. The idea, honey, is you blow smoke up into the holler and you suffocate them bees and then you chop the tree down and split it open and take out that there honey."

"It's a good-sized tree to chop down with a hatchet."

"Hell, it's pretty near rotted through. I believe I can kick it over. Let's have some of that wood, Belle."

The fire burned close to the opening at the base of the hollow and white smoke rose along the tree-trunk, clinging to the bark. Pat tore green leaves from a bush and laid them on the fire and as the smoke began to rise thickly he waved his hat to waft it into the hollow. Belle watched the smoke rise along the tree-trunk and spread into the overhanging leaves of a liveoak tree. She watched the smoke rise against the sky.

"Pat!"

"What's the matter?"

"Look at that smoke. Pat, you oughtn't to take a chance that way."

"Belle, we're miles from anywhere. And anyhow it won't be fer long. Look how thick that smoke is. It's like a chimney, that old tree. See the bees flying out of it now?"

That's the way with Pat and you can't do nothing to stop him. He's just plain reckless and he always has been and if I'd of been there I couldn't of stopped him from robbing that bank. Nothing I could of said would have done any good and that's plain. He'd of give me that smile so sweet and so damned obstinate. When he smiles like that you can't do nothing about it and I remember he had that look on his face the first time I ever seen him at that barn dance where they was playing "Flies in the Buttermilk" and I was stomping out on the floor and I seen him standing in the door with that look on his face and that grin. And right off he come over to dance along with me. Nothing can stop him when he's like that, when he's made up his mind to something, and there just ain't no use to try. It was a spring night I remember and there was a moon just like last night about three-quarters full and that milky color, and it was Fred Lunt's barn with the lanterns burning bright and his hair so red and that grin on his face. I didn't know it meant that nothing was going to stand in his way because he'd made up his mind but it give me that feeling that here was somebody felt like I did and it brung out all the reckless and the wild in me to match what he's got in him. We swung and we pranced and the fiddle was squeaking and the feet was pounding and it was *Flies in the buttermilk and I can't jump Josey, Flies in the buttermilk and I can't git around, Flies in the buttermilk and I can't jump Josey, Hello Susan Brown.* . . .

"Go ahead, Belle. Sing some more."

"Was I singing? I hadn't hardly noticed."

"Sing 'Do-se-do.' Remember that one?"

"Have you forgotten 'Flies in the Buttermilk,' Pat?"

"Of course I ain't. But sing that other one, too."

"All right, sugar."

Smoke was pouring from the upper opening in the hollow tree and there were no more bees escaping with it. Pat knelt by the fire, putting on fresh green sassafras leaves and using his hat as a bellows to blow smoke into the tree. He listened to Belle's low voice behind him as she sang. She stood with her hands clasped overhead on the limb of an oak tree, with her breasts raised and pointing through the cotton shirt.

"That ought to do it," Pat said. "Belle, here she goes."

He kicked the tree tentatively and a shower of bark and bits of porous wood fell at his feet.

"Why, it's easy," he said, and pushed hard with his foot, rocking the tree. It moved and cracked and crashed in a cloud of dusty splinters to the ground. Smoke burst from the fire and from the holes in the hollow tree and Pat stamped on the fire to put it out.

BELLE

"I'll be pleased when there's no more smoke," Belle said.

"That's the last of it."

"It did give off so much, Pat. I know you oughtn't to done it."

Pat brought the hatchet down on the fallen tree and a jagged split appeared in the crusty bark.

"This tree wasn't killed by the drought," Pat said. "This here tree has been dead a long time, Belle."

He swung the hatchet again and again and the dull thudding sound doubled back from the walls of the gully. The tree split open like an over-ripe melon and Pat looked down at the webbing of honeycomb and dried brown wax.

"Some of this honeycomb has been here fer years, Belle. It's old and dried out. But look here, here's a fine chance of honey, all right. This will sure hit the spot with Dad. Belle, what are we going to put it in?"

"There's that pot I cooked the squirrel stew in."

"Will you git it fer me, honey?"

"Right away."

Belle went back among the trees and along the grassy slope to their camp site. She had washed the pot at the spring and scoured it with soapstone and it was clean. She made a nest of green leaves in the bottom of it and carried it back to Pat. She watched him scoop honey from the tree and fill the pot. He licked honey from his fingers.

"How about it, Belle? Want a taste of wild honey?"

"Not now, Pat."

"It sure is good."

"Pat. . . ."

"Yeah, gal?"

"I'm afraid I better go."

He looked across at her. He was not smiling now.

"It's time I started home, Pat."

"Naw, Belle, not fer a couple of hours."

"It's a long ride, Pat, and I've got to git hold of Jay and I aim to bring him out here and we're going to set down and talk this over, the three of us, and figure out what it's best fer us to do."

"Belle, I come a long ways just to see you and I don't want you to hurry off."

"I'll come back, hon, and I'll bring Jay with me."

"When you come back you're going to stay awhile."

"Gee, don't you think I want to stay?"

They walked along the gully toward the camp site and Pat put his arm around her. In his other hand he held the pot of honey.

"Be careful while I'm gone, Pat, and please don't make a lot of smoke."

"Don't you worry, Belle. I'll lay low."

"Please do, Pat. Now don't be reckless."

He put the pot of honey on the log beside the saddle and went to catch the sorrel horse. He saddled the horse while Belle packed the saddlebags. She left him the skillet and the flour and sugar and eggs and bacon she had brought. When she had mounted the sorrel he handed her the pot of honey.

"Belle, I believe I'll walk a ways with you, just down through the woods as far as that old wagon road."

He caught hold of her ankle and held it as the horse started up the slope of the gully. Blackjack oaks grew closely on the flat land of the plateau in which the gully was hidden, and they had to thread their way among the trees. Pat held the bridle-reins near the bit and led the sorrel; Belle sat with the pot of honey in her hand looking down at the V-shape of his shoulders and the curly red hair at the nape of his neck. They did not talk, and the only sound was the brittle snapping of underbrush beneath the horse's hoofs.

Suddenly Pat jerked back on the reins and the sorrel reared.

"Pat, what's the matter?"

"There's somebody yonder in the woods, Belle. You stay here."

"Pat, I don't see nobody."

"I seen a hound dog."

He's gone, and oh my God did they trail me here and find him? It's so quiet and I don't see nobody yonder in the trees. There's only leaves moving and birds singing and there's a crested cardinal, just a spot of red, and there ain't nothing else and where did Pat go to? Whoever's there will see the horse and they'll see me and I'll just set here innocent and say I come into the hills to git some wild honey and I'll show the pot-full of it but I wonder will they believe me.

Pat's voice called her. "Belle? It's okay, Belle."

The bushes moved and a bough of flowering elderberry was shoved aside as Pat stepped into the open. With him was an old man in patched overalls whose straw hat shaded his face.

It's old Haze Thompson. It's only old Haze Thompson. He wouldn't hurt nobody. He wouldn't hurt Pat, I know.

"Hello there, Belle."

"Howdy, Haze."

"I seen smoke off in the woods. I reckon you-all made it, Pat."

"We smoked out a bee-tree, Haze. Got a pot-full of wild honey."

Belle held out the pot and the old man squinted and nodded. His eyes were deep-set and heavy-lidded and he had a genial near-sighted expression. His gray beard grew in a straggle from high on his cheekbones.

"What do you know, Haze?" Pat asked.

The old man looked at Pat, squinting, and it was a few seconds before he spoke. "Glad to see you back home, Pat. Heard about what happened down in Texas."

"Yeah."

"Reckon you're layin' low now?"

"That's right."

Pat looks so watchful. I don't like it and I wish he'd give that grin of his. Everybody knows old Haze Thompson is all right. He wouldn't turn Pat in. I know he wouldn't. And the Law had him once fer selling it and he was in the Mehuskah jail fer six months, I remember.

"You're welcome to hang your hat over to my place, Pat," the old man said. "Nobody won't trouble you there."

"Thanks, Haze, but I reckon I better stay out in the black-jack. I sure do thank you, though."

"Any time you need anything you know where my shack is at."

"I sure do."

Now he's smiling and he gives Haze's shoulder a little shake with his hand. Everybody knows old Haze will stick by the people from the hills. That's the way he is and that's the way most of us are in the hills. We stick together. We got to stick together. Haze has drunk our corn and we've drunk his'n fer all these years.

"Pat's got to be careful, Haze. We don't want nobody to find out he's back in the hills."

"They don't nobody know it but me and my hound dog and we don't talk to nobody but each other, Belle."

"We ain't worried none about you, Haze, and that's a fact. But Pat sure does have to take care. Them Laws want to put him in jail fer ninety-nine years."

"Sure enough?"

"They won't never catch me, Haze," Pat said.

"Not here in the hills they won't."

"How are things, Haze? There was plenty of rain this spring."

"I ain't complaining about rain or no rain. I got no crops to tend."

"You ain't?"

"No, I'm gittin' commodities now, Pat. Any time I want a basket of food I can take and fetch it and they give it to me by the canful in store-made cans. You know, a man's always finding out something. It's the first I ever knowed that bodark apples was fit to eat."

"I never heard that," Pat said.

"That's what they give me, though. I went down to Aldine on commodity day and they give me a big mess of bodark apples. I took and stewed 'em and it was three days before I got the juice out, Pat."

Belle laughed. "Them wasn't bodark apples, Haze. Them was grapefruit."

"Grapefruit?" Haze said. "They looked like bodark apples to me. They didn't look like no grapes. Anyhow I baked 'em and I b'iled 'em and I fried 'em and still they didn't taste like nothin'."

"The relief took and bought a trainload of grapefruit out of the Rio Grande Valley in Texas," Belle said. "You'd ought to ate 'em raw, Haze."

"Well, I never heard tell of that," Haze said.

"She's right, Haze," Pat said. "I've ate grapefruit myself and you eat 'em raw like you would a persimmon."

"Pat," Belle said.

"O.K., Belle."

"I got to ride on home."

"You better go ahead, honey. Me and Haze will talk some."

"I'll come back tomorrow and I'll bring Jay."

"You better bring another jug along, too, and don't you forget my razor."

"All right. Pat, come over here and kiss me good-by."

Belle leaned down to him and old Haze Thompson stood by in silence. She ran her hand through Pat's red hair.

"You be careful, now."

"I sure will."

Pat slapped the sorrel's rump and the horse started forward at a trot. Belle ducked her head under a branch and, laughing, pulled on the reins. She looked back at Pat, for one last glimpse of his red hair and smiling face before the leaves swayed down to shut him out, then she sighed and turned her eyes to the path. It was hardly discernible in the thick summer foliage, but was known to Belle for many years and known to the sorrel horse she rode. It rose from the plateau, winding among slabs of limestone, through thickets of hog plum and sumac, and followed along the crest of a ridge. On the opposite side it descended to a road that had been cleared years ago by Cherokee Indians and little used for a decade. The ruts were overgrown with grass.

It's good to see there ain't no fresh tracks. Not even a wagon has passed over this road since the last rain and yonder are the tracks my horse made on the way to meet Pat yesterday morning. It's plain I ain't been followed and I know Haze Thompson wouldn't do nothin' to harm Pat. I guess them Texas Laws are looking down Mexico way fer Pat and maybe they give him up by now. It ain't as if he'd robbed a big bank or shot somebody and anyhow they caught them others who was with him. That ought to satisfy 'em and maybe they'll let Pat alone. Everybody knows it ain't no use to look fer anybody here in the hills. . . . I got to talk to Jay and I know he'll fix it some way. Jay is so straight in his head. He'll think of something to do and I'll git word to him to come out here tomorrow. You can count on Jay.

The sun was rising high in the east and Belle pressed her heels in the sorrel's flanks. The horse could singlefoot and she held the pot of honey against the pommel as it went swiftly along the slow descent. The road curved around a ridge and came to a crossing with the more traveled road that turned into the valley.

Yonder's Joseph Paul's house on the hillside. He's a good friend, that Indian. He sticks by people he knows, too, like old Haze Thompson, and I reckon I'll stop and let him have some of this honey. They ain't got much and Christine will appreciate some wild honey to sweeten up their supper. I reckon I'll stop.

Belle swung from the sorrel and tossed the reins over its head. She carried the pot of honey up the path, and called out when she had nearly reached the house: "Hey there, Christine."

"Here, Belle, by window."

The Indian woman smiled, showing gold teeth. Her black hair was drawn back to a close knot and her face shone in the early morning sunlight which accentuated the feathering of dark silky hair on her upper lip.

"You wouldn't guess what I got here, Christine," Belle said. "Some wild honey."

The Indian woman left the window and an instant later appeared in the doorway. "Glad you come by, Belle. You don't come enough."

"I thought maybe you could use some wild honey," Belle said.

Christine Paul stood aside and motioned Belle into the house. There was only one room and at the end of it a stone fireplace and a cast-iron cook-stove. Little Emma Paul sat on a cornshuck mattress laid on the floor and looked at Belle from round black eyes.

"It's wild honey," Belle said. "I found a bee-tree, Christine."

"Wherever find bee-tree, Belle?"

"Up in the blackjack."

"Don't see bee-tree fer plenty long time."

"I found it up by Cedar Gully. It's the first I ever smoked out."

Christine looked into the pot at the gluey mass of honey and comb.

I ought to give her all of it but Pat sent it home special fer Crosby and the old man will want it because it come from Pat and because he likes it. He'll believe it was the best honey he ever tasted just because it come from Pat. But Christine ought to have it all. She's got that bottle half-full of molasses on the table and I reckon they use molasses fer sweetening in their coffee when they have coffee and I reckon they don't git much of it.

"Git a dish, Christine. I want to pour you out some of it."

"Belle, you better keep honey."

"I want you to have some of it, Christine. Emma, don't you like honey?"

The little girl smiled slowly, her round dark eyes raised unblinking to Belle. Emma Paul had in her arms a small rag doll that her mother had made, of worn cloth with eyes and pigtail stitched in black wool. The doll had rawhide moccasins and a rawhide dress with a belt of tinfoil; the odds and ends that Christine had been able to collect were the material for the doll.

"Belle, I make somet'ing fer you," Christine said, coming up beside Belle as she poured honey into a bowl.

One of them beaded belts that she makes so nice. Now I wish I hadn't of stopped. If you give her something she thinks she'd ought to give you something back and you can't say no and she could sell this belt at the curio place in Mehuskah and git anyhow six bits fer it and all I got fer her is a little wild honey. And she give me the eagle feather and they don't come by them feathers easy and it was as fine a present as they can make. I wish I'd rode on past.

"Now, Christine, I can't take that nice belt."

"Please, Belle, I make him fer you."

"It's real pretty and you do fine work, Christine, but I oughtn't to take it. You already done give me that eagle feather."

The Indian woman laughed and shook her head. She put her arms around Belle's waist and fastened the belt.

"Joseph made Crosby a walnut stick and Crosby give him two bits fer it," Belle said. "Now you ought to let me pay you fer the belt, Christine, if I do take it."

Christine shook her head and Belle saw the hurt expression in her eyes and sighed.

"I'm sure proud to have it, Christine. You do such handsome work. I'm making me a new dress and this will go fine with it."

"I fix Emma new dress," Christine said. "Today last day

school and Emma got new dress. Pretty soon, Emma, you start schoolhouse."

The little girl nodded, sitting solemnly on the mattress with the doll in her arms.

Belle glanced through the window at the sun, now high in the morning sky. "Christine, I got to ride on home. It's gittin' late."

The Indian woman nodded.

"The belt sure is pretty," Belle said. "I'm right proud to have it."

Belle went down the hillside and caught the sorrel horse, which had strayed a hundred feet along the road. She mounted and started at a trot along the strip of familiar red clay. And as she rode she saw the tracks of an automobile cut deep in the soft ground and a frown came on her face.

There don't no autos come up here and it ain't our little truck. I wonder who could of made them tracks. It might be Jay. I hope it is him and I hope he's at the house now and we can start right out after Pat. I sure do want to talk to Jay and I want him to tell Pat what to do. Jay will know, all right. You can always depend on old Jay.

Belle rode around a bend in the road and saw the lane and the stone fence and the cornfield and the house among the trees. And then she saw an automobile under the post-oak tree near the house. She pressed her heels against the horse's flanks.

But that ain't Jay's car and that ain't Jay on the porch with Crosby. That car has on a U.S. license. It's a Government car and what's it doing out here, I wonder. What business has the Government got with us?

She turned into the lane and the sorrel trotted quickly, with ears pricked up, toward the house.

That's Lamar Baker, that's who it is, and somebody with him. Lamar Baker and some stranger. What business has he got with us?

Belle rode into the farmyard and dismounted.

"Hello, there, Belle," Lamar called.

"Howdy, Lamar."

Belle went toward the porch, with the pot of honey in her hand.

I remember Lamar in patched overalls and a straw hat and he didn't have them fancy silk shirts with stripes and that white Stetson hat and a seersucker suit. And that feller with him is more city than Lamar and he's wearing a necktie now in summer and he looks a little like he don't know how to act with people like us.

"Belle, this here is Mister Smith, Mister Neil Smith from New York City," Lamar said.

"Howdy," Belle said.

He keeps looking at the horse and the saddlebags and the pot of honey and I reckon I'll take it inside the house away from them hound-dog eyes of his'n.

"Belle, I want you in on this here talk," Crosby said as she went toward the door.

"All right, Crosby. I'll be back in a couple of shakes." She went into the house and put the pot on the table. She stood an instant by the table, clutching the edge of it with her hands.

Now what would he be after, all the way from New York City, and what did Lamar bring him fer? It must be Pat and he seen the horse and the saddlebags and he never took his eyes off 'em or off me. I wouldn't trust Lamar much and when he brings a Government man from New York City he's up to something and maybe it's Pat.

Belle heard a soft, fretful cry from the kitchen, and she turned away with a sudden smile on her lips. She went into the kitchen and found Billy sitting on the floor playing with a cardboard box. He was in a patch of sunlight from the window and his tow head was very bright, his eyes intensely blue in his pale face. He smiled at his mother but remained seated on the floor, looking up at her.

"Honey, guess who I seen," Belle said. "I seen your Daddy."

"See Daddy," Billy said in a solemn voice.

"That's right. Mama see Daddy."

"Where Daddy, Mom?"

"Never you mind that, Billy. But you just wait till you see what Daddy sent you. You just wait and see. You sure are going to have some fun."

"Belle," Crosby called. "Come on out here."

"All right, Crosby."

Belle picked up Billy and went out on the porch. She stood with her back against the wall, behind Crosby, who was sitting on the stone step.

"Hello there, boy," Lamar said. "How do you like this hot weather?"

Billy shyly put his face in the hollow of Belle's shoulder and she stroked his white head.

"It's about that lake, Belle," Crosby said. "I just been saying that I don't see the need of it at all. I don't see no need to build a lake out here."

Lamar had a blade of grass between his lips and when he spoke it moved up and down. "Let Mister Smith tell you about it, Crosby. He's the engineer and he come all the way down from New York City to build us a lake."

"For one thing it will put men to work," Neil Smith explained. "There'll be a job for every man in this valley who wants it. We'll put them to work on the dam we're going to build in that draw in the hills back that way. We're going to build cabins and lodges and a regular seashore beach." Crosby was looking steadily at the young man and Lamar leaned against a pillar, stolidly chewing on the grass-blade.

I'm relieved it's only that lake and not Pat they're after. I should of known when I seen that feller with that little black moustache that he don't amount to much and he's just a city feller from New York City. I don't know what Lamar has got to do with that lake but I guess there's something in it fer him.

"We've got to have your land, Mister Strickland," Neil Smith was saying. "The whole valley will be flooded and you'll have to move out. We'll pay you cash for your land and you can buy yourself another farm or we'll resettle you. You can make application for a farm on the good bottom land bought by the Farm Security Administration, and you'll have forty years to pay off the purchase price."

"Is that so?" Crosby said. "I still don't see what they want of a lake."

"People can drive out here from town in the summer months and it will be a vacation resort. There'll be swimming and fishing and boating and places to camp. It will be a pleasure resort for the whole region."

"This country wasn't meant fer no lake," Crosby said. "Us people have lived here a long time. This is our home and we want to be left alone. The Gov'ment ought to mind its own business."

"Look here, we're going to use this lake to reclaim about thirty thousand acres of eroded land hereabouts," the engineer said. He was talking fast, with an anxious expression on his thin, sallow face. "There's only seven inches of soil between us and starvation and we've got to conserve it. We're going to reforest the hills and make terraces and contour ridges to prevent erosion, and we're going to move about two hundred families away from this area. It's a big thing. The W.P.A. will spend a lot of money and it will put five hundred men to work. We're going to make a garden spot of this valley. See here, you have nothing to lose. You'll get a fair price for your land and you can buy a better farm on easy terms from the Government and we'll build you a house and barn on it."

"Say, Crosby," Lamar said. "Jess Cookley has sold out, and everybody else in the valley will follow along. It's got to happen."

"We're going to send Government trucks in tomorrow to move Cookley out, lock, stock and barrel," Neil Smith said. "Let me tell you about the deal he made. He gets a sixty-acre farm and the Government provides him with two teams, a hundred head of chickens, new farm tools, a house and barn and seven hundred dollars in cash, and he has forty years to pay it off in, at three per cent. interest."

"I don't want nobody to come here and tell me what to do," Crosby said in a suddenly positive tone.

"Now, Crosby, we only come here to make a deal," Lamar said. "You'll git more money than your farm is worth."

"I reckon so," Crosby said.

"If you don't sell out there'll be condemnation proceedings," Lamar said. "I'm retained to buy up the land here or else git it condemned and that's what I'll have to do unless you sell out, Crosby. Jesus, man, you can't stand all alone in the way of progress. Oklahoma is building up. These are modern times. The first thing you know these hills will be a garden spot, like Mister Smith told you."

"I got no mind to sell," Crosby said.

Lamar is gitting mad, but so is Crosby. Lamar's face is always red now that he's living rich but I never seen it as red as this. They can't nobody come and talk like that to Crosby and tell him what he's got to do.

"Look here, Belle," Lamar said. "How would you like a new house out in open country, and a barn and chicken coops and land that ain't played out?"

"I like it fine here in the hills, Lamar."

"Well, how would you like some cash money, more money than you ever seen, I guess?"

"We got no use fer money."

"You heard what she said, Lamar," Crosby said. "We like it here and here we aim to stay."

It's funny to look at that little city man. He don't know what to make of us and his face is just as white as Lamar's is red. Like Crosby said, nobody can't tell us what we got to do.

"Crosby, I'm going to give you a little more time," Lamar said. "Mister Smith and me have got to see some other folks here in the valley and we'll come back and talk to you again, maybe today and maybe some other time. Anyhow you think about it."

"Sure, I'll think about it. But I done made up my mind, Lamar."

"You're just going to delay the work," the engineer said. "Eventually you'll have to give up your farm."

"Maybe."

"Anyhow, we'll be back to see you," Lamar said. He went down the two stone steps to the ground, then turned and nodded to Belle.

"Belle, I wish you'd talk it over with Crosby."

"Belle and me talk everything over," Crosby said. "Don't you worry about that, Lamar."

The two men walked toward the car, and the slim engineer kicked viciously at a rock in the grass. Crosby looked at Belle and smiled. They both watched the men get in the car and drive away. Crosby waited until the car was out of sight.

"Belle, did you find him?"

"I sure did, Crosby."

It's good to see his eyes shine and his old face break into a grin and to feel his hand on my shoulder squeezing it and he's a fine old man and he cares as much fer Pat as I do, I reckon.

"Off in the blackjack, Crosby. He met me there yesterday evening. You know where Cedar Gully is?"

"Sure I do. I shot me a deer over yonder once a long time back."

"That's where Pat is."

Crosby nodded. "It's as good a place as any. They won't never find him there."

"Crosby."

"Yes, Belle?"

"Old Haze Thompson seen us."

"The hell you say!" Crosby paused and scratched his chin. "Old Haze is all right, Belle."

"That's what I said."

"Sure, you can depend on Haze." Crosby rubbed his hands together. "Belle, I'm going to ride out yonder and see that boy. How does he look?"

"He looks fine, Crosby. Just himself."

"I'll sure be tickled to see him."

"I reckon you better wait, Crosby. I've got to go after Jay, and Billy can't stay home alone. Pat wants to see Jay and talk to him and I'm going to git hold of Jay and take him up there this afternoon."

"Why can't we all go up?"

"We will, Crosby. Pat wants to see his boy and we'll take Billy along. I thought I'd take the truck and drive to Mehuskah to fetch Jay."

"We're clean out of gas."

"We got enough to make Aldine and I got some money Pat give me."

"Some of *that* money?"

"Yes. He had six hunderd dollars."

Crosby whistled softly, then grinned at Belle.

"Pat sent you something, Crosby. Some wild honey. He found a bee-tree and smoked it out and I got a pot-full of honey in yonder on the table."

"I seen that pot you had."

Belle went into the house and Crosby followed her. She stood in front of the cracked mirror looking at the reflection of the beaded belt and Crosby put his finger in the honey and licked it.

"Sure is good. Belle, what do you suppose Lamar aims to git out of that lake?"

"He's after something, sure enough."

That Lamar is crooked like all them politicians. Pat wouldn't cheat nobody but Lamar would cheat his own kin. But Pat's hiding out in the woods with the Laws after him and Lamar is wearing striped silk shirts and a ten-dollar hat.

"I been thinking some," Crosby said. "With Gov'ment people in and out of here all the time this here valley won't be the same. Maybe we'd ought to move out and locate somewheres off in the hills. Over toward Boggs would be a likely place."

"I wouldn't want to give Lamar the satisfaction."

"We'll make him pay us plenty, and if we move somewheres else it will be safer fer Pat to come and see us." Crosby looked at her. "I know a farm over toward Boggs full as good as this here. It used to have a tenant and he couldn't make it go and the the house is empty right now."

Belle turned her head from the mirror. "How big is it, Crosby?"

"Three rooms. Same as this here. You'd like it, Belle."

"We sure can't live here if they fill the valley up with water," Belle said. "We ain't catfish. I tell you what, Crosby, we'll ask Jay what he thinks about it."

"We'll do that, all right."

"I'm going to git the truck out and go to town now."

Crosby went with her to the barn and slid back the doors. He walked around and kicked the tires of the light truck which he had bought second hand years before when for a time he had tended a truck garden. Crosby bent to the crank and it took several minutes of frequent priming before they could start the engine. Belle backed the truck out of the barn and turned east on the Aldine road. She drove rapidly along the road that climbed the slope of the ridge north of the valley. When she came to the crossroads by the schoolhouse she saw an automobile parked near the well and recognized the United States license.

I guess Lamar come to see that little black-haired woman too. She sure is good-looking but she ain't the woman fer Jay and I wish he'd stay away from her. But she sure is good-looking and I guess Jay is lonely. He works so hard all the time and he needs a woman to look after him. A man can't give all his time to his work and he's got to have a woman but I want Jay to find a woman better fer him than her. She's always prettying herself with paint and powder and she has a different dress on almost every day. It looks to me like that woman belongs in a fancy house not a schoolhouse and I wouldn't want Billy to go to school there and study with her, but I guess by the time he's ready fer school she'll be long gone.

Belle stopped in Aldine for gasoline, at the single pump at the eastern end of the town, then she drove on over the black-top road to Mehuskah.

I ought to changed my overalls. I'd clean forgot I'd be driving along the main drag and I ought to put on that print dress and my new beaded belt but still and all I ain't here to git out of the car but only to find Jay and take him out to see Pat.

She drove along the main business street, crossed the Katy tracks just after a freight train had passed, and turned into the dusty, rough street on which Jay lived. She drove the length of the block to the house by the cornfield and stopped the car. The shades were drawn and the front door was closed. She went up the path to the porch and pushed open the door. She came into a shaded room, looked around her, and saw a Negro asleep on an army cot. He opened his eyes and stared at her.

What's Jay doing with a nigger in the house sleeping on the cot like he belonged here? Maybe Jay moved off somewheres and ain't told us.

"Ain't this Jay Strickland's place?"

"Yes, ma'am."

Belle looked steadily at the Negro, wetting her lips.

Now, what's a *nigger* doing in Jay's house? What right has

he got here, and who is he and why does Jay let him stretch himself out on that cot like the house belonged to him?

"Who are you?" Belle asked.

"I'm a friend of Jay's, ma'am. Name is Rocky Jones."

Jay's got friends everywhere and color don't make no difference to him, white or black, but he hadn't ought to let a nigger make himself easy in his house this way.

"Where is Jay?"

"He done gone out, ma'am." The Negro was standing now, watching her.

"When do you expect him back?"

"He'll be gone till late tonight, I reckon."

"Oh." Belle looked the Negro up and down. He was dressed in new overalls and yellow cowhide shoes with thick soles.

"I got to see Jay. Where will I find him?"

"He was headed lots of places, ma'am. I couldn't say."

"I got to see him," Belle said. "I *got* to find him."

"It ain't no use to look. He was goin' lots of places."

"In his auto?"

"Yes, ma'am."

"I'm Jay's sister-in-law," Belle said.

The Negro smiled and nodded. "Jay gone out on union business and it will keep him late. He gone down south around Jennings County, and he got lots of people to talk to, and I don't expect he come home at all tonight. He'll stay down yonder in the cotton country with some farmer."

Belle sat down in a chair by the table, frowning, and stared at a small china shoe full of matches.

"I reckon the best I can do is leave a message fer Jay," she said, looking over her shoulder at the Negro. "I want you to tell him that Belle was out here. Will you tell him that?"

"Yes, ma'am."

"This is important. As soon as he gits back from Jennings County you tell him I was here to see him and I said it was real important and I got to see him right away and fer him to come out to Aldine as soon as he gits the message. Will you tell him that?"

"I sho' will."

"Remember to say I got to see him, you hear, I *got* to."

"I'll tell him, ma'am."

Belle rose to her feet and the Negro opened the door for her. She looked steadily at his face for an instant, then went out to the truck.

I guess I can count on him. He don't look dumb like most niggers. He looks like he knows what he's about and I expect Jay will git the message in just the way I give it. It's a funny thing him keeping a nigger in his house even if he is a friend of Jay's and even if white and black is all the same to him. He ought to know better than to let a nigger sleep in his house just like he owned it. But Jay knows what he's about and he's straight in his head and he'll know what to do about Pat. He'll have to leave that union business of his and come out to see Pat and he'll want to help and with Jay there we'll know what to do. Some way, somehow, we got to do something. . . .

Jay

✤   ✤

JAY stood by the window of the farmhouse, which overlooked a cotton field and the flat sweep of land toward the Red River not many miles away. He stood with his foot on the rung of a chair looking at the intent faces of the four farmers in the room.

I can do a lot of good in Jennings County with these four men right here. If I can just line 'em up, plenty others will fall in behind and they'll give us good leadership in this here county. They just about make up the compass points of the county. This here farm of Fritz Warner's is south of the county seat. George Burr farms west of town, Ned Bayles is out east and Bill Little to the north. If I can git 'em working in them four districts we'll organize Jennings County solid. . . .

Jay watched big George Burr, who was sitting in a wicker rocking chair reinforced and padded with an old quilt wired to the back and arms. Burr's bald brown head was the tone of the khaki shirt and trousers he wore; his eyebrows were bleached to the color of straw and his eyes were a penetrating blue.

"Now this is the main thing," Jay said. "And this is what we got to put the emphasis on. We got to educate them people. Without education we won't have no organization worth a damn. I tell you, the ignorance of the masses is the only cause we got to live in the poverty we do. If we can just teach 'em that all they got to do is organize and git it, all they got to do is organize and take it. . . ."

"A-*men*," George Burr broke in.

"Listen here," Fritz Warner said. "They ain't enough groceries in this county to last a day if everybody had all they needed to eat, and they ain't enough goods in the stores to clothe 'em." He got to his feet, clenching one fist. His head was bald in front and his black hair was long and brushed forward over his forehead to cover the baldness. His face was pale above a receding chin bluish with beard. "But they's plenty of resources if it was just give out to the people. You could double what this county produces and you could quadruple it and multiply that by ten and we wouldn't have to work more than a few hours to do it. We know it's there and we got to take and git it and by God you're right and the only way we can take and git it is by organization and learning the people that the only trouble is the social order."

Jay grinned, and lifted his eyes to the gleam of sunlight on a bucket jammed into the disused flue of the chimney. He stood by the window with his foot on the chair rung and one hand resting on an icebox adorned with a doily and displayed as an ornament in the shabby farmhouse.

That there German is an old line Socialist but he's trade-union through and through. If I can git him lined up and them others with him we'll have us a union organization in Jennings County that nothing won't stop. . . .

"There's one question I want to ask you," Ned Bayles said. He paused and puffed on his pipe. He sat on the floor, with his knees raised and his paunch resting against his thighs. His hairy hands were clasped on the patched knees of his overalls. "Now down through here they had a farmers' union a while back. Politics busted that up, politics and the fact that there warn't no democracy."

"When they organized an anti Ku Kluck right inside the union that's what tore the guts out of it," George Burr said.

"That's right." Ned Bayles nodded and drew on his pipe. "But it warn't no democracy in that union and I can tell you this, we got to have democracy and if we ain't got democracy we're as bad as what we're fighting."

"The Southern Tenant Farmers' Union is a rank-and-file organization," Jay said. "Rank and file through and through and we decide our action in a body. This here union is founded on democracy and we'll use it to preserve democracy in this here United States."

"Amen," Fritz Warner said.

"And we ain't got no time to lose," Jay said. "In another ten years there won't be no tenant farmers in Oklahoma, the way things are going. You-all won't be tenant farmers, you'll just be day laborers on a mechanized farm. That's what will happen if we don't take and use our organized strength to better conditions, to git long-time land tenure and in the end to git every tenant a piece of land of his own. Tractor farming through here is increasing at the rate of more than twenty per cent. a year and every new tractor means another tenant family throwed out on the road. Are we going to let them machines throw us, or are we going to throw them machines and make 'em work to improve the way we live, that's what we got to decide. The way things is now, them tractors have got us throwed. In some cotton counties half the tenants have took out fer California or Arizona. There just wasn't nothing left fer 'em here and they packed up in old model T's and started west. They claim that most of the ve-hicles moving into California got Oklahoma and Texas license plates."

"That's right," George Burr said. "I got a cousin went out to California. I ain't heard how he made out. — Now look here, Strickland, we're interested in your union. If we wasn't we wouldn't be here. We're union men from the navel up and the navel down. We believe in organization and the way you got the Ten't Farmers' Union lined up it looks like what we're after. But what we want to know is what are you going to do about it? What are you going to do to start it off in Jennings County?"

"That's up to you men," Jay said. "This here is your organization if you join up, and you got to work fer it and work with it. But if you-all join up I'm going to come down here and work with you and we'll put on a drive that will bring in every tenant in the county."

"That's what I wanted to hear," Burr said, slapping his thigh. "Yes, sir, now you're talking, Strickland."

"How much does it cost?" Fritz Warner asked. "We're awful pore folks through here."

"To git you a charter fer a local you got to have fifteen members," Jay said. "The dues is twenty-five cents a month and there's a fifty-cent initiation fee. You give seventy-five cents to start off with and that pays fer your charter, but after them first fifteen members every fifty-cent initiation fee after that stays in the treasury of the local."

Warner nodded. He was sitting on the edge of the one bed in the room, on a candlewick bedspread made of sugar sacks, and leaning back against a nerve-tonic calendar with his hands clasped around one knee and his mournful brown eyes turned up to Jay. "We're as pore as Job's turkey and I ain't got seventy-five cents. I ain't got six bits to my name, but I'm going to join your union and I'm going to git it."

"Amen," Ned Bayles said. "Now tell us just how you aim to go about it, Strickland. I'm hump-shouldered and rough-shod because I never had enough to eat, and I don't want my boys to grow up that way. What do you aim to do?"

"We'd ought to start off with a mass meeting," Jay said, "and then we'll foller it up with meetings in the schoolhouses and I'll talk at each one of 'em and if you-all can git the tenants out I'll guarantee I'll sign 'em up."

"Now you're talking," George Burr said. "I'll sure git 'em out in my district. I'll git 'em out to hear you, and then it's up to you."

"If you git 'em there I'm confident about the rest of it," Jay said. "I don't claim I'm no orator, but I do git results."

"I'll look after my district," Fritz Warner said. "Ned, I reckon you can fill that Sneeden schoolhouse?"

"I sure can."

"I'll tell you men what I'm going to do," Jay said. "I'll just leave this application fer a charter here with you and you can go to work on it. Today is Saturday, and a week from today I'll come back and hold a mass meeting in the courthouse square and then each night after that we'll have us a schoolhouse meeting."

"I'll take Monday night at Wilson School," George Burr said.

"Give me Tuesday at Sneeden School, then," Bayles said.

"And Fritz, we'll put you down fer Wednesday at Rock Creek," Burr said. "That leaves Thursday fer Long Hill School. Can you git 'em out there, Bill?"

Bill Little nodded, but he did not speak. He sat in a corner with a pipe in his mouth and his dusty black hat pulled low on his thin brown face, but it did not shield his burning eyes.

Jay looked at his watch. "Boys, I got a meeting this afternoon in Mehuskah County, over to Tanzey. It's a long drive and I better be on my way."

"Now you got to stay here to dinner," Fritz Warner said. "We're as pore as Job's turkey, like I said, but if we can live on it I reckon you can stand it fer one meal. Anyhow we got black-eyed peas and pertaters."

"I sure do wish I could stay," Jay said. "But I got to make time to git to Tanzey. It's a nigro district and we got to do some work among them nigros. The Tenant Farmers' Union takes everybody in, nigro, white and Indian."

George Burr and Ned Bayles looked at each other.

"That's right," Fritz Warner said. "We got to have 'em. We got to have every working-class farmer, irregardless of race, color or creed."

"Anyhow we ain't got no niggers in Jennings County," George Burr said. "None to speak of."

"Them we got we'll sign up," Fritz Warner said. "Don't you have no fears on that, Strickland."

"This here is your charter application," Jay said. "And this here little green card is the membership card. I'll leave some of 'em with you and you'll see it's got wrote on it the union's program." He looked out the window at the thin rows of cotton plants, at the red clay mound of the storm cellar on the side of a rise behind the house. "Boys, I got to be on my way. It's a long trip to Tanzey and I got to be there on time. I expect to have about five hunderd people out."

"Now look here," George Burr said. "You sure got to be here next week."

Jay grinned. "I'll be here."

He went out on the porch. A cool breeze was blowing across the cotton field, sweeping over the bottom lands. He went down the high steps, the boards of which were engrained orange from the flying dust, and George Burr walked with him out to the car.

"We mean business here in Jennings County, Strickland," he said. "We're behind you and we're coming in with you. We can do a lot of good. Old Fritz Warner likes his moonshine, but he's a union man, and so is Ned Bayles. Bill Little don't say much, but he'll work till he's plumb wore out. Boy, we're with you."

He slapped Jay's shoulder as he got into the car, and when Jay drove away Burr walked back with his shoulders squared to the weather-worn farmhouse with the potatoes and onions piled beneath it, with the broken windowpanes and sagging screens.

With them kind of men we'll build our union and we'll organize this county solid and we'll tie that organization in with Mehuskah County and them counties in between and we'll draw them all together like a purse-string.

Jay crossed an ungraded section-line road, and drove on in deep clay ruts toward the highway, bumping across a rattling wooden bridge. When he reached the highway he turned north toward Mehuskah.

I ain't done so bad and I'll give myself a pat on the back fer it. I covered two counties all since yesterday morning and I talked to lots of people and when I come back this way there'll be crowds out to hear me talk, and I'll sign 'em up in the union, sure as hell. Nothing ain't going to stop us and the Southern Tenant Farmers' Union will git to be a power in this here state. We'll band them tenants and sharecroppers together and we'll demand land fer the landless and a W.P.A. job fer every man that can work and we'll git it. Before we're through we'll abolish land tenancy altogether and we'll build up a class of farmers to hold the place they got the right to hold in this country. We'll build a strong trade union and we'll git them people working together like farmers never worked together before and they'll find out what they can git if they work together and then we can just take and say, now things is going to be this way, or they're going to be that way, and that's the way they'll be. We'll have them people organized solid and supporting one big program and when the time comes to take action by God we'll be ready fer it. But first of all we're a trade union and we're working so that every tenant can have land of his own and make a decent living and there won't be no politics in it until the time comes, but when it comes we'll be ready. . . .

Jay drove fast along the concrete highway, through McAlester, fifty miles; through Eufaula, thirty miles more. He watched the black line in the center of the road spin past beneath his wheels. Sixteen miles south of Mehuskah he turned east toward Tanzey.

I'm kind of late fer the barbecue but this time it's worth it. It's worth it to git the organization rooted down yonder the way I have and to git them old-line union men into it to give us the leadership we need right now at the beginning. Them four has got fire in their hearts, but they still got that disillusionment from that other union dying under their feet. They'll go a little cautious because of that and it will slow them down, but we'll build up new leadership out of the rank and file before we're done.

Jay crossed Big Soapy Creek and turned on a section-line road toward a grove of trees. He saw men under the trees and as he came closer he found that they were nearly all Negroes.

But it ain't five hunderd of 'em. It ain't very many of 'em and I don't see hardly no white men. Some people think a nigro's got no sense, but when it comes to union business he's got more sense than a white man. He knows he ain't got a chance unless he joins up with his friends and the folks like him and organizes. Ever since they was slaves they been scared and hunted like black rabbits but they ain't too scared to join together and fight fer what they got a right to have. They got more sense than a white man that way. I can't figure out why some men won't go out and fight fer their rights, and I wish we had more like George Burr and them other three.

Jay stopped the car under a mulberry tree. Fifty feet away there was a haze of wood smoke from the barbecue pit. He saw Webb Harper coming from the pit with a piece of barbecued goat impaled on a greenwood stick. He wore overalls with broad blue stripes widely spaced. Beneath his straw hat his face was thin, and his long nose and small eyes gave it a sharply focused expression.

"Webb, we sure got to do better than this," Jay said slowly, as soon as Harper reached the car. "Here we got free food and not more than fifty people out to eat it."

"I done everything I could, Jay."

Jay looked out at the small crowd of Negroes and listened to the tuneful rise and fall of voices. "I don't mean to criticize you, Webb, but we ought to have more here."

"I know that, Jay. But I tell you, the last couple of days I been sort of laid up. I baled me some hay day before yesterday and my boy stuck a pitchfork in my heel, a half-inch deep. See here, I had to cut out the back of my shoe."

"You better take care of that, Webb."

"I am, Jay. But what I mean is I couldn't git around yesterday. But before that I called on just as many as I could and they talked like they'd all be here."

"Hey, Jay."

Jay turned and saw Rock Island Jones approaching them.

"Jay, it's time you showed up. How did it go down south?"

"It went fine. We got a sure enough drive starting down yonder. Rocky, this here is Webb Harper. I told you about Rocky, Webb."

"Howdy," Rocky said, putting out his hand. "Jay, I got a message fo' you."

"O.K."

"There come a woman yesterday, said she was yo' sistah-in-law, and said she had to see you right off."

"A big woman with yaller hair and freckles?"

"Tha's her. She had on overalls and a man's hat."

"That would be Belle, all right."

"She said it was impo'tant and she wanted you to come out to Aldine soon's you got the message. If you'd of come home last night I'd of told you then."

Then she found Pat, she sure as hell found Pat. He's hiding yonder in the hills and Belle found him and come to town to git me. He's safe, old Pat is safe and it'll be good to see that perky face of his again and his red hair and freckles. That fool of a boy. . . .

"Jay, I looked fo' a big crowd," Rocky said. "You-all ain't got but forty-fifty people."

"It ain't a good turn-out," Jay said. "But it's a beginning. This is the first meeting here in Tanzey, Rocky."

I got to stay to the end of the meeting. At least I got to git the speaking going and make my talk and then I'll head fer Aldine and look up old Pat.

"Jay, it's too slow," Rocky said. "Like they says in Memphis, it's too slow. And look yonder, I don't see but a couple of white men."

"There's about a half-dozen," Jay said. "This here is a nigro community, Rocky, that's the reason. I tell you what I'm going to do. I'm going to put you out here to organize." Jay bit off a piece of the barbecued meat. "Webb, I reckon you can find a place fer Rocky to stay?"

"Sure I can," Webb Harper said. "I been crippled up the last couple of days, Rocky, and couldn't git around. But we sure do need some help out here."

"Yonder come a few of them Indians," Jay said. He raised his hand in greeting to Joseph Paul. As usual, the Indian's face was wet with perspiration, and the white topi glaringly reflected sunlight. With him were two Indians in overalls and straw hats. Jay got out of the car and went toward them.

"Hello, Joseph. Glad you men could come. You had any of that barbecue yet?"

Joseph Paul shook his head and the other Indians looked toward the barbecue pit.

"Come along with me, you-all. Joseph Paul, this is Rocky Jones, one of our organizers, and I believe you know Webb Harper."

Like Joseph said it ain't going to be easy. Them fullbloods just stand and look without a flicker on them brown faces, and I wish to Christ they had a bigger crowd to look at. But anyhow they come here and with a little hot barbecue in their bellies maybe they'll listen and maybe they'll stop and think and it will do some good. They're always so damned polite and you can't never tell what's in their minds.

"T'is here John Goback," said Joseph Paul. "T'is Red Feat'er."

The Indian named Red Feather smiled and nodded to Jay. His topaz eyes were opened wide. He had a friendly, human smile and his coarse black hair strayed over his forehead like a boy's.

"Howdy," Jay said. "What do you-all say to a little barbecue?"

They went toward the pit, Red Feather walking beside Jay and the other Indian trailing behind Joseph Paul. Rocky Jones was talking quietly: "This crowd ain' very big, but it's jus' the beginnin'. Our strength is in numbers. 'At's what the union is. It's our strength. The only chance we got is got to come from we-all workin' together to help each other and us all."

At the barbecue pit a Negro naked to the waist, with a handkerchief tied around his throat, cut them slices of meat. They went under the shade of a white-oak tree and the Indians squatted on their heels. Jay leaned against the tree, looking at the shifting movement of the crowd, listening to the hum of voices.

It's a good feeling to see that something's doing, even if it ain't but a few of 'em, and all you got to do is bring 'em together and let 'em talk. That's the main thing, just to let 'em talk, and they're all talking union. But it's bad there's so few of 'em and mostly all nigros and hardly any white men.

Along the fringe of the woods there were wagons and a few battered automobiles. Men were sitting on the wagons, on the running boards of the cars, and men stood in groups under the trees, talking.

I reckon that hay wagon would be the best place. I wouldn't doubt that ten nigros rode here on it, and it will make a good platform to talk from. It's time things got started because I got to git away as soon as I can and drive up to Aldine and git off in the hills to find Pat before dark comes on. I reckon he's waiting yonder in the blackjack and expecting any minute I'll show up with Belle.

"Webb, it's time we got started. Let's go up on that hay wagon and you can introduce me and then we'll let Rocky talk."

"Okay, Jay."

"And Joseph Paul, I want you and your friends to come up on the platform with us."

"Don't make speech, Jay."

"No, you don't have to talk. Tell your friends to come on up yonder with us."

The thing to do is to sort of give 'em a share in what's doing. If I left 'em under a tree they wouldn't listen. They'd eat a little barbecue and nobody would talk to 'em and after a while they'd take out fer home.

Jay climbed first to the bed of the wagon, then he reached down a hand to Joseph Paul. The other Indians climbed gravely up beside him. Jay stood looking at the crowd. The faces were turned up toward him and the sound of voices died away.

It's a powerful feeling to see the trust each time at every meeting since the first, since the demonstration we had away back when the relief checks didn't come through on Christmas and after that when I begun to talk union in the spinach fields and we had our first meeting in a tumbledown schoolhouse ten miles west of here and I had heard about what was going on over in Arkansas and I told 'em what I knowed about the union and they listened with that same look you see on their faces, listening like it was the word of God almighty speaking out of a burning bush. And they always come with their families and the women are the most anxious and with kids holding at their skirts and sometimes tears in their eyes and it makes you feel like you got to do something and it makes you feel that you ain't got the strength of a rabbit and then you stop and think that it's all of us together and all I got to do is to tell 'em how to go about it and they got the strength in themselves to do it.

"I'm going to call this meeting to order now," Webb Harper said, raising one hand. "Come a little closer, everybody. This here is a meeting of the Southern Ten't Farmers' Union, an organization meeting. The secret of gitting what you want in this modren world is organization. We been through a bad depression and I can tell you-all that things are going to git a lot worse before they git any better. We got to organize and fight fer our rights, that's what we got to do. The trouble with the farmers is they won't stick together and if they don't they're bound to be the victims of uppression. I'm not talking about *de*pression now, I'm talking about *up*pression. We want to stand on our two feet with our chins in the air and fight fer a living. We don't want to be underdogs. We want to join together in unity and with a little brotherly love, a little of that old-time brotherly love that we ain't got much of these days. We don't want to create no disturbance. We just want to organize and help build this country up. I'm a ten't farmer myself, one of the hunderd and sixty-five thousand ten't farmers we got in this here state, a hunderd and sixty-five thousand out of a total of two hunderd and thirteen thousand farmers in the state. You men think of that. We got a hunderd and sixty-five thousand in this state just like you and me, counting in about five thousand sharecroppers. What we aim to do is to band all them people together and we'll go out together and fight fer our rights. We got the union's organizer here, and I'm going to let him talk to you. This here is Jay Strickland from Mehuskah."

Jay went forward. He took off his hat and held it out between his face and the sun, and he waited for an instant for silence.

"I'm Jay Strickland and a lot of you know me and some of you don't. A lot of you are signed-up members of the Southern Tenant Farmers' Union and some of you ain't, but you're all goin' to be or you wouldn't be here today. You've all heard union talk and it's a new thing to some of you and maybe you want to know more about it and that's why I'm up here, to answer any questions you want to ask. First of all I want to tell you a little about the Southern Tenant Farmers' Union and what it's fer. It's a trade union, founded, organized and chartered as a trade union. We want to abolish farm tenancy and sharecropping and our slogan is Land fer the Landless. The Tenant Farmers' Union begun over in eastern Arkansas, in Poinsett County, back in 1934, and it's been growing ever since and now there are thousands of us joining hands to make our life worth living, to give our kids a chance to go to school and to go to school with a full belly and with clothes on their backs and to have a bed to sleep in and a fire to keep 'em warm. Now don't you-all be discouraged because you didn't git a crowd out at your first meeting, because everything has got to have a beginning and it just takes a little bit to start the ball rolling. Over in Arkansas they had to hold their meetings in secret in the night-time and they never knowed when a bullet would whistle over their heads and the riding bosses would bust the meeting up."

Jay's voice was clear and his words were round as marbles. "But this ain't Arkansas. This is Oklahoma, and we're free to meet here in open meeting and express our opinions without no fear of being victimized. That ain't so in Arkansas or some of the other Southern states. . . . Now some people say this is a radical organization. Of course it's radical. Anything that's right is radical. The Bible is the most radical book ever wrote down because it's radical against sin. When you call anything radical you want to git the explanation of what radical is. Sure we're radicals, but there are different kinds of radicals. Some kinds want to overthrow democracy and set up a dictatorship, and we're opposed to that."

Jay stood on the edge of the hay wagon, holding up his hat to shade his eyes from the sun, but holding it far enough away so that his face could be seen.

"The cotton crop in this United States amounts to a billion dollars a year," he said. "I don't imagine anybody here has thought about how much a billion dollars adds up to, but I can tell you that it's a hell of a lot of money. If a man started out in the year that Jesus Christ was born and spent a thousand dollars a day every day since that time, fer nearly two thousand years, a thousand dollars a day, he'd still have plenty of that billion left, and I ain't even counted in interest. A thousand dollars a day fer two thousand years and there ain't a farmer in this here crowd that can make a thousand dollars in less than three to five years' time, and you all know that. A billion dollars a year the cotton we raise with our work and our sweat brings in and what do we git out of it? What is the sharecropper's share? I don't need to tell you that. His share is a little cornbread and molasses and a side of sowbelly, his share is malaria and pellagra and eviction. His share is hunger and sickness and debt and fear of what's going to happen next year and knowing that next year will sure as hell be worse than the year before. Ain't that so?"

Jay paused, and looked down at the black faces. There were a few low murmurs of "Amen." On the edge of the crowd the white men formed a small group.

"The landlord don't give a damn fer the tenant and he don't hardly talk to him except to cuss him out. He takes more care of a mule. But there ain't nothing the tenant can do alone against the landlord and if he tried he'd be evicted before sundown. He can't do nothing alone but if he gits together with the other farmers, if he joins the union, he's got somebody to help him and work with him. That's why the Southern Tenant Farmers' Union was started and that's why it's growing every day. Here in Mehuskah County we already got a strong organization and more are coming in. We don't have no distinction in our locals. We don't have black locals and white locals. We got just one big union. The white men are coming in, and the nigros and the Indians too. Here on this platform you can see them fer yourselves. Here are three Indians who come down to find out what the union means. Two of 'em are Cherokees and the other's a Creek. They're tenant farmers like the rest of you or else they work day rates in the spinach fields. And they come here to learn about the union and to join up with the white man and the black man to help each other against the landlord. . . . You want to know what the union can do about it and I'll tell you that the union is stronger than the landlord is. The union will git you day workers a dollar a hunderd fer picking cotton and if the landlord won't pay it then we won't pick no cotton and it can rot on the bolls. That's where our strength is. We'll git us a dollar a hunderd or we won't pick no cotton and we'll git us twenty cents a basket fer cutting spinach. And we'll git a square deal from the landlord or we won't farm his land. Now we feel that the tenants should have contracts the same as other union labor. We're coming around to that. That contract is going to say that the landlord has got to pay the tenant wages fer all the work he puts out in improving the property, the work on building fences and repairing wire and every kind of work that improves the property. And that contract will say the landlord has got to furnish fertilizer fer the crops. But the only way we'll git them contracts is to band together, the white

man and the black man and the Indian. We can't have no separate locals and we ain't going to. We're going to build a strong
union and we'll git land fer the landless and right now we'll git
you men who need work a place on the W.P.A. here in Mehuskah County. Now that's the union's program, and if any of you
got any questions to ask I'm here to answer 'em. But first of all
I want to introduce a farmer who's chopped cotton most of his
life. Fer the last two years he's been workin' with the S.T.F.U.
in Arkansas and Mississippi and he's a union man. This here is
Rock Island Jones."

Rocky grinned at Jay and went to the edge of the wagon.
His thin black face shone in the strong light and its planes were
sharp and intent.

"You-all heard Jay Strickland say we can't have no Jim
Crow union. Tha's th' way the Southern Ten't Farmers' Union
was sta'ted and I can tell you-all why. We all got to stick together or we won't git no place. If it's a white union and the
Negroes is left out, all the bosses is got to do when a strike
comes off is to take and put the Negroes to wo'k on the land
and if they ain't in the union the Negroes will naturally go to
wo'k. The white men is got to have the Negroes and the Negroes
is got to have the white men or the union won't amount to
goobers. We got to stick together, and if we sticks together
we'll git what we're after and we'll git a dollah a hunderd fo'
pickin' cotton and twenty cents a basket fo' spinach and we'll do
away with the doodlum books and we'll git a square deal on
settlement day. . . ."

That truck coming in from the road is old Crosby's truck, I
swear it is, and by God that's Belle in it and she's come after
me, but I got to wait until the meeting's over with.

Jay climbed down from the hay wagon and walked around
the crowd. The truck had stopped in the open and Belle was
getting out of it. Jay saw the expression of her face and ran
to her.

"Jay! They got him. They got Pat!"

"Jesus Christ."

"I don't mean he's hurt. He ain't hurt, Jay." She put her hand
on his arm. "But they caught him. A posse of Laws caught him
up at Cedar Gully this morning and took him to jail in Mehus-

kah. Thank God he ain't hurt and he didn't shoot nobody. They took him by surprise and he didn't have a chance to shoot."

"God damn," Jay said. "How did they find him?"

"I don't know. — Jay, I come after you to go to the jail with me. Do you reckon they'll let us see Pat?"

"Sure they will."

"Then let's go, Jay, as quick as we can."

Jay looked back at the hay wagon, at the tall thin figure of Rocky Jones and the three Indians standing in a stolid row behind him.

"Belle, I got business here yet."

"But, Jay, we got to see Pat. We *got* to."

That Rocky is all right. He's good. I reckon I can leave it in his hands and I got to. Him and Webb will have to run this meeting off.

"You wait here, Belle," Jay said.

He went quickly around the crowd to the hay wagon and motioned to Joseph Paul. The Indian squatted on the wagon-bed and leaned down to Jay.

"How did you git out here, Joseph Paul?"

"Come wit' friend, Red Feat'er. Him got old car."

"Will you drive Belle's truck back to the valley?"

The Indian nodded. "Sure do, Jay."

"I'll leave the keys in it. And Joseph Paul . . ."

"Ay-uh?"

"You tell Rocky Jones that I had to go back to Mehuskah and I'll come back later, soon as I can."

"Somet'ing wrong, Jay?"

"They caught Pat."

Jay hurried back to Belle and took her hand. She was pale and the freckles stood out sharply in the sunlight.

"We'll go in my car, Belle, and Joseph Paul will drive the truck home. Come on."

They went at a half-trot toward the mulberry tree where Jay had left his car and Belle said: "Jay, do you suppose it could of been old Haze Thompson?"

"Haze Thompson?" Jay stopped with his hand on the door-handle. "How come?"

"He seen us. Pat was hid out in Cedar Gully, and yesterday

morning early we smoked out a bee-tree to git some wild honey and Haze Thompson seen the smoke and he come over and found us."

Jay stepped on the starter and raced the engine. "I'd hate to think old Haze would do a think like that. It ain't like Haze."

"I know it ain't, but I can't think how else. I know I wasn't trailed up there, Jay. I'm sure of it."

They were on the road now, a dirt road running for two miles between barbed wire fences to the north-south highway. Jay drove as fast as he could.

"I'll be riding up into the hills tomorrow," he said. "I aim to see Haze and I'll find out. But I sure don't think old Haze would do a thing like that."

"Whoever done it I'll kill him," Belle said. "I swear I will."

"Now you forget about anything like that, Belle."

"Jay, it's ninety-nine years in the Pen. Did you know that?"

"Maybe we can git him off, Belle."

"No. How ever could we?"

"If we git a good lawyer. The only thing they got to go on is Pat's red hair and they didn't catch him when they caught them other fellers who was with him. We hire us a good lawyer and maybe we can git him off."

"But if I find out I swear to God I'll kill him, Jay."

They were on the highway now, and up from the plain rose the Mehuskah skyline with its lone tall building thrusting eight stories against the pale sky.

"Never you mind about that, Belle. We'll git Pat off somehow."

She sure enough would kill him too, but I don't see how it could be old Haze and maybe after all they did trail her up yonder. If I was a Law that's what I would of done. I'd of watched Belle and trailed her. I'm damned sure old Haze Thompson wouldn't do it.

Jay stopped the car in front of the police station and county jail, a two-story building of yellow brick one block from the main business street. Belle hung back in sudden apprehension as they went along a cement walk to the entrance of the building. Jay saw her looking at the iron grilles across the windows and took her arm.

"Come on, Belle. Don't you worry none about Pat."

Maybe we *can* git him off, give us a good lawyer. They got to have witnesses who can identify him positively and that ain't easy and we can git witnesses to swear he was right here in these hills all the time. It's the only chance we got, anyhow.

"We want to see Pat Strickland," Jay said.

"You-all have to see the chief. Are you kin to Strickland?"

"I'm his brother and this here is his wife."

"You-all wait a minute."

The son of a bitch, the way he looks at us I'd like to twist his nose fer him. I guess he knows who I am, too.

"You-all can come in."

They went past the guard into the chief's office and a short fat man looked up from his desk. His face was a gray tone against his black shirt.

"You're Jay Strickland, ain't you?"

"Yes, and this here is Pat's wife."

The chief looked steadily at Jay. His fingers twisted a pencil around and around.

He hates my guts and it's plain hate he's looking at me and if he could git away with it he'd throw me right into jail alongside of Pat.

"You can see him fer five minutes," the chief said. "Mac, you take these two back to Strickland's cell."

"Come on, you two."

They followed the guard along a corridor. He wore a cartridge belt of bright Mexican leather, with a keyring attached at one side. He opened a door with a key from the ring.

"Straight ahead now. Foller me."

They were in another corridor and they walked past a row of barred cells and at the last cell in the row the guard stopped and opened the door.

"Only five minutes, the chief said."

Pat was asleep on the narrow bed and a ray of sunlight fell on his rumpled hair.

If he slept like that no wonder they caught him. Not even the opening of the door woke him up. Poor kid, he looks just the same. He'll always look like a boy no matter how old he gits, just a freckle-faced, redheaded boy.

Belle went down on her knees by the bed. "Pat, honey, wake up."

He opened his eyes, startled, and then he grinned and sat upright. He hugged Belle closely, and saw Jay over her shoulder.

"Jay! Hot damn, I'm glad to see you. How are you, boy?"

They shook hands and Jay sat down on the bed.

"What do you know, Jay, they trapped me like a possum. I was sound asleep and I woke up and there was a bunch of men with guns. All I could do was blink my eyes and I guess my mouth was open as wide as a barn door. Ain't that a hell of a thing?"

"I'm glad there wasn't no shooting, honey," Belle said. "Thank God fer that."

"I didn't have no time to grab my gun."

"Pat, I don't know what to do with you," Jay said. "Seems like you can't keep out of trouble."

"Yeah. I'm sure enough up to my ears in it now, Jay."

"Pat," Belle said. "What I want to know is how they ever found you."

"I wish I knowed. The first I knowed of it I woke up and I was looking into them guns. It was the sheriff and they was all Mehuskah Laws. They sure enough knowed where I was at, because they come in two big cars and they left 'em yonder by the old wagon road and come on foot through the blackjack. They knowed just where to come to, all right."

"Nobody knowed where you was at but me and old Haze Thompson, Pat," Belle said.

"It wouldn't be Haze."

"I don't know."

"I don't think it would be Haze," Jay said. "But anyhow I'm going to ride that way and talk to him. I'll know soon as I see him because Haze couldn't look me in the face if he done it."

"You don't suppose somebody else seen the smoke from that bee-tree?" Pat asked.

"Nobody lives up that way but Haze, honey."

"That's right."

"Pat, they can't take you back and put you in jail fer all your life. They just can't."

"Don't you worry, Belle," Jay said. "We'll take care of Pat.

We'll git you off, boy. We'll fight it in the court and we'll win. We'll take and git a good lawyer and he'll muddle up them witnesses and they won't be able to make no identification of you, Pat."

"It ain't going to be that easy, Jay. People knowed me in that town. I used to blow in there payday nights and they knowed me. It's one of them little courthouse square towns in a dry county and it sure was slow. Not even no beer."

Belle sighed and turned her eyes to the barred window and the square of pale sky.

"You'd ought to have better sense, Pat," Jay said. "But, anyhow, give us a good lawyer and we'll git you off. The only thing is we got to have money to pay him and I couldn't even lay my hands on thirty bucks."

"Hell, we got six hunderd dollars, Jay. I give Belle half of it and they took the rest off me when they brung me in this morning."

"I guess I know where that money come from," Jay said, frowning and sitting stiff on the edge of the bed.

Pat laughed and winked at Belle. "Now, Jay, I don't want to hear none of your lectures."

"You ain't."

"Jay ought to been a preacher," Pat said. "Bo, you'd be hell on sinners."

"Now look here, Pat," Jay said. "We got to git you off and we got to git busy. I reckon the best thing you can do is to waive extradition and go on down to Texas and we'll take care of a lawyer fer you and I'll send people down to swear you was here in the hills all the time. Dad and me will swear to it, and maybe Joseph Paul and two or three others. We'll swamp that there jury with witnesses."

"Whatever you say, Jay."

"And damn it, Pat, when we *do* git you free you got to come home and stay home and don't you give us no more trouble."

"Sure, Jay." Pat grinned.

"I mean that, Pat. It's hard on us to have you always in a fix and it sure is hard on Dad. You'd ought to think of Dad, and you'd ought to think of Belle and Billy, too."

"Honey, please you listen to Jay," Belle said.

"I'm a-listening."

"You got to heed him too, Pat."

"I will, Belle. I sure enough will."

The guard looked through the bars at them. "Time's up, you two."

"Now you do like I said, Pat," Jay said. "You go ahead and waive extradition and we'll fight it out in Texas."

"O.K., Jay."

"Come on, Belle," Jay said. "You'll see him again real soon and we'll bring him home to the valley."

I hate to see Belle so cut-up. She's got a lot of guts and he's give her plenty misery. You can't say nothing that Pat will listen to with both ears. He just grins at you and agrees with you and does just what he damn well pleases. But he's got to listen to us now and he's got to do like the lawyer tells him and we got to find us a good one and that will cost plenty and we got to pay witnesses to go down to Texas and that three hunderd won't do fer that. And I don't know as we ought to spend that money. . . .

They came out of the jail into the open and Jay walked ahead of Belle to the car. He got in, but when she was on the seat beside him he did not start the motor.

"Belle we got to scare up some money."

"We got three hunderd dollars, Jay."

"I know, but I don't believe we ought to spend it, and anyhow it ain't enough."

"It's an awful lot of money. More than I ever seen at once before."

"Lawyers come high, Belle. We got to lay our hands on more than that, and money come by in a different way, too."

"But, Jay, there ain't a way in the world we can scare up any cash money. You know that."

"There's one way, Belle, and I reckon we'll have to take it. We can take and sell the farm."

"But, Jay, what would Crosby say to that?"

"I reckon Dad wants to see Pat go free. He'll do anything to help Pat out, and anyhow, Belle, there's going to come a time when we got to sell that farm or else swim out of the valley with our clothes tied around our necks. They're going to make a lake there come what may and if we don't sell out they'll condemn that land and move us off. They got the law with 'em and they can do it."

"Crosby said he knowed a good farm over to Boggs."

"Did he say that, now?"

"Yes."

"Then I reckon Dad has thought some about selling out."

"He don't want to give Lamar Baker the satisfaction."

"It'll cost Lamar plenty," Jay said. "I'll put it up to him, and it will cost him plenty. Belle, what do you say we hunt up Lamar and talk business?"

"Without old Crosby here?"

"I reckon Dad will agree to what I do."

"Sure he will. All right, Jay, let's do that. Yes, I guess we better go ahead and do it."

Jay stepped on the starter and put the car in gear. He turned toward the main street.

Lamar used to hang out at Jed Miller's place and I reckon that's where to find him. He's always there shooting payball pool fer four bits a ball and I guess he could make a living just doing that if he was satisfied with it. One thing you can depend on, you can always find Lamar hanging out with the no-goods.

Jay turned off on a side street and stopped the car. He got out and entered THE SPORTING BAR, a long room open to the street. On his right as he came in was a bar and lunch counter strewn with punch-boards, and opposite it a blackboard on which a Negro was chalking up, inning by inning, baseball scores. Jay went into the back room where the pool tables were. Lamar was not among the group of men around the tables. To Jay's right two men were playing a pin-ball machine.

"I'm hunting Lamar Baker," Jay said.

"He ain't been in all day." The man he had spoken to looked at Jay. He wore his white straw hat on the back of his head and he had sharp, curious eyes that looked Jay up and down.

"Better try his office," the other man said.

"Where is that?"

"In the Cherokee Building."

"Thanks," Jay said.

In the Cherokee Building, in the biggest building in town and up on the eighth floor, I bet. Well, Lamar is coming up, he sure is that, and I reckon pool rooms is a little small-time fer him now-a-days. That man always had his eye out fer whatever would turn up and even when he was just a kid in overalls and bare feet he used to steal mushmelons and sell 'em from a little stand he had built him down on the Aldine road.

"Let's go, Belle," Jay said, getting in the car. "Lamar's got himself an office over in the Cherokee Building now."

"You don't say? I ain't never been in it."

"That's a heap different from a cabin in the hills, ain't it?"

"He still ain't no good, even if he climbs to the top of Jacob's ladder."

Jay turned onto the main street, waited for a green light and a bell to ring, and found a parking space fifty feet from the Cherokee Building.

"You coming in with me, Belle?"

"I want to see the inside of it."

Jay looked up Lamar's name in an index of tenants on the wall. "He's only on the sixth floor, Belle. What do you know about that? I thought he'd be right up at the top."

"I reckon he'll git there yet," Belle said.

"Some day I'm going to have our offices here in this building and it will have the name there in the lobby, the Southern Tenant Farmers' Union right there on that blackboard."

They took the elevator to the sixth floor and Jay paused in front of a door marked in gold lettering: *Lamar Baker, Attorney at Law.* He glanced at Belle and grinned, then opened the door. They came into a small, sunlit anteroom, but it was empty. There was a small desk near the window and photographs of President Roosevelt and the Governor of the state on the wall.

There's his law degree, all framed and under glass, his Tennessee law degree. I remember when he went over to Lebanon after it and all he did was do his heavy drinking over yonder fer a year and they give him a diploma. Anybody can git one of them Tennessee degrees in a year if he works and I reckon Lamar don't know much about the law but he's sharp and he's wise and that's all a lawyer needs to be. He can git ahead of the next man, and that's what makes a lawyer, sure enough.

"Jay, I was never up so high. Look how little-bittey the people are down yonder." Belle turned from the window, smiling.

"I wonder where Lamar is at," Jay said. "Small office, ain't it?"

"There's another door over yonder."

Jay walked over to it and knocked; Lamar's voice answered: "Come in."

Jay pushed open the door and Lamar brought his feet down from his desk and sat erect so abruptly that his swivel chair creaked.

A funny look on that smooth red face of his, a damned funny look. I reckon he never expected I'd walk in his door and it sure give him a surprise and he's dressed awful peculiar fer a lawyer with gold lettering on his door like that. I don't see why he wears old corduroy pants and boots and a hickory shirt.

"Hello there, Jay," Lamar said, wetting his lips. He did not look at Jay's face and his shifting eyes saw Belle. "Hello, Belle."

"Howdy, Lamar."

"What can I do fer you-all?"

"I reckon you heard about Pat," Jay said.

Lamar stood up. Sunlight glistened on his red forehead; sunlight shone on drops of sweat.

"That's too bad, Jay. That sure is too bad."

"They caught him this morning," Jay said.

"Yeah, I heard about it." Lamar moved behind his desk, watching Jay. "Sit down, you-all. Go ahead, sit down. Belle, that chair by the window is real comfortable. Why don't you take that one? Jay, what can I do fer you? I sure am glad to see you. You ain't been around in some time. How do you like my new office?"

I never heard Lamar talk so much. I reckon that's how an attorney at law has got to act but I don't know what he expects to git out of us.

"Say, Lamar, your office is fine, but that's a peculiar rig fer a big-time lawyer to have on."

Lamar looked down at his square-toed boots and Jay looked at them too and saw clay encrusted on the toes and heels.

"Why, I thought I'd go fishing, Jay," Lamar said. "They tell me the cats are biting fine over in the Arkansas. This is Saturday afternoon, you know."

Jay sat down and stretched out his legs. He held his hat in his hand and gazed steadily across at Lamar.

"What's on your mind, Jay?"

"Lamar, what is it you got to do with that lake they aim to build out in the hills?"

"Oh, that." Lamar drew the palm of his right hand across his forehead. "I'm retained as counsel, Jay, to buy up the land and git things organized. There's a young engineer here from New York City and he's fixing to start work on the dam and he aims to build stone cabins and lodges on the ridge around the lake."

"I know all that part of it," Jay said. "I just wondered what you had to do with it, that's all."

It's plain enough why he's got that picture of the President on the wall. Lamar's the kind of a man who wears a tag and he's like a dog that wears the tag of his master and he don't give a God damn who his master is so long as he feeds him. He's just a plain hound dog.

"Belle told me you was out to see Dad about buying his place," Jay said. "I had a talk with Dad but he don't want to sell."

"He give me that idear."

"I believe I could git him to change his mind if the price is right," Jay said. "I suppose it's worth a little more to the Government to settle things up."

"I don't know about that, Jay. How much was you going to ask?"

"Fifty dollars an acre is about right."

"Fer Christ's sake!" Lamar said. "Excuse me, Belle."

"I guess if the Government can spend all that money to build a lake way to hell and gone in the hills, it can pay us fifty dollars an acre and not know the difference," Jay said. "Anyhow, that's our price."

"Now you know that land ain't worth even fifteen dollars an acre," Lamar said. "It's eroded and plumb wore out."

"It's worth fifty dollars to us."

"But, Jay, be reasonable about this thing. Now listen here, I might be able to git you twenty-five."

Jay shook his head.

"Jess Cookley sold out fer twenty, Jay."

"Then he ain't got no sense."

"Now, Jay, you've got forty acres of land and at twenty-five dollars an acre you'd have a clear thousand dollars."

"I don't want to waste my time, Lamar," Jay said. "My brother Pat is in jail and I got things to do."

"I sure am sorry about Pat. I sure am, Jay. I tell you what, and I mean this fer you, Belle, if you're looking fer a lawyer fer Pat why don't you-all call me in?"

Jay looked hard at Lamar, then slowly shook his head, his lips tightening. Their eyes met and Lamar's face became red.

"I wouldn't charge you, Jay. After all, we all come from the hills. We was raised together and I knowed Pat when he was just a little tag-along after you."

"I guess not," Jay said.

Whatever has got into Lamar's head. I know he never did take to Pat and he knows I know it. Pat wouldn't have no chance with Lamar fer his lawyer and what come over him to put his name in?

"Jay, I guess Crosby would take thirty dollars, wouldn't he? We're old friends and I'd like to help him out. What I say goes and if I say thirty Crosby will git it. I tell you, I'll do that fer you, Jay. I'll recommend thirty." Lamar grinned and slapped Jay's shoulder lightly. "How's that, Belle?"

"Make it forty," Jay said.

Lamar looked hard at Jay, then spread his hands. "All right, forty it is, but I don't know, Jay. I'll have to ask the main office. That's a lot of money to spend fer forty acres. I tell you what I'll do. I'll put through a call right now. Sit down, you two, and I'll let you know in a jiffy, just as quick as I can put through a call to Oklahoma City."

Jay sank into his chair, frowning.

It sure is peculiar he should take me up on that without no argument and agree to pay me over all that money, but maybe he knows the main office won't give in to it, and maybe he wants to git something out of it all. . . . Now by God, he's after that county attorneyship and thirty-six hunderd a year and maybe he thinks I'll forget about him bribing that feller at Boggs. Maybe he still thinks he can git the votes I can swing. He'd butter up to a wildcat if he thought there was anything to git out of it.

"Say, Lamar," Jay said. "You still in the runnin' fer county attorney?"

Lamar had the telephone in his hand; he looked across at Jay speculatively, pursing his lips.

"Sure I am, Jay. It looks like I got Mehuskah sewed up."

"Uh-huh," Jay said.

"I don't know about outside, though. I reckon you-all will see me out your way canvassing votes, Jay."

I should of seen it was that and I reckon Lamar figures forty dollars an acre will buy him the tenant farmers' votes just like he figured twenty dollars would buy him that Boggs ballot box.

"Hello," Lamar was saying. "Hello, this is Lamar Baker at Mehuskah. It's about that hold-out in the hills. He come in today and agreed to sell and I beat him down to forty dollars an acre but he won't take less than that. . . . Yeah, I know that. . . . Well, it's either pay him or stall around until we can condemn his land and pay the costs of that." Lamar looked over at Jay and winked. "Sure I recommend we meet his price and git the thing settled. . . . All right, I'll wait."

"What did they say?" Jay asked.

"Give 'em a minute. I guess he has to take it upstairs fer an answer. It looks like they'll pay it, Jay." He put his mouth close to the transmitter. "Yeah, what's the word? . . . Sure, I think so. That's my recommendation. . . . O.K. I'll git the papers signed and forward 'em. Good-by."

Lamar hung up. "There you are, Jay."

"Are they going to pay it?" Belle asked.

"They sure are."

"When do we git the money?" Jay asked.

"First of the week, I wouldn't wonder. I tell you what, that engineer, Neil Smith, moved out to Aldine yesterday and he'll stop by with the papers fer Crosby to sign and he'll bring along the check when it comes through. When can you-all move out, Jay?"

"Pretty soon."

"We'll send in trucks to move you, soon as you give the word."

"Maybe we'll move right off," Jay said. "I don't know what Crosby will want to do. Anyhow, we need that money bad."

"It's fer Pat," Belle said. "We got to set Pat free."

Lamar looked out the window. "Yes, sure." There was a pause, then he jerked his head suddenly around and looked at Jay. "Well, I'm sure glad I could help you-all out. That's a nice piece of change fer Crosby."

"It's a good farm too," Jay said. "I was born on it and Pat was born on it and Dad come there from Arkansas in nineteen-two and bought it off a Cherokee Indian. He's lived there ever since." He nodded to Belle. "Come along, honey."

Dad will sure be cut up about moving away. He come out in nineteen-two and he's lived there ever since and raised his corn and raised his boys and it sure is home to him. He'll hate to move out but he'll be glad to do it fer Pat and that's a lot of money. Sixteen hunderd dollars. That's more than any of us ever seen or had to our names and it's a funny thing it comes to us through Lamar and it's a funny thing he was so quick to give it to us. But he'll do anything to git ahead and I reckon he'll have that attorneyship, but not through no votes that I give to him and there won't be no votes fer him in that Boggs box, just like I told him the first time.

"Gee, Jay, now we gone and done it I don't know."

They were in front of the Cherokee Building, in sunlight, and the anxious expression of Belle's face was plain to see.

"We didn't have nothing else to do, Belle."

"I know that."

They got into the car and Jay started the motor. "Listen here, Belle, that adds up to sixteen hunderd dollars. Have you thought of that?"

"Sure I have. I figured it myself."

Jay was driving along the main street. "I'll take you home to the valley, Belle, and we'll git Dad's O.K."

"All right, Jay."

On the way to Aldine they did not talk. Belle sat looking fixedly at the road ahead of her. She was frowning and Jay noticed for the first time the lines beside her mouth and the tired expression of her eyes. They went through Aldine and took the dirt road to the valley. Turning off by the Sour Tom schoolhouse Jay looked down below and saw men unloading planks from two brown trucks at the dam site.

"Look yonder, Belle, they're fixing to start work already. By next spring they expect to start filling the lake and they say it will only take a few days to do it, just from the water in that creek."

Jay drove on, with only a brief glance at the ocher stones of the schoolhouse, and they descended the slope to the covered bridge and the road that ran the length of the shallow valley. When they reached the farmhouse they found Crosby Strickland sitting on the porch in a wild cherry chair that Joseph Paul had made.

"You leave me tell him about it, Belle," Jay said.

Crosby got to his feet as soon as he recognized Jay's car and came down the stone steps to meet them.

"Jay, ain't it mean? Did you see Pat?"

"Yeah, we seen him, Dad. He's all right. He ain't been hurt."

"I wish I could of been with you, but somebody had to stay with Billy." Crosby turned his eyes mournfully to Belle. "I wanted to see Pat, I sure did."

"I told Pat to waive extradition and they'll take him back to Texas, maybe tomorrow," Jay said. "The first thing in the morning why don't you go to the jail to see him?"

"I sure will," Crosby said.

"And we'll take Billy with us, Crosby," Belle said. "Pat ought to see his boy before they take him back. Where is Billy, Crosby?"

"I seen him out by the barn a minute ago."

"We'll have Pat home pretty quick, Dad, don't you worry," Jay said. "We'll git him off fer sure. Ain't that so, Belle?"

"Yes, Jay. I sure do hope so."

"See, Dad, we aim to git us a big-time lawyer down yonder in Texas and he'll talk Pat right out of jail."

"Lawyers cost money, Jay."

"I know that. They cost plenty. But we got to have one and we got to have the money and I figured the only way to git it was to take and sell the farm to the Government." Jay hesitated, looking at his father's expressionless face. "We went in and talked to Lamar Baker, Dad, and we asked him fifty dollars an acre and I'll be damned if he didn't agree to forty. That makes sixteen hunderd in cash money, Dad."

"That's a heap of money, all right."

"We need it."

"I already thought some about selling, Jay. It looks like nothing will stop 'em from building that lake and I thought maybe we ought to go ahead and move out. I know a place over toward Boggs we could buy fer six-seven hunderd dollars."

"Then I reckon we better buy it, Dad, if that's what you want."

"Sure we will."

Jay looked at Belle and grinned, and her answering smile was wan and mechanical.

So he already made up his mind to it. That makes it a lot easier and I might of knowed that's the way he'd take it. He's got Pat in mind and he ain't thinking about how he lived here and farmed that corn patch since nineteen-two.

"Now we got it settled, let's take and move over to Boggs, then," Crosby said. "My corn is harvested and we got nothing to keep us here."

"Not till we got the money in our hand."

"No, not till then, but I'll ride over yonder and see about that farm. It used to have a tenant but nobody lives there now and the house is empty and ready fer us."

"Right," Jay said. "Dad, I got to be on my way."

"I wish you'd stay awhile, Jay. Can't you wait fer supper?"

"Not this evenin', Dad."

Jay went back to his car and as he drove away he glanced back at the old clapboard house, at the cornfield and the gray-and-green stones of the wall.

Now it's done and there'll be thirty foot of water over it and catfish sleeping there among them stones and the school-house way up yonder on the ridge will be not much above the water level. After all these years. And there'll be fertile land hereabouts and it will be fer rich people to have fun in and the people like us who owned the land will be moved off to hell and gone. Some of them will take them houses the Government aims to build fer 'em and have farms the Government picked out and maybe they'll be a good bit better off, but they won't never git near enough to that lake to wash their hands in it. It sure ain't built fer them, not fer the poor people. It's a rich man's country and a rich man's Government, all right.

Jay drove up out of the valley by the Sour Tom school-house and turned toward Aldine at the crossroads.

I reckon yesterday was the last day of school and the boards is up on the windows. I reckon she'll start back fer Tulsa in a couple of days and next fall I expect there won't be no school. The people will be moved out of the valley and there won't be no need fer the school and she'll be sent off somewheres else. I guess it's just good-by and I ought to stop in Aldine and see her and that's what I'll do.

Jay's foot unconsciously pressed harder on the accelerator. When he entered Aldine he saw an automobile parked in front of the house where Leona lived, and as he drove in behind it he saw that it had a United States license. Glancing toward the house he saw Leona on the porch and with her a slim man with a black moustache. Jay got out of the car and went toward the house. They were sitting on a swing that creaked as it swayed back and forth and bounced up and down with a clatter of chains when they stood up.

"Hello, Jay. I wondered why you didn't come out to see me."

"I've been pretty busy."

"Jay, this is Neil Smith, the engineer who's going to build our lake. He's living here in Aldine."

"Uh-huh," Jay said. "Howdy."

"I met your father and sister," Neil said, putting out his hand. "I drove out to their place with Mister Baker yesterday."

"I heard you did," Jay said.

"Jay," Leona said, touching his arm. "Jay, why don't you-all sell, so Neil can go ahead with the lake?"

I knowed she had something in her head when she touched me that way and used that voice on me.

"You'll have to move sometime," the engineer said. "I can't seem to make people see what a big thing this lake is for the country. You Oklahoma people don't seem to have imagination. Why, we'll build a two thousand acre recreational area, with a lake five miles long, with twenty miles of shore line. We're going to plant a couple of million trees in the hills."

"I don't argue with that part of it," Jay said.

"Then I wish you wouldn't stand in our way. Of course we'll get that land in the end by condemnation, but I wish you wouldn't hold up a half-million-dollar project." Neil leaned back in the swing, looking at Jay. "As far as I can see the only thing you people out here are interested in is politics. I was never in a place like this before. You'll stand for any kind of political thievery and chicanery and laugh it off, but you won't stand behind anything progressive. It's every man for himself out here."

"That's the way Oklahoma was settled," Leona said. "Every man for himself. When they had the Runs people had to rush in and fight for their land sometimes. And there have always been so many bad men that we're used to that."

"I will say this," Neil said, smiling at her. "You've got a lot of friendliness and a lot of tolerance and you don't mix in other people's business. I suppose that's because it's not long since everybody carried a gun. But I wish you people would quit acting like a dog taking care of his own front yard and get behind this lake. It will progress this whole area."

"That lake won't be no particular benefit to the people in the hills," Jay said with a stubborn set of his jaw. "They aim to just move them away."

"But it will be a fine thing for them," Neil said. "They'll be moved out into the world, to better farms where they'll have a chance in life. They tell me those tenants in the hills have an average income of only forty dollars a year and their land is tax delinquent and badly eroded. They'll be moved out where they'll become a part of the life of a community instead of a secret band of hermit people. We'll redeem that land and we'll redeem those people."

Leona nodded agreement, but Jay said sharply: "Them people don't need redeeming. They just need a chance, that's all."

"They tell me those hills are the last stand of the Southwestern outlaws and this lake project is going to open that country up," Neil said. "It's been the hang-out of bad men all these years, and a place for them to hide out, and those hill people take care of them. Lamar Baker was telling me that the National Guard put a dragnet through the hills a few years back and caught seventeen men wanted by the police. He said those men all carry guns, and already six ex-convicts have applied for work on the dam. It was off in those hills that Pretty Boy Floyd hid out, wasn't it? And plenty of others. What this lake will do is open that country up and help clean the bad men out of there."

"Now see here . . ." Jay said.

Leona caught his arm.

"Now see here," Jay said, looking over her head at the engineer. "Sure some of them people have been to jail, and my brother is one of 'em, Mister, and that's because the only way they can make a living is with a gun. The land don't keep 'em and it's pretty easy fer a city man to talk about bad men and all that, because you ain't any idea what their life is like. You say they're bad men and they're mean and some of 'em are. They're mean like some hound dogs are mean. They're mean because they don't git enough to eat and have every sickness a dog can have and still be alive. Now listen here . . ."

"Jay, please." She pulled at his arm. "Jay, listen to me."

That little chicken-drop from the city. By God, I ought to wring his neck like I would a frier, standing there looking at me down that long nose of his.

"Jay, he didn't mean anything personal."

Jay turned away, and she followed him along the porch, still holding his arm.

"He didn't know what he was saying, Jay, don't you see?"

"That's plain enough."

"He's from New York City and he's never been in Oklahoma before, Jay."

"I don't care," Jay said. "I already forgot it."

They were on the path leading to the street.

"Then come back up on the porch, Jay."

"I reckon not. I got to go to town, Leona."

I wonder does she think the same as he does. She's a big-town girl and she's got no idea how people got to live around here. She's got no idea what it's like not to have enough to eat and to be scared of the landlord and scared he'll put you off and git another tenant and scared you won't find another piece of land to plant your crop.

"You can tell him that I done agreed to sell that land," Jay said. "We aim to move out as soon as we git the money. You tell him that."

"I'll tell him. But, Jay, you'll like Neil when you get to know him."

Jay looked at her, frowning.

"He didn't know, Jay. He didn't know about Pat."

"They caught Pat this morning," Jay said. "He's in the Mehuskah jail."

"Oh! I'm sorry, Jay."

"I expect we'll git him off."

"That surely is too bad, Jay. I thought you said he'd gone to Mexico."

"He was yonder in the hills and they trapped him."

Jay started on toward the car and she walked beside him, the top of her head level with his shoulder.

"I guess you're right, Leona," Jay said. "That man's just a fool, like you said."

"I didn't say that, Jay!"

"You said he didn't know how people had to live here and I guess you're right. I got nothing against him except that he's a fool. He ought to see how some people live."

"Jay, you said you'd already forgotten it."

"O.K. I have." Jay put his foot on the running board. "I guess school is out, Leona?"

"That's right. Yesterday was the last day."

"You going back to Tulsa now?"

"Not right away. For one thing I'm going to the stomp-dance next week. I asked Joseph Paul and he said white people were welcome to come. Neil's going to take me."

"I see," Jay said.

"*You* wouldn't, Jay."

"I'm too busy, Leona. It's just only that."

"Jay, you know you work too hard, and you get so little out of it."

"I ain't looking fer nothing. — Listen here, Leona, tomorrow

I got to take a trip. I got to go around and talk to farm tenants
and I'll be a good part of the day driving and if you want to
go with me I'll show you something."

She looked up at his face, her blue eyes expressionless, but
an anxious twist showing on her lips.

"I'll show you how people really got to live around here,"
Jay said. "It will open your eyes, honey. Do you want to
come?"

"Yes, Jay, I'll come with you."

"I'll stop by pretty early. I tell you, Leona, it will open your
eyes."

"All right, Jay. And please, you be more reasonable. Don't
go acting like a wild man."

Jay grinned. "I guess I should of kept my mouth shut. But
it's hard to do it. It sure is hard."

"I know." She took his hand in both of hers. "Don't worry
about your brother, Jay."

"No. I got hopes we'll git Pat off." Jay got in the car and
started it. "Bright and early tomorrow, honey."

"Yes, I'll be ready."

Jay drove away and in the windshield mirror saw her turn
back toward the porch where the engineer was waiting.

The only chance I got is to open them big blue eyes of hers
and let her see fer herself why I got to do what I do. I ought to
of said I'd take her to that stomp-dance when she first asked
me but I got business there. I got to talk to them Indians and
I got to git them to talking union. Anyhow she'll be there and
I'll see her and there are other things I got to think about. Pat's
in jail and we got to git him off and we got to git that money in
our hands to do it and fix it up with a big-time lawyer down in
Texas, maybe one of them sharp ones from Dallas or Fort
Worth. And I got to git busy and talk to more of them white
tenants and git 'em in the union and talk this Jim Crow out of
their heads. And I got to git busy with them spinach workers,
too. Webb Harper has been out there and he knows how to
organize and we got to lay our plans. But first and last I got to
git Pat off. He's depending on me and Belle is depending on
me and so is old Dad. Everywhere I got people depending on
me and I got to win my way and I can't waste no time and

sure as hell I'm wasting time with her. But maybe tomorrow
will open her eyes and if it does she would sure make a fine
wife. If I could git her thinking my way she could work with
me and she'd make me a home to come back to nights instead
of that empty house and that single bed and the meals out of
cans. But I guess I got to stop wishing and do my work.

Jay drove through the Mehuskah business district and turned
off on the bumpy road to his house. Dusk had come and a
lamp was burning in the house and when he opened the door
he saw Rock Island Jones sitting at the table, reading a pamphlet.

"Hello there," Jay said. "How did that barbecue come off?"

"It was sho' too bad you had to run out on it, Jay."

"I couldn't help it, Rocky. My brother Pat is in jail."

"Yeah, that Indian told me. — Say, Jay, I got him signed
up and them other Indians, too."

"That's fine," Jay said.

"We made up a local there in Tanzey, Jay, but it's mostly
colored men."

"Just the same that's a nigro community," Jay said. "We got
a lot of towns like that in Oklahoma, Rocky. We got some
towns where they don't allow no nigros after sundown, and
they got the state university, the seat of learnin', in a town like
that. But still we got nigro towns, too, where white people
ain't welcome. Some day maybe we can break all that down."
Jay sighed and sank into the chair. "We got to be sure enough
strong to do it, and we got lots of work to do."

"We sure is."

"They had to fight it out the same way over in Arkansas.
They had to fight it out in Mississippi. We got to break down
the prejudice of a hunderd years. — Tomorrow I aim to ride
out and talk to as many of them white tenants as I can. Next
Saturday I got a meeting called down in Jennings County and
I'm going to spend a week down yonder, Rocky."

"That sounds like something."

"I'm going to leave that Tanzey district to you and you'd
ought to move out that way," Jay said.

"Okay, Jay."

"We'll go over that after supper. Is there anything to eat
in the house?"

"I got a can of beans heatin' on the stove."

"Good," Jay said. He put his feet on the table and lay back in his chair.

The lamplight was on Rocky's face; he sat facing the lamp with his elbows on the table as he read the pamphlet.

"People write these books got no notion how tough th' work is," the Negro said. "It talk mighty fine on paper but it sho' ain't easy, Jay. I done found that out."

"I told you we had to go slow and git the organization rooted," Jay said.

Rocky put the pamphlet down. "Goin' slow don't come easy, Jay. It don't come easy with me. They tooken my wife's ear off with the flick of a gun back yonder in Arkansas and that don't say go slow to me. That say go fast as you kin and organize so strong you kin tell them bastards what to do."

"Oklahoma is different from Arkansas," Jay said. "The Southwest ain't like the South, Rocky. People here in Oklahoma are live-and-let-live people and each man is lookin' out fer his own oats. The red man and the white man and the black man growed up together in this state side by side and we got independent people here. They won't stand fer no rough tactics. We ain't got no vigilantes and there won't be no trouble here. I'm telling you that, Rocky."

"Maybe you ain't had no trouble because you ain't done much," Rocky said. "You ain't went very far yet." He looked steadily at Jay. "You can't never tell when it's goin' to happen. One place is about like another when it comes to low-down, mean-hearted men and when you start steppin' on their toes you'll find it out. I done seen it happen, Jay, and I know. Over to Arkansas, Jay, I sharecropped on a big plantation, maybe two hunderd families. But befo' dat I'd been to Baltimore and I lived in one of them white-stoop houses on Franklin Street where it sho' was comfortable to live. My pappy was on th' Rock Island and he was in the union, Jay. He brung me up union and when I went home to Arkansas I was union and I joined up with the Southern Ten't Farmers' Union first off. One night they come a-lookin' fo' me. It hadn't been no trouble at all up to then, but they come a-lookin' fo' me and I wasn't to home. My missus said she didn't know whereabouts I was, Jay, and they took and beat her with the butt-end of a gun. I had to take out into Memphis and I never seen nor heard of her fo' a year. — And up to then, Jay, it hadn't been no trouble, no trouble at all."

"That sure is terrible, Rocky," Jay said.

"It's three years past now, and my missus has got a job in a Memphis laundry now. We ain't never been back to Arkansas. Since then I been workin' mighty hard fo' the Ten't Farmers' Union. The rest of my life I aims to do that work, Jay."

"But just the same what I'm telling you is true, Rocky," Jay said. "You won't find no terror here in Oklahoma. It's mostly tenant farmers here, not sharecroppers. They rent their farms and they got their own tools and they got more independence as farmers than them Arkansawyers. And the nigros here are most of 'em come down from freedmen of the Indians. Them Five Civilized Tribes had slaves and they brung 'em along when they was drove out of the South and moved to the Indian Territory. When they was freed them slaves settled down and growed up with Oklahoma just like the Indians and the white men and they had the benefit of three races growing up together. Oklahoma was the Indian Territory up to nineteen-seven, and they hasn't no bigotry or prejudice took root here. Oklahoma has been the melting pot of the redskins and the black skins and the white skins and that's the reason. — I'm telling you Oklahoma won't have no terror."

"You can't never tell till it happens, Jay," Rocky said. "Already they done used tear gas on strikers here in Oklahoma." He looked up at Jay, gave his head a shake, and lowered his eyes to the pamphlet.

Jay stood up with a shrug of his shoulders and went into the kitchen. He took the can of beans from the saucepan and wrapped a towel around it. He bit his lip and reached for the can-opener.

After all that it ain't no wonder Rocky always looks fer the worst to happen. But I'm damned sure we won't have nothing like that here. I know Oklahoma. I was born here and I'm going to live my life here and people here are let-alone people. They give a man the right to think what he pleases and work fer what he wants to. We're going to have plenty of opposition, sure enough, but there won't be no terror.

Jay jabbed the can-opener in the can and a spurt of brown hot juice struck his cheek. He wiped his face with his sleeve.

Some day I'll have a home to come to and a wife to cook my supper and she'll be somebody I can talk to about my work and tell my troubles to and it will have to be that kind of a woman. It will have to be a woman who feels like I do and who gits on fire inside when she thinks of the way some people are treated and some people got to live. She'll have to believe in the union and work fer it and have the union come first anyhow until we git it organized solid as it ought to be and strong enough to tell the landlords what they got to do. When that times comes we can set on the porch and take our ease and maybe farm a little land of our own, but not until that times comes. That's all any man wants is a good wife and a good home and good land to farm, but I wouldn't want it even if I had it until every farmer in the state has got that chance. . . .

$\mathcal{J}ay$ ❦

IF she's got eyes to see I don't have to say nothing more, if she's got eyes to see that old oak bed with the busted slats and that mattress with the lumps in it and the stuffing sticking out of it and that pile of quilts gray as a rat's belly.

"I'm Jay Strickland from the Southern Tenant Farmers' Union. Whose place is this?"

"Bill Mitchell is my husband's name."

And the walls papered with newspapers and that tinted photograph in the frame, I guess of his mother and she had a lace choker at the collar of her black dress and it's plain that times was better then and maybe they wasn't tenants then. If she's got eyes to see that . . .

"Where is Bill, Mrs. Mitchell?"

"He's out in the cotton patch, Mister." The woman's voice was whining, anxious. "What do you want of Bill?"

"I just want to talk to him," Jay said.

She ain't blind and I guess she can see the mends in that gingham dress and I guess she can see them deep hollows her eyes are set in and that thin look of her neck under her ears and that scared look just because some stranger come and asked to see her husband. And I reckon she's scared I come from the landlord and they are probably in debt and they're scared I'm going to put 'em off the land and put another family on it. That's what they're always scared of, even when the land is the sorriest.

"I'm from the union, ma'am," Jay said. "Ain't you heard about the Southern Tenant Farmers' Union?"

"I heard tell of it, all right."

I guess she can hear that dollar alarm clock ticking so loud to git 'em up and at the end of the row by sunrise and they work to sunset and they start in when they're kids seven years old and they never let up and lots of times they don't even have a chance to go to school. And I guess she can see that shabby patch of linoleum on the pinewood floor and that greasy oilcloth on the table and that whisky bottle no more than half full of sorghum molasses and that old bureau with the cracked mirror that some rich man must of throwed away and a long time ago at that and that little kid with his head shaved and that little gingham dress she's made him and the scared way he's hiding behind her skirts.

"I'll tell you what," Jay said. "I'm going to walk out yonder in the cotton and find Bill Mitchell."

"Bill's working, Mister. Bill's real busy."

"I won't keep him long," Jay said. "Look here, ma'am, I'm from the union and I want to sign Bill up. I'm here to help you people, to give you the help that organization can give. We want every tenant farmer in the state to have a square deal and we're going to git it fer him."

"I heard about that union," the woman said. "You better talk to Bill."

Jay looked at Leona. She stood just inside the doorway, where she had stopped when they first entered the farmhouse. Against the streaked gray wall her linen dress was very white.

I guess it's Leona that scares her too. In that white dress she comes out of another world and both of 'em know it and that makes her think I ain't to be trusted and I come from the landlord or somebody up to no good and I don't blame her fer that.

"Come on, Leona," Jay said. He nodded to the woman and they went out into the afternoon sunlight. They followed a narrow path between stalks of corn toward the cotton field, toward the long parallels of it, of the cotton plants green and thick on the flat land, unbroken green across to a narrow strip of woods.

"You've about seen the worst of it," Jay said. "You've seen some people who ain't so bad off and maybe have meat once or twice a week and enough canned stuff to git along and a truck garden and now you've about seen the worst of it. You seen the bed they sleep on, didn't you?"

"Yes, Jay." Her voice was low.

"And that old shack that ain't good fer nothin' but to tack up advertising signs on, and them tin signs help keep the rain out, at that. And you seen them newspapers on the wall and pages from magazines with advertisements of automobiles and radios and vacuum cleaners and things like that they'll never own and never see."

"Jay, it's pathetic."

"Ain't it?"

"Jay, did you see the pussy willows? Honestly, it breaks your heart to see those pussy willows in a preserve jar on the mantel, that little way she tried to make her house a home."

"Now you're saying something," Jay said. "I told you it would open your eyes."

He reached out and took her hand and they walked in separate lanes through the cotton field.

It opened her eyes all right and by God her cheeks are a little shiny in the sun and now she knows that feeling you git when you see humans living worse than a mule and you know that something has got to be done about it and you got to go out and fight to make things better. I seen plenty of it but each time it tears at me like it was the first. And it's hard when you come to help and they don't trust you and don't want your help. Some people are like that and it's because like a dog that's been kicked a lot they don't expect nothing but a kick. . . .

"That would be Bill Mitchell," Jay said. "Bear off to the left a little, Leona."

The man stood up and leaned on his hoe, watching them

approach. A black hat, gray with dust and punched with ventilation holes, shaded his face; and it was a long face with narrow squinted eyes, with deep lines beside the mouth and a surly, suspicious twist at the corners of his lips.

"Hello, there," Jay said.

"Howdy."

"My name is Jay Strickland and I'm from the Tenant Farmers' Union."

The man shifted his weight slightly, still leaning on the hoe, and looked steadily at Jay.

"I was just over to your house and your wife said I'd find you here in the field."

"Where else would you find a farmer when there still is sun? I got to thin out this here cotton."

"That cotton looks mighty nice," Jay said.

"Uh-huh."

"There won't be no drought this year." Jay put a matchstick between his teeth to chew on. "I reckon the drought burned you out last summer?"

"Sure it did."

"It about put everybody in debt," Jay said. "They didn't make no crop and it put 'em in debt fer a year's furnish."

"Yeah."

"Nobody likes to owe the landlord money."

Mitchell laughed shortly; his teeth did not show and his eyes remained dark and cold. "I can't count the years since I been out of debt to my landlord."

"What you ought to do is join the Tenant Farmers' Union," Jay said.

"I guess not." The man looked steadily at Jay. "I ain't joining up with no nigger union."

"Now see here," Jay said, and spat the matchstick to the rich black earth. "What gave you a notion like that? It ain't a nigro union, and it ain't a white union, neither. It's a union of all the sharecroppers and tenant farmers and farm workers in the whole cotton belt, and color don't make no difference."

"Any time I join a union it will be a union of white men like me. I had enough trouble with them God-damned niggers."

"What did a nigro ever do to you?"

"They're lookin' to git this farm away from me. You'd ought to know that. There was two white fellers over to Tanzey and the niggers took their farms away."

"It was the landlord drove them men off," Jay said. "He drove 'em off and put the nigros on because he can work 'em more and give 'em less and treat 'em meaner."

"I know them niggers is working them farms now. I do know that, and I don't want to have no part of a nigger union, Mister. If we're going to have a union it's got to be a union of white men like me."

"If you got that kind of a union the landlords will drive all the union men off their land and put nigros in their place," Jay said. "That's what will happen if you have that kind of a union. If you go on fighting the nigros you won't never git nowhere. That's just what the landlord wants, to keep you-all fighting against each other."

Mitchell shook his head. "My landlord wouldn't stand fer my joining up with niggers and I know he wouldn't, and anyhow I wouldn't do it. Niggers and white men don't belong together and that's something everybody knows."

"They belong together economically," Jay said. "It's economic equality we want fer everybody. We ain't talking social equality."

"I believe they ought to be kept separate, like they are in the churches, like they are in the schools, like they are everywheres. Unions is just the same."

"Look here," Jay said. "You told me you was in debt to the landlord."

"Sure I am."

"And you don't see your way to paying off that debt, no matter how good a crop you make this year, and you don't git enough to more than keep yourself alive and you don't have no oil fer the lamps nor snuff fer your wife or tobacco fer yourself. Ain't that right?"

"That's the plain truth."

"You plant cotton fer yourself because that's a cash crop but you don't never know how much cash that cotton will bring in. You go to the store and buy a can of coal oil and you know just what it's going to cost and the storekeeper knows just what he's going to git fer it. But the farmer don't never know what his crops will bring in. But some day we're going to have a subsidy of crops. The Government will fix a minimum price it will buy all surplus at, and the farmer will know where he stands at. That's one of the things we're after."

"The Gov'ment throwed our hogs in the Mississippi and plowed our cotton under and shot our cattle," Mitchell said. "I don't know."

"The Government ought to of bought 'em instead and fed 'em to the hungry," Jay said. "We all know that. But look here, don't it ever make you feel that you'd like to rear back on your heels and fight fer your rights?"

"Sometimes I'd like to bust that landlord on the nose, sure enough," Mitchell said. His eyes burned in his dust-streaked face and not a muscle of his body moved.

"If you done that, what would happen?" Jay said. "You'd git throwed off this land before sundown. Now see here, you want to fight the landlord and the nigro wants to fight the landlord, too. You both raise the same crops and you both got the same landlord and you both want to fight him. It's plain you'd ought to fight him together and not waste your strength fighting each other. I tell you, the white man and the black man have got to fight together or they won't git no place. If you leave the nigros out of the union the landlord will take and put those nigros on your land and he'll drive you off. That's what he'll do."

"It's just this I got in mind, Mister. Sure I want to fight the landlord and I guess a union is the best way to do it and I'll join up with a white union. Let the niggers have a union of their own and you give us a white union."

"And look what will happen," Jay said. "The landlords will blow hell out of that nigro union and they'll scare the nigros like the Ku Kluck done and then they'll use the nigros to bust your union up and move you off the land. That all happened before, twenty years back, in Arkansas, and they had a black union and the landlords busted it up and killed them nigros right and left."

"I don't know about that, and anyhow it wouldn't happen

here in Oklahoma," Mitchell said, shaking his head. "But I don't aim to join up with niggers."

"You'd join up with Indians, wouldn't you?"

"I reckon so. Why not?"

"The Indians are coming into the union. The white men, the Indians, the nigros, they're all coming in. You don't want to be left out, Mitchell. . . . Now look here, there'll be a meeting Friday evening over to the Tanzey schoolhouse. Why don't you come over and bring your wife along?"

Mitchell shook his head and took his weight off the handle of the hoe.

"People you know will be there," Jay said. "You go and listen to what they say. That's all you got to do. You don't have to join up, but you just go ahead and see who's there and listen to what they got to say."

"Well, I don't know as that would hurt any. Maybe I'll do that."

"See you do," Jay said. "I'll be there and I'll be watching fer you."

"I ain't sayin' I'll come."

"Anyhow I'll watch fer you." Jay put out his hand. Mitchell wiped his palm on the front of his overalls and they shook hands.

"Friday evening," Jay said. "So long."

"So long."

Jay and Leona went back through the cotton fields, past the house with its sagging roof and loose shingles and yellow-lettered advertisement of a laxative, to the road where Jay had left the car.

Now she's seen fer herself and she knows what I'm fighting fer and she knows what I'm up against. I wonder what she's thinking after that and after them pussy willows made her want to cry. She feels the way I hoped she would and I guess she understands more what I'm after and why I got to go on the way I am.

As they drove away Jay waved to the man in the cotton field. He glanced at Leona and said: "I reckon I done a little good. Anyhow, I think he's coming to the meeting at Tanzey."

"Jay, I've been listening to you talk to those people all morning and all afternoon." Leona looked with a frown at the road ahead.

"Yes, honey."

"Especially about the union having everybody in it. Jay, do you have to have the nigs in it?"

"What's that?" Jay said.

"I said do you have to have the nigs in it? It's going to make them uppity, Jay, and now that a nig is the heavyweight champion they're bad enough."

Jay's lips were pressed tightly together, and his hands gripped the steering wheel with all his strength.

Now God damn. Now Jesus Christ. From a man like Bill Mitchell you can understand it because there's some reason, but all of it and all the talking didn't do no good with her and it might of been Lamar Baker who said that and that word *nigs*. That's the dirtiest word I ever heard on a woman's mouth.

"Leona," Jay said.

Now what is there to say? It leaves me with an empty feeling like somebody knocked my wind out. You just can't make no answer to a thing like that. There just ain't a thing to say.

"Yes, Jay?" Leona said.

"Never mind." Jay shook his head.

"Jay, you're liable to cause a lot of trouble stirring up the nigs. I don't think you ought to do it. Why can't they have a union of their own, like that man said? You know in this day and age nobody's going to try to stop it. People don't hurt the nigs now unless they get too uppity and think they're better than a white man. Jay, I think you're making a mistake."

"What time is it?" Jay asked.

She glanced at her wrist watch. "About four o'clock. Why?"

"I reckon it's time I took you home."

"Now you're mad at me, aren't you? But that's the way I feel about it, Jay, and that's the way most people feel. You can't flout public opinion, and people won't stand by and let the nigs get out of hand."

"That's just what I said," Jay said. "That's why we got to have one strong union, and the white men and and the black men will stand together. That's the only way it can be done and that's been proved."

He glanced sideways at her; she was frowning and staring straight ahead at the dusty road that ran between barbed wire fences beyond which was the flat green spread of cotton. Ahead of them was the irregular line of the hills, screened by blue mist.

"We just don't think the same about it, Jay," Leona said.

"Yeah, that's plain enough."

"You go too far some ways, Jay. Please listen to me and don't be sore. You go too far in some things you think. I believe you're right to help those people form a union. They need help and it's terrible the way they live, but you oughtn't to mix up with the nigs, Jay."

"Leona, there's just one thing I wish you wouldn't do. I wish you wouldn't use that word."

"What word?"

"That word, nigs."

"Oh. Well, niggers, then. But really, Jay, you oughtn't to mix up with them."

"I guess I can't make you see we got to have 'em with us," Jay said. "But that's what people got to find out. The union won't never git nowheres if the farmers are fighting each other just because one is black and the other white."

Leona did not reply and Jay waited a moment. Ahead of them were the scattered houses of Okie.

"I want to stop in Okie a minute," Jay said. "There's a man I got to see."

He drove along the main street of the town and turned off beside a filling station toward the railroad tracks. He followed a rough road along a spur track behind the line of houses. The road crossed the track and Jay turned to the right down into a hollow between the spur and the main tracks two hundred yards away. In the hollow were the tents and makeshift houses of squatters grouped around small truck gardens. Jay stopped the car beside a chicken yard with bright new wire, beneath a sycamore tree. There was a woman in a faded yellow dress, barefooted, under the tree, and three small children with her.

"Hello there," Jay said.

"Howdy."

"Do you know Ike Williams?"

"Do I know Ike Williams? Well, I ought to." She paused, looking at Jay with a half-smile on her gray face. "He's my old man."

A little girl with blond hair set in Sunday ribbons approached the car, looked at Leona's wrist watch with her head on one side, smiled shyly and backed away. All three children had the mottles of malnutrition on their faces.

"Whereabouts is Ike?" Jay asked.

"Yonder by the tracks." She raised her voice. "Ike! Somebody lookin' fer you."

A big man came trotting from the direction of the tracks two hundred yards away. The woman glanced at Jay, and then walked toward a house of sheet-iron drums pounded into flat sheets, of boards and box-wood, with tent canvas stretched over it for a roof. Jay got out of the car.

"You wait here fer me, Leona," he said.

It don't do no good to have her with me in that white dress and that wrist watch that the kids looked at. This is just another world to her and she won't never know what it means. . . .

Jay walked forward to meet Williams. The man had slowed to a walk and his eyes were on Jay's face. He wore overalls and a hickory shirt and a dusty black hat with a twisted, curling brim.

"I'm Jay Strickland from the Southern Tenant Farmers' Union."

"Well, I'm glad to see you. I shore am." Ike Williams put out his hand, and his grin showed broken, blackened teeth. "We shore got need of you here in Okie."

They moved beneath a mulberry tree and Jay sat down on a wooden crate. Williams squatted on his heels by the tree-trunk, where the ground was littered with the crushed purple fruit of the tree.

"Are you on the W.P.A.?" Jay asked.

"No, I ain't. I can't git on it, Mister Strickland."

"You can't? You're able to do a day's work, ain't you?"

"I'd hate to have anybody tell me I wasn't. No, it ain't that.

But back on the C.W.A. when we had that strike I was one of the leaders of it and I ain't never been able to git on the W.P.A. I'm gittin' commodity relief."

"Well, now," Jay said. "We're just going to do something about that. What you need to have is organization. The Southern Tenant Farmers' Union is an industrial union now and we're taking in everybody on W.P.A. and we're forming unemployed locals. We're going to build up an organization here and we're going to git you put on the W.P.A. You know as well as I do that the only way to git anything is to organize and bring pressure to git it."

"Bo, you sure said something." Williams showed his blackened teeth. "I done tried to organize a local here, but I couldn't git up fifteen members to apply fer a charter. I've cussed and I've cried and I've tried to do everything to build up an organization. I've wore out a pair of shoes trying. . . . Take me, now: I've only had a week and three days' work since I got out of the cotton patch last fall. We need organization. We sure do. We got to have it. But everybody's scared to make a move one way or another."

"You sure ought to find fifteen men fer a charter," Jay said.

"Now I tell you, Mister Strickland, around here there's so many nigros. That's our trouble."

"Now you just got to take in them nigros too," Jay said. "The Tenant Farmers' Union don't discriminate."

"I know that and I believe in it, too. But some of these boys you just can't make see it that way and they don't want to join up with nigros. I've tried about everything and I did git ten members lined up but we didn't have enough fer a charter and, you know, the treasurer took and spent the two dollars we had in the treasury fer groceries. Now I don't blame him fer it. His kids was about to starve and he just took that two dollars and spent it. But that was the end of our organization, Mister."

Jay looked at the truck garden, with one large sunflower in the center, at the wood-and-iron house in front of which were three buckets planted with wild flowers.

"What we need is a stranger down here to organize us," Williams said.

"I aim to come down," Jay said. "That's why I come by to

see you. I got to do some work over to Tanzey, and then down in Jennings County, and when I'm through there I'm coming back here and help you out. I tell you what I'm going to do. I'm going to hold a mass-meeting to start off with and I want you to git them W.P.A. workers out fer it."

"I reckon early in the morning before they go to work is the best time."

"Whenever you say," Jay said. "I'm going to leave that in your hands. You set the time and the day and I'll be here."

"When did you say you could git down here?"

"How about the second week in July, on Saturday."

"All right." Williams rubbed his hands together. "I tell you, we sure got to have a stranger down here. We tried to organize that local ourselves, but you know, the Chamber of Commerce split us up. The Chamber of Commerce controls this here town. They told me to mind what I was doing and I told 'em to put me in jail. I said go ahead and put me in jail." Williams laughed. "Jail wouldn't be no worse than the way I am."

"The Chamber of Commerce ain't going to split us this time," Jay said. "Don't you worry about that." He stood up. "Ike, I got to go on back to Mehuskah, but I'm going to be here bright and early on the second Saturday in July."

"I'll shore be lookin' fer you."

They shook hands and Jay walked back to the car. As he drove away Leona said: "Jay, what are you going to do with people like that?"

"I'm going to organize 'em, Leona."

"But you can't do anything with poor white trash like that, Jay."

"I don't want to hear no 'poor white trash,'" Jay said. "That man is an honest man and a hard worker and he ain't going to set by and see his kids starve. He's going to organize and git his rights."

Leona did not speak and Jay hesitated an instant, glancing at her flushed face. He drove across the spur track and turned west toward the highway.

"Leona, I got to drive up into the hills and I reckon I'll leave you by home."

She did not speak and he looked at her with his lips drawn tightly together. "Did you see them kids with the pimples on their faces? That's because they don't git the right food. You starve 'em when they're young like that and they'll sure enough be white trash. They won't be fit fer nothing. And you seen that pick-up house. A man and his wife and three kids in that little bit of a one-room house, just made of old rusty oil drums and piece of lumber knocked together. But he fitted in a screen door like a master carpenter." Jay swung the car onto the highway and stepped hard on the accelerator. "Leona, I got to drive up into the hills and I believe I'll leave you by home."

There was a long pause, then she said in a low voice: "Don't you want me to go with you?"

"This ain't union business, Leona. I got to ride up and see old Haze Thompson. It's about Pat."

"Jay, I'm upset about Pat. It's just a shame. What's going to happen to him?"

"They extradited him to Texas first thing this morning," Jay said. "He waived extradition and they took him back and they'll try him in Jackville the next term."

"I hope you can get him off. Do you think you can?"

"We're going to try our damnedest." Jay shook his head. "The thing I can't understand is how they ever caught Pat, and that's why I'm going up to see Haze. He was the only one who seen Pat up in the hills where he was hid out, him and Belle, Pat's wife, seen him too. But still I can't believe old Haze would turn Pat in. Pat took it into his head to smoke out a bee-tree to git some wild honey and Haze seen the smoke."

"You know," Leona said with a nod of her head, "I believe I had some of that honey."

"You did!" Jay jerked his head toward her.

"One of the girls, little Emma Paul, brought me some to school. Her mother sent it for me and we ate a little of it."

"Who do you mean — we?"

"Lamar Baker and Neil Smith. They'd been out there on business about the lake and they stopped by the school."

"Did you know where that honey come from?"

"I know Belle gave it to Emma's mother."

"Listen here," Jay said. "Did them two know that?"

"Well, Lamar asked me where I got the honey and I told him about it and he called little Emma Paul out and talked to her. He was real interested because he said bee-trees were so rare and he asked Emma where the honey came from and she said that Belle had found a bee-tree."

"Did she say where she found it?"

"Some gully somewhere in the hills. I forget the name."

So it was Lamar. He knowed Belle brought the honey and he put two and two together and he knowed Pat was hiding out in Cedar Gully, and of course it wasn't old Haze. That's why Lamar acted so peculiar and looked at me the way he did when we was there to sell the farm and that's why he had on them clothes and said he was about to go fishing and that's why he agreed to sell so quick and pay over all that money and acted like he was doing it as a favor and we was good friends and by God there was nothing in it fer him and it was just a cheap political favor and that's all it was. He sold out his own kind fer a political favor to the Sheriff and they'll swing votes his way in the primary to elect him county attorney. He sold out Pat fer thirty-six hunderd a year, that's what he done. He's a sure-enough son of a bitch to do a thing like that and when I remember that we knowed him when we was kids and we all used to go fishing together. . . .

"Jay, what's the matter?"

"Nothing's the matter."

"What are you looking like that for?"

"I'm mad," Jay said. "I'm burning-up mad."

"At me, Jay?"

"Not at you."

I better not let Belle know or she sure enough will ride into town and shoot that son of a bitch and she can drill a squirrel through the eye every time. I better not let her know and I won't tell Pat but something has got to be done and he ought to be done something to, but I sure better not tell Belle because I know she'll do just like she said and she'll drill out them spying eyes that found out where Pat was and turned him in. . . .

"What *is* the matter, Jay?"

"Don't you see? It was Lamar turned Pat in. He found out where that bee-tree was and he knowed that was where Pat was hid out."

"Do you suppose, Jay?"

"I damn well know it."

"But I thought you-all were friends. I never thought Lamar . . ."

"It was him all right."

"And it's partly my fault. Gee, I'm sorry, Jay. If I hadn't given him the honey and told him where it came from . . . Oh, Jay, you don't blame me, do you?"

"No."

"Jay, honestly. Please don't blame me."

"Of course I don't, Leona," Jay said.

"You mean it?"

"Yes."

She put her hand through his arm and leaned against him, but Jay stared ahead at the road. He had turned off the highway and was on a second grade road leading into the hills.

She's sweet the way a woman ought to be and she's gentle and the only thing is them ideas in her head and that's because she ain't really opened her eyes and her thinking is just the thinking she got from people around her and she thinks the way they do and anything else is new to her and she can't take it in all at once. But when she seen them pussy willows it made her cry and she felt it the way a woman feels it with her heart and someday maybe she'll see with her eyes too and see that people in the South can't go on fer always with them ideas in their heads like calling 'em nigs and keeping 'em always underfoot. Even Belle has some of them ideas and Crosby too and both of 'em think a nigro ain't much better than dirt.

"Jay, I'm not so anxious to go back to Aldine," Leona said. "Take me up into the hills with you."

"I ain't going that way now. I know old Haze didn't do it now and I don't need to see him. I'm going to leave you by home and head back fer Mehuskah, Leona."

"Whatever you say, Jay."

Jay drove on in silence over a back road toward Aldine. Already, in spite of the recent rains, there was thick dust that powdered the trees along the road. When they reached Aldine he stopped the car in front of the house where Leona lived, but she did not at once get out. He turned his head and saw her slight frown, the disturbed expression of her blue eyes.

"Jay," she said.

"Yes?"

"I expect I'll go back to Tulsa Friday. I'll stay here until the stomp-dance and then I'm going on home."

"That's sure bad news," Jay said. "I'll miss you, Leona."

"Well — won't I see you before I go?"

"I guess so, Leona."

She smoothed the skirt of her linen dress. "I'm glad you took me with you today, Jay. I did learn something. I'll never forget it."

Jay nodded. In a driveway beside the house the car with the United States license was parked under a sycamore tree.

"I tell you what, Jay," Leona said. "Let's have a picnic. Look, I'll get some fried chicken and cake and all that and you bring along some beer and we'll have a picnic. Do you want to? We could go over on the Grand River and go swimming, too. Let's do, Jay, tomorrow."

"Do you mean just you and me?"

"Yes."

"It's been a long time since I was on a picnic," Jay said.

"You're coming then?"

"Well, I'll try and make it, Leona."

"Jay, you've got to make up your mind!"

"O.K. I'll be there."

"Tomorrow?"

"Yes, tomorrow."

She smiled and touched his hand lightly. "Sometimes you're very hard to handle, Jay. . . . Listen, you're not still mad at me, are you?"

"I told you I wasn't."

"But you don't act it."

"I got things on my mind, Leona. I got a lot on my mind."

"Yes, I know." Her hand rested on his.

I guess I oughtn't to be so set in my thinking. All that was new to her and she talks the way she does because she always has and that's the way she was brought up and people around her talked that way. Them pussy willows made her cry and it ain't that she's mean-hearted and cruel like most people that talk like she did. It's only that she never found out no better and she don't know yet what life is like fer all them people. She never had to sleep on the floor and she never had a flour sack fer a dress and she never had a black skin to mark her fer everybody to torment.

Jay's hand turned in hers and his fingers closed on her fingers. "I'll be out tomorrow, honey. Right now I got to git back to Mehuskah."

"About six o'clock, Jay?"

"Yeah, around about then."

Jay leaned over and opened the door. When she was standing on the curb she smiled at him and his hands tightened on the steering wheel.

"Good-by, Jay."

"So long, honey."

Jay slipped the car in gear and drove along the dusty street, past the boarded-up hotel and the rusted cotton gin, toward the Mehuskah road.

She only said good-by but it was the way she said it in that soft womanlike way that makes me want to set up and whoop. Maybe today done something. She likes me, all right. She likes me. She sure enough likes me. And it was her took hold of my hand first and she squeezed it. And she had that look in her eyes I never seen before and if she feels like maybe she does then I reckon she'll git to thinkin' different too and she'll learn and with a wife like that to come home to life would be different and I could work like a mule and I could git them tenants organized and I could put an end to all this Jim Crow talk. But anyhow and whatever, I got to do that and nothing ain't going to stop me, but I reckon I can take the time fer a picnic on the Grand. A man has got a right to his spooning whatever work he's doing and he's got a right to have a wife and a home he can come to without that empty house to look at and the cold stove and only a can to heat up fer supper and a nigro by the name of Rock Island Jones setting there and talking about the world to come. I guess she's right that

I work too hard and a man can't make his whole life just work and he's got a right to live fer himself too. You go out and work fer people and you try to git 'em organized and the ones you want to help are fighting against you and they don't trust you and you got to fall back on people like Rock Island Jones who think the same way you do and it's a comfort to be with somebody you know feels like you do but still and all a man ought to have himself a wife. Without no wife there's still that feeling that you're alone in the world and you ain't really close to nobody except only Crosby and Pat and Belle and they don't think the same like I do or believe much in what I'm after. If a man didn't have that empty feeling in his guts he could do better work because he wouldn't have that feeling he was so much alone and if he had a wife who thought like he did they'd stand together and they wouldn't neither of 'em be alone or have that feeling of loneliness. It's like the difference between working on a full stomach and working when you're hungry and I guess I'm sure-enough hungry and it's her I'm hungry fer and it's her I want to be there when I come home and it's her I want to be in bed with me sweet and white and with them blue eyes of hers and that little bit of a mouth and I ain't never tried to kiss it and tomorrow on the Grand River by God I'm going to. I never had a woman like her in bed with me. I never had a woman who wasn't there just fer then, just fer that one night, and who'd put out fer anybody and didn't give a God-damn who it was with her, and it must be terrible sweet to have a woman you're in love with and a woman who loves you and it must be different altogether when it's like that.

Jay had reached Mehuskah now. It was nearly dusk and the street lights had been turned on and the Cherokee Building thrust stark and white against a faintly orange sky. The Cherokee Building dominated the main business street of the town, along which Jay was driving, and he could not take his eyes off it.

I don't know what to do and whatever I do I don't want to act too hasty. There's too much on my shoulders to act too hasty and I got to be careful. I ought to stop right now and go up to the sixth floor of that Cherokee Building and walk into his office and put it to him straight and then by God I don't know what. But it's late and I reckon he ain't there and I got too much on my shoulders to act so hasty.

Jay drove on to the end of the street, crossed the Katy tracks, and turned left on the dusty road that led to his house. The house faced west and the shades had been drawn against the sinking sun. He went into the house and the first thing he did was to raise the shades, now that the sun had set. He found a note on the table, a loose scrawl on a sheet of notepaper, held down by the china shoe full of matches. He picked it up.

Webb Harper was in to see you and he said he'd come back Tuesday. He got a cabin fixed for me over in Tanzey with a family name of Quincy and I'm driving over with him this evening.

ROCKY.

That Rocky Jones is on the job and he'll do good work over to Tanzey. I wish I'd of been here when Webb come by and talked to him about the spinach workers. I got to spend more time with them and there are some Indians among 'em and I reckon at this here stomp-dance I can git things started. Joseph Paul will help out and we got them few Indians signed up and I reckon I can call on them. Along in July we'll hold another stomp-dance just fer the union. I got to talk to Webb about that.

Jay went into the kitchen. He crumpled a copy of the *Mehuskah Clarion and Bee* and built up a fire with kindling and wood from the wood-box and put on a kettle of water to heat. On a cupboard shelf he found some black-eyed peas and a half a loaf of bread wrapped in newspaper. There was a package of tea and a bowl of lumpy sugar beside it. As he was washing the peas he heard the noise of the front door opening. He put down the saucepan and went into the living room. Lamar Baker was standing just inside the doorway and with him was a tall old man in a stiff and soiled Panama hat.

"Hello, Jay," Lamar said.

"What do you want?" Jay said. "I didn't look to find you here, Lamar." He took three slow steps forward, and his hands were clenched at his sides.

"We wanted to have a talk with you, Jay."

"Is that so?" Jay said.

I'm going to stand and listen and I ain't going to do nothing hasty. I'm going to listen to what he's got to say and how he's going to explain it and I ain't going to act without I think about it first.

"Jay, this here is S. W. Boaz. I reckon you know he's got a thousand acres south of town, over by Tanzey. I'm acting fer Mister Boaz and I been retained as counsel by the Spinach Growers' Association."

"Is that so?" Jay said.

Lamar glanced around him. "Anybody else here, Jay?"

"Just you-all and me."

"Anybody out back?"

"No."

"Now listen, Jay, we come here to talk it over with you friendly. There's no reason there should be trouble and if we talk it over friendly maybe we can come to some kind of an agreement."

"Just what do you want to talk about?" Jay asked.

"I guess you know what." Lamar grinned mechanically. "See here, Jay, you and me was kids together back in the hills. We know each other pretty good."

"We sure do."

"Why, we've hunted skins together and we've fished that creek together and we've been up to the same kind of devilment in our day."

"I wondered did you remember all that," Jay said.

"Well, say, a man never forgets his boyhood."

"Just what did you want to talk to me about, Lamar?"

"I guess we can set down, can't we, Jay?" Lamar said uneasily.

"Go ahead."

Lamar sat down on the propped-up sofa and leaned forward, holding his hat between his knees. His striped silk shirt was wet with sweat under the arms and along his shoulders. S. W.

Boaz sat beside him, looking steadily at Jay. His shirt was open at the neck and a white handkerchief was tied around his thin throat. His neck was browned by the sun, but his face was almost as white as the handkerchief, with faint pink mottles on the cheeks.

"Like I told you, Jay, I'm talking fer the Spinach Growers' Association and they thought it would be a good idea if I come in and had it out with you. They don't like this union business, Jay."

"I reckon not," Jay said.

"Them people are happy if you just let 'em alone, Jay, and you oughtn't to go stirring up trouble. They make a living and they need the work and any man's lucky to have work to do in these here parlous times. If you go on with this union business a lot of men are going to lose their chance to make a living. You ain't doing them no favor, Jay."

"You-all are wasting your time talking to me, Lamar," Jay said. "There ain't nothing going to stop the Southern Tenant Farmers' Union and the reason they sent you here is because they know that's true."

S. W. Boaz cleared his throat raspingly, and took off his hat. His short-cut white hair grew close as a skullcap on his head.

"See here, young man," he said in a slow, slurring voice. "I've got a thousand-acre farm out south of town and I've had a lot of tenants come and go in my time. I know that class of people. You ask anybody in Mehuskah and they'll tell you that I'm good to my tenants. But you can't do nothing with people like that. I feed 'em and I clothe 'em and I give them work to do and I don't get nothing for it but shiftlessness. The first chance they get they go on relief. I give 'em a nice house and they take and burn the boards off the porch in the cook-stove to save going a hundred yards to the woods on Big Soapy Creek. I put screens on the windows and they was busted and the house full of flies and mosquitoes the next week. They board up the windows and make whisky. . . . You can't do nothing with people like that."

"I think different," Jay said.

"Now you-all talk about abolishing farm tenancy and you know as well as I do it can't be done." S. W. Boaz glanced at

Lamar for a corroboratory nod. "Them people don't have the initiative to do anything better for themselves. They wouldn't know what to do if they had anything better. Now I worked for everything I got and I'm a self-made man. I never took no help from nobody. But you can't do anything with them people no matter what help you give 'em. Why, I've had tenants come to me, tenants who had their own tools and got a two-thirds of the crop. I've had them tenants come to me and ask to be sharecroppers. They didn't want the responsibility."

"Mister Boaz, I don't know what you-all are after," Jay said. "But you're sure wasting your time."

"Now listen here," S. W. Boaz said. His face was intent, his gray lips pursed. "Last February I needed men to cut my spinach and I got 'em off the relief. I took 'em out to my farm boss and he fed 'em and housed 'em and how many do you suppose showed up at the end of the row the next morning to cut that spinach? Not a one, sir. No, not one. That's the kind of people you got to deal with and they got to find out they can't get something for nothing." He shook his head, not taking his eyes from Jay's face.

"Jay, it's just making trouble," Lamar said. "You know that, and you oughtn't to be so fanatic. Everybody knows this is going to be a good year. There's been plenty of rain and all the crops are coming along fine and they say they're making fifty bushels of corn. It ain't no time to start trouble with a union just when prosperity is coming back again. Everybody ought to co-operate, Jay, and maybe we'll see the end of these hard times."

"Is that all you come to tell me about?" Jay said. "Because listen here, Lamar. I told you nothing could stop the Tenant Farmers' Union and I meant just what I said and I don't want to argue it with you."

"The trouble with you people is you don't know what you're starting," S. W. Boaz said. "It's fire, pestilence, disease and the sword, that's what it is. You take these Reds and they want to give everybody a new house instead of repairing the old one. They want a new order and they don't know what they're going to git. They want to change everything, but you can't change people from the way they was bred any more than you can change a hound dog into a bird-dog. It's just going to bring about fire, pestilence, disease and the sword, that's what it will bring about."

Lamar stood up. "Jay, there was one thing in particular I had to say and they told me to tell you it. A lot of people are watching you pretty close, Jay, and they don't like what you're doing. They told me to tell you to lay off them niggers."

"I'm going right on with my work," Jay said tensely. "You can't buy me off, if that's what you're after."

"Now, Jay, listen here. You oughtn't to be so hos-tile. I've knowed you since you was a boy and I don't want to see you git into trouble. You ought to know that you can't go around stirring up the niggers and the poor white trash and git away with it. The white men of this county ain't going to stand fer it and they ain't going to stand fer your Red ideas about unions and white men and niggers both in it. We know how to handle niggers here and they've got a place and they stay in it and it will be a cold day in hell when we stand by and let somebody stir 'em up with Red ideas. I tell you, Jay, there'll be trouble. Don't you lose your head."

"You heard what I said, Lamar," Jay said.

"Listen here," Lamar said slowly. He put on his creamy Stetson hat and stood looking at Jay with his hands in his pockets. S. W. Boaz stood up beside him. "Them people I was telling you about mean business and they ain't going to stand fer it. You can't go around talking social equality, Jay, and you ought to know it."

"I ain't talking social equality," Jay said. "It's economic equality I'm talking and I reckon if we git that social equality will take care of itself. All we're after is a square deal. We want land fer the landless and a square deal fer the tenant farmer. That's all."

"Now, Jay, it ain't fer myself I'm talking. I've knowed you a long time and I know you ain't no Red. But them people mean business. They told me to tell you to lay off the niggers and they mean it, Jay. Just this evening there was a nigger took care of south of town."

Jay looked fixedly at Lamar's small, squinted eyes and red face.

"He was some Red nigger agitator that moved into Tanzey and he hadn't hardly shook the dust off his feet when he was took care of," Lamar said. "I told you them people mean business, Jay."

" 'Took care of'?" Jay said. "What do you mean 'took care of'?"

"It was on my land," S. W. Boaz said. "I don't know who done it and they oughtn't to done it even if he was a Red but it shows the way people are beginning to feel."

"What did they do to that nigro?" Jay said.

"I just know he was took care of proper and he won't show himself in Mehuskah County again," Lamar said. "I told you they mean business."

It's Rocky Jones they got, sure as hell it's him, and maybe I was wrong to send him over yonder. I'd ought never to send out a nigro organizer without a white organizer with him. It looks like they was laying fer him and waiting and I guess it was from that Tanzey meeting where he talked and maybe that was wrong, too. It looks like I acted too quick without I thought it out right and I got to take the blame fer what they done to Rocky and I got to find out what they done and I got to find him. I don't know what they done to him but we ain't going to stand fer it and we'll serve notice that we ain't. This here is Oklahoma and we'll fight fer our rights and we ain't going to stand fer nothing like that.

"I'm on my way, Jay," Lamar said. "You think about what we told you. I don't want to see you git into trouble."

S. W. Boaz put on his faded Panama and started toward the door. Lamar followed him.

"Wait a minute, Lamar," Jay said softly.

"Yeah?" Lamar turned his red face toward Jay. It was nearly dark in the room and Lamar's eyes shone faintly in the twilight. S. W. Boaz went out on the porch, slamming the screen door after him.

"Lamar, I heard you got a taste for wild honey."

"Wild honey?" Lamar said. It was so still in the room that his breathing was audible. "I don't git you, Jay."

"Maybe you don't know that my brother Pat smoked out a bee-tree and maybe you don't know it was honey from that tree you ate some of out at the schoolhouse."

"Now, Jay, listen here, what are you talking about? I recollect now I did have some of that honey, but . . ."

"You turned Pat in," Jay said.

"Jay, by Jesus Christ, now look here, Pat's my friend. . . ."

Jay hit him with his right fist, beside the mouth, and Lamar staggered back toward the door. Jay's left crushed into his abdomen and Lamar fell against the screen door. It flew open and he teetered across the porch and came up against a pillar.

"Now you git out of here," Jay shouted. His voice was hoarse and his face was suddenly wet with sweat.

Lamar backed down the steps, holding a handkerchief to his mouth, where there was blood. His pale Stetson hat had slipped to the back of his head.

"We ain't going to stand fer none of that and you better know it right now," Jay said. "I'm serving notice, you hear? Now you git going, Lamar."

"That's one more mistake you made, Jay," Lamar said thickly. "The time will come when you and me got to settle up."

I got to let him go and I guess already I acted too hasty. The son of a bitch done it and there ain't a doubt and I know by God he had a hand in Rocky or he wouldn't of knowed about it so quick. He come straight here from Tanzey with old Boaz right after they done whatever they done to Rocky, a crowd of them and they jumped one poor thin nigro who was out there to help people like him to git to live a little better than animals. I got to find him and I got to forget about Lamar. . . .

Jay heard the gears of Lamar's car screaming as he drove up the dusty street. He caught up his hat and ran out to his own car. As he got in it he saw Lamar's tail-light blink as the car turned onto the paved road.

I got to drive out to Tanzey and put myself on Rocky's trail. It's a family name of Quincy and I believe I know where they live. It's on S. W. Boaz' land over on Big Soapy Creek. He said it was his land. It's about all nigros there and Quincy

lives in one of them cabins, if he's still there and if they ain't
done nothing to him, too. Rocky said you never knowed
when it would happen and I reckon he was right. I ought to
of listened to him more. It's a terrible thing and we ain't
heard the end of it and it's just the beginning of trouble like
there was over in Arkansas and like Rocky said would happen
unless we stopped this Jim Crow talk. He was right all the
time and I should of listened to him more. If they scare the
nigros and the white men won't have 'em in the union and
won't join a union they're in, then it just ain't no use and they
can scare the nigros and bust the Southern Tenant Farmers'
Union wide open. That's what they're after and they picked
on Rocky because they can lay it on him he was a Red and
that was the reason. But if this Jim Crow talk goes on Rocky
won't be the only nigro and he'll just be the beginning of it
and all our work will be shot to hell. But we ain't going to
stand fer it and we're going to serve notice on 'em that we
ain't going to stand fer it. They can't do that here in Oklahoma. . . .

Jay was on the highway, driving south toward Tanzey
with the accelerator held down flush with the floorboard and
the old car swaying on the road.

It couldn't of been more than a few hours because Rocky
wrote he was riding over with Webb this evening and it
couldn't of been more than a couple of hours or three because it's only an hour since dusk come on. That means they
knowed he was coming or they seen him as soon as he got
there and I hope to hell Webb Harper is all right. But I guess
if he was hurt too Lamar would of made a point of letting me
know. And all that talk he used about Red. He just meant
union when he said Red and he didn't mean Rocky and they
laid fer Rocky just because he was union but they'll say it
was because he was Red and they'll git people to believe it's
true and it ain't but a step from beating up Reds to beating
up unions and they know it.

Tanzey was a village of fifty houses and beyond it were
the cotton fields. Jay turned off on a section-line road and
the headlights of his car made a pattern of shifting shadows
among the cotton plants. He passed an occasional light in a

cabin set back from the road. He crossed Big Soapy Creek on a narrow wooden bridge and turned right at a crossroads.

This here is part of the Boaz plantation and one of these places is where Quincy lives at. I got no notion which it would be and the next one I come to I'll stop and ask. Yonder's a light and I'll leave the car here by the side of the road.

Jay followed a path among the cotton plants that brushed against his legs all the way to the door of the house. The moon was nearly full and the contour of the land showed plainly; the sagging rooftree of the cabin was outlined against the moon. He knocked on the door.

There's a light in there and somebody's home but they don't answer and they don't come to the door and I guess they're scared and after what happened tonight they don't want to open the door to nobody.

"Whereabouts does Quincy live?" Jay called. Still there was silence. "Listen here," Jay said. "I'm from the Southern Tenant Farmers' Union. I'm Jay Strickland."

He heard the soft sound of bare feet on the floor, then the door was opened cautiously a few inches.

"I'm Jay Strickland and I'm looking fer Quincy's house."

"Please, Mistah, don't stay around heah."

"Where does Quincy live?"

"You ain' goin' to say we told you?" Jay could see the Negro's eyeballs shining in the lamplight.

"Don't be scared of me," Jay said. "Look here, I'm your friend and I'm a friend of Rocky Jones."

"De next house Quincy lives at, about a half mile. You'll see a big oak tree."

"All right," Jay said.

It's no use to talk to 'em now. They'll all be like that and you can't talk to 'em when they're scared as rabbits. This thing will raise hell and by God Lamar Baker ain't heard the end of it and he ain't heard the end of Pat.

Jay got in the car and snapped on the lights. He drove slowly along the ungraded road. He came to a post-oak tree and stopped. There was no light, but when he turned off the headlights he could clearly see the dark shape of a cabin and the trees of the creek bottom behind it. Again Jay followed a path through the cotton, but he did not knock on the door of this house. Instead he whistled softly.

"Quincy," he called. "This is Jay Strickland."

There was a moment of silence, then a chair scraped on the bare pine boards inside. The door opened and in the moonlight Jay saw the outlines of the Negro's face. They spoke in lowered voices.

"I just heard about Rocky Jones," Jay said. "Where is he?"

"Dey done took him off, Mistah Jay. Dey done grab him and took him off. He was settin' on my doorstep and we was talkin' when dey come in a big auto and grab him. I tol' 'em he was my kinfolks from Arkansas way and had come to he'p out wif de choppin', but dey didn't pay me no mind."

"Fer God's sake," Jay said. "What did they do to him?"

"Nobody knows, Mistah Jay. Dey jes' tooken him off. Hit was a carload of men and dey had shotguns and rifles."

"Which way did they go?"

"I got no notion, Mistah Jay."

"Jesus Christ," Jay said.

"Nobody knows what dey done," Quincy said. "Mistah Jay, do you reckon . . ."

"No," Jay said. "But I reckon they beat him up cruel."

God damn, God damn, and here I stand and cuss in the moonlight and shake my fist but there ain't nothing I can do, not a thing in the world. Nobody even knows where they took him or what they done to him, but everybody knows that whatever it was it was shameful cruel and mean. All around me stands the cotton in the moonlight, the green leaves of it black in the moonlight, and row after row of plants growing thick and close together and it's all just because of that. And just because of that cotton people like Quincy got to live like he does without enough to eat and scared of the landlord and the farm boss and just because of that cotton they took Rocky out and what they done to him nobody knows and where he's at now there's no way to find out.

"If anybody talks to you, you don't know nothing," Jay said. "He told you he was your cousin from Arkansas and you never seen him before."

"'At's what I'll tell 'em."

"Now, say," Jay said. "How about Webb Harper? What happened to him, Quincy?"

"He left Rocky off at de main road and Rocky come afoot across de plantation."

"Thank God fer that much," Jay said. "Then I got to find Webb. Maybe he'll know what happened to Rocky and maybe he'll know where to look."

Jay looked at the black shadow where the Negro's face was. It was very still in the moonlight with a gentle breeze swaying the cotton plants and the sound of crickets off in the fields and the lift and fall of bullfrogs croaking in Big Soapy Creek.

"You-all set tight, Quincy, and don't be scared," Jay said. "Just you set tight and don't open your mouth. There ain't nothing going to stop the Tenant Farmers' Union, and don't you forget it."

Jay went back along the path to his car. He turned it around and drove back across the bridge and through the cotton fields to the highway.

It ain't no use talking to them nigros because they don't know nothing and if they did they'd be too scared to tell it except maybe Quincy and he's got guts. I reckon when they took Rocky and ever since they been hid out in their cabins and that's why I don't see no lights and it's plumb dark all over them cotton fields. If they come in a car fer him they might of took him any place and maybe outside the county line and maybe over to Arkansas. It ain't much use to look fer him but still I got to do it. Maybe I'd ought to go home and wait because that's where I'd git news of Rocky when it comes up, but still I got to find Webb Harper and maybe he knows something and I'll drive over and hunt him up. We got to find poor Rocky and see he's looked after and find out what they done to him. That's what I'll do. I'll drive over and find Webb. That Rocky Jones knowed what he was talking about and he was right and it means that now we got to work day and night, day and night, and put a stop to this Jim Crow talk before every nigro in the county is scared to join up. If we don't do that the Southern Tenant Farmers' Union is busted wide open in this here county. . . .

$\mathscr{B}elle$

❦   ⚜

HE looks just wore out with them circles under his eyes and
that black hair of his mussed and thick with dust and his
mouth clamped tight and thin even when he's asleep. When
he come in last night I hardly knowed it was Jay. He had that
wild look and he was so tired and he'd been driving all over
creation, he said, looking fer a nigger. And he was wore out
and sick-hearted and he come home to me and Crosby like a
little boy who'd run away from home and got scared of the
world outside and come home to his folks. But it's good he
can sleep so sound and with something hot inside him he'll
feel better.

"Jay, wake up."

Jay stirred, but he did not awaken. He lay on his side with
one arm thrust straight out over the edge of the cot. Belle put
her hand on his shoulder and shook him gently. Jay opened
his eyes, blue and blank as the still hot sky.

"Jay, I got some breakfast fer you."

Jay sat up, blinking, and ran his hands through his hair.

"Some eggs and coffee, Jay. . . . You said to wake you up this morning."

"Thanks, Belle. What time is it?"

"Pretty near eleven."

"Eleven o'clock!" Jay's eyes opened wide and he jumped out of bed.

"I let you sleep a little, Jay. You sure did look tuckered out."

"Jesus," Jay said. "I got work to do. Jesus!"

"Now you eat your breakfast first, Jay."

He sure does need somebody to look after him or he'll kill himself working the way he does and not thinking of anything else but what he has to do. I don't believe I ever seen Jay set and take it easy like Crosby does, or like Pat. And he ain't got the laughing in him that Pat has and he ain't got that smile of Pat's. Jay is too serious-minded fer his own good.

"Jay, are you awake?" It was Crosby's voice.

"Sure am, Dad."

"Come on in the kitchen, son, and eat your breakfast."

"Now come on, Jay," Belle said.

Jay went out on the porch to wash his face in the pan that stood on a shelf beside an oaken bucket of well water. Belle returned to the kitchen where Crosby was sitting in a rocking chair with Billy on his lap. The solemn, tow-headed boy was playing with the toy gun Pat had brought him. When he pressed the trigger sparks flashed from the mouth of the gun.

"Billy, you're going to wear it out," Belle said. "You oughtn't to shoot it off till you see a squirrel and then you aim it at him."

"Don't never shoot a gun off in the house, Billy," Crosby said, chuckling. He glanced over his shoulder. "Jay, you come eat your breakfast."

"Here I am, Dad," Jay said.

He came in and sat down at the table, with his elbows on the oilcloth.

"What do you aim to shoot with that gun, Billy?" Jay asked.

"Squirls," Billy said. "Bam-bam-bam."

"Pat brung him that gun," Crosby said. "He won't let it out of his sight."

"He sleeps with it in bed beside him," Belle said. "Ain't that cunning?"

But still I don't like to see him with it and if it wasn't Pat brung it to him I wouldn't let him have it. I don't like to see him with a gun, even a toy one, but Pat did so want him to have it.

"Jay, why don't you spend the day?" Crosby asked. "We can set and talk."

"I got too much to do, Dad." Jay drank some of the coffee. "I got to find Rocky Jones. I got to find out what they done to him and then I got to go out and organize that union so strong that nothing like that won't never happen again."

"Now, Jay, you eat your eggs," Belle said.

"Sure I will. Thanks, Belle."

"It's a comfort to have you settin' here with us, Jay," Crosby said. "We don't see near enough of you and it makes me think of the old days when all of us was here together. Someday I hope I can git this family all together again."

"If Pat was here it would be like the old times," Belle said. "Jay, what did you do about that lawyer?"

"Nothing yet, Belle, but don't you fret."

"We want a sure enough good one, Jay," Crosby said. "We got the money to pay him."

"I'll find the best in North Texas," Jay said. "Don't you fear about that."

"I rode over to Boggs yesterday in the truck," Crosby said. "I had a look at that little farm, Jay, and it suits me fine. There's forty acres and a fair enough house and it's our'n fer six hunderd and I told the feller we'd pay it."

"We aim to move over yonder right away and maybe tomorrow," Belle said. "That city feller was in to see us and he'll bring the money this afternoon, he told us."

"That's fine," Jay said. "Soon as we git that money in the bank I'll find a lawyer fer Pat. I'll try and make the time to go down to Texas myself the end of the week."

Crosby sat looking at Jay, one thin hand patting Billy's bare leg. His thin shoulders were bent over the child and his face was gaunt and strained in the full sunlight from the window.

"Jay, what chance do you figure Pat has got?"

"It depends on the lawyer, Dad," Jay said. "Hell, we'll git him off. Don't you worry. We'll bring Pat safe home."

"I been praying every night," Belle said. "And I taught Billy a little prayer too."

He even knows what he's praying fer, too, I swear he does. Down on his little knees with his eyes shut so tight like the sun hurt his eyes and he remembers every word and he says it like it meant something to him and he says *Please, God, bring my Papa back from Texas.* I sure do wish Pat could hear him.

"Ain't it hot?" Crosby said. "Jay, who is this nigger you're huntin' fer?"

"His name is Rock Island Jones and he's been working fer the union."

"I seen that nigger," Belle said. She was standing by the window and she did not look at Jay. "Jay, you don't aim to tell me he was sleeping there in your house?"

"Sure he was."

"A nigger, Jay?" Crosby said. "You let a nigger sleep right in your house?"

"I was right proud to have him there," Jay said. "That nigro is a man."

"But look here, Jay, it ain't right to have a nigger in your house. You're a white man." Crosby leaned forward. "I'm your father and I never made no criticism of what you do but I'm your father and you know that ain't right."

It ain't no use to talk to Jay and Crosby knows it but it's a funny thing that Jay is so straight in his head about everything but still he'd keep a nigger in his house.

"Black and white is all the same to me," Jay said. "A black man needs a place to sleep and he needs food in his belly just like a white man does."

"And so does a pig, Jay," Crosby said. "But you don't go to bed with no sow, do you?"

Jay grinned at his father and shook his head. "It ain't no use to argue with me, Dad."

"Look yonder," Belle said. "Joseph Paul's a-coming up the lane. That Indian's moving pretty fast fer him and he's got a sweat up on that old roan mare. I wonder what's got into him."

"Did you say Joseph Paul?" Jay looked up at her.

"It's him, all right, and in a hurry, too."

Jay left the table and strode toward the porch, with Belle and Crosby close behind him. The Indian swung down from the roan mare and took off his sun-helmet. When he saw Jay he gave a brief nod.

"Me go look fer you, Jay," he said. "Howdy Missy Belle. Howdy Crosby."

"Hello there, Joseph Paul."

"What's up?" Jay said.

"Friend of you stay my house. Him ask fer you, Jay. Pretty sick."

"Who's that?" Jay said.

"Black man damn bad hurt."

"Good God," Jay said. "Do you mean Rocky? The feller that talked at the barbecue over to Tanzey?"

Joseph Paul nodded. "Ay-uh. Me find him today in black-jack. Bad hurt. Plenty blood. Carry him my house and Christine she take him care. Him ask all time fer you, Jay."

"Well, good Jesus, let's go," Jay said.

"I'm coming with you," Belle said. "Crosby, do you want to stay with Billy?"

The old man looked at her plaintively, then shrugged his shoulders. "O.K. Belle."

They got in Jay's car, the Indian sitting between Jay and Belle.

"Plenty men beat black man up, Jay," Joseph Paul said. "Find him pretty damn close dead in blackjack when go cut wood."

Jay was driving as fast as he could along the winding clay road. "I looked everywhere I could think," he said. "I never expected it would be right here in these hills."

Jay jammed on the brakes at the foot of the hill and they went up the path to Joseph Paul's one-room cabin. Christine Paul met them at the doorway.

He sure is beat up cruel. It's terrible to see the way they done him. His back is raw as a chunk of beef out of the chopper and oozing blood still and it must hurt something fearful. But still he can look up at Jay and grin and I guess like Jay says this nigger is a man.

"Rocky, this is sure awful," Jay said. "I looked fer you all night long."

"It ain't th' first time, Jay," the Negro said in a whisper.

"I feel like it's my fault," Jay said. "I ought to knowed they'd lay fer you and I oughtn't to let you talk at that barbecue. Rocky, you was right, and I wish I'd listened to you more."

What ever must they done to him with them red stripes on his black skin and raw as chopped beef? It's shameful to treat a man so cruel even if he is just a nigger and I don't wonder Jay is so mad and can't think of nothing else.

"What happened, Rocky?" Jay said. "All we know is some men in a car took you off."

"I was jus' settin' on the doorstep at Quincy's house when they come, Jay. It was a se-dan car and they had all the winders shut tight and they told me to git in an' I did. It wasn't no use to make trouble there and git Quincy mixed in it."

He can't hardly talk and he breathes like it hurts him. I wonder has he got some broken bones and some ribs stove-in. I can see them men, that carload of men with red faces and little pig eyes and thick necks and shoulders like a bull and I hate every damn one of 'em and I'd like to see 'em treated just like they done him.

"We drove a ways and nobody said nothin' and nobody done nothin'," Rocky said. "Then we turned up into the hills, Jay, where the trees shut out the moon. They had a hold of me tight and then one of 'em smashed me in the face."

It's because his mouth is so swelled that he can't hardly talk. Every nigger has got a big mouth but I never seen one as big as that and swelled up like a mushmelon.

"One of 'em said, 'Take that, smart nigger,' and he give me his knee in the belly and when I bent over they begun to beat me on the back of the neck. And one of 'em kep' sayin', 'You God-damn' uppity nigger, how you like that, how you like that?'"

Jay was squatted on his heels beside the bed, and he kept clasping and unclasping his hands.

"I didn't make no sound, but I couldn't ha'dly breathe with

'em kickin' me and hittin' me and it got 'em mad because I wouldn't say nothin' and when they stopped the car side of the road one of 'em said, 'This here will make you talk, smart nigger,' and he got a piece of half-inch rope in his hand. They took and drug me out of the car and throwed me down against a claybank and then they tore off my shirt and it was already stuck to my back with blood. They tore it off and they started in with the rope and I don't know how long they was at it. I sta'ted off to count but I lost track and pretty soon every time they hit me the rope would stick in my back and it was wet and it swished through the air."

"Did you know any of 'em?" Jay asked.

"I don't know no white men around here but you and Webb Harper."

"I bet by God one of 'em was Lamar Baker," Jay said. "Was there a feller with a red face and a white Stetson hat?"

"Maybe it was, Jay. I don't rightly know."

Lamar Baker? Now whatever put it in his mind it would be Lamar? He ain't that low-down. — But Jay must know or he wouldn't of said that, and if Lamar done it then killing ain't good enough fer him and he ought to be beat up with a blood-wet rope too and smashed in the face and git his ribs kicked in.

"After a bit they went off and left me layin' there," Rocky whispered. "One of 'em kicked me hard as he could in the side and he told me if I ever was seen in this county again they'd take and kill me daid. Then they went off and I crawled up into the woods as far as I could go and I fo'git what happened then until I come to right here where I'm at."

"Joseph Paul found you and carried you here," Jay said. "Rocky, we got to fetch you a doctor."

"Jus' give me a little time to heal, Jay, and I'll be all right."

Jay got up and walked to the door. He turned his head and nodded to Belle and she followed him outside the cabin.

"That boy has got to be looked after," Jay said. "Belle, we got to find a place fer Rocky to stay. They got no room fer him here, and he'd ought to be moved off where it's safe."

"But where to, Jay?"

If he asks me to take him in with us I'll say yes, I sure

will. I'll have to say yes. But still we're moving tomorrow or the next day over to Boggs.

"Off into the hills," Jay said. "Belle, do you reckon old Haze Thompson would take him in?"

"But, Jay, it was Haze seen Pat in the hills —"

"I know damn well Haze didn't turn Pat in, Belle, and I aim to ask him, anyhow. When I tell Haze about it he'll be just as burning-up mad as I am. I'm going to ride up yonder and see Haze."

"All right, Jay."

"Will you look after Rocky while I'm gone?"

"I sure will."

Belle watched him go down to the car and drive away toward the old Cherokee road that led up into the hills.

That's the least I can do is to help Jay out that much and help that poor nigger, too. Even if he is black nobody's got a right to treat him that way and it makes me mad clean through to think about it. Now I wonder why Jay thinks Lamar Baker had a hand in it. I should of asked him that.

Belle went back into the house. The Negro lay prone on the bed with sunlight bathing his raw back and his face turned on the pillow so that as she came into the house his eyes met hers. Belle went over to the bed, and the Negro tried to smile at her.

"What you need to do is to lay just as quiet as you can," Belle said. "Do you want a drink of water?"

"If you please, ma'am."

"I thought you would, you talkin' so much and all."

"Here water is, Missy Belle," Joseph Paul said, bringing forward a tin dipper.

Belle held the dipper for Rocky, watching him drink through the shapeless lips. He sighed and sank back on the pillow.

"Where did Jay go to?"

"He went off to find a place fer you to stay, up in the hills."

Rocky sighed. "I don't want Jay to waste no time on me. He got too much to do. After this done happened he got more wo'k than he can handle and it got to be done quick." He looked up at Belle, his head twisted on the pillow. "We don't want nobody to know about me, if they ain't already. Sometimes it would help a union drive, but here it would jus' start a scare and it ain't goin' to do us no good. Jay sure got his work cut out fo' him to organize this county strong befo' the scare gits too big."

"Now don't you talk no more," Belle said.

He's just like Jay that way. He don't think of himself at all. It's only the union he's worryin' about and that's just like Jay. I don't know what it is makes a man give everything he's got fer something like that and maybe it's like me and Pat because I'd give all I got fer Pat and proud to do it. . . .

"I got to git up out of this bed soon's I kin and show myself back yonder where it happened," Rocky said. "Tha's what I got to do. I got to help put strength and guts into them people and if I can show my face again it will help to do it."

"Listen here," Belle said. "If you want to git up and around again you got to lay still. You hear me?"

"Yes'm." Rocky smiled.

"Well, you do like I say, then."

Rocky grinned.

"Now shut your eyes and sleep," Belle said. "Go ahead, shut them eyes."

She turned away from him. "Where's Joseph Paul?"

"Him go fetch horse," Christine said. She sat by the window in a corner of the room making artificial flowers. On a table of black walnut that Joseph had made she had laid out the materials, cut to pattern, and she sat bent over as she wound wire around the stems of several flowers to form a bouquet. Belle went over to her.

"Fer stomp-dance Wednesday night," Christine said, holding up the flowers. "Pretty, Belle?"

"Real pretty."

"You come stomp-dance, Belle?"

"Where at is it?"

"Back in hills on Red Feat'er farm. You know him?"

"I know Red Feather but I don't know where he lives at."

"Big barbecue, Belle. Dance all night. Every year have big dance. Old religion of Cherokee tribe, Belle. Big dance once each year and white people welcome. You better come."

"Not this year, Christine. I don't feel like dancing."

"Stomp-dance make you forget. Make you happy."

"Next year maybe I'll come, Christine, and I'll bring Pat with me."

"Jay come t'is year," Christine said. "Him talk union to Indian. Joseph in union now."

"How do them Indians feel about the union?" the Negro's deep voice asked.

"Now, you," Belle said, turning her head and smiling. "Remember what I told you."

"Yes'm."

"Indian don't know," Christine said. "Mebbeso. Joseph him talk union and Red Feat'er say him join."

"That will tickle Jay," Belle said. "Any time anybody joins the union Jay is tickled."

Belle watched the Indian woman's deft fingers as she completed the bouquet of artificial flowers. Her head was bent and her black hair was lustrous against the carmine glow where sunlight struck through a jar of pickled beets. On the paper-covered shelf were many jars of preserves, an old hand-painted clock dial, and above it a muzzle-loading rifle that Joseph Paul's ancestors had brought with them when Federal troops drove them from the South to the Indian Territory. On the floor beside Christine was a cardboard carton with the stamp of a Chicago firm upon it. The material was already cut into petals, center-pieces and stalks, and Christine assembled the flowers and was paid piece-work rates for the work. Belle watched her with knit brows.

She gits paid mighty little fer so much work and Pat claims anybody is a fool to work so hard without he plain has to, and I believe Christine could git along without it. Pat always says that a man is a fool to hold down a job, too, because there are plenty of fools to do the hard work, but if Pat had stayed on the job in the oil field he wouldn't be in jail and we wouldn't have all the troubles we got now. But anyhow all them Indian women are making little flowers and I reckon there just ain't nothing else they can do. They got to keep alive and that land of Joseph Paul's is plumb wore out and he has to make a living whittling walnut sticks and making wild cherry chairs and working in the spinach fields and Christine has to make them flowers and sometimes beaded belts and little dollies to sell in the Mehuskah curio shop. The only big thing they got to look forward to is the stomp-dances they have, and Christine will look mighty sweet with that bouquet on her dress and maybe a bright flower in that smooth black hair she's got. I remember I was just a little bit of a girl and Pop took me to my first stomp-dance and I thought it was a heap of fun and there was a little Cherokee boy with a silver hatband I knowed at school and he showed me how to dance and we ate some barbecue and they let me play Indian ball with them, the men against the women. It was fun then, fer a kid, but I don't know now and anyhow I wouldn't want to go up there alone without Pat, and with Pat in jail it ain't in me to go out dancing. . . .

"Him sleep now," Christine said, looking toward the bed.

Belle turned her head and saw Rocky lying with his swollen mouth open, his eyes closed.

That poor nigger. It's terrible to see him laying there with that poor back of his'n and to hear him moaning now a little in his sleep and he never let out a sound when he was awake. He's something like Jay that way, and he needs to be took care of just like Jay does, but neither one of 'em I guess would ever own up to it. It was only last night it happened and still and all he can lay there and worry about the union and sure enough like Jay said that nigger is a man.

"Where Jay go, Belle?" Christine asked.

"Up into the hills, Christine. He wants to find a place fer Rocky to stay."

"Him stay here, Belle."

Belle glanced around the one room of the cabin, at the bed in the corner where the Negro lay, at little Emma Paul's corn-shuck pallet near the fireplace.

"Jay don't want to impose none on you, Christine, but he sure does appreciate what you and Joseph done. Anyhow, Rocky will be safe up yonder."

"Him safe here, Belle."

"You-all sure did take good care of him already, Christine, and that's a fact. It was a mighty neighborly thing to do, to

take a nigger right into your house like that. I don't know as I
would of done it, but I would now, sure enough."

Christine smiled and bent her sleek black head over the
artificial flowers.

"Christine," Belle said. "Did I tell you we agreed to sell
our land and move out of the valley?"

The Indian woman looked up at Belle. "No. You sell, Belle?
Lamar Baker come see Joseph."

"What will Joseph do?"

"Joseph say guess him sell. Lamar say Gov'ment promise
move Indian grave to new cemetery before t'ey take make
lake."

Them Indians think a heap of their graves. Joseph has got
that little clump of headstones up on the hill where his whole
family lays buried. They bury their families in groups and
the Indians got little family graveyards all through the hills.
I reckon Lamar knowed what them graves mean to the fullbloods.

"You hear?" Christine said. "Maybe Jay come."

Belle heard the rasping sound of brakes and went to the
doorway of the cabin. She saw Jay coming up the hill, with
long strides, and went to meet him.

"Did you see Haze, Jay?"

"Sure I did and he said he'd take Rocky in. I had to talk
him into it but he said he'd do it and he'll be waiting up beside the road to meet us."

"I hope it ain't going to hurt him to travel."

"We got to take that chance, Belle. But he'll be better off
when we git him up there."

Jay went into the cabin and crossed to the Negro's bed.

"He's asleep," Belle said.

Rocky opened his eyes, then grinned at Jay.

"We got to move you somewheres else, Rocky," Jay said.
"Old Haze Thompson is going to take you in."

"Tha's good," Rocky said. "He b'long to the union, Jay?"

"No. Haze don't do no work fer anybody but himself. He
owns his own land up yonder and he mostly fishes and hunts
and chops him some wood to sell. . . . Listen here, Rocky,
do you feel like you could stand the trip?"

"Sho' I kin. Long as it don't nothin' touch my back."

"We'll set you so it don't."

The Negro sat up and put his feet down to the floor.

"Where at are your shoes?" Belle asked.

"I seen 'em yonder by th' chimney."

Belle went for the shoes. They were of heavy yellow cow-hide, chipped and scarred, and there were dark stains on the round toes.

Now I was about to kneel down and put them shoes on fer him. I was about to put shoes onto a nigger.

"Here's your shoes," Belle said, and dropped them on the floor beside Rocky's feet.

I wouldn't do it but Jay is and it's him kneels down to help a nigger on with his shoes and he don't give it a thought. Jay sure has changed since I remember him. He even let him sleep in his own house before he was hurt and he was just plain nigger then and not no sick nigger and anybody I guess would take a sick nigger in just like they would a sick dog and it wouldn't be right not to do it. But I wouldn't put his shoes on fer him no matter how sick he was.

"Can you stand up, boy?" Jay asked.

"Sure I kin."

The Negro pushed himself to his feet. He stood slightly stooped over and the muscles of his cheeks twitched.

"I'm afraid this has got to hurt you some," Jay said. "But it can't be helped. Now you take hold of my arm, Rocky, and Belle — you git on the other side of him. You can hang onto us both, Rocky."

They went slowly down the hill to Jay's car and Rocky sat in the back seat, leaning forward and holding to the door-frame.

"I'll take it just as slow as I can," Jay said.

"It don't hurt me much. Go ahaid." Rocky glanced up at the cabin on the hillside as they drove away. "Them Indians is sho' good people. If he hadn't found me I'd still be layin' out yonder in the woods. They treated me fine, Jay."

"Indians is good people," Jay said. "And when we git 'em in the union it ain't going to hurt our union strength none. People say that Indians won't never join up with the white man in a white man's organization, and they never could join together themselves in all their history. If they had they'd of drove the white man out. But I don't know. I'm going to sure enough try, Rocky."

Jay drove slowly along the winding clay road. The trees and underbrush were very green because of the spring rains and the loam of the road was a rich red. On the hillsides there were many wild flowers and along the road was the filmy white of baby's breath and the red-orange blooms of trumpet vines. They reached the crossroads and Jay turned south out of the valley bed. The road was firmer on the slope of the ridge where the soil had been washed thin over a layer of rock, but it was bumpy and the Negro clung to the doorframe and his teeth were clamped together. The road crossed over the top of the ridge and below and beyond was the vast undulation of the blackjack, west toward Boggs, east toward Mehuskah and south toward the Arkansas. The old road was used only occasionally by wagons which had been into the hills to haul cordwood and it was grass-grown and followed the natural contour of the countryside without grading.

"This sure must be hard on you, Rocky," Belle said.

"It ain't but a little bit further," Jay said. "Haze will meet us side of the road where the fork is at. We'll have to go afoot up to his house, Rocky."

"I kin make it all right, Jay."

"Sure you can, boy. Just hang on and it won't be but a little bit."

The car swung around a bend in the road, the wheels slipping in the moist clay, and as it straightened out they saw Haze Thompson ahead of them, sitting on a boulder beside the road with his rifle between his knees. He stood up and raised one hand and Jay stopped the car. Belle jumped down to help the Negro out.

"Just will you look!" Haze said. "Christ, I never seen its beat."

"They laid on him with a rope, like I told you," Jay said. "That's what cut his back up so."

"You pore damned nigger," Haze said.

"How far is it from here to your place, Haze?" Belle asked.

"Belle, I ain't even said howdy. Say, you git better lookin' every time I see you. Like a peach tree in blossom, that's what you look like."

"We got to start on," Jay said.

"My hoss is yonder in the woods, Jay. We can put the nigger astraddle him."

"All right, Haze."

They filed into the woods and Haze untethered his scrawny chestnut horse. Jay helped the Negro climb into the saddle.

The old man led the horse and they started through the woods, along a disused road. Belle walked behind and if she raised her eyes she could see the Negro's back, but she kept her head lowered.

I just don't want to look at it. Here it is summertime and the best time of the year and it's hot but them woods still smell like spring and the wild flowers are blooming and the dogwood is in flower and human beings got to treat each other like they do. It makes you want to go off in the woods and live there like old Haze does and you wouldn't need to have no truck with nobody and you wouldn't even know the cruel way they got to treat each other. All he did was to try to organize a union and he wasn't doing nothing uppity. He was just down yonder with them other niggers trying to organize a union. That's all he done and they took and treated him like they did.

They came out of the woods into a clearing fifty yards in diameter and in the center of it stood Haze's shack, weather-worn and with gaps of light between the boards. They passed an old well-shed where an almost white rope was passed through a rusty pulley.

"Here we are, Jay," Haze said, dropping the reins. "Reckon we better git the nigger into the house."

"Reckon we had, Haze."

They helped Rocky down and Belle followed them into the one-room cabin. There were two iron bedsteads in the room, a table and two chairs, and a cook-stove and sooty stove-pipe with clumsily fitted elbows.

"That bed ain't been touched since the missus died," Haze said. "That was back in the Bull Moose days. But you can have it, nigger, and you're welcome to it, and there's a plenty of corn bread and syrup and rabbit meat. That there is your side of the cabin, nigger, and this here is mine."

"He goes by the name of Rocky," Jay said.

"Rocky, is it?"

"Short fer Rock Island Jones," Jay said.

"All right, Rocky, that there is your side of the house and you can cook your grub on that cook-stove. I'll see you git plenty of batter and fresh rabbit. They ain't no fever in the rabbits around here and it's safe to eat."

"Tha's real kind of you, Mistah Thompson," Rocky said. His teeth showed between swollen lips in a smile.

"They never was a nigger in this here house before," Haze said. "But if Jay allows you're to stay here then by God you sure can stay and you're welcome and you can have all the corn dodgers you can eat."

"Haze," Belle said quietly. "I'd of took him in with me and Crosby if it wasn't we aim to move out of the valley, maybe tomorrow."

"Would you now?" Haze scratched his long chin. "Well, like I said, he's welcome to stay here, nigger or not, and I'll see he gits plenty of batter to bake him corn bread and I'll make a rabbit stew fer supper tonight."

The Negro sank face down on the bed and the dried corn shucks of the mattress rustled. He sighed and turned his face to the wall and they all stood looking at the torn flesh of his back.

"It wouldn't do him no harm if that back of his'n was washed down with warm water ever' so often," Jay said.

"No, I reckon it wouldn't." Haze looked at Jay. "I got a fresh bottle of Sampson 'lixir and I'll give him some of that. It sure is good fer what ails you."

"I heard tell of it," Jay said. "Rocky, I'm going to stop back and see you tomorrow."

The Negro turned his head toward Jay. "It ain't no call fo' hit, Jay. You got wo'k to do and you better go ahaid and do it. Don't you waste no time triflin' with me."

"I want to git you up and out," Jay said. "We got need of you, Rocky."

"That's all I'm after, Jay. I wants to show 'em my face back Tanzey way befo' hit's too late."

"Now you're talking," Jay said. "Okay, Rocky, I'll be on my way and you can depend on it that Haze Thompson will take good care of you."

"I'll see he gits plenty to eat and I'll wash down that back of his'n," Haze said. "And I'll give him some of that 'lixir, too."

It looks like Jay can talk anybody around to what he wants and he's got old Haze eating out of his hand. I never expected I'd hear of Haze washing a nigger's back fer him and cooking him a rabbit stew and giving him some of the medicine he pays six bits a bottle fer and has to ride clean to Aldine to fetch. But he said he'd do it and I know he will and I always knowed you could depend on old Haze and I never should of thought even fer a minute it would be him turned Pat in. Pat was hunted by the Laws and Haze wanted to take him into his house and now here he's took a nigger in just like he was a white man.

"Jay, I got a jug handy," Haze said.

Jay grinned. "Next to Dad you make the best corn in the hills and I always said that, Haze."

Haze went to the corner and returned, grinning, with a jug in his hand.

"How about you, Belle?"

"Don't mind if I do," Belle said.

They passed the jug around and then Haze went outside into the afternoon sunlight with Belle and Jay. He walked with them as far as the well, where he stopped and leaned against the well-shed.

"Jay, what do you aim to do about it?"

"About Rocky?"

"Uh-huh."

"I'm going to serve notice on 'em," Jay said quietly. "We ain't going to stand fer that in Oklahoma. And I got to show them farmers that the way to stop it is to build up an organization strong enough to do it."

Belle and Jay started across the clearing. Haze was still standing by the well-shed when Belle looked back just before entering the woods. Then the glossy leaves of a sassafras tree hid him from sight. She followed Jay along the trail.

It sure seems longer than four days that I was up here in these woods. It was Thursday evening that Pat come to Cedar Gully and here it is Monday and since that time Pat is caught and took back to Texas and we done sold the farm and aim to move out and that poor nigger got treated that way. When things come on you they come all at once, sure enough, and I had enough excitement since Thursday to last me all my days and I hope it won't never be like that again and when we git Pat back home I'll see that it ain't. I'll see we plant corn yonder by Boggs and maybe a truck garden too and I'll see Pat works hard in the field and hoes them suckers and he'll come home that tired by sundown that the devilment will be clean worked out of him but not so tired that he'll forget I'm there like happens to some women. And I'll cook such vittles fer him that he won't never feel that itch in his feet to go some place and when he does we'll take off into the hills and hunt like we always did and I'll cook him squirrel stew with cream gravy and we'll have a jug along and that will make him come home easy in his mind. . . .

They reached the road and Belle followed Jay down a claybank to the car. When she was seated beside him she put one hand on his arm. "Jay, I meant what I said. I sure would of took Rocky in if we wasn't movin' away."

"I knowed you would, Belle."

"Then you knowed more than I did, Jay."

Jay grinned at her and started the engine. He drove back along the grassgrown road, over the ridge and down the slope through a woods of scrub oak to the crossroads, where he turned into the valley. They passed Joseph Paul's house and Belle waved to Christine, who had come out on the hillside to see what car was passing. On the valley road Jay drove faster.

"I'm going to leave you by home, Belle, and then I got to go over Aldine way."

"Jay, why don't you stay the rest of the evening? What business takes you over to Aldine?"

"I'm goin' courting," Jay said, grinning at her.

"Oh. That there schoolteacher?"

"That's right."

Belle gave her head a small shake, but she did not speak.

I sure do wish he would find a woman to take care of him but I don't want him to mix himself up with that one. She's just a prissy one and stuck-up and she ain't good enough fer Jay.

Jay turned into the lane and stopped the car under the oak tree near the house. Crosby was sitting on the porch and he jumped up and came toward them, waving a piece of paper.

"Jay, look here! Belle, look, the money come from the Gov'-ment. Just will you look what it says here — sixteen hunderd dollars!"

Jay took the check in his hands and looked at it, then passed it to Belle. Crosby stood watching them with a proud grin on his face.

"That city feller brung it, Jay, just a little after you-all went off. He said he'd send some trucks in to move us out and I told him to have 'em here tomorrow mornin'. Belle, is that all right?"

"I reckon so. It don't seem right that just this little slip of paper can bring us all that money. It don't look like nothing at all."

"It's just the same as money in your hand, Belle," Jay said. "I tell you, now we're going to set Pat free."

"I sure do hope so, Jay."

"I'll take this here check, Dad," Jay said. "I'll put it in the bank at Mehuskah and then I'll go down to Texas and I'll git that big-time lawyer fer Pat."

"Whatever you say, Jay."

"We sure got lots to do, Crosby," Belle said. "If we move out tomorrow there's a heap of work."

"I figured the best thing to do was to move out and git it over with. The three of us can pack things up in a jiffy."

"Jay ain't going to help," Belle said. "He's got to go over to Aldine."

"Is that right, Jay?"

"I'll stay awhile, till about five-thirty," Jay said. "Gimme that check, Belle. I'll stay awhile and help and then I'll have to be on my way."

"Then we better git at it, boy. I don't know just where to start."

"You-all can start in the barn," Belle said. "You load all you can into that truck and everything else we'll put in them Government trucks."

"Whatever you say, Belle," Crosby said.

"There's one thing you don't want to forget, Dad," Jay said. "Ain't that a keg I see yonder in the oak tree?"

Crosby grinned. "I reckon we'd better git that first off, Jay, and see if it's aged good. What do you say?"

"I say damn right," Jay said.

They started toward the tree and Belle went into the house.

Poor old Jay he ain't never found a woman to suit him. Not like me and Pat. The first time we seen each other at that barn dance it begun. But these years have gone by and Jay ain't found nobody and all he does is work at that union business, and I know that little blue-eyed filly over to Aldine ain't what Jay wants and she's just no-good fer him but I wouldn't want to tell him so. . . .

Jay

✤   ✤

IT'S a good thing to see a river moving by and to stand in the trees and watch it pass and not to think about the men that live along it and the cotton that grows beside it and the spinach fields and the people sweating in 'em with never time to look at the river floating by.

The Grand River was high from the recent rains and water swirled around the bend and was sucked in eddies past the massive stone piers of the railroad trestle where the current was strong. Below the bridge was a great quay of stone, the site of a steamboat landing long since abandoned. Once steamboats freighting supplies for an army outpost in the early Territory days had come up the Arkansas and turned into the Grand at the confluence a few miles below. Jay was putting on his bathing suit behind the screen of a willow tree on the bank above the steamboat landing and Leona was changing in her car, parked a few hundred yards away in a grove of trees. The light was the amber color of late twilight, but the sun had not yet set; it was only blocked from sight by the structure of the trestle and the high opposite bank of the river.

It's like bathing naked in the softest water to stand in this here light and you can almost feel it on your skin and the green water of the river looks dark and cold. The trouble is a man don't have time to just stand by and enjoy living and feeling the life that's in him and all around him. . . .

Jay walked along the stone landing looking at the water. He heard Leona call to him before she came in sight on the path down the riverbank and he watched for her.

In her close-fitting bathing suit with them arms and legs so soft and round it makes my breath catch and she's like a white puppy dog learning to walk when she tip-toes that way with the stones hurting her bare feet but now she's running and she's got that sureness about her again and she's splashing like a spaniel in the water and like she was happy and about to bark and echo on the water.

Jay followed her into the river and they waded a hundred feet above the bridge and swam straight out, carried downwards by the current, by the swift, swirling current that tugged like an animate force at their legs and arms, and they barely reached the first solid buttress. Out of breath, they climbed upon a ledge of masonry.

"What a place to swim!" Leona said, panting. "No wonder they're building a lake."

Jay glanced at her, but did not speak.

"Neil's so excited about the lake, now that he can begin the work," she said. "He says he's going to make a little paradise out of that valley, Jay."

"Uh-huh," Jay said.

"The W.P.A. is doing wonderful things for the country," Leona said. "Jay, there'll be fishing and swimming and dancing — everything but surf-bathing."

"I suppose they're going to charge money fer all that," Jay said.

"Why, I believe so. It's supposed to pay for itself in twenty years. Yes, I guess you'll have to pay to go to the beach and rent the cabins and boats."

"I thought as much," Jay said. "Them Aldine people won't

see much of that there lake. Us people they're moving out of the valley won't git no pleasure out of that lake that's going to cover up our homes. But I don't mean I stand against it. All things considered it will do some good."

"Look, Jay, the moon is just about full." Leona pointed. "It will be full for the stomp-dance day after tomorrow. I wish it were you taking me, Jay."

"Maybe I'll see you up there."

"You mean you're going?"

"Maybe I will."

She stared at him, her eyes bright in the pale light. "Then why wouldn't you take me, Jay?"

"I tell you, Leona. I got to go up yonder on union business, to talk to them Indians. I'm trying to sign them up in the Tenant Farmers' Union."

Leona sighed, and splashed her feet in the water. "Don't you ever think of anything but that union, Jay?"

"That's my work and I got plenty to worry about. — But I think about you some, Leona."

She stood up on the narrow ledge. "Jay, we'd better eat, before it gets dark."

She poised for an instant, then dived in a clean white arc of glistening arms and legs into the dark water. Jay followed her and they climbed out on the steamboat landing. She walked up the path and he went behind the willow tree to put on his clothes. On the way up the bank when he was dressed he gathered wood to build a fire. They had come in Leona's car at her wish because it was equipped with a radio, which now was tuned in low. Jay took the back seat from the car to sit upon and she spread a checked cloth on the ground at their feet.

"Well, well," Jay said. "Fried chicken. And potato salad. *And* beaten biscuit."

"Don't forget the beer, Jay."

"I'll go after it."

He brought a bucket with ice packed around the beer bottles and they drank from the bottles as they ate. They listened to the radio and watched the moon turn a brassy

color as the sun sank from sight. In the trees along the riverbank crickets set up a constant whirring.

"I'm sort of sorry school is over," Leona said. "I don't know
what to do, except I'd like to go up to Colorado. I don't want
to spend the whole summer with my folks in Tulsa."

That easy talk of hers about going to Colorado and the fried
chicken and the beaten biscuits, and lots of people I know
never ate a beaten biscuit and don't git no chicken unless they
steal it. She talks that easy way about going to Colorado and
that shows the difference there is between us and we can't never
git away from it. She would have to have a man who made lots
of jack and took her off places every summer such as Colorado,
sure enough.

"Of course next year we go on a twelve-month basis in the
Indian schools, instead of ten months," Leona said. "I won't
have a long vacation then."

"What do you do all them twelve months?"

"After school is out we supervise community events, and
teach sewing projects and teach the women to can vegetables
from the school garden for the next year's school lunches."

"Can you sew?" Jay asked.

"Now, Jay, of course I can sew — and cook, too."

The fire had burned low and the moon was brighter. Behind them a voice was saying on the radio: *Calling all tourist
cars. Calling all tourist cars. You tourists who have come to
Oklahoma will surely visit Tulsa, the great oil capital of the
world, and when in Tulsa be sure to . . .*

"It's a hell of a thing," Jay said. "Here we set and listen to
somebody tell us where to buy and what to eat and which is
the best auto. Here we set on a riverbank and listen to that by
radio coming from miles away."

"Yes, Jay?"

"Here we set and listen to that and all around us people are
living worse off than in the days of bondage. They never heard
a radio and they never rode in an auto and they don't have
money to buy nothing and they don't git enough to eat."

"Yes," Leona said quietly, and moved her shoulders. "But,
Jay, we're here to have fun. We're on a picnic."

"It's just two kinds of worlds and one of 'em is smooth-talking out of that radio and the other one is talking right here through me," Jay said. "Leona, I believe you belong to that first one."

"I wish you wouldn't say it like that, Jay."

"I reckon it's the truth."

"I don't belong to anything special. I just want to be happy and have fun."

She says it just like a little girl and I reckon that's what she is. She ain't yet a woman and what she wants is to be happy and have fun. But she sure is sweet and pretty with that fire-light on her face and that moonlight on her hair.

Jay put one arm around her shoulders and they sat silent, looking at the embers of the fire.

I wonder would she let me kiss her. I said by God I'd try it when we come out here on the Grand and I sure enough will. Yes, I will.

Jay put the palm of his hand on her cheek and turned her face toward him. He bent his head and his lips touched hers lightly, with only an instant's pressure, the shadow of a caress, and he drew away from her again.

Now by God she let me and she sure is sweet and my mouth still burns from it and I'd ought to reach over and grab her tight as I can and I sure do want to do it.

They sat with clasped hands looking at the brassy moon above the trees. He felt in his pocket with his free hand for a cigarette, and saw her profile in a warm, indefinite light as he struck a match.

"Leona, I sure am crazy about you," he said. "Honey, I can't git you out of my head."

"I'm glad of that, Jay. I'm glad it's not only your union you think about."

"It sure ain't."

This time he held his lips against hers a long time, until she turned her head away to look at the moon. She pressed his fingers gently and because of the sudden intimacy there was nothing to talk about and words stuck in Jay's throat.

For the trailer couple Fleishmeyer's offers a complete line of cooking utensils, tableware and . . .

"I just hate to hear that smooth talk." Jay said.

There's no danger of fire with a Fleishmeyer cooker in your trailer. . . .

She sure-enough likes me and maybe like I like her but I wonder what's in her mind and what she thinks about. She never said right out she likes me but she let me kiss her and she kissed me back and Jesus Christ!

"I been thinkin' a lot about you, Leona," Jay said. "Honey, turn your head around."

His arm tightened around her, but she continued to look at the moon. His lips caressed her cheek; he pressed his face into her hair. She turned her head until their lips met and both his arms went around her, lifting her up against him. There was a long interval of pressure felt and returned, of breathless warmth in their bodies.

"Honey, I'm in love with you," Jay whispered. "I been loving you fer a long time."

He kissed her cheek and her ear, half-hidden by the roll of her hair. Behind them a velvety voice was saying: *Now, folks, we're going to hear a hot number from Benny Harris and his Swing Swallows, playing nightly at . . .*

"Jay." She took hold of both his hands.

"Yes?"

"I like you an awful lot. I guess you know that. I just couldn't help myself. But I wonder, Jay, do we really understand each other?"

"I don't know," Jay said. "Maybe we don't."

"Sometimes I think it will be all right, and that's what I think when I'm with you, but it's the way you talk that makes me afraid we'll never understand each other, Jay. I don't know whether I'm the kind of woman you want. I do want to be happy, Jay, and I want to have fun."

"Sure you do," Jay said. "Just like everybody else."

"I want to get married some day, and I want to be a good wife to the man I marry and I want to be sure that I can. I don't want to take any chances. Do you understand, Jay?"

"I reckon so. What you mean is my union business and maybe you're right. I have to work day and night and like you always say I don't git nothing out of it and never will. But

I got to go on with that work whatever happens, Leona."

"I know you do, and I wouldn't be any help to you, Jay."

"Don't you suppose?"

"I don't know. Listen, I'm a practical woman, Jay. I want to plan my life out and I don't want anything to go wrong. I think it would be wonderful to be with you always, Jay, but I'm not thinking only of myself and I don't know."

"It sure is hard to be poor, Leona," Jay said. "And that's what I'll always be." He stood up. "I reckon you're right and that's the end of it. We better go on home."

"It's not the end of it, Jay." She looked up at him. "Don't say that. I just mean I want a little more time. I want to think about it and I want to know for sure. — Jay, you'll wait a little bit, won't you?"

He looked down at her. "You bet I will."

But it ain't no use and it's just like I knowed it would be all the time. She sure is sweet and it's true as hell I love her but there just ain't nothing we can do. She'll always be like she is and she'll always think like she does and she wouldn't never be the kind of wife I got to have and she wouldn't be happy and she wouldn't have fun.

Jay went to kick dirt over the embers, gouging his toe into the ground. Leona cleared the tablecloth and folded it and Jay picked up the cushion. As he was bending to put it in the car a voice said with startling clearness: *Stand by for a special news bulletin* . . . . an electric pause . . . . *Jackville, Texas: Pat Strickland, notorious Southwestern outlaw, escaped from jail here tonight after killing a guard and the Sheriff in a bloody get-away. Strickland, who faces a possible sentence of ninety-nine years in the Texas courts, is believed to be heading north to Oklahoma. He is a desperate criminal*. . . .

Jay's hand went to his pocket, where the check for sixteen hundred dollars was folded in his wallet, then dropped limply to his side.

$\mathcal{P}at$

THEY may be close behind me but I got to stop. I got to stop and git me some gas before it's too late and it's already just about midnight and most places will be closed. Them lights ahead of me look like a filling station and that's where I'll stop. I got to do it.

Braking with a slow steady pressure of his foot Pat Strickland swung the car to the left of the highway and drove under the shed of the filling station. There was only one pump, in the center, and he could not stop the car with his face wholly in shadow. He sat far back in the convertible coupé and sounded the horn with a tap of his fist on the button. Connected with the filling station was a small store where soft drinks and cigarettes were sold; a woman came through the screen door at the store entrance and her feet made a rattling noise on the gravel.

"Fill her up," Pat said.

"I was fixin' to close," the woman said as she walked to the rear of the car. Although it was hot she wore a man's turtleneck sweater of a green color that made her face as sallow as the moon overhead. "It's past midnight," she said.

Pat did not answer. He sat perfectly still, listening to the noise as she unscrewed the cap from the tank and inserted the metal nozzle; then there came the ringing sound as the gallons were checked off. Pat moved the forty-five a little nearer his body on the seat beside him. Under the dashboard the rifle was out of sight.

"I never seen the bugs so bad," the woman said. "They come up from the Red River."

Pat had not noticed the bugs before. They swarmed around the lights of the station; they struck against the windshield in front of him, a constant whirling swarm surging blindly toward the lights with buzzing wings.

"That comes to a dollar sixty-three," the woman said. "Check the oil?"

Pat hesitated, glancing back over his shoulder. "Yeah, check the oil."

It looks all right back yonder. I don't see no headlights and it's maybe a half-hour now since they was on my tail. I guess I left 'em behind at Gainesville when I turned off and made the break across the Red.

"You could use a quart," the woman said, wiping her hands on a greasy rag.

"Okay."

"What weight, Mister?" She came over toward him.

"How's that?" Pat leaned forward so that she would not see the gun on the seat; his face came into the light.

"What weight oil you use?" She peered in at him and he drew farther away, into the shadow.

"I don't know. I don't care — Gimme a summer oil, and hurry it up."

"About a number twenty?"

"All right. Step on it." He began to beat a nervous rhythm on the steering wheel with the palms of his hands, and now and then he looked back over his shoulder at the highway over which he had come from Texas. Once he saw lights approaching, and his hands tightened on the wheel.

But that must be a truck. It's got that yellow fog light low down on the left side. I reckon it's a truck carrying night freight up to Oklahoma City. I don't like them trucks filling up the road at night when I got to drive so fast, but by God, that's an idear. If they git too close on my tail I can snatch me a truck. They wouldn't look fer me except in a fast auto and I could keep the driver alongside of me. . . .

Pat watched the truck rumble past and when it was opposite him he heard the high-pitched, ridiculous noise of pigs squealing their fright.

The woman had finished clamping the hood in place. "Driving a long ways tonight, Mister?"

"Yeah," Pat said.

Now what's it to her? What in hell is she so curious about? I wonder did she see the guns.

"Over beyond Fort Sill," Pat said.

"That makes a dollar eighty-eight," the woman said. Pat stepped on the starter as she came nearer.

"Charge it," he said, and grinned at her. He heard her cry, "Say!" and then her voice was lost in the rasp of flying gravel as he whirled the car out on the highway.

Jesus, it's good to be moving again, but I can't go fast enough, I can't never go fast enough to suit me. She sure got me jumpy taking so long about it when any minute them lights might of come in sight back yonder. I wonder would those Texas Laws turn back at the Red River? If they're on my trail still that woman will tell 'em and maybe she'll tell 'em I took the Fort Sill road and maybe they'll believe her. But I'll burn straight up the road to Oklahoma City and they'd better not nobody git in my way to stop me because I'll sure as hell blow 'em off the road. . . .

The lights danced on the road far ahead of him and he drove with the accelerator pressed flat to the floorboard. It seemed no time at all until a red light came into view and he passed the truck on a concrete bridge over swampy ground. He swung past it with the tires screeching on the concrete and in the same pitch with the sound he heard the instant's squealing of the pigs. He drove on at top speed toward Ardmore and Oklahoma City, watching the road, with the moon ahead of him.

I can't git it out of my head and maybe to the end of my days I won't git it out of my head but already it seems like it didn't really happen and I just seen a pitcher of it. But I won't never forget Clyde running out ahead of me with the machine gun under his arm and being out in the courthouse square in front of the jail and hearing them shots behind us. Clyde turned around and I run right on past him and it was looking back over my shoulder I seen that splatter of mortar and crumbled brick where the machine gun drawed a line alongside the door where that fat Sheriff was with his gun in his hand. He fell over just like a beef steer in a slaughterhouse that don't make a sound when the mallet hits his head and then Clyde stumbled and dropped the Tommy gun and it was too late fer me to turn back after it. I couldn't run back across that open square to git that gun. It was a hell of a lucky break to find them guns in the first place, just setting there in that linen closet. And I reckon that feller is still laying there by that closet and he's the first man I ever shot and I wonder did it kill him. It give me a funny feeling like that time I was a kid and I shot a squirrel and it was the first thing I ever killed with a gun and I was so puffed up I hit him but then I went and looked and he was dead and I had that feeling. That other guard that brung the supper is all right, I know. We only knocked him over the head and it was just bad luck that other one come along when we was at the linen closet and I had to shoot him. He had that gun in his hand and there wasn't nothing else to do. I had to shoot him and I didn't have time to think about it. I just had to shoot and I won't forget the noise in that little jail like a firecracker exploding in a tin can the way Jay and me used to set 'em off on the Fourth when we was kids. After that we just had to run fer it, right out past the Sheriff's door into the square and then Clyde cut that Sheriff in two with the Tommy gun and somebody shot Clyde down from a window and I had to keep on running with them bullets kicking up dust all around me. It was a lucky break that guy was waiting fer a green light in this here coup. He was some scared and he put up his hands and jumped out as soon as I come alongside and I got going and hit that brick highway north. They kept shooting and it was funny seeing all them people standing around with their mouths open and their arms stiff at their sides. It sure did happen fast and it was all of a sudden I seen there was two cars on my tail and a lot of other cars behind and them other cars stayed way back and all they was out fer was to see it all and see me make my break and to see me git shot down if they'd of caught me. But they won't catch me and anyhow they won't catch me alive. With them two Laws dead they'd shoot me down if they caught up, but son of a bitch, I'd rather be dead than spend ninety-nine years in jail. Ninety-nine years and all I got out of it was a lousy six hunderd bucks! And all because of that Clyde Winter is dead and I got half of Texas on my tail and maybe by now Oklahoma too. They'll figure I'd head fer Oklahoma but they didn't figure I'd turn off at Sherman toward Gainesville instead of burning across the Red at Denison. I'm easy a half-hour ahead of 'em now and it's a good U.S. road and this little coup is boiling as fast as it can go, but it ain't as fast as the telephone. It ain't as fast as the teletype nor the radio. And they'll sure as hell be watching fer me Oklahoma City way. They'll be watching this road and they'll be watching old U.S. 69 too and I reckon before long I'd better turn off and head east on back roads toward the hills. But first of all I want to put Texas away behind me and if I turned east at Ardmore I'd sure as hell run into them cops who went on across the Red at Denison on the Durant road, and I reckon that's the way they went. . . .

The windshield now was splattered with insects. Pat turned on the windshield wiper, but it left a greasy smear across the glass and he turned it off again. There was a slight mist rolling close to the ground, dimming the penetration of the lights. For a long time now he had driven without meeting another car. On the right of the road he saw a hotel advertisement on a billboard, ARDMORE 4 MILES, and for the first time he slackened speed.

It sure gives me a stiff neck stretching to see through that greasy windshield and it hurts my eyes too but I got to drive at least a hunderd miles before it's safe to turn into the woods to wait out the day. Along near McAlester, in the river bottoms of the Canadian, would be a good place to hide out, and I know that country. But some place I got to git another car. The license number of this here will be broadcast all over the Southwest by this time.

Ardmore already; the few late lights blinked ahead of him, dimly through the smear of night insects on the windshield. He decelerated to forty miles an hour, the motor singing as it slowed. Entering the town he saw the glare of an automobile's headlights on a side street. The car was parked, with its bright lights burning, and on the opposite side of the highway was another parked car; the lights of the two met at an angle on the road, forming a cross-fire of brilliance through which he must pass. As soon as he saw the lights Pat's foot stepped on the gas. His breath came faster, as if accelerated by his pounding heart. An instant later he shot through the lights and his eyes went to the mirror above and it reflected blinding light.

Both them cars has started after me and they been waiting there and watching fer the license number and I guess they're waiting fer me on that other highway out of Denison too. But by God there's a truck ahead of me swinging out to block the road and it's a trap and it sprung when them two cars behind me blinked their lights turning out of that side street.

Pat jammed on the brakes and swung the car to the right; the rubber whistled on the pavement and he turned the corner with only inches to spare, skidding nearly to a stop. He had turned east, the only road open to him, and he was driving now on the highway toward Durant.

And they'll be watching fer me at Durant, and there'll be a posse out to hem me in, sure as hell. Them Texas Laws have had plenty of time to git to Durant, too, and maybe by this time they're on the road to Ardmore, heading straight toward me on the same road and maybe they got the road blocked down the way. Sure as hell I'll be caught between here and Durant unless I do something. It's a good road and this coup is stepping fast as it can, but them lights stick close behind me, too God-damned close. This coup can make time and it's traveling light but it can't step away from them big cars behind. So far they ain't fired a shot and by God that means they ain't trying to catch up with me yet. They're waiting me out, waiting until I run spang into them other Laws ahead of me and it means that sure as hell they got this road blocked up ahead. On the next side road north, by God, I'll have to turn off. I wouldn't dast turn south into the Red River bottoms where they'd circle me and bring bloodhounds down from the McAlester Pen to smell me out. Yonder's a crossroads sign but it points right and that means south and I ain't going to slow down fer that. There's got to be a road pretty soon, and on a rough side road I'll git away from them Laws in their heavy-loaded cars. It won't be such smooth rolling on a country back road.

Another crossroads sign — black letters on a yellow shield. Pat's eyes turned from the sign to the road ahead. There was a gravel turn-off to the left, near at hand now. The tires screamed as he put on the brakes and the lights behind him flashed nearer in the mirror, then he swung off into blackness, off to the left in the direction of the moon, the car careening and fence posts slipping by under the lights. He had barely made the turn and the tires skidded on the gravel road as he fed gas to the engine again. Behind him the pursuing cars had missed the crossroad, and he saw a flash of distant light on trees as they turned around on the highway.

Looks like I gained a quarter-mile on 'em, and now there ain't no Laws ahead of me. But I wish to Jesus I knowed where this road is headin' to! There was some signposts at the turn but Christ, I couldn't make out what was on 'em. I reckon it bears up north toward Ada and it will take me to the banks of the Canadian and I can find cover there tomorrow through the daytime. . . .

The road was narrow, and there were sharp curves around which the car slued in flying gravel that rattled against the fenders. There were trees close on both sides and the headlights glowed in a tunnel ahead of him with the road dancing toward him drunkenly as the car slipped in the gravel. Occasionally there were drainage dips in the road in which the body of the car landed with a staggering jolt on the springs, but Pat hardly slowed down for them. He was well ahead of the police cars now; the mirror above was dark, with only a faintly reflected glow from the dashboard lights.

Suddenly the motor coughed, and there was a long, sucking

sigh. Pat had just turned a bend in the road and had pressed the foot throttle again, but the engine did not respond for an instant. Then it caught again, jerkily, and the car bucked forward, ran smoothly for a few hundred yards, then coughed again. The gauge showed the tank was nearly full of gasoline.

Damn that woman, now God damn her, there's water in that gas, sure as hell. It's just cheap gas and she put water in it. Maybe the fuel pump is blowed — but this coup is this year's model and it wouldn't be that. Maybe it's a clogged feed-line; but no, by God, it's that woman and her gas with water in it, sure as hell. . . .

The motor was sputtering as the car ran across a narrow steel bridge. Down below there was a brief glint of water in the Washita River. Again the sucking sigh, the abrupt deceleration. Pat's decision was instantaneous. He put on the brakes and turned the car to the side of the road. There was no fence and he drove across a shallow ditch and in among the trees. But there the motor died. He could drive no farther and the car was still visible from the road.

"God damn it, now God damn," Pat said.

He snatched up the rifle and kicked open the door. He leaped into the brush and started at a run into the woods.

I'm on the east of the road and I'm running right back toward where it's hot, but maybe that's the best thing I can do. They'd figure me to head west away from all them Laws.

Behind him there was a flash of light and he heard the rumble of a car passing over the bridge. Above the snapping of brush underfoot, the rasping of leaves catching at his feet, he heard the screeching noise of brakes. The underbrush was high and he had to hold the rifle up away from it as he ran east in the thick woods through which moonlight came sparsely. It was light enough to see the trees ahead of him, to see the form of the bushes, and to search out the easiest way to run. But it was dark enough so that he could not himself be easily seen, and he had a good start.

That bitch in the green sweater she knowed she was giving me watered gas and just to make a few extra pennies she's that low-down. I wish to Christ I had her here now and I'd pour that gasoline down her throat and if it hadn't been fer her I'd of got clear easy and I'd be hiding out in the woods of the Canadian before sunup.

Pat came to a barbed-wire fence and scrambled through it, ripping his tan shirt at the shoulder. He had run on twenty yards before he felt the sting where a barb had gouged him. Off to his right he saw the sheen of moonlight on the water of the river, which bent in toward him. He bore to the left, crashing through a thicket where tough dogwood slapped at his face. He was breathing in spasmodic gasps that tasted of blood deep in his lungs. His shoulder was hurting and he stopped by a tree and turned away from the moon, looking in the direction from which he had come. At that moment the gashed shoulder was a greater annoyance than the officers behind him. He dabbed at the wound with a handkerchief, leaning against a tree. His face was flushed with sweat and he dried it with a motion of his biceps across his forehead; the damp shirt-sleeve passed coolingly over his face.

I can't hear nothing but my own breath. I reckon I must have run all of a mile from where I left the car and that tank full of watered gas that yellow bitch in the green sweater put in. I run a full mile along the river and the river flows down to the Red and if I follow it I'll come to a traveled highway and I'll have to take that chance and maybe I can git my hands on another car and git away and head north again. I ought to took that truck when I first seen it or when I passed it on the Ardmore road. I'd be half-way to Ada by now if I had, and nobody would think to look fer me in a slow-moving truck full of hogs. But if it hadn't been fer that woman and her watered gas I'd of made it and I'd of run away from them Laws on that third-grade road and I'd of been safe at the Canadian before sunup. I'd of been back in the hills tomorrow night and then they'd never catch me. I'd lay low and I wouldn't take no chances and me and Belle could go off in the woods and make camp and wait our time to git clean away. By God, I got to git back to them hills, and son of a bitch, I got to see Belle again.

The handkerchief was wet with smeared blood and Pat crumpled it in his fist and threw it on the ground at his feet. He picked up the rifle and with a deep-drawn breath started off again at a run. But ten strides away he came to a sudden stop.

I left that handkerchief there where they'll sure by God find it and they'll have the bloodhounds out from some prison farm and they'll smell it. They don't have nothing now fer the hounds to git my scent from without that handkerchief and I got to find it.

Pat ran back under the dark trees and feverishly began to search through the brush, kicking in the grass. The moonlight came down like shattered glass, broken in a thousand pieces, with here and there a space of light on the ground, of glinting light that looked like handkerchiefs spread beneath the trees. But when he came nearer there was only moonlight shivering on the grass. In the distance he thought he heard a shout, and he stood perfectly still, listening, but it was not repeated. Whatever it was, it was not repeated. But as he stood there the ghostly call of a screech owl sounded near at hand. Pat turned away.

I got to leave that handkerchief go and if I can't find it neither can they, I expect. But in the daytime, tomorrow when they got the dogs it will be easy. I got to be way to hell and gone by morning. If I follow the river there ain't no danger of coming out into the open and that's all there is fer me to do. I got to follow the river all the way to the Red if need be. I got to keep going all night and grab a car if I can and be far enough away so I can hide out all day tomorrow without they find me. I got two guns and enough bullets to make a fight of it if they do catch up and if I can't git away. I'll sure as hell kill me some of them Laws. I never shot nobody before but now I done it and if they catch up I got to do it again. That guard in the jail corridor grabbed his stomach and looked at me with his eyes popping. He slid down to his knees with his head on one side like a man about to drink sweet water from a mountain spring and he went over on his face like a man bending down to water and then he stretched out flat with his hands under him and blood wetting through his shirt where the bullet blowed clean through him. I never shot nobody before but I had to do it. He had that gun and he would of shot us. I had to do it. God damn it to hell there wasn't nothing else to do and Jesus, I had to shoot. Jesus Christ! Things happened so fast and I had to shoot and we had to run. I had to shoot that guard or git shot myself and Christ Almighty if it had been me with the Tommy gun I'd of had to turn around and let the Sheriff have it and it would of been me shot down like Clyde was. God knows I was lucky and I was lucky to find that coup waiting fer the red light to change and I'll be lucky again and I'll git in the clear I know damn well. I'll shoot it out if them punks ever catch up with me and I'll make my break again like I done already and they won't catch me asleep in broad daytime like they done in the hills. I'm just as sure of that as I am that big blue moon will keep shining down to show me the way through the woods. They won't never catch Pat Strickland and they won't never plunk me in jail fer ninety-nine years to hoe potatoes on a prison farm. . . .

Pat stopped again, out of breath. He had been running steadily, plunging through the underbrush, and it was very quiet when he halted in a patch of moonlight beside a tree. His tan shirt was dripping wet and was stuck to his shoulder where the gash was; it stanched the wound and now there was no bleeding. He leaned against the tree, listening, and this time he heard a progressive humming sound and suddenly saw a flash of light, to the north of him and only a hundred yards away. Pat's mouth opened soundlessly and he drew back close against the tree. The lights of an automobile moved swiftly along a road; he heard the swish of tires on gravel.

By God, there's a road running side by side of the river and here I'm trapped in a strip of woods just a few hunderd yards wide between the river and the road. I got to git across to the other side and quick as hell before them Laws git out of their car and begin to beat back toward me through the woods. But Jesus, if I cross the river I'll come to the east-west highway just a mile or so beyond and there's plenty Laws there and they'll git me sure. I got to turn north and I got to cross that there road. . . .

Pat turned around and trotted among the trees toward the place where he had seen the automobile headlights. He stumbled over a root and nearly fell. He ran against a tree, jarring his shoulder, and then he realized that it was dark. He looked overhead for the moon and saw no sign of it in the black sky.

My luck is still holding and thank God fer that stormcloud that come up so sudden and hid out the moon. I can git across to the woods on the other side without they see me and all I got to watch out fer is if that car comes back or another follows it along the road while I'm crossing of it.

He came to a barbed-wire fence, saw it just before he walked into the wires. He was aware of the lighter tone of the road in the blackness ahead of him. As he climbed the fence he felt a cool wind drying the sweat on his face; he heard the rustle of the wind in the trees and smelled a freshness in the air that had not been there before.

Any minute now it's coming on rain and that will mean my tracks will show plain as hell and they can trail me when day comes on. And when day comes on I got to be plenty far away. I can't hide out in these here woods and I got to make the Canadian before day.

Across the fence Pat broke into a run, hurdled a ditch on the opposite side of the road and stopped with his hand out, feeling for a fence, expecting each instant a burst of searching light from an automobile on the road. His hand touched a fencepost, clutched it with relief, and he put his foot on the bottom strand of wire and vaulted over. He ran on, stumbling over rough ground, and he was still on open land. His ankles turned in furrows and he gasped for painful breath. His feet caught in plants, nearly tripping him, and he knew that he was running across a cotton field. There might be a half mile of it, a hundred acres of it, and he was in the open. He felt a cold splash on his forehead.

Now the rain is coming and thank God fer it. In the rain the lights won't come this far if a car goes by. I'm safe from sight but still and all my feet leave clear tracks in this soft topsoil. . . .

The rain came down steadily, the water beating noisily on the leaves of the cotton plants, on the clodded black earth. It hurt Pat to breathe, but he could not stop running.

I got to go on and I got to git into the woods again. I got to make the Canadian somehow. I got to git back to the hills and find Belle. We can hide out somewheres in the hills and hell, I know places not like Cedar Gully where they won't never find us and we can make camp fer a month and maybe two. We can live on squirrels and rabbits and roasting ears and then some night we can git us a car and head West. As soon as the hunt is over we can head West and we'll git away and them punks won't never catch us. We'll head out West, me and Belle, and we'll lay up safe this winter, maybe in California.

Pat stopped running, just in time. Ahead of him was a fence of bare poles and beyond it, perhaps a hundred yards away, he saw a light. He crouched by the fence, the rain beating down on his face. The light was a steady warm glow through the rain.

That light comes from a coal-oil lamp and I reckon it's a house yonder and the farmer who works this cotton and maybe he's got a car. That's about the one chance I got and I got to take it. I got to git me a car and leave these river bottoms behind me and I got to git on the road to Ada and the Canadian. Sure as hell that's all there is fer me to do and I'll take that chance.

Pat climbed over the fence and walked slowly toward the light, the rifle ready in his hands. He came to another fence, of pickets, and walked along it until he found a gate. The hinges squeaked, and then his feet made a sucking noise as he walked along a muddy path to the house. A woman's voice called shrilly: "Who's that?" Pat set his jaw and walked on toward the house.

"Now you can't have no more hosses," the woman said. "You already took every hoss we got. Fred, you go tell 'em that."

"Who's out there?" a man's voice asked. "You already took our hosses." Pat heard a heavy tread on the floor inside and a man came to the door as Pat climbed the two wooden steps to the porch.

"You'll never catch that feller a night like this," the man said.

"I don't want no hoss," Pat said. "You-all got a car?"

"I can't let you drive my car into them river bottoms a night like this and git it mired. No, sir!" The farmer did not open the screen door. He stood peering at Pat, at the gleam of light on the barrel of his rifle.

"You got a car, though?" Pat asked.

"I got a light delivery truck, but I told you . . ." The man's mouth dropped open and he looked at the barrel of the rifle, pointed at him now.

"Git it," Pat said.

"You don't belong to no posse," the farmer said. "Say, you're . . ."

"That's right," Pat said. "Git that car."

"My God," the woman said. "Fred, is it *him?*"

"It's him, all right."

"I ain't waitin' long," Pat said. "Where's that truck?"

"In the barn, Mister."

"Fred, don't you give it to him." Pat saw the woman in the glow of light behind her husband. She was wearing a quilted kimono over a cotton nightgown. She walked aggressively into the light, then saw the rifle in Pat's hands. She screamed, catching her husband's arm with both her hands.

"Shut her up," Pat said, moving the rifle forward. The farmer put one hand over her mouth, the other around her waist, but she jerked her head free and stared at Pat.

"He's got red hair," she said. "They said he had red hair."

"Come on out to the barn," Pat said. "Bring that lamp."

"The rain will put it out, Mister."

"You got a flashlight, then?"

The man nodded and Pat said grimly, "Git it." He stepped forward and opened the door. Standing in the parlor of the farmhouse, water dripped steadily from his clothes to the floor. He kept the farmer in sight as he took a foot-long flashlight from a drawer.

"Out the back way," Pat said. "Step on it."

The woman flattened herself against the wall as Pat passed her. "You keep your mouth shut, lady," he said.

They followed the glow of the flashlight to the barn and Pat held it while the farmer slid back the doors. The delivery truck was last year's model and in good condition. Pat nodded in satisfaction.

"Git in and back her out," he said, and stood aside, holding the light on the farmer as he climbed in and started the engine. When the truck was out in the rain Pat got in beside the farmer. In the dashboard light the man's face was sallow.

"I'm going to let you drive," Pat said.

"Me? Say, Mister, don't make me go with you. Say, I'll keep my mouth shut. I won't . . ."

"You bet you'll keep your mouth shut," Pat said. "Call to your wife."

"Call *her*? Now see here." The man swallowed, his eyes wide and fearful in the dim dashboard light.

"Tell her to keep her mouth shut," Pat said. "Tell her you're going with me and if I git caught up with I'll let you have it. Tell her if she wants you back to keep her mouth shut and forget the license number of this here truck. Understand?"

The man called in a shaky voice: "Sweets, I got to go with him."

Pat screwed up his mouth as if to spit.

"Don't say nothing, Sweets, please," the farmer pleaded. "Don't tell 'em where I've gone. He says he'll kill me. Don't tell 'em the license number, please. Do you hear?"

The woman stood in the doorway, moaning, her face filmed by the rain.

"Listen, Sweets, I ain't kidding," Pat said hoarsely. "If you behave I ain't going to hurt him. But if you don't!"

The woman put one hand to her face and her voice said thinly, "Fred!"

"Okay, Fred, drive on," Pat said. The man's foot trembled on the clutch and the car moved forward jerkily.

"Which way you going, Mister?"

"I got to go to Ada — by a back road. You take me there and you take me straight. If it comes to shooting the first slug goes to you and I mean just that."

"Yes, sir." The man turned left into the lane. "There's a road to Ada that turns off over by Tishomingo."

"How far?"

"A couple of miles. Maybe more."

"All right. Step on it." Pat leaned the rifle between his knees and took out the forty-five, easier handled in the close quarters of the cab. They turned off the lane onto the road that ran parallel to the river, the road the police car had passed on.

"If anybody tries to stop us, step on the gas," Pat said. He felt in his pocket for a cigarette and took out the package. It was soaked through. "Got a cigarette?"

The farmer shook his head. "Sorry, Mister." His voice trembled and he cleared his throat loudly after speaking.

Pat grinned. "If you behave yourself and if we're lucky you'll git back to Sweets, all right. Just take it easy. I got no wish to hurt you. Say, I've got a wife myself."

But she's a real wife. She's a woman with some spunk to her, Belle is, and she rates better than most men. If she was driving now I'd feel a lot easier.

"Yonder's the turn-off, Mister."

"Okay." Pat bent forward, looking along the road. He saw no lights. The car swerved around the turn and Pat leaned back with a sigh.

"Headed north again," he said. "Open her up, Freddie." He laughed. "Yeah, open her up. Maybe you'll see Sweets again, after all."

Belle

❧   ❧

IT must be even worse fer old Crosby. He built this old house
himself and added to it when he got married and when the boys
was born and he always lived here since way back in the beginning when he come to Oklahoma from Arkansas. It sure
must be worse fer him to leave it than it is fer me but still and all
it gives me a low-down feeling. It's only been four years fer me
but now it seems like forever and it seems like I've always been
wife to Pat and living here with him and old Crosby.

The rain had stopped before dawn and there was bright
morning sunshine drying the trees and the ground. They were
moving the furniture out of doors to be stowed in the trucks
when they arrived. Crosby had carried out the mattress from
Belle's room and placed it on the porch and Belle was taking the
bedstead apart. Billy sat on a chair by the window, watching
her, with sunlight on his white hair and his blue eyes round and
solemn.

This bed was new then when I come here and Billy was born
in it here in this room and Pat always slept with me here in this

room and it sure was lonesome when he went away and it will sure be lonesome to be in another room without everything to remind me. That very first night we had a jug of corn whisky and Crosby sat with us drinking it till all hours and we like to never got him out of the room so we could go to bed together and that was what we was after. And I still want to just as bad as I did then that first time with Pat and on a night like last night when we could lay in the moonlight and then when the storm come up and there was lightning and rain beating hard on the roof and he could hold me tight. I got to have him back again with us and there just ain't nothing to do but pray that we can git him off and all that money will do it fer us.

"Bam-bam-bam," Billy said.

"Honey, can't you think of nothing else to do but play with that little gun?"

"Bam-bam. Squirl dead, Mom. Squirl killed dead."

"I reckon he's just as good a shot as his Maw and Paw," Crosby said from the doorway. "I ain't heard him miss yet. . . . You know, the hunting is pretty good over toward Boggs. That's what they tell me."

"You hear that, Billy?" Belle said. "You can shoot you lots of squirrels. But I wish he wouldn't always be thinking of his little gun, Crosby."

"He takes after his Dad."

"That's just the part I don't want him to take after."

"He gits it from you too, Belle. You're the best woman rifle-shot I ever seen."

"It was Pat taught me how."

"Uh-huh. Belle, what is there fer me to do now?"

"Did you load everything out of the barn?"

"It's all in the truck. I'll have to come back some other time and haul that corn out of the crib. I hope we can make as good a crop over to Boggs as we done here this year."

"We'd ought to take along that new well-rope and bucket."

"That's right. We shore ought. I'll git it." Crosby put on his faded hunting-cap for the short walk through sunlight to the well.

If we could just take the house with us too like we can take the well-rope and bucket and if we could just take this room and these four walls where so much has happened then I wouldn't care where we moved off to. I won't never have another window where the moonlight will come into just like this one and I won't never have wallpaper where I counted every flower like I done this here when Billy was born and when I was laying there waiting in between the pain and Pat was setting in the kitchen with a jug and a lot more scared than I was and coming to the door ever so often to look at me with sweat standing out on his face and that red hair rumpled. I know I counted every one of them flowers on the paper and now I don't remember how many but I sure did know then. I wonder what the new room will be like and Crosby says it's a house with three rooms just like this here but it couldn't be just like this here. I know every board that creaks and every place that's liable to leak in a rainstorm and every window that sticks when the wood swells and every tree in the yard and just about every stalk in the cornfield. And I know which way the wind blows to make the chimney smoke and I know where to look fer hen eggs in the barn and that special place in the hay where that Plymouth Rock hen always goes and her special cluck when she's laid an egg and I never seen a hen who laid more than she does. All that I got to find out all over again at the new place and I got to start out all over again and without Pat and it just couldn't be the same. If we can just only git him off and git him back that's all in God's world I want. If we can git him off, God, I won't ask another thing, not never. . . .

Belle heard the screech of the well-winch and through the window she could see Crosby stooping to unfasten the rope from the bucket, with his thin figure bent like a jackknife.

I'll miss just looking out the window at the old well and I'll miss the shape of that ridge and the sun rising over it and I'll miss the color of it when it sets t'other side. But we been here a long time and Crosby since nineteen-two, and it will be kind of exciting to move off somewheres else, if only Pat was here moving with us. I wonder what the wallpaper is over yonder and maybe we can git it papered new and I'll pick something out with lots of flowers and maybe pink and it will be like living in a candy box. And it'll be a new kitchen to put the dishes in and the windows will look out on something else and maybe we'll

like it right fine. And it's a new town to go to and a new store
to buy at and it ain't so far from home as Aldine. But I'll miss the
store in Aldine and we always done our business with Jack
Wheeler and I don't know will I like the new store and I don't
know will I like Boggs. It ain't as big as Aldine and it's a long
ways from Mehuskah.

"Belle," Crosby called. "I see them trucks comin'."

He was standing by the well with his hat in his hand and the
sunlight full on his thin white hair. She went nearer the window
and saw two khaki-colored trucks turning into the lane. Crosby
walked past the window, turning his head to grin at her, and
she went out on the porch. Two men got out of the first truck.

"Howdy," Crosby said. "I reckon you're from the Gov'-
ment?"

"You the family movin' over to Boggs?"

"That's right. This here is our b'longings and there's still some
sticks in the house."

The men went to work and Belle stood on the porch where
she could watch them load the furniture on the trucks — the
bedsteads and the oaken cupboard and the bird's-eye maple
dresser, the mahogany what-not that had belonged to Crosby's
wife, the mounted stag's head with one eye missing, the plow
and harrow and the coops with the chattering chickens in them.
In the second truck the two horses were loaded and Crosby led
them up an incline of boards into the truck. Billy sat on the
mattress behind Belle, watching with his round, solemn eyes.
Belle sighed and went into the house.

And now it's so empty that the smell is even different and it
ain't the same house at all it used to be with the furniture here. It
smells empty now and dusty and it looks so small, too. It just
ain't the same and it makes me heartsick to look at it and I'll be
pleased when we're on our way and I can go hard to work set-
tling in the new place. But we got to take that stove along or we
won't have no supper tonight and I'll tell Crosby.

"Crosby!" She went to the window. "Crosby, the cook-stove
is still here."

"We'll come after it, Belle."

She sighed and returned to the porch just as an automobile

turned from the road into the lane, a car with a United States license and two people in the front seat.

It's that city feller and I believe that's Jay's schoolmarm with him. Yes, that's who it is, all right. I don't see what business they got with us now that we done sold our land and all that and we're moving out like we promised him to.

Belle went down the steps to meet the car, taking the dust-cloth from her head.

"Hello there," Neil Smith called.

"Howdy, you-all."

"How are you, Mrs. Strickland?" Leona said.

"I'm fine, Miss."

"We drove out to see how you were getting on," Neil said. "Wanted to make sure the trucks got here all right."

"You see 'em there, and we're about ready to go," Belle said. "Crosby, don't you see we got company?"

Neil got out of the car and helped Leona to the ground. She wore a pale blue scarf over her black hair, tied beneath her chin, and a yellow sweater and linen skirt.

She sure is a good-looking woman and I reckon that's why Jay can't keep away from her. I don't blame him fer that because she is sure handsome, but still and all she's just a no-account little big-town girl and she ain't got nothing in her head but clothes and picture shows and I wouldn't wonder she can't even boil coffee.

"You know, I've been looking for a belt like that one," Leona said.

Belle glanced down at the beaded belt around her waist. "A Creek woman give it to me — Christine Paul."

"Yes, I know her. Emma Paul's mother. Is that your little boy?"

"Yes, that's Billy."

"Say, he's a big boy. How old are you, Billy?"

"He's three," Belle said.

"Why, he'll be going to school pretty soon. And he's big for his age, isn't he?"

"He's going to be a big man like his daddy, all right," Crosby said, leaning over to pick the boy up.

"I'm so sorry about your husband, Mrs. Strickland," Leona said.

"Uh-huh," Belle said, looking at her coldly. "But you don't need to fret yourself about Pat. We're going to git him out of jail and bring him home."

"You're going to get him out of jail?"

"Sure we are. We got a big-time lawyer."

Leona looked at Neil, then her eyes turned back to Belle, with an expression Belle did not understand. "Then you mean you haven't heard about it?"

"Heard about what?"

"Your husband broke out of jail."

"What's that you say?" Crosby moved nearer. "Did you say Pat made a break?"

"Yes. Last night."

Oh Jesus God what did he go and do it fer, just when we had a big-time lawyer and was going to git him off free and he knowed we was going to git a lawyer and bring him home from Texas and why did he go and do it? Oh, if Pat only wasn't like that and he'll take and do anything that comes into his head and he don't never stop to think. He's just reckless and wild and he'll do whatever he takes a mind to and he knowed we had a big-time lawyer and he talked it over with Jay and it was all settled and he knowed it. . . .

"Here's a chair," Neil said. "Why don't you sit down a minute."

Belle raised her eyes; everyone was looking at her. She drew a deep breath. "Tell us about it."

"It was on the radio last night and the morning paper had it," Leona said. "He broke out of the Jackville jail and got away."

"If Pat broke out you can depend on it he got away," Crosby said. "That's Pat."

He got away and it means he'll be hunted again and this time not no big-time lawyer will do a mite of good. Now he's got to stay hid out and like Jay said before we have to git him out of the state and he won't never come home to live with me and Billy in the new house over to Boggs and he'll have to hide out in the hills all over again and we're back where we was only worse off even than we was then. . . .

"Have you got that newspaper with you?" Crosby asked.

Leona looked at Neil. "No — No, I don't think so. Have we, Neil?"

"I left it back in Aldine," Neil said, biting his lip. "I remember I did."

"I wonder if Jay knows about it," Crosby said.

"Yes, he knows." Leona glanced at Crosby, then at Belle. "He was with me yesterday evening and we heard about it on the radio."

"Now, why didn't he let us know?" Crosby said.

Jay knowed it since last night and he ain't told us and we ain't heard from him at all and the first thing he ought to done was to come here and tell us. But I know Jay feels most as bad as I do. Pat is his only brother and they always been so thick and Jay would do pretty near anything fer Pat and Pat would do the same fer him. But still and all he knowed it all last night and since yesterday evening and you'd think he'd come and tell us.

"Belle, I want to talk to you," Crosby said. He took her arm and they moved over beside the oak tree and the old man leaned against its trunk with his hands in his pockets, staring out over the cornfield.

"Belle, I don't know what to do. Do you reckon we ought to go on over to Boggs?"

"I just can't think, Crosby. I don't know. What do you say?"

"If we move over to Boggs how in hell will Pat ever find us? I don't know what to say."

"I wish Jay was here. Crosby, why do you reckon Jay didn't come and tell us last night? Why do you reckon?"

"Honey, I got no idear. You'd think Jay would do that, you sure would."

"Look here, Crosby, it ain't no use to stay here in the valley. Pat wouldn't come back here. He'll look to find me off in the hills and I know places to go and look fer him and I know whereabouts he'd leave a message and whereabouts I can leave a message fer him, and not in Cedar Gully never again."

"What I hope is Pat went down Mexico way," Crosby said. "He'll be better off if he done that."

"I ain't so sure," Belle said. "I reckon Pat will head back home to the hills. . . . Crosby, look here, it ain't no use to stay in the valley. We got to move, sure enough, and let's go ahead with it."

"I can't but say yes. I reckon like you said it ain't no use."

It ain't no use of nothing the way things is and we can just move over to Boggs and we'll git ourselves settled in the new house and then I'll take off into the hills and I'll git some of that money off'n Jay and I'll find Pat sure enough and with money in his pocket he can clear out of this part of the country and go somewhere it's safe and I reckon like he said California is a good place and in time me and Billy will go out that way too and we'll meet up with Pat and he can git him a good job and use another name and we'll just have to say good-by to the hills fer all our days. It ain't no use of nothing else and that's what we'll do.

"Them trucks is full loaded, Belle," Crosby said. "Suppose you ride off in one of 'em and I'll drive our truck over to Boggs?"

"Whatever you say, Crosby."

Belle walked back to Leona and Neil. "Well, Mister, we're ready packed and fixing to start out," she said. "This here farm is yours now and you can go ahead and cover it up with water."

"I don't like to move you people off," Neil said. "But that's progress. You won't know this part of the country a few years from now."

"I reckon I won't want to neither," Belle said, and turned away. "Come along, Billy."

"Mommy, where my bam-bam?"

"What you want, honey?"

"My bam-bam, Mommy."

"Your little gun? I packed it away fer you, honey. You can have it when we git to Boggs. We're going off to a new home, Billy, and they's lots of squirrels yonder and you can hunt 'em with your bam-bam gun and I'll make you a squirrel pie and a little suit out of the squirrel skins and a little squirrel tail fer a feather on your hat. Won't you be high and mighty, though?"

Belle lifted the boy to the seat of the truck, where the driver was already waiting, and climbed up beside him. She settled herself with Billy in her lap and resolutely turned her head and did not look back as the truck drove away from the farmhouse. On the floorboard at her feet was a newspaper and Belle pushed it away with one toe. She saw that it was a copy of the *Mehuskah Clarion and Bee* and the headline caught her eye: OUTLAW ESCAPES FROM TEXAS JAIL. She bent and snatched up the paper. *Pat Strickland, Oklahoma desperado and bankrobber, escaped from jail here today after killing the Sheriff and a prison guard as he fought off pursuing officers.*

Pat, Pat! *Killing the Sheriff and a prison guard as he fought off* . . . killing the Sheriff and a guard. . . . He killed them. Pat killed two men. But he couldn't and it just ain't true. I know it ain't true. . . . *After killing the Sheriff and a prison guard as he fought off pursuing officers.* I know it ain't true. Pat wouldn't kill nobody. He just wouldn't. He just couldn't. But it says *Jackville, Texas, (AP)* and my God *Pat Strickland, Oklahoma desperado and bankrobber* — and Pat ain't no desperado and he's just only wild and reckless but he wouldn't kill nobody — *escaped from jail here today after killing the Sheriff and a prison guard as he fought off pursuing officers.* . . . It can't be like that, it just can't be, and I know Pat wouldn't kill nobody and it's mixed up somehow and it just can't be the truth, but he's so wild and reckless and maybe without thinking, maybe just to save himself, maybe he just had to do it and maybe without he thought he had to shoot. . . . *The prison break occurred just after the prisoners had been given their supper at six o'clock, when Strickland and his cell-mate, Clyde Winter, who was Strickland's companion in the hold-up of the Public State Bank ten days ago, overcame a guard and seized guns.* . . . It was that other one put him up to it like he put him up to robbing that bank and it was him killed them men. I know it was him and they blame it onto Pat. That's what it is. . . . *In a bloody gunfight Winter was killed.* . . . Oh, Jesus, was Pat hurt? It don't say. It just says he got away and I reckon was he hurt it would say so. They'd brag on it if he was shot. . . . *After a long chase Strickland eluded officers near the Red River and up until late tonight Texas police had been unable to locate his trail.* . . . Then he got clean away and he ain't hurt and he's heading back to the hills and I'll see him again. I'll find him and I'll go off into the hills and find him and I'll know whether it's true he killed them men. But I know it ain't true and it was that other one done it, I know, and anyhow Pat got clean

away and he ain't hurt and he'll come home again to the hills
and I'll go off and find him. But now it just ain't no use because
they'll lay it onto him he killed them two men and now it
wouldn't be ninety-nine years in the Pen, it would be . . . Oh
God, it would be just the end of everything and all the money
we got wouldn't git him off free and no big-time lawyer could
do it and it's just too late fer that, but still we can use that money
to git him away safe and he can go off to California and have a
different name and git himself a good job and Billy and me will
go out yonder and maybe someday we'll have that little stucco
house he wanted and we'll forget all about Pat Strickland and
he'll be somebody else and I'll be somebody else and we'll say
we come from somewheres far off like Kansas or Louisiana. . . .

"Say, ma'am, that feller wants you, it looks like. He give me
a hail."

"What's that?" Belle crumpled the newspaper in her hand.
The truck was grinding to a stop and the driver motioned back-
ward with his thumb. Belle looked out and recognized Jay's old
car on the road and saw Jay getting out of it.

That's why Jay didn't come out and tell us because he knowed
about them saying Pat killed two men and he didn't want to
tell us about it and that's just like Jay. But I know he don't believe Pat done it. He knows Pat wouldn't ever kill nobody.

"Jay, I only just found out. I just seen the *Clarion*."

"Where is Crosby, Belle?"

"He's coming in the other truck. We're headed fer Boggs,
Jay."

"Well, look here, you and Billy come git out and ride with
me and I'll drive you over yonder."

"All right, Jay."

He put up his arms and lifted Billy down to the ground. They
walked back to Jay's car and the truck started on.

"I heard the news last night," Jay said, starting the engine. "I
wanted to give you another night of peace, Belle. It sure is a
terrible thing."

"Jay, you know Pat didn't do it. They just want to lay it on
him that he killed them men."

"I'm sure hoping he didn't do it, Belle."

"But, Jay! Don't you know Pat wouldn't kill nobody?"

"Not unless he plain had to. But it sure is a terrible thing and I don't know what there is to do, Belle."

"But, Jay, we got to git him out of this part of the country, like you said before."

"I reckon so."

"Well, we can do it, can't we?"

"We can sure enough try."

"Jay, you scare me. Now you don't think Pat killed them men, do you? Jay, you know he didn't!"

Jay glanced at her briefly, then turned his eyes back to the road. "Of course he didn't, Belle. Pat wouldn't harm nobody."

"I know he wouldn't. They just want to lay it on him, Jay."

"That's right. That's the way the po-lice work."

"But Pat got clean away, Jay. The *Clarion* said he got clean away and he'll come back here to the hills and we can take and give him that money, Jay, and he can slip off to California."

"Belle, honey, listen to me."

"Yes, Jay?"

"I hate to tell you, but it ain't so sure Pat got clean away. It looks like they got him trapped. He had to leave his car and take off afoot in the Washita River bottoms and they aim to track him with bloodhounds."

"Oh, dear God!"

"It was on the radio and the afternoon paper had the story today. . . . But don't you worry, Belle, they ain't caught him yet."

"But he's afoot then, Jay?"

"Yes, he's afoot."

"Oh, I feel so bad. . . . Jay, it's just the end of everything and I swear I don't know what to do."

"That poor Pat," Jay said. "He just ain't never growed up, and it sure is terrible to see him in such trouble and I wish to hell I was with him right now. He always had that devilment in him but he sure ain't bad and it busts me up to have it happen this way. How did Crosby take it, Belle?"

"Jay, he don't know."

"He don't know!"

"He knows Pat made a break but he don't know the rest. He don't know they're trying to lay it on him fer them two men that feller Clyde Winter shot."

"We got to tell him about it."

"I didn't know until I seen the paper, Jay."

"Did you read that there editorial, Belle?"

"No, where is that?"

"On the inside. They call it 'Hillbilly Hero.'"

Belle opened out the newspaper on her lap and Billy playfully began to slap at the spread pages. "Now, Billy, don't you do that. Be still, now."

This here is it. . . . *The near-by hills have bred yet another bad man, Pat Strickland, the Public Enemy Number One of the Southwest. Strickland, facing trial for armed robbery, broke out of jail and killed two men yesterday in Jackville. . . .* They all try to lay it onto him. They don't want to give him a chance and it's like Jay says the papers is mostly full of lies. . . . *In the annals of the Southwest there have been many celebrated gunmen — Jesse James, Billy the Kid, the Dalton Boys — whose exploits have filled the pages of romantic narrative, but today's criminal is a different and more vicious product. He kills venomously for the joy of it and he skulks in the hills like an outlaw panther, and Pat Strickland is one of these — cruel, vicious and quick to kill. Born to be a troublemaker. . . .* Now it ain't fair. It's just mean and cruel to say that about Pat and to lay it onto him when it couldn't be the truth. . . . *It is a sad commentary that a criminal of the Strickland type should be a sort of hero in the hills that bred him — a hillbilly hero. For there is nothing heroic about such a killer; there is none of the Robin Hood in him. He is a thief and a killer and an enemy of society. Pat Strickland is the brother of Jay Strickland, who has been attempting to stir up trouble among the tenant farmers of this district with talk of union action at a time when bumper crops and farm prosperity seem sure. That is the type of men who are bred in our near-by hills — criminals, agitators, enemies of society. The W.P.A. project to build a lake in the hills and open up this last stand of the Southwestern outlaw is a worthy one, but we believe that the only way to deal with our anti-social criminals is to shoot before they shoot and kill before they kill.*

. . . It just ain't fair to do that to Jay and it just ain't fair to use Pat to low-rate Jay and to lie about Pat the way they do and to lie about Jay. It's mean and cruel.

"Jay, it makes me feel bad to see what they done. It sure does make me feel bad the way they use Pat to low-rate you."

"Just forget about it, Belle. I shouldn't of showed it to you. But it made me burning-up mad when I read it, and I can tell you they ain't going to stop my work that way, and that's what they're after."

"Pat ain't like that, Jay. Everybody that knows Pat knows he ain't like that. He's just wild and reckless and I know he didn't shoot them men."

"Of course he didn't, Belle."

"Jay, tell me what you think, and tell me straight out. Is Pat going to git away? Have they really got him trapped down yonder?"

"I only know what the paper said."

"Jay, what do you reckon, I mean if they find him, what do you reckon they'll do when they catch him, I mean, if they do?"

"Don't you trouble yourself about that, Belle."

"But would they shoot him, Jay?"

"I hope Pat gits clean away and he's smart enough to do it. Don't you worry about Pat. He'll git away from 'em, sure enough."

"I sure do hope so."

But Jay don't think that and he's just saying it fer me and he thinks they'll catch up with Pat and they won't wait fer nothing and they'll blow at him with sawed-off shotguns and they'll shoot without waiting fer no questions just like they laid it on him that he killed them two Laws.

"Belle, this here is Boggs," Jay said.

They were on flat land between two low ridges and the thirty houses of Boggs were spread over a hundred acres in the valley. The road widened out to the main street and on the right as they entered the town was a canvas tent with a sign *The Traveling Cinema.*

"It ain't as big as Aldine," Belle said.

"No it ain't, fer a fact."

"Billy, we're coming to your new home," Belle said, tightening her arms around the boy's body. "You just watch out close and you'll see it."

"See new home," Billy said.

"That's right, see new home. Jay, we turn off on the first road north after we pass the river."

"All right, Belle."

The car crossed the river on a narrow bridge and mounted a slow incline with trees growing to the road's edge. They entered the shadow of the woods spread across the road, the silence of the woods, and Belle held her son tightly.

Somewheres in the woods down along the Washita Pat is hid out and they got bloodhounds after him and hunderds of men beating through the trees with guns just to catch poor Pat. If I only knowed. . . .

"Jay, turn right here."

"Yes, Belle." Jay turned upon a narrow dirt road that mounted into the woods and the tires slithered on soft clay.

"Jay, please, just as soon as you find out anything let me know."

"Sure I will."

"I mean don't wait till the next day like you did. I want to know right off, Jay."

Jay nodded, and both of them watched the road. The car ran along beside a rail fence, then turned a bend — and on their right was cleared land and a house set far back.

"This is it," Belle said. "Billy, this is your new home."

The house sets solid on that brick foundation and like Crosby said it's in pretty good repair. It needs screens put on, though, and that porch roof sags some. And it's an upland farm and we won't make the crops we did back yonder in the valley. The barn is solid too and that house is right nice, all considered. First off I'm going to take and clean it good, before we put the furniture in. I'm going to take and put myself to work and I'm going to try to take the heaviness out of me and I'm going to stop fretting about Pat and I'm going to try to hope and hope and hope. . . .

$\mathscr{P}at$

❦   ⚜

PRETTY soon now it will come dark and I'll start out again and by midnight I'll be home in the hills. But I got to do something about Fred. I don't know what. I sure can't take him back to the hills along of me.

Among the trees of the riverbank Pat could not see the setting sun, but the color of it filtered over the sky above and was reflected in the slow, malignant waters of the Canadian, in pale pink color edging the wide areas of darkening water. It was very still; occasionally he heard a fish flip to the surface, heard the resonant splash, sounding wet as raindrops. The current of the river swept away from a bank of red sand and was swift close inshore, swift and very deep there where the water lapped at the downthrust dead branch of a half-uprooted tree. Pat sat on a tree stump a few yards from the river with a whisky bottle leaning against the stump between his feet, and Fred Oliver, his pale hostage, crouched cross-legged at the base of a liveoak tree. The green leaves, the feathery underbrush, pressed close about them and there was a sense of complete shelter and safety there on the riverbank, as if there were a roof overhead instead of the gently swaying boughs, as if there were four solid walls around them. Pat watched the twilight settle over the river, shining silver on the blood-red water, creeping away into the shadow of the riverbank, the darkening shadow that closed in around them. The brighter river became more and more the focus of their eyes, and both of them watched the swirling current.

Soon as it gits dark I'm on my way. I'll sneak back to the edge of the hayfield where we left the truck and I'll drive back across the field to the road and I'll turn east again, east to the hills. . . .

Fred stirred, and Pat saw him take a package of cigarettes from his pocket.

"Don't strike no match," Pat said sharply.

The man put the package away with shaking hands and Pat stared at him morosely. He picked up the whisky bottle and took another drink. Then he grinned sourly. "Say, does Sweets know you keep your liquor hid out in the truck?"

Fred shook his head miserably and Pat laughed, then the muscles of his cheeks slowly tightened into a steady, grim expression. He sat and stared at the face of his hostage, becoming a pale blur now in the dusk.

I'm sick of the sight of him always looking at me in that scared way and this has been the longest day I ever put in. He sure is yellow but he come in handy and he saved my neck down yonder on the Washita. And he bought them cigarettes at that roadhouse and Jesus, he was scared, and he knowed I had the forty-five ready and was watching every move he made but he was too damned yellow to take a chance and he bought them cigarettes and come right back to the auto. He come in handy, but now what will I do with him? It's so dark I can't hardly see his face and I reckon it's time to start but I got to start alone. I got no more need of that punk.

Pat stood up and walked two paces nearer the river. He looked down at the water, red-black now, and in the silence heard the ripple of the current around the dead limb of the tree. He heard Fred breathe a deep sigh and glanced at the pale oval of the man's face.

"Git up, Freddie," Pat said.

"Now listen, Mister. . . ." The white face was turned up to Pat. "You wouldn't throw me in the river?"

"Git up," Pat said contemptuously. "That's what I ought to do."

The man struggled to his feet. They were near together, looking at each other, their eyes dark formless holes in their faces. Fred's face was suddenly edged with crimson, with a pale reflection of brilliant light.

"Look," he cried. "Look yonder, Mister."

Pat did not need to turn his head to know that there were lights behind him on the river. His hand clenched the butt of the gun and slowly he pivoted toward the water. The lights danced on the surface of the river, forming crossing lines of crimson. Torches. They were the torches of fishermen in shoal water across the river.

"They're after catfish," Fred said with relief in his voice.

"I reckon. We got to git out of here." Pat put one hand on Fred's shoulder and grinned. "What do you know about that? I was about to leave you go."

"Say, I won't talk to 'em." Fred's voice dribbled from his loose lips. "I won't go near 'em. I promise I won't, Mister."

"You bet you won't," Pat said. "Git started."

They went along a path through the woods, away from the riverbank, and they walked into the orange light of the rising moon. Fred's figure became clearer ahead of Pat, as if seen through colored mist. They were near the edge of the woods, the hayfield beyond. They walked across the open field toward the grove where they had left the truck. The smell of alfalfa was lung-filling and oppressively sweet. Pat still held the flashlight but he did not use it in the open and they stumbled across the field in the shadow of the trees. In among the trees he flashed the light, once, and picked out the truck deep in shadow. Fred was a step ahead of Pat. He had put out one hand to open the door of the truck and he had one foot on the running board. Pat shifted the forty-five in his hand, gripping the barrel.

I hate to do it but I got to. If I leave him go he'll run straight to a telephone and he'll call up Sweets and that will be the tip-off and they'll be laying fer me. I got to do it. That guard in the jail corridor, I had to do that and it was self-defense. It was him or me. And I can't take him back to the hills with me and I can't leave him go. I just got to do it.

Biting his lip, Pat flashed the light and struck, but not with all his force. He brought the gun down on Fred's head, and he fell without a sound at Pat's feet. The light on his face showed his mouth open, showed drops of blood on his forehead.

He couldn't be bad hurt and I reckon in an hour or so he'll come around and by then I'll be safe away and by the time he gits hold of Sweets I'll be back home in the hills. . . .

Pat flicked off the light and stepped over Fred's body. In the truck his hands fumbled with the ignition. Hurriedly he stepped on the starter and flushed the carburetor with gasoline by the choke. The motor hummed, and still choking it, he backed out into the hayfield.

I better not turn on the lights till I'm on the road and I don't want to see that punk laying there. He'll be all right. I didn't hit him hard enough to crack his skull and when he comes around he'll git back to Sweets again and anyhow I'm rid of him now and I can head back to the hills.

Pat drove across the field with only moonlight to guide him to the gate through which he had driven that morning. He missed it by several yards and got out of the car with the flashlight to find and open it. When he had driven through to the road he did not stop to close the gate. He turned on the bright lights and fed gas to the engine. He was traveling over rough road, under construction, and he covered seven miles of it before he reached black-top road and a signpost showing that it was twenty-five miles to McAlester.

That's a laugh. I'll go right by the Pen and turn north toward the hills. Right by the Pen where the bloodhounds are. Right past where I done my time and past that prison candy shop they had me working in. Making fudge in a candy shop, Jesus Christ!

The black-top was in fair condition and Pat drove fast. In half an hour he descended a long incline to McAlester, crossed the Rock Island tracks near the depot, and drove slowly out of town on U.S. 69.

One good place to eat is a mining town and Jesus I am hungry. I don't know why it is but the food is always good in a mining town. I remember the first thing I done when I got out of the Pen was to eat that two-bit plate dinner in that cafe by the depot. Man, it was good, and it would taste like that if I had it now.

Outside of town Pat opened the car up again, but soon there was more construction work to delay him, and black-top road torn into ripples that jarred the car.

I done a little work on this road once. They been working on it off and on fer a long time. I guess it was five years ago I worked on the road gang here because it was a little after that, when I was laying low in the hills, that I run onto Belle. It's funny I don't remember her as a kid when we was at school together. I can't connect her up with none of them skinny little gals, not that big good-looking blond woman with that walk on her like an Indian with a basket on her head and swaying like a willow reed. The first I remember of her is that time at the square dance away back in the hills and I remember I rode there with a quart of corn on my saddle and I had come out of hiding and I sure was lonesome and wanting fer a woman. She had on that pink dress and white shoes and she danced with her skirts held up and them white feet flashing like brook trout striking in that haze of haydust rising up from the floor of the barn. It was "Do-se-do" they was dancing to when I first come in and the fiddle was screeching and whanging and the air just shivered from all them pounding feet. *Do-se-do to your best liking, do-se-do to your best liking, do-se-do to your best liking, you're the one, my darling.* Even the engine is humming that tune and she's running sweet and if it goes on like this I'll be back in the hills sooner than I thought. *Do-se-do and don't you touch her, do-se-do and don't you touch her . . .* That Belle has got guts all right. Right off I tried to kiss her out there on the floor in the hay-smell and she jolted me with a slap of her open hand and she stood there laughing with them freckles shining on her forehead and by Jesus I had to laugh too. *Do-se-do and a little more do . . .* By God there's the Canadian again, and I been traveling faster than I thought. Eufaula is just ahead and fifteen miles more and I'll turn east toward the hills.

The boards of the long wooden bridge over the South Canadian rattled under the speeding car. Pat swung off the narrow bridge and slowed speed on the way down a winding hill road.

At the bottom there was a mile of rough gravel road, then a sharp turn into Eufaula. He drove slowly through the town and at the other end came upon the concrete highway. A few minutes later he crossed a steel bridge over the North Fork of the Canadian.

Inside an hour I'll be halfway home and inside of two I'll see Belle again. *Both hands around to your best like-em, you're the one, my darling* . . . white slippers in the hay, freckles in the lamplight, pink dress spinning, white feet dancing. . . . *Do-se-do and don't you touch her* . . . pale face against mine in the moonlight, soft lips on mine, round arms around me, Jesus Christ! . . . *Do-se-do and a little more do.* . . . Yesterday I was in jail with ninety-nine years of it ahead of me, ninety-nine years of hoeing potatoes on a prison farm, and now I'll see Belle again. Inside an hour I'll be home with Belle. . . . And yonder's the turn-off already and it begins to look like home. I could drive blindfold from here to Aldine. I know every turn of the road and it's the road home and the road to Belle and the road to the hills where I can lay up safe and I guess now I'm in the clear. *Do-se-do and a little more do.* I can't keep that song out of my head. I sure got to sing and that road is just a fiddle string a-humming of it. *Do-se-do* . . . Too bad Fred's liquor is done run out and what kind of a wife is that you got to hide your liquor so she won't know you got it? Who the hell would want a wife like that? When I git home we'll finish off a jug, me and Belle and Crosby. We'll finish off a jug and we'll drive this here truck into a gully and me and Belle will take off into the hills to hide.

The Arkansas River and a steel bridge with the aluminum paint shining in the moonlight; he was nearly home. He turned off the highway onto a wide dirt road where he had to drive more slowly. The scrubby limbs of blackjack oak rose up around him, closed in around him, as the road ascended into the hills, away from the river bottoms into the hills. There were no cars, no filling stations, no signs of commerce or life; only occasionally the light of a farmhouse showed far back in a field. The bright lights ahead of him picked up a square white signpost.

That will be it, Aldine 3 Miles, and I'll take the back road. I don't want to pass through the town and I'll take this here back road.

He turned off a half-mile before he reached Aldine, and he was back on the gravel road a mile beyond Aldine, the road that circled the base of the ridge and led him at last to the valley and the ocher schoolhouse and the ungraded road of red clay that wound through the woods. The road was rough and the ruts were wide and deep. In the bright lights he saw the marks of heavy treads, the tire marks of trucks with great double wheels that had driven heavy-loaded over the soft clay. Near at hand, on the right, he saw a light.

Now there never was a house here. What the hell! Nobody ever lived here at the mouth of the valley. I better slow down and I better be careful. It's a shack yonder and a light in it and that big black thing is sure as hell a steam shovel. Now what the hell does a construction gang want of a steam shovel way out here in the hills?

Pat drove on, leaning forward over the steering wheel to watch the road ahead of him. Entering the deepness of the woods, where the oak trees twined their upper branches in a screen, the moon was shut out and the road was dark; walls of shadow pressed in around him.

Yonder's Jess Cookley's house and he's already to bed and the lights out. I sure better go slow because they might be laying fer me and they might know I got clean away down on the Washita.

Pat strained forward and watched the lights slipping from tree to tree, falling on the swaying stalks of the cornfield. He slipped the car out of gear and let it coast to a stop. Now he heard the sighing of the wind in the drooping leaves of corn, but there was no other sound, and he saw no light beyond the cornfield where the house was. He put the car in gear and drove past the lane. He turned a bend in the road, a hundred yards from the lane, where his lights would be hidden from the house. He snapped off the lights and turned the ignition key. In the silence and the sudden darkness he sat for a moment with his hand caressing the butt of the gun.

I can't just set here. If it's a trap laid fer me I got to take that chance. Dad and Belle and Billy are just across that clearing and by God I'm going after them.

He got out of the car and closed the door as silently as he

could, then walked cautiously back toward the lane, his feet sinking noiselessly in the soft clay. He hesitated at the entrance to the lane.

They sure might be laying fer me there, but by God I ain't come this far and I ain't escaped from that posse on the Washita just to be trapped at my own house. My luck is still holding and I know it and I reckon it's so quiet because they're to bed. But I sure would like to hear a horse whinny or a dog bark or even a hoot-owl yonder in the woods. But I come this far and I got to take a chance and I got to see Belle again. . . .

He walked in the shadow of the cornfield, where he could not be seen from the house, and he walked as softly as he could, from tree to tree along the lane. At the last tree he stopped. His hand was clenched on the gun and he saw the looming form of the house ahead of him. A splatter of moonlight burnished the roof, fell upon a window, and was reflected toward him.

I got to take that chance and I'll walk slow and I'll keep the gun ready and I'm in the open in the moonlight and I can plain be seen now but nothing happens and I reckon I'm just plain too God-damned jumpy. And now I'm on the steps and still they ain't a sound and by God all the windows is closed tight and the door too and in this here heat.

He went on tip-toe upon the porch and across it to a window. Peering through it, he could make out nothing in the darkness. He flattened himself against the wall, drew in his breath deeply, and whistled. The sound was penetrating in the night. He whistled only a few bars and he whistled *Do-se-do*.

But there ain't no answer. They ain't a sound and it's so still and hot and I can't wait no longer and I got to find out and I got to take that chance.

He turned abruptly to the door and threw it open and walked into the blackness of the house. He put out his hand for the table and felt nothing. He walked on three slow steps and his out-stretched hand touched nothingness. Now his eyes were accustomed to the darkness and he could see a little; the brighter rectangles of the windows, a path of moonlight on the floor.

But the floor is bare as a pig's bottom and the table is gone and the chair is gone and that old what-not and the oak cup-

board and there ain't a damned stick in the room. It's empty
and not even that old stag's head. What the hell!

Pat stirred, and the floor creaked underfoot, a startlingly alive
sound. He had left the flashlight in the car. He felt in his pocket
for a match and struck it on his thumbnail. In the flare he saw
the dusty floor, the bare floor. He saw the empty walls and the
soiled wallpaper. He walked through into the next room, a bedroom.

It's empty and it's our room and it's empty. Where is she and
where is Dad and where is Billy and why ain't they here to
meet me? I thought she'd be here waiting and we'd finish off a
jug together and we'd take out into the hills. . . .

Pat breathed through his teeth and the sound was almost a
sob. He walked on and the match burned his fingers and went
out. He struck another as he entered the kitchen and the first
thing he noticed was the round dark hole in the wall, the black
recess of the flue where the stove-pipe had been.

Not even no stove, they ain't left even the stove and all the
furniture is gone and not even no stove. What in hell! Why, this
is home, and it's empty and this is the house I was borned in and
I worked in the cornfield yonder and I killed snakes up the
branch and me and Jay have hunted fox-squirrels in the woods
and fished the creek together and I growed up here and I brung
Belle home here to be my wife and now they're all gone and
without no reason fer it and I got to find out.

Pat walked slowly back through the house and out upon the
porch. He stood looking at the sweeping silver leaves of the
cornfield in the moonlight.

I got to find Belle. There must be some reason fer it and sure
nothing could of happened to 'em and I got to find Belle. I got
to know.

He ran across the porch and leaped over the stone steps to the
ground, then he sprinted along the lane toward the road, running toward the dark shape of the car. He got in and snapped
on the lights, and with the return of brilliance to the familiar
road, to the dark line of trees, he felt more sure of himself.

I'll go by Jess Cookley's house and he sure as hell will know
the why of it and it's plain they moved off somewheres and I

got to know where and I got to know why. Maybe there's been some kind of trouble and I got to know.

He backed the car to the lane and turned around, then he drove very fast back as he had come, over the twisting valley road to Jess Cookley's house. He turned without caution into the lane and drove up to the house.

It's dark too and it's quiet and by God the windows are down and the door is closed. Jesus Christ, what could of happened here in the valley? What in hell could it be!

He jumped out of the car and ran upon the porch. He threw open the door and flashed the flashlight.

Not a stick of furniture, not even a chair and my feet echo like only in an empty house and the bedroom is empty and the kitchen too and where in hell is Jess and his wife and them two kids? And where is Belle and Billy? Sure as hell something has happened here in the valley and I got to find out. I wonder where Jay is and could I find him. Jay will know and he can tell me where Belle is at.

Pat ran back through the house to his car. The motor still was running and he threw the car in gear and drove back to the road. He turned toward the entrance to the valley, driving as fast as he could on the slippery, winding road. When the structure of the steam shovel loomed up out of the night he swung the car toward it, over toward the shack on the bank of the creek. There was still a light, the shaded light of an oil lamp. Pat stopped the car and got out. With the gun in his hand he approached the shack, walking cautiously. He came up to it in the moonlight and his hand touched the smooth boards. He went along the wall to the window and peered in. There was a Negro sitting alone at a table, an oil lamp beside him with a homemade shade of wrapping paper. The Negro was reading the Mehuskah evening newspaper and Pat saw the streamer headline: OUT-LAW TRAPPED IN WOODS.

By God that's me. That's me all over the front page and they still think they got me trapped down yonder on the Washita and I reckon they got bloodhounds on my trail. I don't see no picture and thank God fer that. They ain't got a picture of me to put in the paper.

Pat pulled his hat farther down over his eyes, to conceal his

red hair, and walked around to the door of the shack. He opened
it without knocking and the Negro turned startled eyes, the
whites showing widely.

"Hello," Pat said.

"Yas, suh?"

"What's going on in this here valley?" Pat asked. He remained outside the shack, in shadow, holding the door wide
open.

"You mean heah? Dis camp? We's building a lake, Mistah."

"A lake?" Pat said.

"Yassuh. De W.P.A."

So it's that Goddam lake and I reckon Dad sold out and they
moved away because they aim to make a lake of the valley
and I remember Belle talked about that lake and thank God
there ain't nothing happened to her or Billy or Dad but still I
got to find out where they went. I got to find Belle.

"I'm just passing through," Pat said. "Lookin' fer some friends
of mine."

The Negro nodded, his mouth open, watching Pat.

"Whereabouts are the people that live down the road yonder?" Pat asked.

"Dey done move out. Most everybody done move out dis
yeah valley. It's de re-settle."

"The what?"

"De re-settle."

"Where in hell did they move to?" He was holding the gun
behind his body where the Negro could not see it.

"Diff'ent places. Some ovah yonder way, some ovah yonder."

"Where did Jess Cookley move to, do you know?"

"No, suh. He move off some place. Mistah Smith, he know."

"Where did Crosby Strickland go?" Pat's voice dropped a
little when he spoke his father's name.

"Mistah Stricklan'? He only jus' move out, dis very day. It
had some trouble makin' Mistah Stricklan' move."

"Where did he go to?" Pat asked harshly.

"I couldn't say, Mistah. Mistah Smith, he know."

"Who's this here Smith?"

"He de 'gineer. He de boss man."

"Where do I find him? Come on, I'm in a hurry."

"He live ovah to Aldine City. In de hotel."

Pat abruptly shut the door and returned to the truck. As he turned on the lights he saw the Negro's face at the window. He started the engine and drove on toward Aldine.

I got no time to waste now. I got to find where Belle went to and I got to go after her before day comes on and we got to take out into the hills. I sure got to make time to do it.

On the right of the road the lights flashed on a white sign: ALDINE, POP. 380. On the main street of the town there were only two lights, one in the filling station, the other in the hotel.

They already done took the sidewalks in. That car in front of the hotel, it's got a U.S. license. That's the Government, the W.P.A. That's him all right and he's in yonder and I got to go right in that hotel after him. It's a damn fool chance to take but he knows where Belle is at and I got to find out and I got to find Belle.

Pat drove in behind the car and stopped. He could see into the tiny lobby and an old man asleep in a chair in the office. He put the gun in his pocket and got out on the boardwalk. When he opened the door the old man awoke and sat upright.

"I'm from the lake," Pat said.

"The lake?"

"I'm working over there — one of the foremen."

"Oh, sure, that dam."

"That's right. I want to see Smith."

"I reckon he's in bed asleep." The old man rubbed the palm of one hand over his eyes.

"I got to see him right away. This is important."

"Something wrong over to the dam?"

"Maybe. What's his room number?"

"Fourteen. One flight up."

"Okay." Pat turned toward the stairs.

"Say, what's wrong at the dam?"

Pat did not answer. He went quickly up the stairs, and in the dimly lit corridor that smelled faintly of ammonia he took out the forty-five as he looked for number fourteen on the row of closed doors. When he found it he silently turned the knob and opened the door. A light cord was dangling and he pulled it.

The man in bed was awakened by the light. He threw one arm across his eyes and turned his face to the wall.

"Git up," Pat said quietly. He caught Neil's shoulder and shook it. "Wake up, and don't make no sound. Catch on?"

Neil turned his head and the light fell full in his eyes. Now he was awake. He sat up in bed and his mouth opened when he saw the reflection of light on the barrel of the gun.

"What's the matter?" he mumbled.

"If you open your yap I'll crack your skull," Pat said in a husky voice. "Git up and put your clothes on."

Neil raised his eyes from the gun. Pat stood over him with his shoulders looming broad and threatening in the stained tan shirt. He stood braced with his feet wide apart, with the black hat shading his face except for a fuzz of reddish beard on his chin.

"Who are you?" Neil said. "What goes on?"

"I work on the dam. I'm one of your foremen. Remember me?" Pat put his face closer, and a fantastic grin split his rust-red beard. "You're going to git dressed and you're coming downstairs with me and you ain't going to open your yap. I'm one of your foremen and there's something wrong at the dam and you remember that. Got it?"

"Yes," Neil said, looking at the gun. "I got it."

"Now put on your clothes."

"Listen," Neil said. "If it's money you're after . . ."

"It's you I'm after, Mister. Now git dressed and quit stalling. Here." Pat took some trousers from a chair and tossed them on the bed. "Put on your britches."

Neil's fingers fumbled with the buttons of his pajamas.

"Never mind that. Put your clothes on top. — Come on, we got to hurry."

Neil pulled on the pants over his pajamas, then put on the shirt Pat threw beside him. Pat kicked his shoes toward him and Neil put them on without socks. As he was fumbling with the laces Pat caught his elbow roughly.

"Never mind that, Mister. Come on."

Neil kept looking at the gun and Pat put it in his pocket. Neil's eyes remained on the bulge of the pocket.

"Remember now, I'm your foreman. We're going outside and into your car and drive away. Don't you open your yap, you hear?"

"Yes."

They went together down the creaking stairs and at the bottom they found the old clerk waiting. "Say, Mister Smith, what's wrong at the dam?"

"Nothing," Neil said, barely above a whisper. "It's not important." He walked on beside Pat and out to the boardwalk.

"We'll take your car and you're going to drive," Pat said. "Climb in."

Neil slipped behind the steering wheel and inserted the ignition key. Pat said quietly: "Drive straight ahead. Straight out of town."

"Yes. All right." Neil put the car in gear and glanced helplessly over his shoulder at the hotel.

"I guess with this U.S. license nobody won't stop us," Pat said, grinning. "No, sir, we're on Gov'ment business now."

"What do you want with me?" Neil asked, wetting his lips.

"You're the feller in charge of that Gov'ment job in the valley, ain't you?"

"Yes."

"You done moved all them people out of the valley, they tell me."

"That's right."

"I come back and my home is gone because some little Gov'ment chicken-drop wants to build a lake," Pat said harshly. "God damn it, people ought to mind their own business. Now listen here, whereabouts did you move my wife to?"

"Your wife?"

"Belle Strickland, and my Dad. You moved them out of our home in the valley."

"You're Pat Strickland!" Neil said, turning his head. The car started for the side of the road and he had to spin the wheel to keep out of the ditch.

"Okay, I'm Pat Strickland, all right. Where did my wife and Dad go to?"

"I don't know."

"God damn it, you *got* to know!" One of Pat's hands closed on Neil's wrist with crushing pressure.

"Over by Boggs somewhere," Neil said quickly. "I don't know exactly which farm it is."

"Ain't you any idear?"

"It was a vacant farm and your father bought it. It's a few miles the other side of Boggs — in the hills."

"Maybe I know that farm," Pat said slowly.

"I think I know the road it's on. I don't know the house, but I think I know what road it's on."

"Then step on it. Fer Christ's sake, this car can do better than forty, can't it?"

Neil's foot jammed on the accelerator. "It's on that road north of Boggs," he said. "I'll find it."

"Yeah, I know that road. And maybe I know the house, too." Pat looked out at the moon. "Say, what time is it?"

"It must be about one o'clock."

"That late? Step on it, Smith. We got to cover a lot of ground before daybreak."

It ain't much time and we got to move fast and I got to find Belle and we got to take out into the hills before it gits light. I might of knowed Dad would move some place like Boggs still in the hills because he belongs in the hills and I might of knowed I wouldn't find him nowheres else. But I know where they're at now and I'll find Belle and we just about got time to git away safe before sunup.

The lights danced on the road ahead of them and the shadows rushed crazily toward them. The car pitched and slued in gravel. Moonlight flooded the road, on which there were pools of shadow like moving dark water. The air was fresh and Pat breathed deeply, his head thrown back.

"That air sure feels good," he said, blowing out a deep breath. "I like the feel of it. I like the smell of it. It's good to be back in the hills again. . . . Say, you're only doing fifty."

"There's a curve ahead."

"That's all right. Keep moving."

"When we get to Boggs . . ." Neil began. His voice was only a whisper and when he raised it the sound was unnatural. "When we get to Boggs what are you going to do?"

"I'm going to git my wife," Pat said, and then he looked at Neil closely.

The son of a bitch is scared. He's yellow like that Fred was and I wonder has he come to by now and is he out telephoning to Sweets. I don't know what makes 'em so scared of me and I reckon I just run onto two of 'em who are yellow.

"I ain't going to hurt you, Mister," Pat said. "I don't want to hurt nobody. All I want is to git my wife and git clean away."

And now he takes a deep breath like it was the first time he filled his lungs in a week and I wonder what he thought I would do to him.

Pat laughed. "Keep your mouth shut and do like I say and you won't git hurt. But you behave yourself."

"I will."

Pat lit a cigarette and settled back; a bit of hot ash blew stingingly against the other man's cheek.

"I ain't no killer," Pat said. "I never harmed nobody. All I want is to git away. But there better not nobody stand in the way to stop me."

They drove on in silence, mile after mile through the woods, and in the moonlight each turn seemed familiar, each bend was like the one before. Whenever Neil slowed the pace Pat said: "Come on, open her up."

When they approached Boggs Pat took the forty-five from his pocket and turned his eyes to the road. In the flat land between the ridges the thirty houses of the town were spread out in the moonlight. The road widened and the car rushed upon the main street, past a canvas tent which was dark and unlit. The only light in the town was at the filling station.

"Keep moving," Pat said. "If anybody tries to stop us, keep going."

Neil slowed speed in driving through the town but as soon as they were past the filling station he fed gas again to the engine. They were still on the highway, the gravel highway that ran through a long valley. The land was flat around them; corn and cotton fields were spread out in the moonlight, with beyond the looming dark shapes of the hills.

"It can't be far now," Neil said. He took his foot off the accelerator. "It's a little beyond this bridge we're coming to, on the right."

"Okay," Pat said.

They crossed a narrow bridge over the Illinois River, saw a brief glint of moonlight on the water down below. Then they climbed a grade and near the top the lights revealed a break in the trees, a road opening to their right off the highway.

"This is it," Neil said. He turned off the highway and ahead there was a steep hill. As he shifted to second gear Pat held up his hand. "Hey!"

"What's the matter?"

"Look at that road."

Neil glanced down at the broad tiremarks in the clay. "This is right," he said. "Those are the tracks of our trucks. We moved your family up here today."

"All right, go ahead, but drive careful."

Pat shifted a little to one side and held the forty-five ready.

"It can't be more than five miles," Neil said.

Just five miles and Belle will be waiting there and we got plenty of time before sunup and we'll take out into the hills. It sure has been a weary time since last I seen her and since we was last alone together in the hills but now it's only five miles and we'll be together again. Five more miles and I'll see Belle again. . . .

✿ *Belle* ✿

IT sure is lonesome here and it just ain't the same in this here room and in the moonlight that bird's-eye maple dresser Crosby give us fer a wedding present looks just as strange to me as it did that day he brung it home in the wagon.

Belle lay sleepless on the bed, across which the moonlight cast the barred shadows of the metal bedstead. Moonlight flowed like water into the room and gave softness and bulk to the familiar objects in it, but the room was not familiar.

So much has happened in such a little time and I got up this morning in the same bed but it was in the old house and that house is still home and it don't feel right laying here. I guess maybe it's just only that I'm tired after packing up to move and unpacking again to settle down and with all that other it sure has been a day since that schoolteacher first come out with Mister Smith. That girl has got it in her eye that she wants to git married and I reckon Jay had better watch out fer that city feller even if he can't stack up to Jay. I guess maybe he's smart in the head but he's got no heft to him — not like Pat. . . . I ought not to think about Pat and I tried not to but I can't help it and I can almost hear the sound of them bloodhounds down on the Washita. I know he didn't kill them two men and I wish they wouldn't try to lay it on him that he done it. Pat couldn't never kill nobody. He's kind and he's gentle and he never treats anybody mean. I wish I could just not think about it and it was so easy all day when I was moving furniture and scrubbing floors but now I just can't sleep, I can't sleep, and Pat, Pat, Pat. . . . And his red hair and that chin of his stuck out and that smile of his and them strong muscles and I know he'll git away because he's just got to and he'll find his way back to the hills and I'll be on the watch fer him. . . .

The moonlight brightened in the room, a sudden flash, and Belle held her breath. The light paled, then flashed again. She knew it was caused by the lights of an automobile shining into the window from the road. She lay quite still, hearing the sound of the automobile close at hand now, turning from the road toward the house. Instantly Belle sprang from bed. She snatched up a kimono and ran into the living room of the farmhouse, across it to the door, and as she ran she saw lights through the window and saw that there were two cars coming.

Then it ain't Pat and I might of knowed it wouldn't be him but I got to keep on hoping that he'll git away safe. But maybe it's Jay and maybe he knows something. . . .

She threw open the door and saw a man climbing upon the porch, silhouetted by the lights of the cars behind him. He wore a gray shirt and gray trousers and there was a badge pinned on his shirt over the heart.

"What do you want?" Belle asked.

"Are you Pat Strickland's wife?"

Belle nodded, watching his face, waiting for him to speak. He turned his back. "Drive them cars around behind the house, boys, into the trees," he shouted.

It's po-lice and what do they want of us? Just because I'm Pat's wife and Crosby is his Dad it ain't nothing to them and they come and act like they got a right to do just what they take a want to, without no by-your-leave.

The automobiles hummed in low gear and the bright lights flashed past them and then it was dark.

"Strike a light a minute," the man said.

"What do you want?"

He pushed past her into the room.

"Git out of here," Belle said. "Crosby, wake up! — What are you-all after?"

"Lady, I'm the Sheriff." He struck a match and in its flare saw the oil lamp on the table. He went across to it and removed the glass chimney. As he held the match to the wick the light came from below upon his face, forming insolent shadows on his cheeks.

The door to Crosby's room opened and the old man stepped out with a shotgun in his hands, his white hair in scanty tufts on his head.

"Hey," the Sheriff said, "drop that gun!"

"What comes off here?" Crosby's eyes were half-closed with sleep. "What do you want?"

"What do we want here? Well, three guesses, old-timer."

"You won't find my boy here, if that's what you're after," Crosby said.

"No?"

"Of course he ain't here," Belle said.

"Well, now, maybe he'll be here, though. What do you think? Did you see a paper today?"

"I don't need to," Crosby said; "I know he got out of jail and you won't never catch him."

"Take a look." The Sheriff drew a folded newspaper from his pocket and tossed it on the table.

OUTLAW TRAPPED IN WOODS. That's like Jay said and that's the paper he seen but if it says that and they're here then he ain't trapped and he got away. He got away!

"So he got away," Belle cried. "So he ain't trapped! That's why you're here."

"Smart girl."

Belle went to the table and opened out the newspaper, and Crosby came and stood behind her.

A posse of three hundred Texas and Oklahoma officers closed in today on Pat Strickland, Southwestern desperado who yesterday escaped from the Jackville jail after killing two men. . . .

There they go laying it onto him again. They just do their best to lay it onto him and everybody knows Pat wouldn't kill nobody. . . . *Strickland was forced from his car into the woods near Ardmore and police chief J. G. Clement said it was only a matter of hours until he was caught.* But they ain't caught him and he got away just like I knowed he would. . . . *A pack of bloodhounds from the McAlester Penitentiary is leading the searchers in the strip of woods along the Washita River bottoms where Strickland is believed to be hiding. Officers found his abandoned car on the bank of the river and followed his trail into the woods. The heavy rainfall which was general in eastern Oklahoma yesterday hampered the search, but Chief Clement said that with the coming of daylight the outlaw's trail was easily followed. "Strickland is a desperate man and I don't think he will be taken alive," Chief Clement said.* . . . And they'd like to kill him just like they laid it on him that he killed them two men and that's the way they are, like Jay said, but he got clean away and they'll never catch him and they're just plain fools to come here because Pat will head off into the hills and I'll go out and find him. . . .

"Better blow out that light," the Sheriff said, and Belle looked up. The room was filled with men, some in uniform, some in plain clothes, but all with guns. She glanced at Crosby. The Sheriff came over to the table and as he bent to blow out the light Belle's eyes turned to the sawed-off shotgun in his hand.

"He got away, all right," the Sheriff said. "That time, anyhow." He grinned at Belle, then blew out the light. "But we figured he'd head this way and sure enough he did. He stopped over to Aldine and a nigger in the construction camp spotted him and tipped us off. He's on the way here now. I hope he finds the road."

Some of the deputies laughed and Belle leaned against the table, her face burning, her fists clenched.

I hate 'em and the mean cruel sound of their laughing and with all them guns they got I hate 'em and they're here just to kill Pat. It couldn't be that he'd come here. He'd ought to have the sense to take out into the blackjack but he's so wild and reckless he might like they said come here to git me. But I know he wouldn't take a chance like that, not even Pat. . . .

"Now both of you two lay low," the Sheriff said. His voice

came from the direction of the window and Belle saw him sitting in a chair in the moonlight, facing the road. The barrel of the sawed-off shotgun shone faintly.

"I don't want to hear a sound from nobody," he said. "Say, did you take the gun off the old man?"

"Yeah, I got it," another voice said.

Crosby sat down heavily in a chair beside the table, but Belle stood perfectly still in the center of the room, facing the window.

"We got a pretty good start on him," the Sheriff said. "It will be maybe a half-hour before he gits here."

"I reckon he won't be expecting no reception committee."

The room again was filled with laughter and the Sheriff said warningly: "Okay, quiet down." After a pause he added, "Hey, you — Miz Strickland. You better go in the back room."

"I'll stay here," Belle said.

His voice softened. "I think you'd be better off. You wouldn't want to see. . . ."

"I'll stay here," Belle said fiercely. "You can't make me."

"All right." He laughed. "But you stay quiet. . . . Tom, you better keep an eye on her."

"Okay, chief." A man stepped up beside Belle and his fingers closed on her wrist. She jerked away.

"You keep your hands off me."

"She oughtn't to be here, chief."

"Maybe not. Take her in the back."

"You can't do it," Belle said. "You can't make me."

Two arms went around her from behind and she kicked backwards with her bare heels. She started to scream and a hand was clapped over her mouth. Two men held her, dragging her to the door, into her bedroom. Billy awakened and began to cry and suddenly Belle gave up struggling and threw herself down on the bed. She buried her face in the pillow, lying still with her hot face pressed deep into the pillow, her arms stiff at her sides.

"Now just be easy, sister," one of the men said. "Lay quiet."

Belle did not reply, and the two men returned to the living room, the room full of guns and waiting men. They left the door ajar and Belle could hear their breathing. Through the crack of the partly open door she could see the figure of the Sheriff at the window, the moonlight on the sawed-off shotgun.

They stay so quiet like fishermen waiting on the riverbank and Pat is their fish and they're waiting to kill him and they act like they know and they said he stopped and talked to a nigger and maybe he's going to take that chance and come here and I got to do something. Some way I got to warn him and turn him back before it's too late.

She heard a slow deep voice from the next room. "Don't take no chances, men. Wait until he gits out of the car and then when I give the signal let him have it."

"Wait till you see the whites of his eyes," another voice said, following with a nervous laugh.

"I mean it. Don't fire until he's out of the car where we can take good aim."

"Okay, chief."

"He ought to be here pretty quick now."

Again there was silence, fearful, unbearable silence, except for a sleepy whimper from Billy's crib. Belle raised her head from the pillow. She sat upright and looked out the window toward the road. She saw only moonlight on the round tops of the blackjacks, the vast shadows of the woods beneath, and a small strip of moonlit road.

I got to warn Pat. I got to git away and warn him somehow. If he's coming this way I can't let him drive up to this house full of Laws waiting.

She lowered her bare feet to the floor, then slowly put her weight upon them. There was no sound, no warning creak of the floor, and she filled her cramped lungs deeply and paused a moment because her knees were weak.

It's good I'm barefoot but if it was the other house I'd know which board would creak and I wouldn't have to go so slow on tip-toe to the door and it wouldn't take so long and oh my God I got to hurry. Maybe he *is* coming like they think and if he is I got to warn him. I got to.

There was a slight, metallic sound as she turned the doorknob, but it was unnoticed by the men in the living room. She opened the door inch by inch, and there was no noise. She left it open and went quietly across the floor of the kitchen. At the rear of the house there was a screen door and the rusty hinges squeaked as she opened it.

God, the noise is so loud and I can't wait to see if they heard and I got to go on and the grass is cold and wet with dew and I'm alone now and I'm in moonlight and I got to git to them trees before they see me. . . .

She ran across the open space behind the house toward the woods. Stones cut into the tender soles of her feet but she hardly noticed the pain, although instinctively she limped. The shadow loomed ahead of her; it seemed to reach out to enfold her, and safe in the darkness she leaned gasping against a tree. She looked back at the indistinct form of the house, at the dark windows.

I ain't been missed or I'd hear something and he said *He ought to be here pretty quick.* . . . That's what that Sheriff said and I got to go and I got to hurry and I got to git down to the road and be waiting there to turn him back and I got to go fast as I can and no matter. . . .

She started off through the trees toward the road, now deep in the shadow of the woods. Her bare feet were bruised by stones, pricked by twigs; her toes burned from stubbing against the roots of trees, against rocks unseen in the darkness. She felt her way from tree to tree, always toward the road. She passed the house, and still it was fifty yards to the road, parallel to the lane leading to the house and barn. Briars scratched her legs and once the barb of one of them sank deep into her foot. She cried out and stopped to rub the wound.

But no matter and I can't delay and I got to make the road before it's too late and they're waiting there and watching with the whole room full of guns. . . .

She pushed on through the woods. Her kimono caught on bushes again and again and at last she slipped it off and left it, going on in her cotton nightgown toward the moonlit road. She was sobbing now, partly from pain, partly from agonizing fear.

I got to make the road before Pat comes, oh Jesus God I got to do it, and I'll run down it until I meet his car and I'll turn him back and then we can go on together off into the hills to some far-off place Pat knows where we can hide out safe. And that's the road just ahead and moonlight on the rail of the fence — but *it's a car coming* and I can hear it. It's Pat coming. . . .

She ran on and struck hard against the fence. She was hurt by it, nearly knocked breathless by it, but she did not pause. She swung upon the fence and she was astraddle it when the lights flashed near at hand, when the car came abreast of her on the road.

"Pat!" Her voice was high and shrill, but it seemed without volume in the night. "Pat, it's Belle!"

The car passed her by and she saw the red tail-light. She jumped from the fence to the road and ran after it. She was full in the moonlight now, a white figure in the moonlight. She slipped on the soft clay and her scream was broken by the sobbing in her throat, "Pat, it's Belle!"

The car had stopped and was waiting for her and as she came near it she saw Pat leaning out, looking back at her.

"Pat, drive on." She stumbled alongside the car. "Drive on. They're . . ."

The guns went off with a great explosion, the sawed-off shotgun at the window, the rifles behind. Belle fell to her knees, as if she had been tripped up.

"Run, Pat, *run.*" She saw him open the car door and get out on the road. "I'm all right, Pat, run, run, run . . . !"

Belle looked up at him, and then she fell forward on her face, at his feet.

Pat

✦   ✦

SHE'S shot. Belle is shot. And she's all over blood and she lays still and Jesus God she's bad hurt. She's limp in my arms and she don't move and her eyes, Christ, her eyes and the moonlight on her eyes. . . .

Again the guns blazed and there was the ripping impact of slugs striking the body of the car. Men were running from the house.

"I got to go and leave you here. Belle, honey, I got to leave you here on the roadside. Jesus Christ, where is my gun?"

Pat jumped on the running board and snatched the pistol. The forty-five made a smashing sound and there were darts of flame in the night. Neil jammed the car in gear and stepped on the accelerator in a panic. The car roared on up the hill, guns flashing behind, and as they drove in among the trees Pat looked back at the white blur on the road where Belle lay, looked back until it was hidden by the trees. He got in beside Neil and slammed the door. The car was veering from one side of the road to the other, rushing madly into the black tunnel of the trees.

They was waiting there laying fer me and she come out to warn me and they shot her and God, if she's dead it's plain murder and they done it because they seen she come to give me warning. But I know she ain't dead. She ain't dead but there was so much blood. Oh Belle, honey, why did you do it and why didn't you stay safe in the house and I'd of shot it out and they never would of caught me. Can't you see they never would of caught me?

Sweat was all over Pat's face. His body was wet with it and his shirt stuck to his skin. His hands trembled. He turned and stared at the white face of the man beside him.

"That was my wife, Mister," he said, almost screaming above the noise of the engine. "Did you see what they done? They shot her down and maybe she's back there dying."

Just because she run out to warn me. She's got guts and she come out to tell me them Laws was waiting and she come out just in her nightgown and they shot her down. It wasn't me they shot at and I ain't even scratched. But she was shot and she was all over blood and she's bad hurt and she might be dead but that just can't be and Belle won't die but them eyes and the moonlight on them eyes . . . and if she dies they ain't nothing fer me and Christ, I got to know how she is and I can't take off into the hills alone and not know how she is.

Pat stared ahead of him at the light on the nest of tree trunks along the road. His hand clenched and unclenched on the butt of the gun.

"It was that damned nigger done it," he said. "He telephoned them Laws and they come up here to wait fer me and Belle tried to git to me first and when they seen her they shot at her."

"Maybe she's not badly hurt," Neil said, with a glance at Pat's face. "We were a long way from the house."

Pat's eyes were large and cloudy and his face was white. There was a spasmodic twitching of the muscles of his cheeks.

"She was limp all over, Mister. All the back of her was blood. I felt it. She was hit by slugs from a sawed-off shotgun."

The road was climbing, winding, toward the top of a ridge.

Pat turned his head and saw behind and below them the glare of lights, the headlights of two automobiles.

"They're on our tail," he said. "Keep going fast as you can. They ain't going to catch us."

"You bet," Neil said.

"How are you? You ain't hit?"

"No."

"Well, keep going fast as you can. This road runs straight fer maybe six miles more, then we come to a turn-off, on the left. Take it."

Neil nodded. For a moment they were on the crest of the ridge, where there were fewer trees and the moonlight was bright, then again they were in thick woods, descending the ridge on the opposite side. The car rushed down the narrow road and there were rocks and occasional deep ruts to avoid. They came to the bottom of the hill, shot across a bridge over a creek, and veered to the right beside a deep ravine. Pat looked back and saw the lights of the police cars descending the hillside.

"We're holding our lead," he said. "You're doing O.K., brother."

Pat picked up the rifle and swung around in the seat. They were on a straight stretch of road and he waited for the other cars to reach the bottom of the hill and turn upon it. He held the rifle ready and when the first lights flashed full in view he fired. But the lights were a quarter of a mile behind them and he shook his head.

"They're a little too far back," he said.

"That's where I'm going to keep them," Neil said through his teeth. His voice still was shaky.

"You're all right," Pat said.

"I don't want to get shot, that's all."

Pat leaned forward. "Any minute now that road turns off. Keep your eyes open."

They both stared ahead. The road was rough and seemed to bound toward them, to roll toward them in waves of red clay.

"Yonder she is," Pat cried. "Hold her down."

Neil put on the brakes and swung the car off on a side road which had been concealed by the trees until they were nearly upon it. The car careened into a shallow ditch at the side of the road, then bounced back upon the roadway and Neil stepped on the gas again. Pat turned to look. The road was climbing again, up a gradual grade, and he saw the lights rush past the turn-off, then heard the scream of brakes.

"We gained a bit," he said. "You'll find another turn-off, I remember, say five miles from here, on the right side of the road. We'll take that one."

The road rushed on under their wheels, mile after mile of red clay and ruts and stones and sometimes pools of water, mile after mile of black foliage and gnarled tree trunks and a forbidding stillness and quiet. There was no wind in the trees, never a movement of the leaves, and never a sign of life on the lonely road.

"Hold her," Pat said, and Neil applied the brakes. "Ahead there, on the right."

The brakes shrieked, and this time the turn was made more safely. They raced on again.

"They won't catch us," Neil said grimly.

"That's the way to talk. We'll git away, all right." Pat was silent for a moment. "But if they do catch up, I don't care. I got some shootin' to do."

Neil's foot pressed harder on the accelerator, pushed it flush with the floorboard.

"There's a sharp turn ahead, I remember," Pat said.

Neil slowed, and the car bounced around an abrupt curve, with an immediate ascent beyond.

"I don't see no sign of 'em," Pat said. "We must be easy a mile ahead."

They came to the top of the hill and far below there was a flash of light. "Look!" Neil cried.

"I know. That's the highway again. We doubled back to the highway. Turn left at the bottom. We're going back Aldine way."

At the bottom of the downgrade the road met the gravel highway. As Neil turned left Pat said: "We left them Laws in the hills somewhere. We got a good start now. Let's go."

Neil opened the car up on the straight gravel highway and in a few minutes they overtook the car whose lights they had seen from the hilltop. It was a truck with a load of poultry, with crates of poultry roped staggeringly high.

"It's plenty late," Pat said. "It will be daybreak the first thing we know." He hesitated. "I reckon we better turn off the highway into the hills again. We got to lay low in the daytime."

They had passed the truck and left its lights far behind and the miles spun by under their wheels.

"We'll take the next road into the hills," Pat said. "The next road on the west of the highway, away from them Laws."

Neil drove on in silence. Pat tried to light a cigarette but the match went out in the wind and with a cry of anger he crushed the cigarette in his hand and threw it away. He remained silent, watching the road, and fifteen minutes later he touched Neil's arm.

"It looks like there ought to be a road where that old schoolhouse is. Slow down, Smith."

They passed a boarded-up schoolhouse and a hundred yards beyond it came to a dirt road. "This goes into the hills somewhere," Pat said.

The road turned at a gradual angle from the highway and followed the course of a creek into the hills. It was a narrow, rarely-traveled road and the ruts in it were wagon ruts.

"I ain't sure where this road goes to," Pat said.

"It looks abandoned."

"Yeah, not traveled much. Go ahead."

The night was beginning to lift, detectable only on the horizon above the line of the hills, which now became more distinct. The clay road wound with the creek into the hills, flanked by deep ditches on each side, and covered with a layer of reddish dust.

"We left them Laws away back," Pat said. "They won't trouble us again tonight. There ain't been much rain here and the road is dried out and our tracks won't show."

Neil could not drive fast on the rough road, with its many blind turns. It required close attention to drive and he was very tired. His eyes ached in their sockets. The miles rolled by, and they had been driving half an hour when they reached a crossroads. Neil stopped the car.

"I don't know," Pat said. "I reckon we'll take the one on the left. It's got grass growing in it and I reckon it will take us where it's wild enough to hide out. Yeah, turn left."

Neil drove on. It was much lighter now and the air was acquiring the color of the dawn. A clear warm light came among the trees. On the left of the road was a deep ravine; the soft shoulder of the road stretched to its very edge, and on the right the rocky hillside. It was dangerous and he drove carefully. The road followed the contour of the countryside, dipping with every depression, rising with every slope. Now the clay turned a deeper red with the coming of dawn; there was color in the green of the trees and the headlights washed into the light of approaching day. The road turned away from the ridge after it had skirted the ravine and moved into flatter land in the direction of a hill a mile away. After a while they came to a gradual slope and at the top of it the road forked. Neil took the right fork and they came out into an open space, circled by trees, into which both forks led and abruptly ended. Neil stopped the car.

"What the hell," Pat said. "We ought to took that other road back yonder. This one ends right here." He looked back at the road over which they had come. "It's daylight now. We better lay up here, Mister. Turn up into the woods and drive as far as you can."

Neil drove in low gear, winding among the trees, crashing through underbrush. He drove two hundred yards into the woods, until the tree-trunks became too close to proceed.

"O.K.," Pat said. "We'll stop here." He sighed, and the two men looked at each other. Pat was pale and there were deep lines in his cheeks beside his mouth. His face was drawn and his eyes had a glazed look, an expression of suffering. Pat took the ignition key and got out of the car. He was stiff, and he kicked to straighten the kinks out of his legs.

"I could sure use a cup of coffee," Pat said. "I ain't had a thing to eat fer thirty-six hours, about." He took off his hat and his red hair flamed in the dawn. He sank into deep grass at the base of a blackjack oak, leaning against the tree trunk. He closed his eyes, and now he heard the birds, the busy vibrant twittering of them, the call of a crow far away. The light was growing steadily brighter; he could feel it through his eye-lids. Soon the sun would rise above the hill to the east. He heard a creaking sound and opened his eyes.

"What in hell is that?"

Above the sound of the birdsongs he heard a steady, progressive, rattling noise, then the *clop-clop* of horses' hoofs on the ground. Pat picked up the rifle. He looked steadily at Neil, his eyes narrowed and dark in his white face. "Remember now, keep quiet. You been all right tonight. You stay that way."

"Yes," Neil said.

"It's a wagon and team," Pat said.

He could see nothing but trees and deep grass and a straggling covert of sumac. He started stealthily among the trees, then stopped and turned. "You better come with me. Be careful, and stay out of sight. Don't make no noise."

Neil nodded and Pat walked on ahead of him. His tan shirt was streaked with sweat and stained with blood where it was ripped at the shoulder. When the clearing came into sight Pat held up his hand and stepped behind a tree. The open area was below them and a hundred yards away and peering down through the foliage Pat saw a wagon near the center of it, beside a mound of ash-colored earth. Climbing down from the wagon-seat was a man in a beaded buckskin jacket almost the color of the clay road. He wore a black hat, and two white eagle feathers, black-tipped, were thrust at an angle in the hatband. There were four men, and all wore eagle feathers in their hats, but only one wore buckskin; the other three were in overalls. Even from the distance Pat saw the coppery color of their skin in the dawning day.

Now what do them Indians want away out here? I reckon they been up to something and they stole something and they don't want me to see them any more than I want them to see me.

One of the Indians was piling wood on the mound of gray earth, dry brittle wood for kindling. Pat saw several logs stacked near at hand. The first bright flame rose from the wood on the gray mound of earth and a thin spiral of smoke drifted against the green background of trees. The Indian in the fringed buck-skin jacket walked slowly back to the wagon. He stepped on the wheel-hub and reached into the wagon-bed. When he stood erect there was something white flapping in his hand — a chicken.

A white chicken. Now I know. It's a white cockerel. They sacrifice a white cockerel at dawn and I remember all that and it's a stomp-dance. They're fixing to have a stomp-dance here and that means these woods will be full of Indians all day long and all night too.

The Indian carried the cockerel to the fire and Pat saw the flash of a knife, then the cockerel flapped in the Indian's hand. He flicked the bird over the fire, scattering drops of its blood on the mound of earth, as a priest scatters holy water. Now the Indians moved away from the fire on the ash-gray mound and there came again the creaking sound as the wagon rolled on toward a lean-to among the trees on the opposite side of the stomp grounds. Pat saw two of the Indians get into the wagon and lift down the dressed carcass of a calf, then a goat, and another goat. The Indian in the buckskin jacket stood beside a shallow pit in the ground and watched while another man built a fire. Slow wood smoke rose in a pale bluish mist.

"They're fixing to barbecue some meat," Pat whispered. "Come on, we got to git back into them woods."

Neil walked ahead of Pat, back among the trees, through the thicket, to the car. Pat looked in the back seat and found a coil of copper wire.

"Go on a ways further," he said.

They kept walking, over uneven ground, into the depth of the woods where blackjack oaks grew thickly and thrust crusty and misshapen limbs across their path. It was close in the woods, and both men were sweating. They had walked about five minutes when they came to a grassy glade with a limestone boulder almost in its center.

"This will do us," Pat said. Neil dropped to the ground and stretched out his arms and legs.

"You know what that is?" Pat said. "They're fixing to have a stomp-dance."

"A stomp-dance?" Neil raised his head. "Say, this is the stomp-dance I was coming to, then."

"You was?"

"I had a date to come here."

"Well, here you be," Pat said. "We got to wait here through the day and tonight we'll git away." He leaned against the boulder. "Anyhow, they won't be looking fer me at a stomp-dance, and the traffic on that road will cover up our tracks. There'll be plenty of Indians rolling in here before dark."

Pat leaned over and picked up the coil of wire he had brought from the car.

"I got to git some rest." he said. "I'm going to tie you up, Mister."

Neil looked at the wire.

"Don't like to do it," Pat said. "You been all right tonight. But stick your hands out."

Pat knelt and bound Neil's wrists and ankles with the wire. "Okay," he said. "Just lay easy and rest some. We'll have a long time to wait."

Pat went over to the boulder and sat down beside it, leaning against it. He sat staring fixedly over Neil's head into the tree-tops.

I'm sure tired and I'm sore in every muscle and my head is aching but I don't want to stop moving and start thinking again and Jesus I wonder how bad she's hurt and I reckon Dad has got her in the house and they'll take care of her and he'll git her a doctor and somehow I got to git back that way and find out how she is. I got to know if she's all right but there was blood all over the back of her and my hands are stained with it. My hands are stained with Belle's blood and her eyes was open in the moonlight. But it just couldn't be that Belle would die and I ain't going to think about that part of it. I just got to wait until I know and somehow I'll git back there to that house and I'll git word to Dad and I'll know. . . .

Jay

YOU give a man a gun and you give him the law on his side and he's going to shoot it off and he'll kill and he don't need to have no reason to kill. You give most men a gun and the law behind them and they want to kill somebody and they git a lot of pleasure out of it and I've seen it happen before but to shoot a woman down like that, it ain't even human.

"Jay, it was terrible," Crosby said. "I was in that room in the dark and all them men was there with guns and we seen the lights of his car coming around the bend. Their aim was to wait until the car turned into the lane and Pat got out and then they aimed to let him have it when he wouldn't have no chance to git away. You could see that strip of road yonder and the moonlight was on it and they was all watching that road and we seen the car come around the bend and then there was that little spot of white on the road and I never knowed it was Belle. I never knowed it was Belle until I heard her voice and she was telling Pat to run and then them guns went off. Every gun in the room went off and I seen the car drive away and I never knowed they'd shot Belle. I never knowed it until they'd packed themselves into their cars and started off after Pat, and then I went out after them and I seen Belle laying there on the road and they hadn't never made a move to pick her up."

They were standing in tall weeds beside the porch and Jay had not yet been into the house.

"I went over to her and I called her name and she didn't answer and I bent down and I seen the blood and I knowed then she was dead, Jay. I picked her up and I carried her into the house and I laid her out on her bed and she's laying there now. . . . Jay, do you want to view her?"

Jay looked at his father. "Poor Belle. She'd do anything fer Pat and I never seen two people better suited."

"She run down through the woods in her bare feet, Jay, and I want you to look at them feet, where she bruised and cut 'em."

In the house Billy began to cry; they heard the low, fretful sound of his voice.

"That poor kid," Jay said. "Billy, come out here, boy. Come see your Uncle Jay."

Jay went upon the porch and over to the door. Billy was sitting cross-legged on the floor of the living room, crying.

"Don't you cry none, sonny," Jay said. He went into the house and knelt beside the boy. "Look here, you've growed too big to cry like that."

"Where my bam-bam?" Billy asked. Sunlight from the window fell on his tow hair and tear-stained cheeks.

"What is it you want, Billy?"

"I want my bam-bam."

"Crosby, what is he after?"

"I don't rightly know, Jay."

"Honey, we'll git you whatever you want if you can tell us what it is," Jay said, picking up the child.

"Mommy got my bam-bam."

"You poor kid," Jay said. "Dad, we got to git him his bam-bam. Billy, what is your bam-bam? What do you do with it?"

"Kill squirl dead. Bam-bam."

"Oh, say," Crosby said, "it's a little gun Pat brung him. You pull the trigger and it makes a flash like a gun shooting off."

"I remember I seen it. What do you suppose was done with it, Dad?"

"I got no notion, Jay. We just only moved yesterday and I got no notion where things was put."

"Well, don't you fret, Billy. We'll find you your bam-bam and we'll shoot us lots of squirrels."

Jay put the boy down and looked at Crosby. "The poor kid don't know."

"No, he don't."

"Christ, Dad, this is the worst I ever heard of."

Crosby sank into a rocking chair by the window, then jerked his head toward Jay. "It was right here the Sheriff sat his fat rear-end last night, Jay. He sat here with a sawed-off shotgun, and he was the first one fired."

Jay walked slowly away from his father, across the room to a closed door. He glanced back over his shoulder and Crosby nodded. Jay opened the door.

She's just the same with that quiet look and the freckles on her face and that cornsilk hair and it's good it didn't hit her face . . . and her feet with them blue marks and them scratches and cuts. God Almighty! What a woman poor Belle was and what a wife she was fer Pat, running out in her nightgown to save his life, and now that she done it we got to make sure that Pat gits away safe. Me and Dad have got to do that fer her. . . .

Jay went out and closed the door. Crosby raised his eyes. He was rocking slowly by the window.

"Dad, I went to the bank first thing this morning and drawed out that money," Jay said. "I figured one of us might git in touch with Pat and we could give it to him."

Crosby nodded.

"I'll give you half of it and I'll keep half," Jay said. "Either one of us gits in touch with him can give him the stake. . . . Dad, there's just one thing I want to do and that's to git Pat safe away and I want to do that fer Belle as much as fer Pat."

"I'm glad we got that money," Crosby said. "I'm glad we sold out the farm and got that money because now we can lay Belle away good."

"We'll lay her away the very best," Jay said.

"Do you reckon Friday, Jay? That's day after tomorrow, ain't it?"

"Yes."

"Then how about Friday over to the graveyard in the hills?"

"All right," Jay said.

"I aim to git some fine rented autos from Mehuskah, shiny ones with white tires, and a white hearse. Like you said, Jay, we're going to lay her away the very best."

"Yes," Jay said. He walked to the window.

"Jay, do you reckon Pat got clean away?"

"If he'd of been caught we'd know about it by this time. It looks like he run off and left 'em, Dad."

"Maybe he's laid up safe in the hills."

"I wouldn't wonder. . . . Dad, do you suppose he was hit?"

"Jay, I don't know. They sure did fill the air full of slugs and I never heard such a ruckus as all them guns blowing off."

"If he's in the hills we'll find him," Jay said. He put on his hat. "Belle would of knowed just where to go after him."

"She sure would."

Jay looked steadily at his father, his clenched fists thrust in his pockets.

I don't want to go off and leave him alone with Belle laying in yonder dead and with Billy crying fer his bam-bam gun, but I got my work to do and I got to do it. It sure is hard and you can see the difference in him and he ain't the same old man he was just two days ago at Aldine. Now he looks old and broke-down like a harness-sore horse.

"Dad, I got to leave you fer a spell," Jay said.

Crosby did not answer, and Jay looked at his pale and watery eyes, the droop of his mouth. Crosby wore his green-faded hunting-cap on the back of his head and his face was sharp as a knife-blade beneath it.

"I got to go to that there stomp-dance," Jay said. "I wouldn't go if I didn't have to, Dad, but it's union business and I got to do it."

"All right, Jay."

"I'll come back this way when it's over with, Dad."

"You'll find me waitin', son."

Jay reached out and touched the old man's shoulder lightly; his fingers tightened on the bone and stringy muscle, then he turned away and went down the steps toward his car. As he drove away he glanced back and saw Crosby leaning against a pillar with his corncob pipe hanging from his mouth and his hands in the fore-pockets of his overalls.

I feel near as bad about Dad as I do about Billy. Nobody could of thought more of Belle than him and I don't believe they ever crossed each other from the time Pat brung her home from the wedding. And poor Pat. Jesus God, what are we going to do?

Jay followed the clay road down to the gravel highway and turned west toward Boggs. He drove for several miles along the highway, parallel to a low blue ridge.

Joseph Paul said I'd know it by a tumbledown schoolhouse and that looks like it. Yonder's an old road with grass in the middle of it and it must be the one. Yes, because there's been plenty of people over this here road. The tracks is fresh and it's automobiles and wagons and horses and I ain't any too early. There ain't been no rain up here and sometimes it looks like it just rains county by county here in Oklahoma. It sure makes a lot of dust and I guess it's a car where that haze is up ahead of me. . . . If I can git them Indians lined up today and git 'em talking union, if I can just do that! I got Joseph Paul to help me and that Red Feather friend of his, and that other one that Rocky signed up at the barbecue. John Goback he calls himself. That poor Rocky, I got to git up yonder to Haze's shack and see how he is. I got to do that today. I got so much to do and so much has happened I don't hardly know where I'm at. . . . I never seen a worse road with the dust and the rocks and the holes in it and I guess it ain't used but this one time each year.

Jay drove carefully along the soft shoulder of the road on the edge of a deep ravine, and when he came to the crossroads he turned across the plateau, following the signs of traffic. The sky had become overcast. Silvery clouds drifted across the sun, which occasionally broke through with a blinding blaze of light, and it was shining through a break in the clouds as Jay drove into an open space of hard-tramped, dusty ground and stopped the car under a tree. Around him there were many wagons, a few automobiles, and horses tethered under the trees. He sat a moment looking at dark brown faces and straight black hair, with here and there the flash of an earring, the brilliant color of a woman's skirt. But there were not many people at the stomp grounds, except for a small crowd at the barbecue pit, and the fire on the earthen altar had burned low, red embers in ashes the color of the piled-up dirt. Off to the left Jay saw Joseph Paul seated under a tree. Jay waved his hand and went over toward the Indian. It was hot and Joseph Paul was perspiring. His fat brown face was wet and he wore his pith helmet far back on his head, showing a forelock of black hair on his forehead.

"Hello, there," Jay said.

"Howdy." The Indian pushed himself slowly to his feet.

"Where is everybody, Joseph?"

"Powwow start, Jay. Yonder in woods." The Indian looked at Jay, his black eyes clear and expressionless. "Pat come back."

"Yeah, he come back. . . . I reckon you heard the rest of it, too?"

Joseph Paul bent his head.

"We got work to do," Jay said, with a twist of his shoulders. "Joseph, I want to talk to every Indian here before the day is over."

Joseph Paul smiled. They walked over to the barbecue pit and the Indian raised his hand in greeting to a man in a buckskin jacket. They shook hands and Joseph Paul introduced Jay. "T'is here Jay Strickland. T'is him chief."

The chief was a pale old man with stooping shoulders and hollow cheeks. He wore gold-rimmed spectacles and his black, intelligent eyes were magnified by the glasses.

"Joseph Paul told me you come stomp-dance," the chief said. "Pretty soon powwow begin. You come along."

"I sure will," Jay said. "I guess you know why I come up here. I want to talk to your people and I want to tell 'em about the Southern Tenant Farmers' Union. I'd appreciate it if I could make a little talk at the powwow."

The chief did not take his eyes from Jay's face. He was stroking two eagle feathers he held in his hand along his wrist.

"I want to sign your people up in the union," Jay said. "The busy season is coming on and if we build the union strong we'll git a good price fer the work."

"White man never helped the Indian," the chief said quietly. "Long time ago Indian find out him better off stay with him own people."

"You and me are talking about a different kind of white man," Jay said. "The kind of white man I represent works with his hands in the cotton fields and he gits two bits a hunderd fer picking cotton and he works in the spinach fields fer four cents a basket, just like your people do. They only work in that season and they drift along from field to field and they ain't got no way to pertect themselves. But if all them workers join together in the Southern Tenant Farmers' Union the union will talk fer 'em and the union will git a dollar a hunderd fer pickin' cotton."

"Powwow Indian powwow," the chief said. "Today Indian day. Some other time you talk about union."

"I wouldn't take but five minutes."

The chief shook his head. They were standing near the barbecue pits, where the meat was suspended on hogwire above the coals, and Jay smelled the pungent spices. Occasionally a wagon drove into the arena and across it to a clearing among the trees where there were many wagons grouped around a well. They came by families, with the women and the girls and the children in the wagon-beds, with stolid men perched high on the wagon-seats.

"You see," the chief said. "Today Indian day. Cherokee day. Once a year Indian day and every other day white man day."

"All right," Jay said. "I ain't trying to force myself."

"But you come see powwow. Come listen."

"I'll do that," Jay said.

The chief gave Joseph Paul one of the eagle feathers to put in his sun-helmet and as they walked away Joseph Paul said: "T'is not my tribe, but every year me come. Chief give me feat'er. After powwow play Indian ball — *on-g'las-ka-lishka*. Maybeso you like him, Jay. Chief say today Indian day. Okay. You stay. Have good time Indian way."

Jay smiled and touched the Indian's shoulder lightly. They started along a lane among the trees, part of a slow-moving group. On several of the trees campaign posters had been tacked up. Jay looked at them with a curl of his lips. There was a picture of the Sheriff in a ten-gallon hat, of Lamar Baker. They came to a rail fence and crossed it where two rails had broken down. Then they were in tall yellow grass in a clear space among the trees where two hundred Indians were seated facing a large post-oak tree. The men were dressed in overalls and most of them wore straw hats, but some of the younger men had black felt hats with bands of silver or bright beadwork. Many had black-tipped eagle feathers. In the dresses of the women there was color; purple skirts with a glittering sheen in the sunlight, red and yellow skirts and embroidered jackets, pendant earrings dangling against brown skin.

Yonder she is and all this time I know now I been watching out fer her. Sun on her blue-black hair and that green sweater and such a little bit of a woman settin' on a stump. . . .

Jay walked up behind her. "Hello, Leona."

"Jay!" She caught his hand. "So you did come after all."

"Sure I did." He sat down beside her in the grass, his shoulder against the stump she was seated on. "Where is that New York friend of yours?"

"He hasn't come yet. He can't get off from his work until five o'clock and he's going to drive up this evening."

The chief in the orange-colored buckskin jacket stepped over the rail fence and walked slowly toward the lone oak tree where several older Indians were squatting in a half-circle in the shade.

"Lots people come stomp-dance this year," Joseph Paul said. "More come tonight."

"Hello, Joseph," Leona said. "Where is Christine?"

Joseph Paul smiled and pointed to his wife, seated in the grass only two yards away. The chief had begun to speak, and there was a hush in the grassy clearing. He stood a little away from the tree and his voice flowed evenly, it seemed with hardly any variation in sound, except that each sentence ended in a rising inflection, nearly a shout. His words were pronounced partly through the throat, partly from the nose, and several times he stopped to spit into the grass at his feet, the only interruption in the steady singsong of the language.

"I wish I knew what he was saying," Leona said. "Do you, Jay?"

"No, I don't know the language. What's he saying, Joseph?"

"No say much." The Indian shrugged his fat shoulders.

Seated almost at Jay's feet was Christine Paul, with a bright red scarf around her shoulders. She held little Emma Paul in her lap. The child's oval face was expressionless, her round dark eyes staring, and her mother was plucking black-eyed Susans from the weeds around her to make a bouquet. The voice of the chief flowed on monotonously, soporifically. Many of the Indians were chatting among themselves, and only the older men squatting under the oak tree paid close attention. Christine completed the bouquet of yellow blooms and tied the stems with a piece of string. The child took it from her and transferred her quiet stare to the yellow flowers.

"Jay, are you going to stay for the dance tonight?" Leona asked.

"Are you?"

"Of course. I don't want to miss it."

"Then I reckon we can have a dance together," Jay said.

"Sure we will. Jay, have you heard anything from your brother?"

"Ain't you heard?"

"No. What? They didn't catch him, Jay?"

"They laid fer him. They laid a trap fer him last night and they shot and killed Belle, his wife."

"Killed her, Jay?"

Jay looked up and saw her open mouth, the contraction of her eyes, and just then the chief finished his speech with a final spit into a patch of milkweed and there was a burst of applause.

"That poor, beautiful creature, Jay. She was so fine."

"The very best," Jay said.

"Jay, I can't believe it."

"I know," Jay said. "Well, that's what happened." He turned his head away and said sharply: "Joseph Paul, what was it all about?"

"Him talk a lot," Joseph Paul said. "Don't say much. Take long time say little. Him talk about big t'ings tribe do. Him talk about big men long time ago. Him talk about Sequoyah, John Ross. Him say young Indian ought to do like grandfat'er. Him say Indian got go back to old way, to old tribe way and religion and leave white man way to white man. Him say Indian got to stay to himself like grandfat'er." He smiled, his broken tooth showing. "The past always pretty fine. Today not so good."

Now a man was speaking in English and Jay jerked his head around.

Now fer God's sake it's Lamar Baker and he's making a speech and they let him make a speech and they wouldn't let me. He knowed Lamar was going to make a speech and he ruled me out and then he told them Indians they ought to stick to themselves. Lamar got in there and that son of a bitch don't never miss up on anything and he comes way to hell and gone in the hills to make a political speech on the chance he'll win him a few votes. That left side of his jaw is swelled up and a piece of court plaster there and I'm glad I done it.

"I'm always glad to come and talk to my Indian friends," Lamar was saying. "And I'm always glad to see any one of you who drops into my office in Mehuskah. On this great day I don't want to take up much of your time." His voice filled the grove with a stereotyped cadence of sound, the oratorical volume of practised usage. "But I do want you to know you got a friend in Lamar Baker and when I'm county attorney . . ."

Jay looked at Leona. "He don't ever miss a vote."

"That's just like Lamar," she said, smiling.

Lamar's voice rose and fell untiringly, but little attention was paid as the Indians accepted his speech as something that must be endured. Jay lay back on the grass at Leona's feet and looked up at the sheen of sassafras leaves against the gray sky. He closed his eyes, and his mouth clamped tightly shut as he listened to Lamar.

"I want the opportunity fer service," Lamar said. "I'm a young man and I want to go in and make a record fer myself, and after I've made that record you can decide fer yourself whether I ought to go on in office. My opponent is eligible fer an old age pension and he ought to retire. He ought to retire and give the young man a chance and I want you to vote

me in and retire him. Let's pass these county jobs around. What
I say is if it's a good thing let's pass it around and if it ain't then
it's too big a burden fer one man to carry, and an old man at
that."

When Lamar finished talking there was a polite scattering
of applause and one of the old Indians rose and stepped out into
the open. He began to talk without preliminary and the old men
whose ranks he had left sat stolidly waiting their turn. Jay
saw Lamar moving behind the circle of the crowd and sat upright. Lamar walked toward them, toward the stump where
Leona sat. He did not look at Jay.

"Hello, there, Leona. Gittin' full of Indian lore?"

"That's right."

"Mind if I sit down alongside?"

"Please do. You know Jay Strickland?"

Lamar looked down at Jay, with his feet spread. There was
an intense silence, then Lamar moved his shoulders slightly,
and grinned. "Oh, what the hell, howdy, Jay."

"Hello, Lamar," Jay said.

"There'll be hours of this, Leona," Lamar said. His hand went
to the patch of adhesive beside his mouth. "Say, Joseph Paul,
when is the ball game?"

The Indian shrugged. "Pretty soon. Maybe one hour. Maybeso two. Indian don't hurry."

Lamar smiled. He was wearing boots and corduroy pants
and his creamy Stetson hat on the back of his head. He sat
chewing a straw and talking to Leona and Jay lay back and
did not listen. The old Indian spoke for twenty minutes and
when he had finished the sun was shining through a rift in the
gray wash spread over the sky.

"Dear souls," a loud and oily voice said. Jay sat up and
looked toward the oak tree. A white man in a gray shirt, with
a cowlick of black hair falling over one eye, stood with his
arms stretched out. "Dear souls, I feel like I'm one of you today
in this solemn gathering. Maybe we got some differences in
the way we worship, but underneath it all it's the same religion,
ain't it?" The unctious voice rose higher. "Dear souls, we're
gathered here in the eves of God, and it's the same God fer us
all. It's the same great Power watching over us and looking

down with love and kindness at our little gathering here today. I want you dear souls to think of that, to remember that He is up yonder . . . "

Lamar stood up. "Leona, what do you say we go back to the dance grounds? This goes on fer hours."

"I suppose so," Leona said. "Jay, are you coming?"

"No," Jay said. "I'm going to set awhile. I'll see you later, Leona."

"Good-by then."

"So long."

Jay watched her walk beside Lamar to the rail fence and cross it. They passed from sight among the trees.

"We got to gather together in the service of the Lord," the evangelist was saying. "Today, with infidelity, atheism and communism sweeping the land we got to stick together fer God. We got to fight against them isms. We got to show the world that the word of God can still prevail. Now ain't that true? In these days we can't have no lightning-bug religion. You-all seen a lightning-bug, brothers, flickering on and off in the night-time, flickering when the night is pitchest black. Some people git religion that way and they flicker on and off just like a lightning-bug. They flicker bright when the preacher comes around, but when he's gone the light goes out and they pull down the shades and nobody knows what they're up to and maybe they're playing cards and the women smoking cigarettes and they make themselves easy with the instruments of the devil in hell. That ain't what we're after. We don't want no lightning-bug religion. I tell you, some folks got patches on the seat of their pants from backsliding. . . ."

They let Lamar talk about his politics and they let that soul-saver talk about religion but they don't want nobody to git up and talk union. They don't want nobody to tell 'em how to fight the landlords and better themselves in this world. . . .

"Down in West Texas, where I was partially raised, now down in Texas, I tell you, where I was a little boy, they had a lake there and I used to go out and swim in it. It was the old swimmin' hole. Now a couple of years ago they took and drained that lake and what do you suppose they found? They found thirty-six baby carcasses in it. That's what they found down

in Texas. Now I ask you grayheads, did you ever hear of
mothers deserting their babies in your day? Did you? Did you
ever hear of mothers drownding their babies in the lake? No,
sir, you didn't." His voice rose higher; his forehead glistened
with sweat and his gray shirt was stained dark under his up-
raised arms. "I tell you, my friends, we got to come back to
God, we got to make the crooked places straight. I ain't
ashamed to say it. I was a bad man and I stole. Yes, I stole.
Would you believe it to look at me now? But it's true. Absolute
fact. I stole a bag of sugar and two pounds of coffee and I was
headed fer a life of crime. But there come a good man, a man
of God, and he talked to me and he showed me the evils of my
ways and he helped me to make the crooked places straight
and he brung me back to God. He brung me back to the old-
time religion."

The evangelist was walking up and down under the oak tree,
while two hundred stolid brown faces were turned toward him,
black eyes watching.

"And I tell you, dear souls, there's too much education in
this world today and not enough of that old-time religion. We
need more of the old-time plowboy preachers, that's what we
need, more of the old-time plowboy preachers. That's what
the whole world needs. We've all got to come back to God. The
nations that have left God have gone to hell. Now who believes
that the world is gittin' any better? If anybody believes the
world is gittin' any better I'd like to see him hold up his hand."

He paused, looking at the unresponsive faces. "We *know* the
world ain't gittin' any better. We all know that. Now right in
the Holy Book the Apostle Paul told us about this pleasure-mad
age we're livin' in now. The Apostle Paul told us about the
autos and the airplanes and the radios we got in this world today
and he warned us agin 'em and I tell you, my friends, the
Apostle Paul had the right idear. We need more of that old-
time religion. It's the staff of life, that old-time religion. We got
to depend on it more and more. These are the days of infidelity
and isms and too much education. People read something in a
book and they think it's true but the only true book ever wrote
down is the Holy Scripture. That's the Book fer us, dear souls,
that's the Book we put our faith in. . . . And now we're going

to sing a hymn, folks, and we'll sing that old favorite you all know: 'O mother dear, Jerusalem.' Anybody who don't know the English words, sing it in your own language. Now, all together. . . ."

"*O mother dear, Jerusalem. . . .*" The Indians straggled through the hymn, standing, and Jay too stood up. "*When shall I come to thee? . . .*"

There ain't nobody makes disagreement with religion, and politics is just like food and drink to lots of 'em, but they sure do change their tune when union business comes up. *When shall my sorrows have an end? Thy joys when shall I see?* I don't see why I should set by and take it and by God I ain't going to do it. *In Thee no sorrow can be found, Nor grief, nor care, nor toil. . . .*

The voices died away like a sigh of relief and Jay suddenly jumped upon the tree stump.

"Just a minute, everybody!" The brown faces turned toward him and the chief in the beaded jacket got to his feet under the oak tree. "You heard a little politics and you heard a little religion and now you're going to hear a little union. First of all I want to invite everybody here to a barbecue a week from Friday. A week from Friday the Southern Tenant Farmers' Union is going to hold a barbecue right on this very spot fer you-all, and it will be a stomp-dance too. It will be a stomp-dance fer the union and I want you-all to come and hear what we got to say and eat our barbecue and dance all night long. A week from Friday, and don't forget it. That's about all I got to say except that when you go down to the spinach fields you'll git twice as much money fer your work if you join up with the union. You'll all have black felt hats and silver hatbands and eagle feathers in 'em if you join up with the union and if you want to know more about it you come to that stomp-dance a week from Friday. Don't forget it, a week from Friday right here."

Jay stepped down from the stump and walked away. He heard a murmur of voices, but he did not look back. He stepped over the rails of the broken-down fence and went through the trees toward the stomp grounds.

I'm glad I done it and maybe it'll do some good and I'll talk to that Red Feather and Joseph Paul and we'll sure as hell have that stomp-dance a week from Friday and we'll git every Indian we can to come to it and by God we'll git 'em to talking union.

At the stomp grounds a few men loitered around the barbecue pits, from which a slow, steaming haze rose, and at the far end several men and women were gathered around a tall pole, at the top of which was a crudely carved fish, about eighteen inches long. Jay found Leona sitting on the running board of an automobile under a persimmon tree with Lamar. Her face was flushed and her blue eyes very bright.

"Jay, he makes me so mad," she said as soon as he came within hearing.

"Does he?" Jay looked steadily at Lamar.

"He thinks I take it too seriously."

"I don't know what you're talking about, Leona."

"The Indians. They're never left alone. They've been mistreated for generations and they accept it with the patience of Job. And when they have their own celebration, their tribal festival, the white man comes in and tries to take it over."

"I guess she means me," Lamar said, grinning.

"Well, I do, kind of."

"Say, I don't think you like me very much."

Jay sat down in the grass and looked up at the sky through the shiny leaves of the persimmon tree.

"Well, you do annoy me, Lamar," Leona said. "I like you, but you sure do know how to get under my skin."

"I guess that goes fer Jay, too," Lamar said. "Listen, Jay, everything else aside, I was sure sorry to hear about Belle. She was a fine woman and it broke me up to hear about it."

Jay nodded but did not speak.

"Why, I've knowed Belle since school days," Lamar said.

Jay got suddenly to his feet and walked away, across the stomp grounds toward the road. He called sharply: "Haze!"

The old man had come from the road and was walking toward the barbecue pit when Jay called him. He turned and bent his head. "I was lookin' fer you, Jay."

"How is Rocky?"

"That pore nigger. That's why I wanted to see you, Jay.

It looks like he's got worse. I done give him a whole bottle of my Sampson 'lixir, but it ain't done a lick of good."

"Is he pretty sick?"

"He's worse than pretty. Jay, them cuts on his back is festered and most of the time he's out of his head. He spits blood, Jay, like you and me would spit terbacco."

"I hope he ain't hurt inside." Jay shook his head. "He said they kicked him in the side hard as they could. I should of took him to a doctor the first thing."

"Uh-huh. I come up here today to git hold of Joseph Paul and send you word, Jay. It ain't but about three mile back through the woods to my place, so I come afoot to tell Joseph."

"I sure do appreciate it, Haze. Yonder's that Indian now."

Joseph Paul came toward them, wiping his face with a purple handkerchief. Behind him Jay saw other Indians coming from the woods.

"Ball game now, *on-g'las-ka-lishka,*" Joseph Paul said. "Howdy, Haze."

"Hello, there."

"Jay, chief damn plenty mad."

"I ain't surprised about that," Jay said, grinning.

"Couple men talk to me," the Indian said. "Say come stomp-dance week from Friday."

"You keep talking it up, Joseph."

"Ay-uh, Jay."

"And where's that Red Feather?"

"Him here, Jay. Don't know where."

Joseph Paul nodded and walked on toward the ball field. At the base of the tall pole a group of men and women stood; vigorous laughing women with large round arms and strong backs. Each man had two sticks, looped at the ends and laced with rawhide, like small lacrosse sticks. The men played against the women and only the men used sticks. The men and women formed a circle around the pole and the game began when a small rawhide ball was tossed toward the pole by the chief. The men then tried to pick up the ball with their two sticks and throw it at the fish, while the shrieking women caught at the sticks, tried to intercept passes thrown among the men, and when they got possession of the ball threw it themselves with

their hands, at the fish. Sometimes the women were whacked
on the wrists and arms as they fought for the ball, and there was
always laughter, and shrill, playful cries. Joseph Paul, still wearing the pith helmet, stood at the edge of the circle and waited
until the ball came his way; otherwise he did not exert himself.

"Jay, do you reckon anybody's got a jug here?"

"You ain't supposed to bring no liquor around Indians, Haze."

"I know that, but anyhow I reckon I'll take a look."

"All right. Haze, I'll have a doctor out yonder bright and
early tomorrow."

"That's good, Jay."

Jay walked over to the barbecue pit. One or two Indians
glanced at him curiously, and a young man wearing an eagle
feather in the hatband of his black felt hat smiled and came
toward him.

"Hello, Red Feather," Jay said.

"Hello."

"Did you hear my talk?"

The Indian nodded, still smiling.

"Maybe it was the wrong thing to do," Jay said. "I ain't sure.
But we're going to hold that stomp-dance, like I said. I'm going
to put it in your hands, Red Feather. I want you to talk about
it to everybody you know and I'm going to leave it in your
hands."

"Indian like stomp-dance, Jay. Maybe come."

"I sure do hope so."

"But maybe come just fer dance, Jay. Indian new to union.
Union white-man way." Red Feather pursed his brown lips.
"Listen, Jay, you got plenty barbecue?"

"I'll look after that part of it."

"Plenty squirrel now. Me tell Indian kill lots damn fox-
squirrel. Roas' squirrel okay."

"All right," Jay said. "I'll rustle up a little meat, though, just
the same."

"Union do like say, Indian maybe join union," Red Feather
said. "Indian say Land fer Landless good. Indian say plenty
good, go git land. Indian have land one time, now git back.
White man give Indian land fer long as water flow and grass
grow, then steal land away. When we git land back, Jay?"

"Now that ain't going to come overnight, Red Feather," Jay said, looking at the young Indian with his head on one side. "Our plan is to have the state sell the school lands, fer one thing. They got those school lands laying idle since the time they was turned over to the state when the townships was laid out and we figure there's enough land fer over a thousand families. That's just a beginning, but our ultimate objective is to git land fer the landless."

Red Feather's bright black eyes watched Jay's face. "Some slow fer Indian, Jay. Indian want land damn quick now. Indian land once and Indian say time come take land back."

I got to be plenty careful with them Indians. Them fullbloods is mighty independent people and they git a notion in their heads and it's hard to git it out. I got to watch that Land fer the Landless or they *will* go right out and take it, sure enough.

"When we're organized solid it will be time to take our action, Red Feather," Jay said. "But we can't do nothing until we got that strong organization."

The rise and fall of shrill voices abruptly ended and Jay saw that the ball game was over. The Indians were deserting the south end of the arena, trooping toward the barbecue pit where the wood smoke made a faint haze against the trees. Some of them had red-lettered cards in their hatbands.

"Jay, you like *ka-nah-chi?*"

"What's that?"

"Come see."

Jay followed Red Feather to a lean-to of fresh oak boughs near the pit. The Indian dipped a gourd cup in an iron pot and held it out to Jay. Jay drank some of the fluid. It had a bitter taste, and Red Feather, who had been watching his face, laughed.

"What is it?" Jay asked.

"*Ka-nah-chi* Indian drink, Jay. Boil hominy in ashes to take hull away. Beat hickory nut, whole nut, plenty fine, cook in water and strain and pour into hominy. You got *ka-nah-chi*." Red Feather laughed, and slapped Jay's shoulder. "Give me, Jay. Me drink *ka-nah-chi*."

Jay gave him the gourd. "I got to circulate around, Red Feather. I'll talk to you later."

"Okay."

Jay went to find Leona. Walking through the crowd he passed the Sheriff, a short man in gray shirt and trousers, with a ten-gallon hat. He looked steadily at Jay, his brown face expressionless, and Jay passed him by.

He's here with them deputies of his that he always has along with him, his deputies and vote-getters. Maybe he's up here like Lamar to git votes and maybe he's on the watch fer Pat and he's got his eye on me fer that reason. Pat ought to be up in Missouri by now, unless he's still hiding in the hills. If he's still here Crosby and me will hear from him. I reckon he'll hide in the hills until after Belle is buried and I hope to God he'll have the sense not to come to the funeral.

Jay found Leona under the persimmon tree with Lamar and Joseph Paul. Lamar had a stack of cards in his hand, lettered in red *Lamar Baker for County Attorney*.

"All finish now," the Indian said. "Not'ing more till night come."

"Say, Jay," Lamar said with a faint smile, "I heard you made a little talk."

"That's right," Jay said, stiffening.

"Don't you forget they're my constituents, Jay."

"I ain't interested in their votes, Lamar. All I'm interested in is the union, and if you had any sense you'd string along with me. All we're after is a square deal fer the tenant farmer. You ain't against that, are you?"

"We talked that over once," Lamar said, touching the patch of adhesive beside his mouth. "Of course I'm fer the farmer, but . . ."

"Then why don't you act it?" Jay said. "Why don't you go out and campaign to have the school lands turned over to the tenant farmer on an easy-purchase plan? You string along with us on that and it won't do you no hurt."

"I believe I could support that," Lamar said, pursing his lips.

"Let's don't talk politics, Jay," Leona said. "What are we going to do about food? Could we have some of that barbecue, Joseph?"

"Maybe. Me go see."

"That'll be fine," Lamar said.

"Hold on," Jay said. "They only got a calf and a couple of goats to feed all them people. Leona, I reckon you and me better rustle up something fer ourselves."

"We could rob us a cornfield," Lamar said. "We could build up a fire and cook us some roasting ears."

"Steal corn taste best," Joseph Paul said. His small eyes watched them with an inscrutable expression.

"We ain't stealin' no corn," Jay said. "Lamar, I'm going to take Leona back down the road."

Lamar met Jay's eyes, then bit his lip. "Okay. Leona, you and me are going to have a dance tonight."

"All right, Lamar."

"I got to talk to a man," Lamar said. "So long, you-all."

Jay watched Lamar walk toward the barbecue pit with a strong, assured stride, the white Stetson hat on the back of his head. He saw Lamar put his hand on the shoulder of an old man with a high-crowned hat of brown straw.

"That's old man Binch," Jay said. "He runs a general store and they put the box there on election day. He marks the ballots fer a hundred and fifty people and he's got those hundred and fifty votes right in his pocket. Watch Lamar butter up to him, Leona."

"Jay, there's been enough politics." Leona looked toward the cars parked among the trees. "Neil ought to be here by now."

"Now look here, are you hungry?"

"You bet I am."

"Well, what do you say we drive back Boggs way and we'll rustle up something to eat?"

"I have to wait for Neil."

"There ain't but one road and like as not we'll meet him on the way out."

"Well—all right, Jay."

Already twilight was at hand, with no afterglow of sun in the overcast sky. They walked among the trees to Jay's car.

"We'll recognize Neil's car when we meet him," Leona said. "It has a U.S. license."

They drove eastward, away from the stomp grounds, with the darkness thickening in the trees around them. A fresh wind had come up and it was cool. Leona tied a green scarf around her hair to hold it in place and Jay grinned at her.

"You look like an Indian yourself, honey," he said.

There was a monotonous sameness about the road — the rust-red loam overlaid with fine dust and the green trees darkening in the twilight. They met several cars and the dust was so thick that Jay was blinded each time and had to stop the car. When at last they came out of the woods upon the highway Jay sighed in relief and turned east toward Boggs.

"We ought to have met Neil," Leona said, frowning. "I don't want to miss him."

"We'll find him all right."

"He ought to have been here by now. He planned to leave the dam a little early, and he's usually on time. Neil is a very dependable person."

"Uh-huh," Jay said.

It's funny she would like a skinny little city man like him. There ain't no fat on his bones and he's got that little black moustache and he don't look to me like much of a man.

"How about this place?" Jay said. "Fried catfish. How about that?"

They crossed a steel bridge over the river and on the right, perched on the riverbank, was a small frame building. *Fried Catfish Dinners* was painted on a sign beside the road.

"All right. We can sit near the window and keep an eye out for Neil."

Jay drove off the road upon a gravel parking space. Below them was the narrow green river and a skiff moored to a willow tree. Inside the building there were four tables and a counter beyond which shelves were stacked in a confusion of groceries. A woman came from the kitchen in the rear.

"We want some supper, ma'am," Jay said.

"We got catfish and corn dodgers."

"That's fine. Set down, Leona."

"Over here by the window, Jay, where I can see the road."

"Anywhere you want." There was an icebox near the door and Jay raised the lid and fished out two bottles of beer, then went to the kitchen for glasses.

"I'm sure we've missed Neil," she said when Jay returned.

"If we have we'll find him at the dance, honey," Jay said. "Look here, you forget about him fer a bit."

She turned her head from the window and smiled.

"Looks like you're more dependable than ever he is," Jay said.

The woman brought a tray from the kitchen and put plates of fried catfish and round greasy corn cakes before them.

"It's seven o'clock now," Jay said. "Looks like he ain't coming."

"Y'all goin' to the stomp-dance?" the woman asked. "Them catfish are right out of the river, catched this afternoon. Y'all goin' to the dance?"

"Reckon we are," Jay said.

"I never been to one of them dances. Sometime I'm goin' to. Lots of people went up last year but I couldn't git off. They say them Indians dance all night up there. They been passin' by all day in their wagons, dressed up like you never seen 'em."

A car flashed by on the road. It was nearly dark and Leona put her face close to the window. "Jay! That car had a white license plate."

"I seen it," Jay said. "It was a Missouri car."

"It don't look like they'll have a moon fer it tonight," the woman said. "Want some more corn dodgers?"

"Yes," Jay said.

"I'll put some more on the fire, then. They *are* good, ain't they? My husband sure did like my corn dodgers. Wouldn't eat catfish without 'em, he wouldn't."

"Jay, I think we'd better go," Leona said. "Really, I've got to meet him."

"All right," Jay said. "Never mind that other batch."

He paid the woman and they went out to the car. As they drove away Jay said slowly, "Right up the road on the right, a few miles yonder, is where they moved to. That's where Belle is now."

"Oh, Jay, it's really terrible. I don't know how to say it. . . ."

"It ain't no use to talk about it, honey."

They drove on in silence. Ahead of them a car turned off on the side road toward the stomp grounds and beyond it they saw the tail-light of another car. Jay drove slowly along the rough road, with the headlights seeping through the dust ahead of him. He had to drive in second gear and they were a long time on the narrow hill road before they saw lights in the dust ahead where the stomp grounds were. As they came nearer the light suddenly brightened and Leona looked overhead.

"The moon," she said. "It's not very bright, but it's the moon."

The moon was a hazy disc that seemed translucent as it shone from a misty sky; it seemed that the light was behind it, shining through it as through soft knitted wool. There were many cars at the stomp grounds now and Jay had to drive well off the road, over rough ground. They struck against a tree-stump and the engine stalled.

"Now let's look for Neil," Leona said. "It ought to be easy to find his car. It has — "

"A U.S. license," Jay said sourly.

They walked together among the cars, under the trees. The moonlight was bright enough to see the license plates if they bent down to them. They made the circuit of the grove, wherever there were cars, and they did not find Neil.

Them are Laws under that oak tree, a couple of Laws standing there watching, and they wasn't there before. Standing there with their gun-belts on and their arms folded watching a stomp-dance. They're from the state highway patrol with them brown shirts and caps and the dark brown stripe on their pants and it's plain the Sheriff got 'em here. That's why they're here. It's because of Pat. They're still after him and they're watching me. That boy, I hope he's way to hell and gone by now. . . .

In the center of the arena there was a soft white blur, of shirts and faces and pale dresses in the moonlight, in the firelight. Suddenly there was a shout, low-pitched and husky, followed by the rhythmic beating of a drum.

"Looks like the dance is started," Jay said. "Let's go look at it, Leona."

They found men and women standing four deep in a great circle and Jay pushed ahead, making way. There were several white people around them. They came to the inner edge of the crowd and before them was the light of the altar fire flickering on a press of faces. An old man with a gourd rattle in his hand stood near the altar. He called something in Cherokee and several old men went forward. They fell in behind the man with the rattle and began to walk slowly around the fire. The long-handled gourd rattle began to shake in the old man's hand and his voice rose in a chant, "*Hah-you-wah-nee*," and the men behind him responded, "*Na-na-yo*." More Indians had come forward and fallen in line and the circle was completed about the altar fire. "*Hah-no-wee-eh-hey*," the leader chanted, with the chorused response, "*Hah-nah-wee-yeh*." There was a pause while the drums pulsed, then the chant again. The tempo became faster and Jay heard the shuffle of feet on the bare-baked ground and a progressive rattling noise like the shaking of a toneless tambourine. There were three concentric circles of dancers now and they moved steadily in lockstep around the altar, dancing with a rhythmic motion, half a shuffle, half a dog-trot. All the time the drums were beating and the occasional chant rose in perfect unison, although now there seemed to be no signal for it. The dancers swept past them a few feet away, and they saw the firelight on the brown faces, on the round arms of the women as they danced with their hands on the shoulders or waists of those ahead of them.

"You notice they don't have no dress-up clothes," Jay said. "That's how poor they are. They don't even have no special dress-up clothes fer their stomp-dance. They don't have nothing and most of their land is mortgaged to Kansas City banks."

The misty moon shone dimly down and now and then there came the glimmer of heat-lightning far away. The crowd of watching people, of which they were a part, became a vague and shadowy background for the steady flow of motion around the altar, the swiftly passing figures, the feet scuffling in the dust, the black hats and straw hats at jaunty angles, the beaded hatbands bright in firelight. Jay saw that some of them wore Lamar's campaign cards in their hats. And all the time the drums were beating and the feet were shuffling and the chant rose, spontaneous and musical: "*Hey-he-yey, hey-he-yey*." Jay watched one strong girl, bare-footed, in a printed cotton dress. She danced with a liquid motion of her hips and legs, her torso hardly swaying, and timed with her movements was the brisk clatter of the rattles she wore, like a snake's warning in the grass — rattles of dried tortoise shells strung together and fastened to one of her bare ankles. Her head was raised and the light slanted on the broad high planes of her face; she seemed to move like a princess among her people, yet in harmony with them and with the lifting chant, the beating drums.

"Look at ol' fatstuff," a girl's voice said. "Attaboy, fatstuff."

Jay turned his head and saw that it was a young Indian girl who had spoken. She stood near him, wearing blue slacks and a man's red shirt. She was chewing gum, her black eyes fastened on the dancers.

"Come on, let's stomp," she said. "Wanna stomp?"

The girl with her said lazily, "No, I like it to go faster when I stomp."

"There's old fatstuff again," the first girl said. "Look at him."

Jay looked at the dancers and saw it was Joseph Paul they were watching. The firelight shone on the white crown of his pith helmet, the black-tipped eagle feather in it. He trotted heavily in the outer circle of dancers, and after he had gone once more around the altar he dropped out, near Jay and Leona. He turned to Jay, his face impassive in the uncertain light, his eyes soft dark shapes. He was puffing and his face glistened with sweat.

"Go ahead, Jay, you dance."

"Is it all right?" Leona asked. "They don't mind?"

"Go ahead. White people welcome."

"How about it, Jay?"

"Sure."

"Step right in," Joseph Paul said. "Plenty room."

Jay took her hand and they moved out away from the crowd. They found places among the dancers and trotted away.

"Dance on the balls of your feet," Jay said. "Just sort of slide along."

His hands were on her waist, holding her, and they danced around the great circle with the glow of the altar fire on their left, with the misty moon overhead, with the heat-lightning flashing regularly like a lighthouse on a foggy night. The rhythm of it entered into them and they felt rather than heard the beating drums, the quivering sound of the rattles and the lifting chant. They joined in the chant. "*Hi-yah. . . . Ho-he.*"

. . . Leona's mouth was open and her eyes were bright as glass reflecting the glowing light. Around and around they danced, with the massed faces of the watching crowd a continuous pale strip against the black tree shadows. The sound of the shuffling feet on the hard bare ground became a part of the rhythm of the drums and the rattles and the chanting voices. They trotted dizzily and timelessly in the stream of humanity, a part of the electric bond that joined it in the selfless abandon of the dance. In the liquid motion, the rhythmic sound sequences, there was complete forgetfulness, even for Jay. But then with a shrill, high-pitched shout the dance ended and they were left standing together among the Indians. Jay gave her a great hug.

I wonder does she feel like I do. It ain't much to watch but when you're out here it gits into your blood and you can shut your eyes and it's like a dream and I got the feel of her waist and it's warm to my hands and I want to squeeze it. . . .

They moved slowly back into the crowd, leaving the central space bare around the gray altar. Many people around them were white, Jay saw, and looking over his shoulder he saw the lights of more cars approaching through the dust on the narrow road from Boggs.

"We'd better look for Neil now," Leona said.

Jay did not reply. He was watching the old Indian in the black hat walk across the arena to the crowd on the opposite side, where the drums were. The Indian began to form people in line for the next dance, shaking his long-handled gourd rattle.

"Come on," Jay said.

"But I ought to . . ."

"All right. After this dance."

They went out to join the dancers, lined three abreast around the altar. They found places and Jay put his hands on her waist again. They stood listening to the hum of many voices; close on their left a log on the altar made a snapping noise and sent up a brief Roman candle of sparks. Then the drums began to pulse, the voices rose in a shout, "*Hey-he-yey*," and they were in motion again. A young Indian ahead of Leona had a hand rattle, pebbles in a dried gourd, and he shook it in time with the dancing. Their feet shuffled on the hard ground and now even the earth seemed to beat with the pulsation of the dance.

Jay's hands tightened on her waist; his eyes were half-closed. The dance was all rhythm and contact for him, musicless. There was contact with the earth, with the moving muscles of her waist; his fingers were strongly clasped around her. And always there were the drums and the rattles and the drums and the rattles and the shuffle of feet; the soft beat of feet on bare ground, the resonant beat of the drums, the dry high clatter of the rattles. Jay chanted with the rest, "*Hi-yah*," opening his eyes to look up at the soft woolen moon above the trees. The moving faces around him were warmed by the altar fire, the whole scene was colored by it. Now Leona was chanting. He heard her voice soft and low-pitched and he laughed deep in his throat and held her more tightly. Then the dance ended with the sudden shout and they went back to the crowd and stood breathless in a mass of people. It was almost painful to breathe and it seemed unreal with the misty moon making indistinct the faces around them. Leona looked unfamiliar, her features blurred in the soft light. He put his arm around her, and she looked up at him, then bent her head.

"Honey, I'm crazy about you," Jay whispered.

Leona pulled away. "I should really look for Neil." She turned her head toward the road.

"Wait a little. Let's have one more dance."

"But he may be here in the crowd."

"We'll look and see." He took her arm and they walked inside the circle of the crowd, looking at the mass of faces. When they had gone nearly around the altar the drums began to beat again and the dancers swayed past them. Jay took her hand and led her toward the altar. Then they were in the swing of it again, his hands on her waist again, the rattles and the drums and the shuffle of feet beating with their pulse again, the rattles and the drums and the shuffle of feet. And the drums and the rattles and — "*Hi-yah*," Jay chanted with the rest. Ahead of Leona moved the plump Indian girl in the printed dress, with the rattles of dried tortoise shell quivering on her bare ankle; on each side of her were young Indians with beaded hatbands, in overalls. Leona swept around the circle behind the plump girl, it seemed as part of her retinue as she moved regally with her head erect, her arms lifted. Jay watched the Indian girl's

supple shoulders as she danced around and around the altar.
There was something primitive and stirring about her; she
identified herself with the dance. Jay's blood flowed fast, his
heart pounded, and there was never enough air in his lungs as
he breathed shallowly in the mounting excitement . . . around
and around the altar with the glow of the fire, the misty disc
of the moon, the glimmer of heat-lightning far away. Jay gave
himself entirely to the motion of it, the flow of sound and the
great harmony of movement; he embraced the crowd, with a
warm feeling of affection and identity for the lithe young men
around him, for the sinuous girl with the tortoise-shell rattles.
In these continuous revolutions around the altar he was one of
them; he moved with them, felt with them. His voice rose with
theirs in the chant and he beat his feet on the ground. His hands
were tight on Leona's waist and he watched her as she floated
around the circle as wraithlike as the moonlight.

She must feel it like I do *Hi-yah* and she must feel my hands
the way I feel her waist *Ho-he* and Christ I know she feels
like I do and I'm crazy about her and I love her *Hi-yah* and she
loves me *Ho-he* she's got to *Hi-yah* Leona, honey *Ho-he* I'm
just goin' to grab you *Hi-yah* and hold you *Ho-he* and I ain't
never going to turn you loose *Hi-yah* and just you and me together *Ho-he* holding each other *Hi-yah* stamp stamp *Ho-he*
stamp stamp *Hi-yah* stamp stamp *Ho-he* stamp stamp *Hi-
yah*. . . .

Suddenly the dance was over and they were left together
among the Indians. Her eyes were closed and he saw the glow
of firelight on her face. She stood with her eyes closed and her
arms hanging limp at her sides and when Jay kissed her she did
not stir. His lips fluttered mothlike on her cheek, then on her
lips. His arms tightened around her and his lips pressed hard
against hers. Jay could hardly breathe and there was a great
pressure in his lungs as if they were filled to bursting with air.
Then she raised her hands against his chest and pushed herself
away. They walked back to the crowd, neither of them speaking, and he held her hand in a tight grip. They went through
the crowd and came out into near darkness under an oak tree.
He kissed her again, holding her close.

"Honey, I love you," Jay whispered, and kissed her ear.

"I love you too, Jay."

He hardly heard her; the whispering voice was strange and unfamiliar. Behind them the dance had begun again and they heard the drums and the rattles and the shuffle of feet and he held her very close under the oak tree and kissed her eyes and her cheeks and her moist lips.

"I can't hardly believe it," Jay said. "Honey, come away with me, away from all them people."

His arm was around her waist and he led her out into the moonlight. They threaded their way among parked cars away from the stomp grounds and they came to where the woods began, turning away from the road on which there was a steady stream of lights — car after car on the way from Boggs, as far as they could see, all the way to the bend in the road, cars a few hundred yards apart bumping over the rough road in a pall of dust toward the stomp grounds. They stopped in tall grass under a sassafras tree and Jay caught her again and kissed her. She was supple, almost limp, and her body clung to his. Whispering to him, her mouth open, her face pressed against his, her eyes closed. Her arms were around his neck, her body almost suspended, and when he sank to his knees she was beside him in the tall grass and her body yielding in his arms.

"I love you, honey," Jay whispered. "Christ, you'd never know."

The dance had begun again and there came the sound of the chant, the beat of drums and the whispering sound of feet on the dusty ground. They lay together in the tall grass in deep shadow beneath the sassafras tree with their hot faces pressed together, and behind them were the drums and the rattles and the shuffle of feet and the drums and the rattles and the shuffle of feet and "Hi-yah, Ho-he," and the rattles and the drums and the rattles and the drums. . . .

In the tall grass the crickets were chanting a stomp-dance of their own and the leaves of the sassafras tree whispered above. Jay heard her sigh and opened his eyes, looking at the moon breaking through the black leaves overhead.

"Honey, what are you thinking about?" He found her hand and held it.

"Nothing."

"You keep so still. You ain't regretful, Leona?"

"No."

"I'd sure feel bad if you was regretful."

"I'm not, Jay."

He put his head in the hollow of her shoulder, sighing.

"Jay."

"Uh-huh?"

"We've got to get up. Somebody's liable to come along."

"We're deep in shadow here, honey."

She sat up and began to arrange her hair; Jay could see the pale blur of her face against the tree-trunk.

"I'm crazy about you, Leona, and I'd sure hate to think you was regretful," he said.

She touched his hand. "You're very sweet, Jay."

There was a crackling sound in the underbrush, but Jay hardly noticed it. "I'll sure be happy when we're man and wife," he said.

The noise grew louder and Leona said: "Somebody's coming, Jay."

She got to her feet and an instant later a dark shape broke through the bushes and bright lights flared blindingly in their faces. They stepped back against the tree as an automobile passed them, rolling slowly over the rough ground toward the road to Boggs. The car went past and just above the tail-light Jay saw the white license plate and the initials *U.S.*

"It's Neil," Leona said. "Oh, goodness, it's Neil. Do you suppose he saw us, Jay?" She called after the car, "Neil!"

"Let him go, Leona," Jay said.

But she had started after the car toward the road, calling over her shoulder, "Come on, Jay."

Jay remained under the sassafras tree with his hands thrust in his pockets. He saw her come alongside the car as it crossed a shallow ditch onto the road. The car stopped after it had crossed the ditch and Leona was poised for an instant beside it, then the door was opened and Jay saw her get in. The car drove away.

Now what did she go and do that fer? I don't see why she's got that interest in that little engineer. She just wants to be polite and after all this I don't see why. Jesus Christ she sure is sweet and maybe if I'd of just gone that way about it before it would have happened before. How are you going to know? She said she loved me and now she's my woman and I'm going to git myself hitched up to her quick as I can and we can sure be happy, just us two, like nobody else ever was . . . except maybe Pat and Belle. They was happy that way and she was sure a good wife fer him and now she's laying dead and poor Pat, God knows where he is and I can see now how he must feel about it. That poor boy, that poor reckless Pat, so deep in trouble now and with the Law after him and the Sheriff and a posse right here in the hills, here at this stomp-dance and with Belle shot and killed. . . .

$\mathscr{P}at$

✤   ✤

"KEEP your yap shut," Pat said.

He sat in the front seat beside Neil, half-turned toward Leona, and light gleamed on the barrel of the forty-five in his hand. He kept his face turned from the lights of the approaching cars as they drove away from the stomp grounds. The moon, shining through clouds like shades of muslin drawn across it, was further dimmed by the drifting dust clouds caused by car after car moving slowly over the bumpy road from Boggs. Neil had to shift to low gear and drive on the very edge of the road to pass the cars they met, and the dust rolled in so thickly that he could see only a few feet ahead and the approaching lights glowed redly and without penetration.

I ought to of started out sooner, just as soon as it got dark. It looks like I waited too long and it looks like my luck has clean run out. Now I got two of 'em on my hands and one of 'em a woman and you can't never tell what a woman will do and I sure wouldn't shoot a woman the way they shot Belle. . . . I got to git out of these woods and I got to git back somehow and find out about Belle. I got to know and I can't go on alone without I know.

"You keep going fast as you can, Smith," Pat said. "Never mind if you scrape a fender."

"I can't see," Neil said.

The approaching lights shone dimly through the dust and Neil watched the side of the road for guidance. Most of the cars stopped to let them pass, and there was hardly room to do so. The dust sifted into the car chokingly. And steadily the lights kept coming, every few hundred yards on the narrow, slippery road. In ten minutes they had hardly gone a mile. Pat was uneasy and his hand was clenched on the butt of the gun.

"Look," Neil said. "Now what will I do?"

He stopped the car and Pat saw on the right of the road a deep ravine, obscured by the blown dust, on the left a hillside. There was not room for two cars to pass, and immediately ahead of them were the lights of a car, another behind it, glowing through the dust.

"What will I do?" Neil asked, staring into the white night. The driver of the car ahead sounded his horn.

Pat glanced behind him. "We got to turn back," he said through his teeth. "Okay, back up to that wide space and turn into the trees."

Jesus God my luck has run out. I can't git past that ravine and I can't make them other cars back down the road into that dust fer a mile or more, with all them other cars coming in. I got to go back again. . . .

Neil put the car in reverse. Fifty feet back along the road he backed the car over a ditch and into an opening in the trees. There was just room enough to get the front wheels off the road.

"Go on," Pat said. "We can't stay here with them state highway patrolmen on this road."

Neil swung the car around on the road again, in the direction of the stomp grounds.

"Later on we'll try again," Pat said. "If anybody yells at you, don't you answer. Understand?"

This stomp-dance has sure been bad luck fer me, and it was sure bad luck to come up here out of all places in these hills.

The dance is just now gittin' off good and them people will be coming in to watch it fer hours to come. They say the dance goes on till dawn.

Neil followed the dust-clouds back to the stomp grounds and turned right at the fork in the road. The car climbed up through the lane in the parked cars and onto the stomp grounds at the northern end. They drove through a crowd which scattered before the lights and Pat sat half-turned, watching Leona. Neil turned off into the trees and the car plunged through underbrush for a hundred yards, then came to a stop. He snapped off the lights. Pat got out of the car and stood in the moonlight with the gun in his hand.

"Okay," he said. "Git out."

The misty moonlight broke through the trees and shone on the barrel of the gun in his hand. He stood a yard from the automobile and watched them as they got out, Neil first, to open the door for Leona. As she stepped down to the grass Neil held one of her hands and his low voice said: "Don't be afraid."

"Keep quiet," Pat said harshly, and they both looked at the forty-five in his hand.

"We'll go back to where we was before," Pat said.

Leona turned away and suddenly Neil threw himself forward. Pat was only a yard away and he was taken by surprise and Neil knocked up the hand that held the gun. The two men grappled with each other.

"Neil!" Leona screamed, and an instant later Pat freed one arm and brought the blue barrel of the gun smashing down on Neil's head. He fell on his face at Pat's feet. Leona screamed again and, too late, turned to run. Pat jumped after her. His arm swept roughly around her and his hand was crushed across her mouth. The scream was choked in her throat and she stood with wide eyes staring at Neil on the ground beside the car.

"Keep your mouth shut, you hear?" Pat whispered. "Are you going to keep still?"

She nodded and he took his hand away from her mouth.

"If anybody heard that it's just too bad." He released her and she slipped to the ground beside Neil.

"Damn you," she whispered. "You've killed him. Oh, you've killed him."

"He ain't hurt much."

She lifted Neil's head to her lap. "There's blood all over him." She was sobbing. "He's covered with it."

"He ain't hurt," Pat said uneasily. "I didn't want to do it. I got nothing against him. But he oughtn't to jumped me that way."

Leona looked up at his face, in shadow under the brim of his hat. "I know who you are," she said hoarsely.

"Keep quiet," Pat said. He leaned over and picked Neil up in his arms. "Now you start out ahead of me, Miss. Go on."

Leona started through the woods, looking back. They pushed through underbrush, following a narrow trail of moonlight, and came out into a moonlit glade. Pat put Neil gently on the ground. He kicked in the grass and found the copper wire.

"What are you going to do?" Leona whispered.

"Tie him up, and maybe you too."

"But you can't tie *him* up. He's hurt."

"He'll be all right. I'll leave you loose, Miss, and you can take care of him. He'll come around in a minute."

Pat knelt and bound Neil's hands and feet. Neil lay with his head in Leona's lap, breathing heavily. Once he moaned. She took the handkerchief from her hair and dabbed at the wound.

"It ain't but a break in the scalp," Pat said.

It was very still in the glade, with only the softest whisper of wind in the trees. The moon spread a steady soft light over them, and now from the distance came the beat of drums as the dance was resumed.

"Is there any water here?" Leona asked.

"There's a brook over yonder in the brush. Come on." Pat walked with his hand on her elbow, the leaves rustling under his boots. He tramped through a thicket toward the sound of flowing water.

"Here it is," Pat said, and watched her kneel down and soak her handkerchief in the brook. He walked beside her back to Neil. She mopped the blood from Neil's head with the wet handkerchief. The moonlight was full on his face and they saw his eyelashes flutter like shadow on his cheeks. Then his eyes opened.

"Oh, Neil, are you all right?"

"How did it happen?"

"He hit you over the head. How do you feel?"

"My head hurts some. You all right, Leona?"

"I didn't want to do it, Smith," Pat said. "You shouldn't of jumped me that way."

"Neil, how did you get here with him?" Leona asked.

"Doesn't everybody know?"

"No."

"He took me hostage last night — came into my hotel and got me."

"That's enough," Pat said harshly. "I reckon you're all right now, feller. You better come away from him, Miss, and keep your yap shut." He bent over and examined the wire wound around Neil's ankles and wrists, then looked at the handkerchief with which Leona had bandaged his head.

"How you feelin'?"

"I'm all right."

"I didn't hit you hard. Come on, lady." He took her wrist and led her away. He stopped near the edge of the glade, twenty feet from Neil. "Okay, set down."

"That man's injured," Leona said. "I'm going to stay with him."

"No you ain't. Set down."

She started away and his fingers closed hard on her wrist. She kicked at him and he laughed and neatly tripped her up.

"You want to be tied up, too?" When she did not answer he added: "Well, you better lay quiet."

He sat down in the grass beside her, still holding her wrist. He looked at her, grinning.

"You're contrary, ain't you?" he said. "But you're okay. You got some guts, sister." He released her wrist. "Now you be quiet and stay where I can watch you and we won't have no trouble." He lit a cigarette, striking the match on the sole of his shoe. Through the trees he could see a faint glow from the stomp grounds, and he heard the drums and the rattles and the occasional chant.

"Them Indians git on my nerves," he said. "They been at it fer hours now." He sat cross-legged, with the forty-five in his lap, looking at the glow of the distant fire and listening to the drumbeats. "Eating and talking and dancing all day and night, just talking and dancing and eating."

He tossed the cigarette away and it glowed in the grass.

I ain't ate in two full days and God, I'm hungry. I'd like to git some of that barbecue but I can't take that big a chance, not with my luck run out. I could go and git it easy as not but I can't take that chance. It's so close I can see the firelight and pretty near I can smell that barbecue but I got to set here and starve myself and I can't take a chance like that with my luck gone. I got to git back Boggs way and find out about Belle and git in touch with Dad or Jay. Maybe I ought to take out into the hills afoot and lay up safe but then I wouldn't know and I'll go crazy if I don't find out. . . .

Pat sat staring at the distant glow of firelight. His eyes were sore and his mouth drooped at the corners. Looking at the fireglow, listening to the rattles and the drums, his heart was so heavy that he could hardly fill his lungs and he took a deep breath. He looked at Leona, sitting pale and silent beside him.

"Listen, you don't need to be scared of me." He shook his head. "Say, I wouldn't hurt you, and I wouldn't never hurt a woman. I sure enough wouldn't *shoot* a woman."

Pat took off his hat and dropped it in the grass beside him; in the moonlight there was color in his red hair. He glanced at her and she moved a little nearer him in the grass, receptively nearer him and nearer the glint of the forty-five in his lap.

"I wouldn't hurt nobody," Pat said. "All I'm after is to hide out safe in the hills and find my wife. It's because of her I come back here. I broke out of jail in Texas and headed back fer the hills."

It ain't no use of talking but I just got to and it's so heavy on me I got to talk. I just can't stand it no longer setting here and thinking about her and not knowing. . . .

"I read about you in the papers," Leona said.

"Yeah? What did they say?"

"It was on the radio, too."

"What did they say about me?"

"They called you a desperado," she said quietly. "They said you were a desperate criminal and a killer and that you'd never be taken alive."

"I ain't no killer," Pat said sharply. "Listen, lady, all I wanted was to git away. I was in jail in Texas and they was going to send me up fer ninety-nine years. Ninety-nine years! Even with parole that would mean all my life in prison. All I wanted was to git away and find Belle. Say, I ain't no killer."

He felt in his pocket for a cigarette and the cellophane rustled as he opened the package. He lit a cigarette and drew a deep inhalation, then breathed the smoke out with a sigh.

"Listen, Miss, I ain't no killer. All I wanted was to git away, I tell you. I had to do that."

"They said on the radio you shot two men," Leona said steadily.

"That's just a lie." Pat clenched his fists. "I never fired a shot. It was Clyde done it and they try to lay it onto me. And listen here, lady, I wouldn't even shoot a dog in cold blood like they done. Listen. . . ." His voice broke and he looked at her. "Them Laws laid fer me last night and they shot my wife down with a sawed-off shotgun. I don't even know how bad she's hurt. You listen here, I made a break in Texas and there was some shooting and they chased me, but I got away and I come back to the hills to find Belle." He clenched and unclenched his hands and there was sweat shining on his forehead in the moonlight. "I picked up Smith to lead me to where she'd moved to and we was coming up a dirt road and we turned a bend and I heard her calling to me. She had run out in her nightgown to tell me the house was full of Laws and they seen the lights of our car and they seen her on the road and they opened up and shot and it was her they shot at." His voice trailed off and he raised the crumpled cigarette to his lips. "That was Belle. She run out of the house to warn me and she run right under their guns and they shot her. That's the kind of a wife I got, lady. That's Belle."

Pat put his hat on again, pulling the brim low over his eyes. It was very still in the glade, with only the distant beat of drums and the quiver of rattles coming faintly to them. Off in the woods crickets were whirring in mechanical monotony. Leona sat with her eyes half-closed, listening to the drums and the rattles, to the crickets among the trees behind her. After a long time she said quietly: "I saw your wife yesterday."

"You did!" Pat's head snapped around. "Why didn't you say so? Tell me about it. Where did you see her?"

"It was over by Aldine. I drove there with Neil to your father's house and . . ."

"You seen Dad, too?"

"Yes, and I know your brother." She paused an instant. "I'm a good friend of Jay's."

"You are? Well, why didn't you say so? How is old Jay?"

"He's here at the stomp-dance."

"Here? Tonight? You mean now?"

"Yes."

"Christ, I got to find him. Jay will know. I got to find him. Jay will know about Belle."

Pat started to his feet, then sank back to his knees. He gazed at her steadily in the moonlight and slowly his hand went out and caught her wrist. His fingers closed tightly around it.

"Tell me," Pat said. "Go ahead, tell me."

"Belle was killed," Leona said in a whisper.

"She's dead?" His voice sucked in the words.

"Yes."

I been afraid to think of that but I knowed it all along. She was all over blood and she was hit by slugs from a sawed-off shotgun and Christ God she's dead. . . . And I can't never forget the way she died, running out to warn me, running out in her nightgown through the woods to tell me the house was full of Laws and then them shooting at her and she laid there on the road covered with blood and all the time she was dead and I never knowed it and I didn't want to know it. . . .

"Tell me about it." His hand closed on her wrist again.

"I don't know any more. Jay told me she was killed."

Pat sank into the grass beside her, still holding her wrist. The pressure of his fingers slowly relaxed, and at last he said quietly: "But you seen her yesterday. Tell me about her. How did Belle look?"

"Oh. She had on a pink dress and white shoes and she looked real pretty. She had nice hair."

"Yeah, like corn tossels. That was the first thing I noticed about her." Pat paused, and cleared his throat. "It was at a square dance and she was out there in the middle under a coal-oil lamp and the light was on her hair. She had that strong body and she was stamping her feet and laughing. And her hair was like corn tossels in the lamplight."

Pat dropped the cigarette in the grass and ground it out under his heel. He drove his heel viciously into the ground several times.

"She didn't know then you had escaped," Leona said. "She had on that pink dress and one of those beaded belts the Indians make and her hair was tied up in a dustcloth."

"In a dustcloth," Pat said. "I can see her. I can see them freckles on her nose that used to plague her so. She wrote off once to a mail-order house fer some stuff to git rid of 'em and it like to took her skin off. Did you notice them freckles?"

"There weren't so many of them."

"They gave her a pert look," Pat said. "I liked them freckles myself, but they sure plagued Belle. Go on, what else did she say?"

"She didn't want to leave there, but you know, your father is a shrewd man. He drives a good bargain. He got the top price for his farm and he wouldn't move out until he had the check in his hand."

"Good fer Dad," Pat said. "How much did he git?"

"Forty dollars an acre."

Pat whistled softly. "Good fer Dad." He was silent for a moment, listening to the drumbeats from the stomp grounds, then he said: "She didn't know I'd got away, you said?"

"Not until I told them. They were sure you'd escape and wouldn't be caught."

Pat took off his hat and the moonlight fell on the nest of wrinkles on his forehead and the long lines drawn beside his mouth in the stubble of reddish beard.

"She must have been very loyal," Leona said gently.

Pat nodded, sucking in his breath. "In some ways she was almost like a man. We used to go squirrel hunting together and take a jug along. We'd lay up in the hills fer two or three days. That was what I aimed to do this time. All I wanted was to find Belle and git away. I didn't want to hurt nobody. We could of took out into the hills, Belle and me, and lived on game and green corn. I know places where they'd never catch us and you know, she could make a squirrel stew like you never tasted, with cream gravy and spices like you never saw."

Pat cleared his throat and gave his head a shake. He wet his dry lips. "We used to go off together whenever we felt like it. It was always that way, from the first time I seen her. It was because of her I made my break. I *had* to git out of jail. They'd of sent me up fer ninety-nine years, sure as hell."

Pat reached for a cigarette and struck a match. His hand shook. The instant's flare of light showed the weary droop of his mouth, the lines of strain in his face.

"What are you going to do now?" Leona asked.

Pat shrugged his shoulders. "Pretty soon I'll have to be on the move again. I'll leave your friend tied up yonder." He looked at her. "I'll take you with me."

Leona stiffened, and the fingers of one hand clutched a tuft of grass.

"We'll wait until along about two o'clock," Pat said. "By that time the road will be clear."

He looked at her and saw that she was trembling, heard her small, quivering voice: "What about me?"

"Oh, say." He smiled. "I wouldn't hurt you, lady. I'll turn you loose somewheres down the road and you can tell where Smith is. I told you I wouldn't hurt nobody."

"Oh," Leona said, and closed her eyes. When she opened them she looked steadily at the gleam of moonlight on the gun, in the grass beside Pat.

"I'm in trouble, and I guess I'm no good," Pat said. "But I ain't mean. I always done what I pleased and I stole, but a man has got to live and a man don't want to go on relief work even if he can git it. A man has got to have some comforts and he's got to have something special to give to his wife. A woman wants a man who'll care fer her right."

His voice broke off in a sob, and in the glade they heard the beat of drums from the stomp grounds where the Indians were circling in primitive rhythm around the altar fire, to the sound of the drums and the rattles and the shuffle of feet. They listened to the cadence of it — the drums and the rattles and the rattles and the drums and the musicless chant.

"All I had was Belle," Pat said slowly. "That's the reason I wanted to git away and that's why I come back to the hills. Coming up the road I knowed she'd be there waiting fer me and I was looking fer the house when I heard her calling me. Then I knowed it was all wrong and I knowed what was going to happen almost before them guns went off. I never even had a chance to say hello. The Laws done that fer me with their guns. But she was thinking of me and she tried to warn me off. She told me to go on off and leave her and she said she wasn't hurt. But she was laying there and I picked her up and there was blood on her but I didn't know she was dead. She was an easy target in the moonlight, in that white nightgown, and a sawed-off shotgun spreads its slugs. It's plain they aimed at her."

Pat dropped his head to his hands, his fingers spread over his face. The forty-five lay unnoticed in the grass beside him, gleaming like mica in the moonlight; Pat sighed, and suddenly a startling sound split the silence — like the screech of an owl, the howl of a wolf, but metallic and without crescendo — the steady flow of noise from an automobile horn, very near them. Pat jumped to his feet.

"It's that car of ours and somebody's leaning on the horn and I got to stop that God-damned quick before the whole stomp-dance is on my neck."

He whirled around and his mouth opened and his hands clenched into fists. Leona was sprawled out on the grass and her hand had closed on the butt of the gun. She rose to her knees, two yards away from him, and the gun was pointed at him.

"Stay there," her dry, toneless voice said. "Put up your hands."

Behind Pat the automobile horn sounded again and he looked over his shoulder toward the noise.

"Put your hands up," Leona said. "I'll shoot."

"I reckon you would," Pat said. He slowly raised his hands. "Well, you fooled me. I clean forgot about that gun." He took one step toward her.

"You stay where you are," she said, and her voice was stronger now.

"Leona, have you got his gun?" It was Neil's voice. "Good girl!"

She backed away toward Neil and Pat followed her step by step.

"You stay there," she said nervously. "Don't come any closer."

"Shoot if he does, Leona," Neil called.

"I reckon she'd shoot," Pat said. He was still following her step by step. "Or would you?" His footsteps were slow in the grass. "I was wrong about you. You said you was a friend of Jay's. I never thought you'd try it."

"Leona," a voice called from off in the woods. "Yoo-hoo, Leona."

Pat kept walking toward her. His steps were slow, deliberate. She stared at his white face in the moonlight. Her finger was on the trigger and she held the gun pointed at his heart. But he walked on toward her, nearer now.

"I'll shoot," she said, and her voice was nearly a scream.

"Leona, yoo-hoo." It was Jay's voice calling from the woods.

Pat did not stop. He came on toward her, his hands above his head, a looming figure against the dark trees. He did not take his eyes from the gun in her hand and he came on, step by step.

"Give me that gun," he said hoarsely.

The gun was pointed at him but he sensed that it was held in nerveless fingers. It was held out as if she were offering it to him. He swooped forward and his hand swept down and struck her wrist. There was a flash of fire and a thundering noise as the gun went off. It fell to the grass at her feet and Pat picked it up.

"Now you done it," he said. "Jesus Christ, what a noise it made."

They heard the voice in the woods again, nearer now, calling Leona's name, and Pat turned toward the sound.

"Don't you recognize it?" Leona cried. "That's Jay calling."

"I believe it is," Pat said.

Leona dropped to her knees beside Neil and Pat walked slowly across the glade. He saw a dark figure in the trees, heard the rustle of bushes.

"Jay, is that you?"

"Yes — Good God! Pat?"

"It sure is me."

My brother Jay and it's good to feel his hand and see that face of his'n and know that old Jay is with me again. It makes it different just to see old Jay again and maybe he can tell me what to do. Jay will know.

"Bo, how did you git here?"

"I was looking fer my girl and I seen the car and that's why I honked the horn. Pat, fer God's sake!"

"She's over yonder. She's all right."

"Pat, they sure as hell heard that gun go off. Jesus, what was it? What happened?"

"It was an accident."

"You got to run, Pat. That gun made a hell of a noise and I seen lots of Laws out yonder and they're liable to be here any minute. The Sheriff's there and Lamar Baker and some state Laws. Pat, why don't you run?"

They heard the noise of men crashing through the woods.

"I'll go with you," Jay said. "Come on, Pat."

"No, Jay, you keep your hide out of this. I'll go alone and I'll lay up somewhere and . . ."

"Then fer God's sake, Pat, run!"

"Okay." Pat grinned and turned away. "So long, Jay."

Pat ran across the glade and into the bushes, running toward the east, toward the lowering moon.

Jay

❦   ❦

ALL this time he's been here in the woods while I was out there at the stomp-dance and I never knowed. It was him in that car and that's why she run off without saying nothing to me and it was him in that car when they come back and I seen it turn up into the woods. All that time it was poor Pat hunted and looking fer a place to hide. . . .

"It's Jay Strickland," someone shouted, and suddenly the glade was filled with men. Their faces were dark against their lighter clothing, their hats were haloed by the moon.

"Say, Jay, what did you shoot off your gun for?"

"I took a pot-shot at a squirrel, Lamar," Jay said.

That's the Sheriff with him and some of them others have got guns. Pat better be running as hard as he can but that reckless boy, you never can tell what he's up to.

"There's a feller over here tied up," a man said. "Yes, sir, tied hand and foot with copper wire."

"How come, Jay?" Lamar asked.

"Listen, you men, it's Pat Strickland." Neil's voice rose high and excited. "Get this wire off me, will you? It's Pat Strickland and he ran out that way just before you got here."

There was a murmur of voices and Lamar strode across toward Neil. "What was that you said, Mister? Why good God, it's Neil Smith!"

"That was Pat Strickland," Neil said. "I've been his captive since last night."

"Neil!" Leona said.

"Which way did he go, Neil?"

"Yonder." Neil pointed eastward. "He's only got a couple of minutes' start, Lamar."

"Fellers, let's go," the Sheriff shouted.

Lamar ran across the glade, and as he passed Jay he turned his head and laughed. The laughter came bubbling up from his chest. He ran on into the trees.

Leona came through the moonlight to Jay. "I'm sorry, Jay."

"It's all right, honey. I reckon Pat can git away in them woods."

"I got his gun away from him but I couldn't shoot, Jay. I just couldn't. But it's my fault it went off."

"It's all right, Leona." Jay looked over his shoulder. "Listen, I got to follow after 'em. Maybe I can help somehow and I'm going, too."

"Leona, I wish you'd help me get loose," Neil called.

"So long," Jay said, and ran into the woods.

If he keeps running Pat will git away but they must be a dozen of 'em after him and most of 'em got guns and the moonlight is bright now. I wish to God I'd knowed he was yonder in the woods all that time while I was dancing around the fire and I'd plumb forgot all about him and about Belle. . . .

Blackberry bushes caught at Jay's feet and he stumbled. He knocked against trees, and swinging branches struck across his face and chest. Ahead of him he heard shouts and the noise of men crashing through the brush. There was someone on his left, panting, swearing as he ran.

Pat's at home in these hills and if his start is only good enough he can git away. If it wasn't so bright. All night long there been clouds across that moon and now when we need pitchy night it comes out clear and bright and not a cloud in the sky and even deep in these trees I can see plain where I'm going. And all that time all night and all through the day, too, he was laying up yonder in that clearing and I wasn't but two hunderd yards away and while I was at the powwow and at the stomp-dance too if I'd of raised my voice and yelled he'd of heard me. And if I'd of knowed it I could of gone to him and we'd of figured a way fer him to git clear and I could of give him the money. I promised Belle I'd git him away safe and I got to do it fer her and if I follow after maybe I'll find him after they done give up. God damn that little city chicken-drop. He told 'em where Pat run to and who he was and if he hadn't Pat would of had a good start. But she didn't tell and she never would of let on, I know.

Jay ran with his hands ahead of him to push aside the swaying branches of elderberry and dogwood. He broke through a thicket of blackberry bushes and his face and hands were scratched. Several times he fell, and other men were falling, for he heard the noise of it in the underbrush and always he heard the shouts ahead of him.

"Come on, you-all, we're catching up."

The guiding shouts were all around Jay. There were men in front of him, more behind, and he heard their voices.

You'd think it was a coon hunt with the laughing and the yelling and the only thing is there ain't no hounds and thank God there ain't no hounds to track him. But they're after him like he was a coon and they're about to git him up a tree. Lamar and that Sheriff are leading 'em and both of 'em know if they catch Pat they'll damn sure win on primary day. That's what they're after. . . .

"I believe I seen him," someone shouted.

Jay ran on harder, crashing through the brush. He stumbled and struck his knee against a limestone boulder and gasped in pain, but he ran on without knowing that he was limping and his pace had slowed. Suddenly he heard the ringing, echoing sound of a rifle shot close ahead, then two more shots. A voice called: "I swear I hit him. I had a clean bead on him and I believe I hit him."

"Whereabouts? Whereabouts did you see him?"

"Yonder the other side of that gully. He was just climbing up the bank."

"I believe I seen him too."

Jay plunged through a screen of bushes and came out on the bank of a ravine where there were several men. One of them was the Sheriff and Jay saw a rifle in his hand.

"I know damned well I hit him," he was saying. "Come on, let's git acrost that gully."

The cedar trees were black down below and the opposite side of the gully rose sheer and bare of growth and the top of it was bathed in milky light.

It's near and that light is clear but it's tricky and not even no good shot like Pat or Belle could be sure they'd make a hit. But Jesus God I hope he didn't. . . .

Men were sliding down the bank into the gully and Jay followed them. The shale was dislodged by his feet and he slid down hard against a cedar tree and his face and hands were scratched by the brittle bark. But he did not stop. He pushed himself clear and started on through the cedars. There were men ahead of him and more were sliding down into the gully behind him. Needles slapped his face and the smell of them was in his nostrils. He plunged on through darkness and then came out of the trees into milky moonlight at the base of the slope. Above him men were climbing and moonlight shone on the barrel of a rifle, on the cartridge belt of the Sheriff. Jay heard him swearing as he labored up the bank. Jay started after him, bending forward to catch at rocks and tufts of weeds, and when he had nearly reached the top he heard the Sheriff's voice, loud and triumphant.

"I told you I hit him. Look here. Here's a speck of blood on this here rock and yonder's another. You see I hit him sure enough."

Jay reached the top and saw the circle of bright light from a flashlight on the flat, stony ground.

"Come on, you-all, we'll git him now," the Sheriff shouted.

"He won't run so God-damned fast with a thirty-thirty slug in him, sure enough."

Someone laughed, and there was a sob in Jay's throat as he ran on into the woods, following the bulky figure of the Sheriff. They were in dense trees now and could not run so fast, but always from ahead there came eager shouts. Around Jay was the constant noise of other men running, their voices shouting, cursing, laughing.

"I think I seen him."

"Spread out some more. Spread out, you-all. We're catching up."

Jay gasped for painful breath and his heart beat against his ribs. His knee was stiff where he had struck it against the rock, but he ran on after the Sheriff.

If it was blood on that rock they got him. If it was blood and a thirty-thirty slug he's bad hurt and he can't run far and they'll catch him sure. If that was blood it's all up fer my poor brother and they'll shoot him down like they shot Belle. . . .

Jay ran on. Sometimes he was in darkness in the dense woods and sometimes he ran across a glade where the moonlight was bright. He could hardly breathe and as he ran his eyes were hot and wet with blinding tears.

Somewhere up ahead Pat is running all alone and maybe with a thirty-thirty slug in him and he can hear 'em shouting back behind him like I can hear 'em shouting up ahead. If that was blood and if he's got a slug in him I'm afeard he can't go on much more. We run already maybe three mile and with a slug in him I don't see how he can go much further. Pretty soon he's got to stop and they'll close in and they'll shoot him down like they done Belle. . . .

Far ahead there was the sound of a shot, a singing noise and a flat report, and then another. Jay's teeth grated. Then he heard shouts, concentrated like the baying of hounds, localized, and several more shots.

Them shots is all in one place and they're shouting to the rest to come on and that means they got poor Pat. They got him treed and like hound dogs they all come together and they got him treed. Jesus, what am I going to do to help him? I got to git there and I got to do something. . . .

Jay ran in the direction of the noise and he heard more shots. He fell against a tree, righted himself, and ran on, and suddenly he came from darkness into bright moonlight and he saw the solid figure of the Sheriff and a line of men in the moonlight and a clearing bright with light and a cabin with a sagging roof-tree silhouetted against the moon.

"He's in yonder," the Sheriff shouted. "Spread out around that shack and we'll smoke him out."

From the dark window of the cabin there came a flash of fire and the smashing noise of a forty-five. Several men dropped flat on the grass, but Jay stood with his mouth open staring at the cabin in the moonlight.

It's Haze Thompson's house and Rocky's in there sick and Pat with a thirty-thirty slug in him. I guess he couldn't go no further and he run in there with Rocky. Jesus God!

A man ran forward, bent over, and ducked behind the well-shed. Jay saw the shine of the moon on the barrel of his pistol. He saw the pale crown of his Stetson hat and recognized Lamar Baker's solid torso. And as he stared at him Lamar stood up with his hands cupped to his mouth.

"Strickland," he shouted. "We got your surrounded and you better come out and give yourself up. Come out with your hands up. You better listen to me, Pat."

His voice died away and there was silence, and Jay strained his eyes in the moonlight, looking at the black window of the cabin.

"This here is Lamar Baker, Pat," Lamar shouted. "Your old friend, Lamar. You better come on out, feller."

There was another flash of fire from the window and Lamar cursed and ducked behind the well-shed. "The bastard tried to plug me."

"Let's don't trifle," the Sheriff said. "Let's blow him the hell out of there."

From the screen of the woods where Jay stood he could see the moonlight on the cabin and the dark trees all around, and all at once from the trees fire flashed and the sharp ringing sound of shots rose to crescendo. Lamar rose to his knees behind the well-shed to shoot. Flashes were coming from the dark window of the cabin. Near Jay the Sheriff knelt beside a fallen log to steady his aim and the noise of the rifle smashed loud in the sound of gunfire. Jay turned away and leaned against a tree. His eyes were closed.

"I believe we got him," a voice said clearly.

Jay became aware that the firing had ceased and it was very

quiet. He heard someone groaning and cursing, viciously and methodically cursing, out in the moonlight, and he recognized Lamar's voice.

"What's the matter?" the Sheriff called. "Are you hit?"

"In the leg. The bastard got me in the leg. Jesus Christ, you got to stop the bleeding."

"Somebody give him a hand," the Sheriff said. "I sure enough believe we got him." He raised his voice to a shout. "Strickland, you hear me?"

He paused and there was silence. "Okay, men, let's give him another round."

The air was filled again with the incredible noise; it was unreal in the moonlight, and the flashes of fire seemed improbable and without menace. Jay leaned against the tree. His knees were weak.

They filled that shack full of slugs and it's just thin boards and it wouldn't stop them slugs. I heard it said that a thirty-thirty pointed steel jacket will shoot through twenty-six three-quarter-inch pine boards laid together. Or was it seventy-six. It was seventy-six. Seventy-six three-quarter-inch pine boards. Pretty near five feet. Jesus God, what wouldn't it do to a man and what wouldn't it do to that frame shack and Pat in there and Rocky in there too, just a poor sick nigro and I reckon it's the end of it. I hope Pat knowed he hit Lamar. It would sure tickle him to know he done hit Lamar.

"Hold your fire," the Sheriff shouted. He walked forward into the moonlight, the rifle in his hand, and from the fringe of black trees other men moved into the light. No shot was fired and the window of the cabin remained dark and silent. The Sheriff walked on alone, his boots shining in the moonlight. He walked toward the door of the cabin, deliberately, with the rifle ready in his hands. He went on step by step and it was very still and even Lamar had stopped groaning. He reached the cabin and put out his hand and opened the door. There was an instant's pause and then a flash of bright light.

"Son of a bitch, there's two of 'em here!" His voice was deep and unshaken. The flashlight moved along the wall of the cabin. "There's a nigger in here, too." He stepped into the dark cabin and Jay saw a glow of light at the window, then the shadow of the Sheriff's heavy shoulders. He shouted through the window. "It's okay. Both of 'em is dead."

Jay looked into the darkness of the woods, into the darkness to ease the pain of his eyes. He tried to spit and his mouth was too dry and the muscles of his stomach were tight. He felt like retching.

"Come on, you-all," the Sheriff shouted.

Jay turned back toward the moonlight. In the grass beside the well-shed Lamar was lying. Jay walked past, looking at him, at the man bending over him.

"You was itchin' fer it and now you got it, Lamar," Jay said. His voice shook. "I'm God damned glad. You'll git elected now and that's Pat's vote."

He walked on toward the cabin and the man behind him asked: "Who in hell was that?"

"Jay Strickland."

Jay went through the moonlight toward the cabin. There was a group of men crowded around the doorway and Jay pushed forward.

"Take your time, feller."

"Quit shovin'. Everybody will git a look."

"Git the hell out of my way," Jay said.

The Sheriff was standing in the doorway, the flashlight in his hand.

"Let me past," Jay said.

"Who the hell do you think you are?"

"That's my brother you killed," Jay said. "God damn it, let me past."

"It's Jay Strickland," someone said in a subdued tone.

"You killed him," Jay said. "What more do you want?"

"Okay, come on inside." The Sheriff stood aside. "You can have your brother." He flashed the light in Jay's face. "Say, I'm sorry. We had to do it."

Pat's shoulders leaned against the foot of an iron bed and his head was thrown back and the moonlight was on his face. Rocky's body was on the floor beside the other bed. Jay saw the formless shape of the table and went to it. He felt for the lamp and found it; the chimney had been shattered by a bullet and the table-top was dusted with broken glass. Jay struck a match and lit the wick and the flame flickered and cast grotesque shadows on the walls. In the light Jay did not look toward Pat. He turned his eyes first to the body of the Negro, partly in deep shadow beside the bed. Rocky had been shot through the head. He lay on his face with his arms stretched out and light fell on the raw flesh of his back.

I guess he never knowed what it was. He was laying here sick and he never knowed what the shootin' was about. Haze said he was out of his head part of the time and laying there so sick and then they begun to fill the cabin full of holes and maybe he got down on the floor to hide and maybe he got shot first and fell off on the floor and he never knowed what it was. He was a good nigro and he had guts and he didn't want nothing but to git out and do the work he felt like he had to do.

Jay turned his head slowly. Pat's hair was red in the flickering light and his face was very white. He seemed to be at ease with his shoulders against the bed and his head bent back. Below his shoulders his tan shirt was wet and stuck to his body. Jay could see where the holes were. He went down on his knees.

This morning it was Belle I seen laid out with them freckles brown on her white face and her feet cut and bruised from running through them woods and tonight here is Pat. And it ain't but six days ago that they was both together in the hills and we had some hope then that we could git Pat away safe. All he was after was to git Belle and go off somewheres and poor Pat he broke out of jail and killed them men and one thing come on another and he never had no chance. They was bound to git him and now that Belle is dead I reckon Pat is better off the way he is. That smile of his'n I won't never see no more and it was that smile that always made me remember Pat when he was just a boy, and it was that smile that kind of said to you that Pat was still a boy and he wasn't bad and he didn't really know how he come to be in such a fix. It was just the way one thing followed on another and he never had a chance. He was just that kind of boy that wants to have himself some fun and some excitement. He always hankered to be in some kind of a ruckus and in school he was always the one to start a fight or play hookey or snitch some watermelons and there was always a couple who would foller after him. Sometimes he would listen to me and maybe part of it is my fault. I don't know. That time he stole an auto in Mehuskah it was just plain devilment and he'd been working with a road gang and he had some money in his pocket and he was full of corn whisky. Pat had always listened to them stories of bad men in the hills and what they done and he admired them the way a boy does but he wasn't never bad and that time it was just the liquor in him. And when he come back from the Pen he was changed a little and maybe a good bit harder but he still had that smile of his that said he was just a good-hearted kid. And then he had Belle and nothing was too good fer Belle and there was Billy and he thought a heap of that boy. Things was so bad, Christ knows, and Pat thought he sure had to do something. God knows he tried. Clyde Winter come along and said he knowed of jobs in Texas and him and Pat thumbed their way down yonder and they did git jobs and Pat aimed to save his money and send it home and then it was that recklessness again. His job petered out and I guess he didn't want to come home broke and Clyde was a no-good bastard and I reckon it was his notion to stick up that bank. Pat went along with him because of that devilment in him. Without that Pat might of been different and he might of joined up with me and helped with my work but he couldn't never see it that way. It was his red hair, I reckon, and like Dad said he wanted to go out and kick the world in the pants and git what he was after. But he didn't do it because he was bad and he never was no killer. I never seen him do nothing mean or low-down. . . .

Jay was alone in the cabin with the flickering wick spreading fleeting shadows over Pat's bloodless face. Outside he heard the sound of many voices, eager with the ease of tension that follows on excitement. Several men were at the window looking in at Jay.

"I don't know where that nigger come from. Who's he?"

"First time I ever seen him."

Jay turned his head. He saw the curious faces watching him, heard the murmur of voices outside. He started to speak, then turned his eyes back to his brother.

I can't leave him settin' here like we was talking to each other and I reckon I'll lay him out on the bed. Them slugs sure tore hell out of him and I wonder did he have that thirty-thirty slug in him all the way from the gully. His black forty-five is still in his hand and his fingers sure are tight on it. I wonder if he knowed he hit Lamar. . . .

Jay lifted his brother upon the bed and stretched out his limbs. When he stepped back to look at Pat he glanced at his own hands and they were wet and sticky with blood. Someone touched Jay's shoulder and he turned his head. It was Haze Thompson, his face pinched and gray with the unsteady light coming upon it from below.

"Jay, it sure is too bad," Haze said.

Jay looked down at Pat's white face and red hair, now partly in shadow.

"Pat never had a chance, Haze," he said. "He never had a chance."

Haze whistled softly. "What they done to my cabin! Jesus, they sure filled it full of slugs."

"It's good you wasn't home, Haze," Jay said.

"I was over with them Indians and I heard all that shootin' and I come on the run," Haze said. "Jesus, man, what a lot of shootin'." He came forward a step and peered down at Rocky. "That pore nigger too. He was a good nigger, Jay, if they's such a thing."

"That Rock Island Jones was a man," Jay said.

Haze looked toward the window. "Jesus, Jay, there's fifty or a hunderd people outside and more comin'."

Jay nodded. "You got a wagon, Haze?"

"Sure I have. It ain't much good, though."

"I'd like to have the loan of it," Jay said. "Come dawn I'm going to take Pat home."

"All right, boy," Haze said. "I'll ride along with you." He looked suddenly toward a corner of the cabin. "Now by God, the jug wasn't hit. Jay, you and me had better have a drink of corn."

"We sure had," Jay said.

✤ *Jay* ✤

THE axles creaked and the wagon swayed on the narrow road in the hills. The wheels sank deep in the soft clay and the chestnut horse sweated under the load and its hide turned red as blood in the morning sunlight. Jay sat on the high wagon seat beside Haze Thompson and he did not look back into the wagon bed at the two blanket-covered objects there. The road had turned up from the black walnut and hickory of the bottom lands to the cedar and scrub-oak of the hills and the wagon rolled on in an enclosing silence.

"It's just around the next turn, Haze," Jay said, without taking his eyes from the road.

Haze Thompson spat tobacco juice into the weeds beside the road. "Jay, what do you aim to do with the nigger?"

Jay stared at the road. His eyes were red-rimmed and underlined with green shadow. He gave his head a slight shake and said quietly: "I aim to bury him, Haze."

"Uh-huh." Haze looked at Jay, his lips pursed, then resumed chewing his quid of star tobacco.

The wagon followed the bend in the road and the farmhouse came into sight beyond a rail fence enclosing a field of broomweed and sunflowers.

"Somebody there," Haze said. "Couple of wagons and a auto. — Giddap."

"That looks like the undertaker's car," Jay said. "I believe that's what it is."

As the wagon rolled along the lane Crosby Strickland came out on the porch. He shaded his eyes with one hand to look at them, and then he started down the steps to meet the wagon. The chestnut horse stopped under an oak tree, flicking its head to free the reins, and bent down toward the grass. Jay looked steadily at his father.

"I brung Pat home, Dad," he said.

"I been waitin'," Crosby said. "Joseph Paul come here from the stomp-dance and told me what happened, son. Him and Christine are yonder in the house now, and she's fixing to cook some dinner."

Jay climbed down from the wagon seat. He met his father's eyes, and then Crosby turned away and went nearer the wagon. He stared at the gray blankets.

"He looks just the same, Dad," Jay said. "You can look at him."

Crosby lifted up a corner of the nearest blanket.

"But poor Rocky was shot through the head," Jay said.

"My son Pat," Crosby said. "Jay, I reckon I always knowed it would end this way but somehow I never reckoned that day would catch up with us. But now it is, and Belle, too." He looked at Jay. "She's done been laid out, son."

"Yonder comes another wagon," Haze Thompson said. "Looks like plenty folks will be calling, Crosby."

"Belle had a lot of friends," Crosby said. "And so did Pat."

Jay started toward the house, and Crosby followed him. Jay went into the living room where sunlight fell on the dusty floor, on the familiar furniture that seemed out of place in the unfamiliar room.

"Where is Billy?" Jay asked.

"He's playing out by the barn, son."

Jay sat down in his father's rocking chair and looked blankly at the stag's head on the wall, at the dark hole where one eye was missing.

"I reckon we all better have a swig of corn," Haze said. "You got a jug handy, Crosby?"

"Yonder on the table, Haze. If it was a snake it would bite you."

"Where is that Indian?" Jay asked.

"In the kitchen, I reckon. . . . Hey, Joseph."

"I'll go after him," Jay said.

I can't set quiet. I ain't slept all night and my eyes are sore and my skin feels like sandpaper and I'm shaky all over but I can't set quiet and I can't set with Dad and see that look on his face. I better leave him and Haze with the jug.

Jay went into the kitchen. A fire was burning in the stove and Christine Paul was cooking, leaning over the stove with perspiration on her smooth forehead and the downy hairs at the base of her neck. Her hair was drawn in a black sweep back from her face, her turquoise earrings dangled, and she still wore the bouquet of artificial flowers. Joseph Paul got to his feet when Jay came in and held out his hand.

"Christine cook coffee, Jay. Better take some."

"Thanks, Joseph. I sure will."

"Ready quick now," Christine said.

Jay went to the window and looked out at the yellowed grass of the clearing and the woods beyond, at the shabby unpainted barn gray against the black trunks of the blackjack trees.

Yonder's little Billy playing all alone with a strap of his overalls busted and not knowing that his mother is dead and his daddy too. It looks like he's found his little bam-bam gun and he's out there making believe he's shooting squirrels.

"Jay," Joseph Paul said. "Plenty Indian talk about union stomp-dance."

Jay turned his head. "Is that right?"

"Red Feat'er him say plenty Indian come."

Jay looked closely at the Indian's still brown face. "Maybe you're saying that to make me feel better, Joseph," he said with a twist of his lips. "But it sure is good news."

"Indian like dance," Joseph Paul said. "Maybe him don't join union, Jay." He spread his hands. "Pretty soon find out."

"Coffee ready, Jay," Christine said.

Jay went to the table, and as he was spooning sugar into his cup a stout man with straw-colored hair came into the room. He had a round face and solemn, serious eyes.

"Hello," Jay said.

"I'm the mortician — the Dabney Funeral Home. Everything is ready with the young lady, Mister Strickland, and I'm going to Mehuskah for another casket for your brother."

Jay nodded. "We'll need three all told. You'll have to fetch another one."

The man's pale eyebrows went up. "Three?"

"There's a nigro out there we want to bury," Jay said.

"All right. I suppose a plain box. . . ."

Jay sipped some of the coffee. "I reckon so. I reckon a plain box is just what Rocky would want, all right."

"I'll have to go to town, then, and I'll bring it out this afternoon. Whereabouts will the interment be, Mister Strickland?"

"Over by Aldine, back in the hills. The old graveyard there."

"Jay." It was Crosby's voice calling.

"Yes, Dad?"

"Come out here a minute, son."

Jay pushed back his chair and walked through to the front room. Crosby and Haze Thompson were seated at the table and there were several other men in the room. Jay saw more people outside on the porch and heard their voices, the scraping of their boots on the boards of the porch.

"A feller here to see you, Jay," Crosby said.

Jay looked at the young man in the doorway. He had a thin pale face and wore horn-rimmed glasses. In the pocket of his seersucker coat Jay saw a rolled-up newspaper.

"I'm from the *Clarion and Bee*, Mister Strickland," the young man said, coming forward a step.

"Let's have a look at that newspaper," Jay said.

The reporter gave it to him and Jay opened it out on the table. The streamer headline said: PAT STRICKLAND KILLED: *Mehuskah Attorney Wounded in Gun Battle: Negro Partner of Strickland Slain.*

"He wasn't no partner of Pat's," Jay said. "That was Rock Island Jones."

"The nigger?"

"Yes."

"How do you spell his name?"

"Just like the railroad." Jay watched the reporter scribble on a double-folded sheaf of copy paper.

"Well, how does he fit in?"

"I'll tell you," Jay said. "But your paper ain't going to print it."

"Of course we'll print it."

"You watch and see," Jay said. "Rock Island Jones was an organizer fer the Southern Tenant Farmers' Union and he was working over toward Tanzey and Sunday evening a gang of men jumped him over on the S. W. Boaz plantation and they beat him up cruel. They beat him near to death. Now you know that ain't goin' to git in your newspaper."

"It sure is, Mister Strickland. But what proof — I mean how are we going to know it's true?"

"Do you want to take a look at Rocky? You come along and I'll show you what they done to him."

"Well, no. I'll just hang it onto you. But say, how did he come to be up there with your brother?"

"He was in that cabin, laying there sick, when Pat run in there last night. Pat never even knowed Rocky."

The reporter glanced up from his copy paper, studying Jay's face. "When's the funeral going to be?"

"Tomorrow afternoon over by Aldine."

"And how about the nigger?"

"Same place," Jay said. "Same time."

"You don't mean along with your brother and her?"

"That's just what I mean."

The reporter returned the copy paper to his pocket.

"Now wait a minute," Jay said. "You come outside with me."

He went ahead of the reporter to the door and out upon the porch. Men there spoke to him, called his name, and the buzz of conversation ended abruptly. There were automobiles and wagons in front of the house, horses tethered under the trees.

"Come on, you-all," Jay said. He walked through the sunlight to Haze Thompson's wagon where the bodies lay beneath the blankets in the hot noon sun.

Jay climbed to the wagon seat and faced the house. The

crowd was straggling toward the wagon, and Jay saw the reporter's sallow face. "Come up here, son," he said. "Yeah, I mean you."

The reporter approached him slowly.

"Stand up there on the wheel-hub," Jay said. "Go ahead, I want to show you something."

The reporter put his foot on the hub and swung up beside Jay. Jay leaned over and folded back one of the blankets.

"Look at that," he said. "Why don't you put that in your paper?"

There were flies in the noon sun and Jay dropped the blanket back in place. He looked hard at the gray face of the reporter, then turned to the silent group of men beyond.

"Listen here, you-all," Jay said slowly. "Let me tell you about Rock Island Jones." He paused, and his eyes searched for his father, found him standing with Haze Thompson under a black-jack tree. Jay drew the back of his hand across his forehead. "Rocky Jones come here from Arkansas," Jay said. "He was borned over to Arkansas and he was just about borned in a cotton patch and he had himself a wife over yonder. And that Rock Island Jones had a lot of sense. Somewhere he got himself a little education and he learned how to read and write. Anybody can learn to read and write and all it takes is a little schoolin', but Rocky Jones learned to think and that's a thing not many of us troubles himself with. Rocky chopped his cotton and he thought a good bit and he thought union and when the Southern Tenant Farmers' Union was started Rocky Jones was one of the first and he joined up and then he set to work organizing fer the union. He worked on a big plantation, maybe two hunderd families, and they was mostly nigros. Everybody knows it's easy to scare a nigro but there wasn't nothin' Rocky Jones was scared of. He knowed what he had to do and he done it. But one night they come a-lookin' fer Rocky. He wasn't home and his missus said she didn't know where to find him. They told her she better find him God-damned quick and she didn't say nothing and they told her if she was a smart nigro she would talk and she didn't answer 'em nothin'. Then they took and beat her with the butt end of a gun and Rocky told me that one of her ears was took off with just one flick. But she didn't open her mouth. Somebody got to Rocky in time and told him about it and he took out and he never seen her fer a year. He went up across the Mississippi and he was up Memphis way awhile and then he come down here to Mehuskah County to work fer the union. We had a barbecue at Tanzey Saturday and he made a speech and Sunday evening he went over Tanzey way to locate and he hadn't hardly shook the dust off his feet when they got him. They was laying fer him and they took him off in a car and they beat him with a rope. They beat him near to death."

Jay paused, and heard the murmur of hushed voices. The hot sun glared from the bare ground into his squinted eyes and sweat was on his forehead and dew-like on the bristles of his chin. "That Indian yonder on the porch found him. I reckon most of you know Joseph Paul. He belongs to the union now. Joseph found him and took care of him and then old Haze Thompson took him into his cabin and that's where he was laying about to die when my brother Pat run in there last night. Both of 'em was killed."

Jay looked down into the wagon bed at the gray blankets. "They're laying there together now, my brother and Rock Island Jones. One of 'em broke the law and they claim he killed two men. I don't know. My brother Pat wasn't no killer and you people know that. He got into trouble and they killed him. And yonder in the house his wife is laying dead and they killed her, too. She didn't do nothing except try to save her husband's life. And Rocky Jones didn't do nothing at all. He never broke no laws. If it comes to a question of law the law was on his side and them others broke it and it goes to show that the law is the law of the landlord and it ain't our law. Rocky Jones didn't do nothing but try to organize a union and the law says you got a right to do that and nobody can't stop you. But you seen what they done. Are we going to stand fer it? I ask you, what are we going to do about it? Are we going to stand fer that?"

"We sure ain't," Haze Thompson called, stepping out from the shade of the blackjack tree, and the cry was taken up by several men.

"You bet we ain't, and we're going to serve notice on 'em that we ain't," Jay said.

"Wait a minute, Jay," Haze Thompson said, pushing through the crowd. Jay reached down a hand and helped the old man to the wagon seat.

"Let me tell 'em something," Haze said. He faced the crowd, and spat tobacco juice on a nearby sunflower that bobbed under the impact. "Listen here, you-all," Haze said strongly. "That nigger was a good nigger and like Jay said he was a man. There never was a nigger in my house before but I took him in on Jay's say-so. That nigger didn't have but one thing in his head and that was union and he was always claiming that the white man and the colored man got to join together and by God I think he was right. Everybody that work in them cotton fields and them spinach fields and everybody that farms tenant land has got to jine together in the same union and that means white and black both, and the Indian too. If you do that maybe you'll git you a square deal from the landlord and maybe you got a chance like Jay says to git a dollar a hunderd in the cotton patch this fall. And if Jay says we got to have the white man and the colored man in the same outfit I'll take it so just on his say-so."

Jay put his hand on Haze's shoulder. "You heard what he said, you-all. We ain't going to have no Jim Crow union. We ain't going to have no Jim Crow nothing. And I'll tell you this here right now and I told that feller to put it in his paper and that is we're going to take and bury Rocky Jones tomorrow afternoon along with my brother Pat and his wife, Belle, over to the grave-yard in the hills back of Aldine. It's going to be the God damnedest funeral you ever seen and it's going to be a union funeral fer Rocky Jones and I want to see the same faces there that I'm lookin' at now, and the faces of your friends."

Jay dropped his hands to his sides and looked down at the up-turned faces. An old man in the front row said: "I'd like to take a look at that nigger."

"Come and look, Henry," Jay said.

The old man climbed up in the wagon and went down on his knees. "Glory be to Jesus, look at that! It looks like they whacked him with a length of bobbed wire." Men drew nearer the wagon, and the old man said: "Look how they done him, will you."

Jay got down from the wagon and started toward the house. Someone touched his arm. "Anyhow, Jay, that brother of your'n shore did lead 'em a chase. He shore did that."

"Old Pat was the toughest man in all these hills," another voice said. "He was a hellbender, all right."

Jay went on toward the house, and Crosby joined him. They climbed the steps and Jay went into the shaded living room. He sighed and sank into a rocking chair. His face was dark with beard and his eyes had a strange glow in the shaded room.

"Jay," Crosby said. "Did you read that there newspaper?"

"I only looked at the headlines, Dad."

"They laid into you again, Jay. They said you was there helping him and you'd ought to be investigated fer aidin' a criminal to escape."

"I reckon they expected me to arrest my own brother and take him down to the county jail," Jay said. "I tell you this, Dad, that paper ain't going to print what I said about Rocky."

"You reckon not?"

"You watch and see." Jay stood up. "I knowed they'd use this to try and break me down, but they ain't going to do it, Dad, they ain't going to do it." He went to the window and drew back the shade. "Look at them people, Dad. They come here just to take a look at Pat. Like that paper said yesterday he's a hill-billy hero, all right."

"People are too God damned curious," Crosby said. "Jay, pass me that jug. It makes me sick to my stomach. Let's have that jug, Jay."

Jay leaned over and picked up the jug. Crosby took it in both his hands.

"Jay, I don't know what you're after. Do you aim to leave Pat out there in the wagon until the undertaker gits back?"

Jay looked at his father in surprise. "It never come into my head. Dad, we better bring him in the house."

"I reckon we had."

Jay went to the doorway. "Look at all them people. . . . Dad, when will that undertaker ever git back?"

"A couple of hours, he said."

"Haze," Jay called. "Bring that wagon over here to the porch."

"All right, Jay."

Crosby came up behind Jay. "Son, let's you and me carry him in. Just us two."

"Yes, Dad."

Jay went down the steps and Crosby followed him, out into the sunlight.

"Stand aside, you-all," Jay said. He climbed into the wagon and slipped his hands under Pat's shoulders, without moving the blanket. He drew the body to the rear of the wagon, and climbed down to the ground.

"He's stiff already," Crosby said. "Jay, he sure is stiff."

"We better carry him in the blanket, Dad."

"I reckon so."

Jay waved two men aside. "We'll carry him in. You-all can bring Rocky Jones."

In Belle's bedroom there was a walnut coffin on the floor. They put Pat's body on the bed and Jay took away the blanket. Crosby stood looking at the gray face of his dead son, at the tangled mass of red hair. Tears rolled slowly down his face. "I said I wanted to git the family all together once more," he said. "Well, Jay, here we are."

"Dad, you better help yourself to another drink of corn," Jay said quietly.

"I reckon I better."

"And see they lay Rocky somewheres."

"He can have my bed," Crosby said. "Jay, what's he going to do about that face of Rocky's?"

"What's who going to do?"

"The undertaker. It's got that big hole in it."

"He'll have to build it up with wax, Dad. That's what they do."

"Won't it melt though, son? It sure is hot."

"He'll take care of that, Dad."

"I reckon he uses black paint, don't he? He's got to make him look like a nigger."

"Dad, go and git yourself another drink, you hear me!"

"All right, son. Yes, I reckon I need a drink."

Jay looked down at his brother. He leaned over to fold Pat's hands across his chest, but they were very stiff, and cold, and Jay dropped them.

There's been a terrible lot of blood. Three people killed. Belle and Pat and Rocky Jones. And the headlines in the papers are black and all they tell is lies and they call him another Pretty Boy Floyd and another Clyde Barrow, and Pat never was mean and cruel like them and he never was a killer. And they call Rocky Jones his partner and they know damned well that he was just a working man building up a union like the law says he's got a right to do. They ain't said a word about the way they done him and they never will I know. It makes me burning-up mad to see it. They sure won't never print the truth and that's a fact. They got the law on their side and when the law ain't on their side they don't pay no mind and they don't have to because they got the Laws on their side too. The poor man don't never have a chance and if he tries to make something fer himself he gits shot and killed like Rocky was and like Pat was. Only Pat was thinking just about himself and his kin and Rocky was thinking of everybody like him who didn't have no chance and he wanted to help 'em all. And whichever way you go about it you run up against the rich man's law. There ain't nothing going to come out of this kind of a world fer the poor man and anybody but a fool can see that. Rocky knowed it. He'd be singing in a cotton field now if it wasn't so. He'd be singing in a cotton field if this kind of a world could only let him live like a man. But everybody knows how hard times is and everybody knows there's less money in cotton every year and every year there's more people throwed out on the road and them that still has land to farm is treated worse than they was the year before and the next year will be worse again. It's the croppers and the tenants that git the dirty end of the stick and they always will the ways things is. And there ain't nothin' left fer the day worker but relief, the way things are going, with tractors in the fields and the cotton-chopper coming and the cotton-picker doing the work of forty men. We got to have a day of reckoning. If we organize and build our union strong we'll be better off fer a little time and we'll have us red meat to eat, but Rocky knowed that sometime somehow the day would come when it would have to be a change. You got to change the whole God damned set-up that can bring about three people killed and all that blood and only because they was poor people in a rich man's world. Rocky knowed that and he told me so and that nigro was smarter than most white men. He told me you never could tell when it would happen and he was right and now it has happened. I was just thinking the way my hope was and hope made me blind. But Rocky knowed that we won't git no place so long as they got the guns and the law behind 'em and he told me so. If you could just make people see that, too, and someday, by God, they're going to see it. . . .

$\mathcal{J}ay$

❖   ❖

I KNOWED people was curious and I seen them black headlines in the paper but I sure didn't look fer no crowd like this
here. Soon as we went through Boggs they begin adding on and
now I reckon the lines of cars is easy three mile long and more
coming. Some of 'em is people from the hills and they come to
see their friends buried and to mourn 'em, but mostly they come
out of curiosity to see a dead bankrobber and a public enemy
like they called him and to see that bankrobber's kinfolks and to
watch us at his grave. . . .

The funeral procession stretched out along the gravel highway between the ridges; polished cars from Mehuskah and Tulsa
and from towns for many miles around, and cars of uncertain
date and varying stages of disrepair from the hills. The procession moved along the highway at about thirty miles an hour and
Jay drove close behind the white hearse. Billy was asleep on the
seat between Jay and Crosby, his white head resting against the
shiny, greenish cloth of Crosby's old black suit.

They come from Mehuskah and they come from Tulsa and

they come from Okmulgee and all them towns and they come because of Pat and because of what they printed in the papers. He was just a reckless boy and even if he did shoot them two men he wasn't no gunman and he wasn't no killer. It's just them newspapers that make him out that way to put news in their papers and all them people read it and they come out to see us bury him. To read them papers you'd never know that Pat was just a good-hearted boy and he had him a wife and son and he thought the world of them and he wanted to fix it so they could have a little something to make their life better and he couldn't git it no other way so he took him a gun. And the way they called Belle his moll when she was just a wife like anybody else's wife, like the wife of the president of the Mehuskah bank and she stood by her husband and they killed her fer it. They don't print nothing but lies and I knowed they wouldn't print nothing about Rocky except that he was with Pat when they was killed and that he was Pat's partner. There wasn't a mention about the way they done him over to Tanzey and I knowed there wouldn't be.

Beyond Aldine the procession turned off into the hills at a crossroads where there was a group of people and a state patrol car. On the clay road the cars had to move more slowly and the hearse ahead of Jay swayed from side to side, the square body lunging on the springs. They turned along the side of the ridge, at another crossroads beside the Sour Tom schoolhouse, and now they moved in clouds of reddish dust, through which the limestone schoolhouse showed darkly yellow.

I ain't seen her since at the stomp-dance and I ain't even thought of her to now. She won't never be in that schoolhouse again. She won't be a schoolmarm no more, and when we're married we'll live in Mehuskah and she can take Belle's place with Billy. She can be a mother to him and he's only a youngster and he'll forget. She sure did look scared when I come on her in the woods and she had took Pat's gun away from him but she come over and said she was sorry and she never would of told 'em which way he run to. She stood by him and she stood by me and it was sure sweet yonder at the stomp-dance under the sassafras tree and it'll be again, and again and again. I'll put my head on her shoulder and maybe I can forget like Billy will and

she will sure be a comfort and a wife to come home to and help
me in my work. She's got a lot to learn but she wants to try to do
it and that's a plenty. Someday we'll have us a little house and
some land to farm and we can settle down like man and wife and
there'll be a corn patch and a truck garden fer her. I never
knowed a woman that didn't like a truck garden and like to go
out in her sunbonnet and a pair of gloves on and tend her radishes
and beets and sprinkle her lettuce fresh and have lots of turnip
greens fer the table and boast to the neighbor women that she
put up twenty quarts of tomatoes. She'll want that and I'll see
that she has it just as soon as we got a strong union and I can
take a little time. But I got to do that first and I can't let nothing
stand in my way and I couldn't never rest easy if it did. And I
got to begin right now and put all this out of my mind, put all
this out that's happened in the last five days. I got to begin back
where we was when Rocky went over to Tanzey Sunday, before
he was beat up, and before Pat made his break and before Belle
was murdered and Pat was killed. The papers said there was a
thousand men hunting fer poor Pat down along the Washita and
there was more on the watch fer him here in Mehuskah County.
Fer two days he was clear of 'em and he'd of got away sure if
he was mean and a killer like they said. They'd never of caught
him if he wasn't just a boy and wanted to come home to the hills
to his wife and son. I guess Leona knowed he was just a boy
and he wasn't no killer and I sure wouldn't want her to think
about my brother the way them papers said and I got to show
her that they didn't print nothing but lies. Just as soon as I see
her I'm going to show her that, and I sure do want to see her
again. Maybe she'll be out to the graveyard and I sure do wish
she'd found the time to come out to the house to see me yesterday. . . .

The hearse ahead of Jay turned to the left upon a grass-grown
road in lessening dust and moved so slowly that Jay had to drive
in low gear. In the mirror above the windshield he saw reflected
the twisting line of automobiles behind him, and he recognized
far back Red Feather's battered seven-passenger car, in which
there were nine Indians. The road traveled along the side of a
ridge, and then turned away from the trees, and suddenly there

was a crowd of people, with the scattered headstones and dusty Bermuda grass of the graveyard beyond.

All them cars and all them people. There must be a thousand of 'em. It's like I thought, there'd be a crowd, but I didn't look fer it to be so big. Women in linen frocks and men in city suits and them overalls and sunbonnets sure do stand out and I believe it's union people in them overalls. It's Webb Harper and maybe fifty with him come out here to bury Rock Island Jones. And by God a few of 'em is nigros and it's good to see that.

Jay stopped the car under a tree, among many cars. He saw the license plates, the familiar black on yellow of Oklahoma, black on white for Texas and Missouri and white on red for Arkansas. He got out of the car and Crosby awakened Billy. The boy stared with wide blue eyes at the mass of people. Automobiles were turning into the open space behind Jay, where there were already many cars and wagons and saddled horses. Webb Harper came toward Jay.

"Jay, we been waitin' fer you. I sure am sorry about your brother."

Jay nodded and they shook hands. Webb leaned down and took Billy's hand, and murmured to him. His angular face was very serious, with deep lines beside his mouth.

"Look at all them people coming," Jay said. "It's because of Pat."

"It sure is."

"They made him out the Public Enemy Number One of the Southwest. That's just a God-damned lie."

"Everybody knows it is," Webb said. "Jay, people begun to drift in last night and some been up here in the hills since early this morning. They brung picnic dinners."

Jay shook his head and looked at the automobiles, at men and women getting out in the grass, men in linen suits and seersuckers and women in sports clothes. Here and there he saw a sunbonnet where people were packed close around the white hearse. Jay turned away from the curious eyes and put one hand on Crosby's shoulder. "Come on, Dad."

They walked through the graveyard together, and Webb Harper and the men from the union fell in behind, fifty of them filing silently among the slanting gravestones in the dusty, yellow-tipped Bermuda grass. On the other side of the cemetery, near a line of blackjack oaks, there were three open graves.

I didn't come this year to the graveyard working but last spring I was here with Pat and Belle both and now I'm standing by their graves. It was a fine day like today with lots of sun and we had the graveyard weeded before the day was half done and yonder by the woods the women had laid out the food and Belle had brung along some fried chicken that she cooked so good and there was cornbread and cake and cold black-eyes and everything fine and we cleaned the graveyard mighty well and then we set down to eat. And afterwards we put some flowers on Maw's grave and the last I'd ever of thought was that the next time I'd be burying Pat and Belle. . . .

"Hey, there, Strickland."

Jay turned his head and saw a large man in khaki shirt and trousers, with a dome-shaped head bald and brown in the sunlight, with bleached eyebrows and a clear, penetrating gaze from pale blue eyes.

"George Burr," Jay said. "Howdy."

"I read them newspapers and I come up here from Jennings County," Burr said. "Fritz Warner would of come along, and Ned Bayles too, if they'd of had the bus fare."

"Now if you're wondering about my coming down to Jennings County tomorrow," Jay said, "I'll be there. I'll be there like I said."

"I counted on that, Strickland, but I just wanted you to know that this ain't going to make no difference in Jennings County."

"What ain't?"

"This here about your brother. It ain't going to make no difference at all with us."

"Oh," Jay said.

"The papers can print what they want, Strickland, but don't you let that worry you none."

"I won't," Jay said. "George, this here is Webb Harper."

"Jay told me about you," Webb said. "Now I think to say it, Jay, we got that meeting over to Tanzey this evening."

"Yes, I know." Jay turned his eyes from the graves, and looked with a frown at the cars still turning in from the road.

"I'm going to take me a couple of cars of good union men along right from here, Jay, and we'll organize that there local."

Jay nodded. "I ain't goin' with you, Webb, not today. You come back Mehuskah way and let me know how it goes."

"Sure I will."

"Jay," Crosby said. "Look at all them people. Will you just look at 'em, Jay!"

"It's because of what them papers printed, Dad, all them big black headlines and the lies they printed."

"But Pat sure would of enjoyed it, son, now you know he would." Crosby's pale eyes brightened.

"They even got the po-lice here, Dad," Jay said. "Them po-lice got to be here even after they shot him. They ain't done yet and they got to be at his funeral."

People were coming across the graveyard; they were gathered around the white hearse. Jay heard the sound of their voices. His lips tightened and he looked down at the three open graves. Raising his eyes, he saw opposite him the group of union men Webb Harper had brought and in the crowd around him there were faces he recognized, the solemn faces of the hill people who had known Pat all his life.

"Kind of a commotion over yonder, Jay," Crosby said.

Jay turned his head and saw a surging mass of people around the hearse. Fine dust rose against the leathery green leaves of the blackjacks and the hearse rocked on its axles.

"What goes on there?" Jay said. "Hey, Webb!"

"My God, they're like to tear that hearse to pieces," Crosby said in a high voice. "Jay, we ain't goin' to stand fer that."

"You bet we ain't. — Come on, Webb. Come on, you-all."

Jay started running among the gravestones, panting, sobbing in his throat.

The good fer nothings, the God-damned good fer nothings just come here out of curiosity and tearing that hearse to pieces. People just ain't human. . . .

Webb Harper came alongside Jay and caught his arm as they ran. "Jay, boy, you stay out of this. We'll take care of it. Now you and Crosby stay back."

Jay stopped beside a mossgrown headstone and stared at the hearse and the close press of men and women in the dust. It seemed unreal with the sudden motion and the mist of dust above it and the strange absence of sound. Men ran past Jay, following Webb Harper, and pushed solidly into the crowd; it gave way and Jay watched them slowly clear a space around the hearse. The dust cloud rose free and blew across toward the trees on the other side of the graveyard. Jay saw a short fat man with thick gray hair that drooped over his ears stagger into the open, away from the crowd. His black frock coat had been pulled half off his shoulders and his face was pink and sweat shone on his long upper lip.

"Over here, Brother Andrews," Jay called.

"Goodness me," the minister said, taking off his black hat. "Where did all these people come from, Jay? Goodness me!"

"Ain't it awful the way they act?" Jay said.

The crowd had turned away from the hearse and moved toward Jay, among the stones, trampling on the graves. Jay stared at the eager, intent faces, then turned to the minister.

"We're burying 'em over here," he said. "Come along, Brother Andrews." He took the preacher's elbow and steered him toward the open graves. "You knowed my brother and I reckon you know what kind of prayer he needs," Jay said. "And you knowed Belle. I want you to say a prayer fer them two and then I want you to say a prayer fer Rock Island Jones. He's a nigro and he's black but he worked to help them that couldn't help themselves and that's a Christian way to live. I don't know what religion he had but he was a good man."

Jay glanced over his shoulder and saw the pallbearers, in overalls with their straw hats in their hands, walking slowly through a lane in the crowd formed by the men from the hills and the men from the union. Sunlight shone on their sweaty foreheads as they carried a walnut coffin.

"That's Belle," Crosby said, looking at Jay.

"They took and beat him up just because he was working fer the union, Brother Andrews," Jay said. "He never done no wrong."

"Goodness me," the preacher said, and looked down at the mound of reddish earth, at the dark coffin resting on yellow-tipped grass beside it. The pallbearers went back through the crowd, which now had gathered close around the graves.

"You baptized me, Brother Andrews," Jay said, not looking at the curious faces on every side. "It was you who married Pat and Belle in the Aldine Community Church. You knowed them and you know me."

"Jay, I never expected I'd say a service fer a nigro."

"That Rocky Jones was a Christian man," Jay said. "If there's such a thing, it's him. It's my brother Pat there dead and his wife and I want to bury Rocky along with them."

The pallbearers brought another walnut coffin through the crowd and lowered it beside the second grave.

"If it goes against your conscience, we'll bury Pat and Belle first," Jay said. "And then we'll take and bury Rocky."

The minister raised his eyes to Jay's face, and then he glanced across at the six pallbearers.

"Bring along that other casket," he said quietly.

"I appreciate it," Jay said. "And I just want you to remember this, Brother Andrews. Rocky Jones never done no wrong. He was organizing a union like the law says he's got a right to do and he was working to help people who can't help themselves. Some men come and beat him up cruel and he was like to die and it was just chance my brother Pat run into that cabin where he was at and both of 'em was killed." Jay glanced over his shoulder, seeing the eyes that watched him and hearing the drone of low-pitched voices. The corners of his mouth drew down and he said quietly: "I'd like to have you tell that part of it to God. You tell Him that Rocky never done no wrong and you tell Him that Pat was a sinner but he sure enough knowed not what he done, like the Scripture says."

The pallbearers carried Rocky's coffin forward. The plain pine box was light in color against their blue overalls and against the walnut coffins. Jay looked at the three graves and the mass of men and women in the sunlight. The preacher took off his black hat and sunlight fell on his tangled gray hair. His fat chin drooped over the stiff collar he wore and the black string-tie made a tiny bow beneath it. Jay's eyes were on the three coffins.

Pat and Belle and Rocky Jones and just two days ago they was all three alive and now they're three corpses in three boxes and we put 'em in the ground and cover 'em up with dirt and we go away and forget. We try to forget. But we don't want to forget Rocky Jones and what he done. If there was only some way to make men remember the world would be a better place to live in and we got to remember Rocky Jones and what he was doing and what he worked fer. Whenever I hear Jim Crow talk I aim to tell everybody about Rocky Jones. . . .

"You men take off your hats," Webb Harper shouted.

Jay raised his eyes and saw the preacher standing at the head of Belle's grave, with one hand uplifted. He stood with his head well back, his eyes raised, and his gray hair ruffling at the back of his collar like a parrot's feathers. His eyes were lifted to the pale sky and his voice rose full and deep: "Forgive them, for they know not . . ."

"Hey," a voice shouted. "Don't we git to see the bodies?"

"Yeah, give us a look at the bodies. That's what we came up here for."

Brother Andrews looked uncertainly at the crowd, then turned his eyes to Jay.

"No," Crosby said in a high, thin voice, "my boy ain't here fer anybody to see that takes a want to."

"This here is a funeral," Webb Harper shouted. His face was red with anger. "Nobody asked you-all here and you can either keep still or go."

"Go ahead, Brother Andrews," Jay said quietly.

"Forgive them for they know not what they do, the Lord said." The preacher's voice shook at first, but gained strength as the murmur of the crowd died away. The coffins were being lowered into the ground. "In every man's life there comes a turning of the road and some men listen to the devil and they look along the road he points out to 'em and they see a stretch of fresh-paved blacktop and trees growing green along it and it's an easy road to follow. They see people dancing and making merry with corn whisky and a fiddle and they see the good things of life a-promising. Sometimes they know it's the road straight to hell and sometimes they don't. Today we're burying a boy who didn't know it. He knew not what he done. He listened to the devil in hell and he was lost and he took up a life of crime and now he's dead and he's paid that penalty. He didn't know what road he was taking, and we can stand here and lift our eyes to the Lord and say from our hearts, forgive him, for he knew not what he done."

Brother Andrews lowered his eyes to the graves. "By his side lies his true wife, Belle. Sister Belle was a good, pure woman and she was known fer her good qualities all through these here hills. There never come a turn in the road fer Sister Belle because the devil couldn't never git her ear to tempt her. She was a good wife and a loyal wife and if it hadn't been so she might be here alive today. But the Lord in His wisdom seen fit to take her away and she's laying there beside the man she loved and comforted. Oh, how our hearts are brimming over like a filled cup when we think of Sister Belle and we remember her kindness and her goodness and her faithful service of God. If the Lord took her away it was because He wanted her up yonder in Heaven above with Him and not because of any sin of hers on this here earth. Sister Belle was a true servant of God and she has passed on to greater service and maybe so that up yonder she can pray fer the salvation of the man whose wife she was. The Lord took them away together and He must have had a reason fer it."

Brother Andrews looked down at the coffins. He had stopped talking and the silence for an instant was intense, then Jay heard the rustle of feet in the grass and louder noises from the back of the crowd, where a man was coughing. Brother Andrews looked over his shoulder.

"Now please you-all stay back," he said quietly.

He paused, and from behind someone shouted: "Git a loudspeaker."

The preacher turned his eyes back to the graves. "Over here lays the body of Rock Island Jones," he said. "This man was a black man but he was a Christian man. He followed the teachings of Jesus Christ our Lord and he tried to help his fellowman. Maybe he was wrong. Maybe it's wrong to organize a union and stir up trouble, but he thought it was right and he done it to help his fellowman. It sure ain't no sin and maybe it's the Christian thing to do. Only God in His infinite wisdom can tell that. But I know God don't look down from heaven above and countenance the way a mob of men set on this here black brother and beat him. . . . In the book of John, the Saviour said that *If the world hate you, ye know that it hated me before it hated you. If ye were of the world, the world would love his own: but because ye are not of the world, but I have chosen you out of the world, therefore the world hateth you. Remember the word that I said unto you, The servant is not greater than his lord. If they have persecuted me, they will also persecute you.* . . . We're burying Rocky Jones along with Pat Strickland because that was Jay Strickland's wish, and now let's raise our voices in prayer and song fer these three who have gone into the valley of death, fer that good woman, Sister Belle, and fer her sinning husband who took that wrong road, and for this here black man who was set on by the Philistines."

Jay looked down at the three graves, then closed his eyes, listening to the rise and fall of the preacher's voice.

In my Father's house are many mansions. . . . I reckon it will help 'em to remember and I can't never forget. I can't never forget Pat and Belle and Rocky and the way they done 'em. *If it were not so, I would have told you. I go to prepare a place for you.* . . . Last spring we was here together the three of us and we ate them friers and Pat claimed he picked more weeds than anybody else and he was here laughing and giving Belle a hug and I never thought then it could happen this way. *And if I go and prepare a place for you, I will come again, and receive you unto myself.* We was all happy together and Pat hadn't been in no trouble fer so long. We believed he had changed and settled down and when he went to Texas to find work we had a lot of hope in Pat. . . .

Jay raised his head as a hymn began. The voices of the farmers were raised like a choir and as they sang men spaded dirt into the graves. *Jesus, Lover of my soul, let me to thy bosom fly.* Jay watched the dirt fall and crumble on the coffins. *While the nearer waters roll, while the tempest still is high.* The walnut coffins were covered first; the lighter color of the pine box still showed through the red and yellow subsoil. *Hide me, O my Saviour, hide, Till the storm of life be past; Safe into the haven guide, O receive my soul at last.* All three coffins were covered over now. Jay looked at his father and saw that he was sobbing. He put one hand on Crosby's thin shoulder.

"My boy never hurt nobody," Crosby said. "Jay, you know he didn't."

They're covered up now and they're laid away and it's only Crosby and little Billy left and I got to be a father to the boy now and he don't even know what happened and that he won't never see his mother no more. I'm going to see to it that I raise him up to be the man Pat could of been. . . .

"That was mighty fine, Brother Andrews," Crosby said in a husky voice. "It was a good service and a fine prayer."

Jay leaned over and lifted Billy in his arms. The boy looked at him with solemn blue eyes and put one arm around Jay's neck. His body pressed close against Jay and now he noticed that it was suddenly noisy in the cemetery. Flowers were being placed on the graves and Jay saw a wreath with S.T.F.U. on it. He saw Christine Paul bend down, her purple skirt brilliant in the sunlight, and place a bouquet of artificial flowers on Belle's grave. The crowd surged forward and the sound of voices was high-pitched and insistent. Jay saw a man with an angular face and small eyes, with a grizzle of black beard on his chin. He stood only a yard away, looking steadily at Jay.

"Say, I seen you before," Jay said. "Where was that?"

"Over Tanzey way. My name is Mitchell."

"Bill Mitchell," Jay said. "Sure, I talked to you Sunday. That was the same day they got Rocky Jones."

"Uh-huh."

"That meeting comes off at Tanzey this evening. I heard you say you'd be there."

"Shore, I know that. But I already made up my mind to join up with your union."

"Is that right?" Jay said. "Well, say!" He smiled and his fingers closed on Mitchell's.

"What are we goin' to do about that nigger?" Mitchell asked. "We ain't going to stand fer that kind of business."

"We sure ain't," Jay said. "We're serving notice on 'em. We're going to organize strong and we're going to serve notice. We're going to band together, every tenant farmer in the state, and nothin' like that ain't never going to happen here again."

"You bet it ain't."

There was a half-circle of men around Jay, watching him,

and beyond was the larger circle of the crowd, around the graves. Crosby touched Jay's shoulder.

"Son, let's go home."

"All right, Dad."

Men were coming up to speak to Jay, to shake his hand, and they had to raise their voices to be heard in the noise. Jay turned his head and he could no longer see the graves. Men and women were all around them, pushing toward them, trampling over the grassy mounds in the cemetery, standing on the headstones. Jay heard laughter and occasional shouts.

"I don't like the way they're doin'," Crosby said. "People oughtn't to act like that at a funeral."

Jay called to Webb Harper. "Webb, git the men together and let's clear them people back some."

Quick hands were snatching up the floral wreaths, tearing them apart. Leaves and ferns and flowers were scattered on the grass and ground into the dirt. Jay saw only hands and feet. The faces seemed composite, but the hands were swift and individual, tearing at the souvenirs; the feet were moving in the dust. Webb Harper ran forward with an angry shout and the union men followed him, a solid group in faded blue overalls and hickory shirts, in hats of straw and worn felt. They moved forward like a company of troops behind Webb Harper and the crowd gave way. Jay saw the heavy shoulders of George Burr among them, his khaki shirt streaked dark with sweat.

"Move back, you-all," Webb Harper shouted. "This here is a funeral. Now you-all move back."

Crosby's hand was insistent on Jay's arm. "Son, I want to go home."

"All right, Dad."

I didn't see before how Dad is taking it. He's so white in the face and he's trembling some and I guess he only sees the shame in it all, his boy laying there buried and a bank robber and killed by them Laws and all them snooping people pushing in to git a look at the bank robber's father and his brother and to see the graves and it don't matter to them if they tramp all over 'em and all they want is a souvenir and they tear them flowers to pieces. I guess poor Dad can't think of nothing but that and he don't want to see it.

"Webb, we aim to start home," Jay called.

"All right, Jay." Webb Harper came over to him, his straw hat in his hand and his forehead wrinkled. "Listen, I'll go over to Tanzey this evening and then I'll come back by your house. And don't you-all worry about this here. Some of us will stand guard until the crowd is gone. We'll take care of them graves, Jay."

Jay nodded, and his eyes were drawn again to the mounds of red earth where the flowers had been crushed. The bouquet of artificial flowers on Belle's grave was soiled and scattered.

Christine made them flowers fer Belle and them Indians sure been good to us and good to Rocky too. Yonder Joseph stands with them other fullbloods and he signed 'em in the union, him and Red Feather, and he brung 'em here today and he'll turn 'em out fer that stomp-dance next week and anyhow that's a start. It ain't going to be easy to sign them fullbloods up and it will take time, but someday it will come about, and . . .

"Jay, let's us go," Crosby said.

"Sure, Dad. I reckon if we foller along by the trees we can keep out of that crowd."

They walked along the edge of the cemetery, beside a low stone wall, skirting the crowd, and they came out behind the mass of people where the cars were. Jay saw empty bottles on the ground, and paper napkins and plates. The white hearse was driving away and Jay watched it move out of sight among the trees. When they got in the car Crosby looked back at the crowd, but Jay did not. He drove slowly over the rough ground toward the road.

"Dad, I'm going to take you and Billy into Mehuskah with me," Jay said. "You don't want to go back to Boggs."

"No, I don't, Jay. Not just now."

"You better come in and live with me altogether, Dad."

"Whatever you say, son."

"We got to take care of Billy, you and me, and maybe I'll take and git married and there'll be a woman to look after the boy."

"Is that so, Jay?"

"I might do that."

Jay glanced obliquely for an instant at his father's pale, intent profile. Crosby stared with a squint at the road ahead.

"You ought to git married," Crosby said. "Jay, you ought to been married a long time back."

"It ain't never too late fer that."

"I guess not," Crosby said. "Son, you won't never find a woman to match Belle. Her kind don't come in litters."

"Belle was mighty fine, all right."

"Belle was the best. Nobody won't never take her place, Jay."

They had come down from the ridge and Jay turned off into the valley on the familiar clay road among the blackjack oaks. Deep ruts had been cut in the clay by all the traffic that had passed that day and the car slued from side to side. They passed Joseph Paul's cabin on the hillside, and when they came to the crossroads Jay turned to the north to avoid the road that passed by the old farmhouse.

I don't want to see it now. I don't want to see the house and the cornfield and the old stone fence I helped to build. It's the land I was born on and the land I belong to but I don't belong there no more and water is going to cover it up thirty feet deep. That part of me is gone already like Pat and Belle is gone. We got no more roots here in the valley, none of us, not no more. I don't know, maybe I won't never have no roots no place again the way the world is today, but some day maybe we'll have us a little farm and a cornfield. I got to hope fer it, anyhow, after my work is done. I'll just go on living in a rented house until that time comes and the harder I work the sooner it will come. I got to have some place where Billy can grow up, where he can have a fence to help build, too, and a house he knows every board and shingle of and a little creek and a hillside and plenty of oak trees to give him that feeling that a little corner of God's earth was made fer him. Everybody has got that feeling that he wants a little corner that belongs to him and he belongs to. Everybody wants some place to plant his roots and some place he can always come home to and know it will be just so and no matter how different the rest of his life turns out that there part will be just so. I guess especially when you're as old as Dad you feel that way and I know he don't like to think of the valley filled up with water.

Jay turned off at the Sour Tom schoolhouse and looked down into the valley where a steam shovel was gouging ocher-colored fill for trucks to haul to the dam site. Already the dam was beginning to take form. Crosby too looked down at the dam site, then his eyes met Jay's briefly. Jay drove on, and a few minutes later they were in Aldine, passing the white boardinghouse set back under the dusty trees. Jay slowed speed, hesitating.

I reckon I won't stop by now, but when I git Crosby and the boy settled in Mehuskah I'll come after her. I'll close this day off and then maybe we can begin another day together and it will sure be sweet, just us two. I'll go up to her house and I'll knock on the door and I'll say, here's a man looking fer a wife. Do you know of a likely woman to be Missus Jay Strickland, I'll say. She's got to be real pretty, I'll say, and she's got to have black hair and blue eyes and a willing disposition, and she's got to be a good cook, too. And then I'll just have to grab her and tell her it's her I come after and tell her, honey, I sure do love you and I want you to be my wife. I want you and me to live together fer the rest of our days and I want you and me to share our work together and share our plans together and share our thoughts together and what you want I'm going to want and what I want you'll want and it will be like that fer the rest of our days. And someday we'll have us a three-room house in the hills and a truck garden. It won't be no big farm, but just a place where we can be together and be man and wife. We'll set on the porch and we'll watch the sun go down over them hills and the mocking birds will sing the songs of all the birds in the blackjack trees. They'll sing their songs fer just us two. . . . *Coffee grows on whiteoak trees, The river flows with brandy-O, Go choose someone to roam with you, As sweet as 'lasses candy-O. . . .*

"Jay, you oughtn't to be singing," Crosby said.

"I reckon not, Dad. I forgot myself."

"I remember that one," Crosby said. "Belle always used to sing it. She sure did know a lot of tunes, and it was a sweet voice she had."

"I forgot myself sure enough," Jay said. "But, Dad, I got that singing feeling in me, too."

"She sure did have a sweet voice, all right," Crosby said slowly. "Pat used to set and listen to her all evenin' through."

They had reached the outskirts of Mehuskah, where the smooth city paving began, and Jay drove along the tree-lined streets of the residential section. Crosby sat silent with Billy in his lap. Jay leaned his elbows on the steering wheel. He was very tired, and the waiting period for each traffic light in the business section seemed interminable. His eyes ached and his skin was dry and rubbery on his face. They crossed the Katy tracks and turned onto the dusty street where Jay lived. He stopped the car in front of the house, snapped off the ignition, and sighed.

"Dad, I sure am tired."

"You'd ought to have some sleep, son. You was up most of the night last night."

"And all night the night before," Jay said. "Last night I just couldn't sleep. I couldn't lay still. And I sure am tired now."

They got out of the car and Jay carried Billy to the house. Crosby opened the door and they came into the shaded living room, with its one table and two chairs and the propped-up sofa. Crosby looked blankly at the colors of the calendar on the wall.

"Jay," he said. "Don't you think we laid 'em away good?"

"Sure we did."

"There was all them people there, but still and all . . ."

"It was a fine funeral, Dad. Absolute fact."

"I thought it was, too." Crosby looked around at the bare walls of the room. He sighed. "Jay, I reckon I'll take Billy out back and set in the sun awhile."

"I'm going to take me a cat nap," Jay said.

Jay went into the next room and threw himself down on the cot. He lay prone, with his face buried in his arm and his eyelids pressed against the texture of his shirtsleeve. He heard Crosby walk through to the kitchen, and then the slam of the screen door at the back, then there was silence, an oppressive, tangible silence.

It's over now and like Dad said we laid 'em away the best we could. . . . Jesus, I sure am tired. I got to keep my head quiet and not think no more about it and try to git some sleep. . . . He looked real natural, just like he always did, with that red hair and her with that little sprinkle of freckles. And now they're six feet under, six feet under, six feet down there in walnut coffins, six feet . . . Christ, I got to git some sleep and I got to lay still and do that. . . . That preacher said almost what I told him to and he said it loud enough so everybody heard him. He never said a service fer a nigro before, but there never was a nigro like Rocky Jones, not that I ever seen. . . . Rocky said that riding boss in Arkansas lopped off his wife's ear with just one flick of a gun. The son of a bitch. . . . I wonder will I ever sleep again. I just can't lay still. . . . I'm going to miss that Rock Island Jones. He sure would of done me lots of help. People can be so God-damned cruel. Just one flick of a gun. And the way they beat him with a rope and stomped on his ribs. Some men got that dirty mean streak. . . . Now I'm going to sleep and I ain't going to think. I ain't going to think until tomorrow and then we got to start to work and we got to plan out what to do and we got to stop the scare and we got to organize that union strong. . . .

Jay heard a step outside and sat upright. From the window he could not see the tiny porch, but in the street in front of the house he saw an automobile parked behind his own. Jay went to the door and his mouth opened soundlessly when he recognized Leona. Then he grinned.

"Honey!" he said. "Hello, honey."

"Hello, Jay."

"Come inside, Leona. I sure am glad to see you."

Jay held the door open wide, but she lingered on the sill. Her blue eyes met his fleetingly.

"Jay, I want to talk to you."

"Sure thing. You come inside. You've never been in my house before, have you?"

"No."

"Come in," Jay said. His eyes kept watching her, and his smile eased the lines of strain in his face. "It ain't much, but what it needs is a woman's hand. It's just a house and it needs a woman to make it a home. It sure does."

Jay took her hand and held it tight. He led her into the house and inside she drew her hand away and took a handkerchief from her belt.

"It's just a buzzard's roost fer me," Jay said. "I guess it looks like it. If I'd knowed you was coming I'd of swept it out, anyhow, but fer the past few days . . ."

"Yes. Don't talk about it, Jay."

"I can talk about it."

She glanced briefly at his face. "You've . . . It's all over with now?"

"Yes, we buried them today, up in the hills, up in the hills that Pat and Belle loved. There was a thousand people at the funeral, Leona. — Say, why don't you come in the parlor and set down? I want you to meet my Dad and Billy."

"Jay, I have something to tell you," Leona said. She had rolled the handkerchief into a tight ball in her hand. "I've just got to get it over with."

Jay looked at her with his head on one side. The smile had left his face. "What's the matter, honey? What's got you so worried?"

"Jay, you know, at the stomp-dance . . ."

"Yes?"

"I don't know what to say, Jay. I don't know how to tell you and you'll never forgive me. I know you're going to hate me."

"Now look here," Jay said, taking a quick step toward her. "I couldn't never hate you, Leona. What are you talking about?"

"Jay, I'm going to be married." Her hand was clenched tight on the handkerchief.

"Sure, but . . . Listen here, honey . . ." Jay stared at her. "You mean not to me?"

She bent her head and he stood staring at the part in her black hair. He wet his lips. "Listen here," he said. "Say. . . ."

She raised her head with a jerk. "I can't help it, Jay. It's got to be this way. I'm going to marry Neil Smith. He asked me the other night and I said I would." Her voice trailed off and she shook her head slightly. Jay could not see her eyes.

"Leona, up there at the stomp-dance — you said you loved me — and up there at the stomp-dance . . . Listen here!"

"I couldn't help that, Jay." She looked up at him and moved back a step. "I owed you that, Jay. I owed it to both of us."

"And you just said that. You don't love me, is that it? You

never did." Jay's hands dropped to his sides. "Yeah, I can see you never did."

"I want you to understand, Jay. That's why I came here to-day. I've thought about it. I haven't thought about anything else. You know how I feel, Jay, you can see that. I've felt that way all along, and I've been running away from it. I know it wouldn't work out. I haven't anything to give you, Jay, don't you understand? I haven't anything for you."

"Leona, you got all in the world I want." Jay reached out and caught her hand. "You know that."

"You feel that way now, Jay, but after six months, a year — you'll know I'm right." She pulled her hand away uneasily. "You don't really need me, Jay, not me. You need a different kind of woman. We wouldn't either of us be happy."

"I don't know where you git them notions from," Jay said. "I thought we got along fine."

She looked at him, shook her head slightly, then looked away. Jay followed her gaze, to the automobile in the street. His lips pressed tightly together.

"Leona, listen to me. Are you in love with him? I never even knowed you gave him a thought. I never paid no attention to him. Are you in love with him?"

"We do understand each other, Jay. Oh, I don't know how to say it. I admire him and respect him and there's a very fine companionship and I value it."

"But don't you love him?"

"Please understand me, Jay. I know this will work. I'm sure of it. We want the same things and we think in the same way."

"And up yonder at the stomp-dance, that didn't mean a thing?" Jay's voice slurred lower. "It was just moonlight and drumbeats and it didn't mean nothing, is that it?"

"I told you what it meant, Jay." Her voice was very low.

"And you aim to marry him anyhow?"

"Yes. He's waiting outside in the car for me."

"I see," Jay said. His face was rigid and masklike, but his eyes burned bright.

"We're going to stay here until the dam is finished and then maybe we're going up to New York City."

"Uh-huh," Jay said.

"Don't be like that, Jay."

"I don't know what you expect me to be like."

"But, Jay, think about me. You know I'm right. You'll see that. And please don't hate me."

"No, I ain't going to hate you."

"And we can still be friends, can't we?"

Jay looked at her and shook his head. "We won't never be enemies, anyhow. He's waitin' fer you, Leona, and I reckon we better say good-by."

"Does it have to be good-by, Jay?"

"Yes. Yes, it sure does."

Jay went past her and opened the door. She walked out upon the porch, then turned to look at him. She started to speak, then shook her head and turned quickly away. Jay stood at the door and watched her walk across the grass and get into the car. As it drove away he saw the United States license.

I ought to grabbed her and told her she couldn't go. I could see it in her face that she likes me and I ought to grabbed her and I don't know why I didn't do it. If I'd of done it she'd be here now and she'd stay here and I know it.

Jay stepped back and slammed the door hard. He heard Crosby calling to him, and went into the kitchen. The old man had spread a quilt in the back yard and he lay in the sunlight with his grandson. The boy was laughing and rolling on the quilt.

"Jay, who was that you was talking to?"

"Nobody, Dad," Jay said. "Nobody at all."

Billy sat up beside Crosby. "Mommy come back, Jay?"

"No, Billy, not yet. She's gone away fer a long time, son."

"Come back tomorrow, Jay?"

"Day after tomorrow, maybe," Jay said. "Yes, day after tomorrow, Billy."

"Day after tomorrow." The child parroted the phrase with a wise nod of his head.

He don't know what that means, day after tomorrow, and it will always be day after tomorrow fer him, and most things you want are day after tomorrow, sure enough. And I was thinking she would be a mother to Billy and making my plans and hoping

fer a little house and a truck garden and just us two and it ain't
never going to be that way and there ain't even no day after tomorrow. . . . But I got my work to do and I aim to do it and
that work will always go on and it ain't never going to be that
truck farm in the hills. I guess I knowed all along she wasn't the
woman fer me. She's like she is and I tried to make her over different and I reckon I couldn't never do that. She belongs on
the other side of town and I belong on this here side. She belongs over yonder with the Chamber of Commerce and the
Spinach Association and I belong over here with the working
man and the union. She belongs to that kind of world and I
belong to this kind and she wouldn't of never been the wife fer
me. And she wouldn't of never been the woman to take care
of Billy.

Jay looked at the sunlight on the tow head of the child,
sprawled on the quilt beside Crosby with a sunflower in his
hand, then he turned away and went back to his cot. The room
was quiet and depressing with the shades drawn in the western
windows. Jay stretched out on the cot with his head in his
arms.

She wouldn't say she loved him and it ain't that and he won't
never see the look in them blue eyes that I seen. I reckon she
was thinking only about herself and anybody thinks only about
herself ain't fer me. She was making her plans fer a long time
to come, and she'll be going to New York City and that's what
she wants. She wants fine clothes and plenty of silk stockings
and moving picture shows and she ain't the kind of woman
would put on a Mother Hubbard and her hair done up in a
dustcloth and go to work to make a home fer a man. She ain't
the woman fer me and I reckon I knowed it all along. I knowed
it when she used that word nigs the way she did. She looks at
things different from me and she looks at things from the top
down and I look from the bottom up. That word nigs is sure
a dirty word on a woman's tongue, but Jesus Christ up yonder
in the hills it was *I love you too, Jay,* she said, *I love you too,
Jay.* And she was so sweet and she was my woman then. But all
that time she had made up her mind. I always knowed she was
the kind of woman with lots of wants and she would want fine
clothes to wear and she talked like she did about going to Colo-

rado fer the summer and now I reckon she wants to go to New
York City. I reckon that's it. She's got more wants than I could
begin to give her and that kind of woman couldn't never git
along with me. She belongs on that other side and I'm on the
side that does the hard work. She wants to be where the money
comes easy and it won't never come easy to me no matter how
much I sweat. Fer a long time I done too much dreaming and
I got to quit that. I been dreaming about a wife and a farm and
a truck garden and I know God-damned well it ain't going to
be like that. I just got to do my work and forget about that part
of it. . . . But someday I'll find me a woman who believes like
I do and she'll help me in my work and we'll have us a home
and wherever we are that will be our home, maybe with no roof
but the sky and nothing to warm us but the sun but it will be
our home. She'll be a good woman and a real woman and she'll
take care of Billy and we'll have us kids of our own and it will
be a woman who will want that and won't have no wants like
silk underwear and Colorado Springs and New York City. It
will have to be a woman strong as a whiteoak tree, strong as an
oak tree planted in the river bottoms, and she won't never forget the earth she sprung from. She'll work the way God made
man and woman to work and she'll work along with me and
she'll believe in what I believe in and I won't have to teach her
nothing. Someday I'll find that woman and I reckon she'll be a
little bit like Belle and that's the kind of woman I got to have.
All that other part I got to forget. And I got to git some sleep
and when I wake up maybe I won't have that empty feeling
like I swallowed my stomach. . . . I'm just going to do my
work and I'm going to forget all that part of it and I ain't going
to do nothing but my work fer the union and someday when I
ain't thinking about it I'll come across that woman and it will
be in doing my work that I'll find her and she'll be one of people
like me. I know that now and I damn well know she ain't the
woman fer me and I knowed it all along and she knowed it too
and that's why she was always hanging back from me. She
knowed she wouldn't never fit in and that's what she was saying
to me and one thing about her is she had the guts to come out
and say it that way. She just as good as said *Jay, I ain't got the
guts to marry a union organizer and live a life like that,* and sure

enough that's what she meant. She'll marry that engineer and she'll go to New York City and she'll go lots of places, I reckon, and life will be easy fer her but when she's all done what has she got? I couldn't live like that. If you're just going to pick the easiest way fer yourself and live as high and mighty as you can then you ain't living. You're just using up your time on God's earth. I ain't going to set by and just use up my time. I'm going out and do my work and fight fer what I believe in and when I'm done I'll know I wasn't just using up my time. . . . But she was sure sweet and that black hair and that laughing look on her face. . . . I got to forget all that and I got to sleep. I got to forget it, forget it. . . . I got to forget her and keep my mind off her. I'm going to git some sleep and when I wake up I won't never think of her again. . . . I got to forget her, and that's what I'll do, forget her . . . forget. . . .

When Jay awakened it was dark in the room. Someone was shaking his shoulder and he opened his eyes to darkness.

"Jay, wake up."

Jay saw a dark figure bending over him, silhouetted by the glow of the oil lamp in the adjoining room.

"Is that you, Dad?" Jay sat up. "Have I been asleep?"

"It's me — Webb Harper."

"Howdy, Webb." Jay yawned and rubbed his eyes with his fists. "I sure have been sleeping."

"You needed it, Jay. — Listen here, I just got in from Tanzey."

"Set down, Webb." Jay was wide awake now, alert and tense. He moved over and Webb sat beside him on the cot. "Let's have a cigarette," Jay said.

In the flare of the match as he lit the cigarettes Jay saw Harper's face, relaxed and grinning at him.

"Let's have it," Jay said. "What happened over to Tanzey?"

"We organized that local. Bo, we sure enough organized that local."

"Webb, that's fine. Jesus, that sure is good news. Did you tell 'em about Rocky Island Jones?"

"I didn't have to tell 'em nothin', Jay. Every tenant farmer in this here county knows about Rocky. I didn't have to tell 'em nothin'. Jay, forty white men signed up."

"Oh, that's good," Jay said. "I tell you, Webb, they made one hell of a mistake when they done Rocky that way."

"Man, did they! We'll organize that district solid, Jay. There was black men and white men in that old schoolhouse this evenin' and they all signed up, every last man, black and white. And everybody knowed about Rocky Jones and they was burned-up mad. Everybody knowed about your brother. I guess everybody in the whole Southwest knowed about him, and now they know about Rocky, too."

"And how they done him?"

"They sure do."

Jay drew deeply on his cigarette and leaned his head back against the wall. "Rocky done his work, Webb. Alive and dead he done his work. He didn't just use up his time."

"How's that, Jay?"

"I just mean to say Rocky Jones was a man."

"He sure was that. Jay, I wish you'd of been there. I wish you'd seen 'em crowd up to join that union and I wish you'd heard the talk."

"I sure do wish I had," Jay said. "I ought to been there, too."

Crosby came to the doorway, the lamp glow behind him outlining the stoop of his thin shoulders. "I fixed supper fer youall, Jay. You can come and git it."

"That's fine, Dad. Is Billy still up?"

"I put him to bed awhile back. I'm glad you got some rest, son."

"I feel fine, Dad," Jay said. "I sure do. Dad, there ain't nothing going to stop the Southern Tenant Farmers' Union now. I tell you, we're on our way."

"Ain't we, though?" Webb Harper said.

"I reckon you can stop long enough to eat your supper," Crosby said. "Come and git it, you two."

Jay laughed and followed Webb into the lamplit room. Crosby had set the table for three and Jay went into the kitchen for another chair. In one corner the child was asleep on a mattress laid on the floor and covered with the faded quilt. Jay walked over and looked down at him.

He don't even know yet that he won't see his mother and his dad no more. He don't know they're gone and I reckon he thinks they're lost like his little bam-bam gun and tomorrow or the day after he'll find 'em. But the day will come when he'll know and he'll hear about his dad and how he broke out of jail and killed two men and was shot down by a posse in the hills. He'll hear all that and they'll tell him he's a criminal's son, but I'm going to tell him different. I'm going to tell him how Pat growed up like he did and was just a good-hearted boy that got into trouble because he went the wrong way. He went alone, and that's the wrong way. This here little boy is going to grow up union and he'll learn to stand along with other little boys like him. And I'm going to tell him that he had a dad he can be proud of, and he don't need to be ashamed that Pat was what he was. The Southern Tenant Farmers' Union is going to grow big and strong and everybody will stand together, nigro and white man and Indian, and there won't be no Jim Crow. We won't hear Jim Crow again. And that's because of a nigro name of Rock Island Jones and a little bit that's because of Pat. He done wrong and he went the wrong way, Pat did, but sure enough he left something to remember him by. Pat left us something to remember him by. . . .

"Jay, come and eat your supper," Crosby said in a petulant, commanding tone, as if he were speaking to a child.

Jay grinned and walked into the lamplight.

THE END